The Rise of Farson Uiost

W. Mahlon Purdin

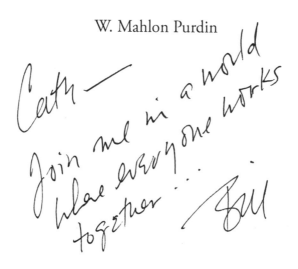

Cath —
Join me in a world where everyone works together . . .
Bill

THE SCREENMASTERS (Volume One)

FRONT AND BACK COVER PHOTO:

"EARTH ON THE MOVE" BY DENIS TABLER

ISBN-13: 978-0692025185 (Legend, Inc.)
ISBN-10: 0692025189

www.legendinc.com
www.wmahlonpurdin.com
www.emerald.earth

1.7

Dedicated to

my father

for his gift:

imagination.

Dedicatory Poem

THOSE IMAGES

by W.B. Yeats

What if I bade you leave
The cavern of the mind?
There's better exercise
In the sunlight and wind.

I never bade you go
To Moscow or Rome.
Renounce that drudgery,
Call the Muses home.

Seek those images
That constitute the wild,
The lion and the virgin,
The harlot and the child.

Find in middle air
An eagle on the wing,
Recognize the five
That make the Muses sing.

(1937, 1938 C.E.)

Foreword

by Farson Uiost

There is a world where humanity is finally free from suffering, where everything and everyone is in union.

All the cravings, anger, and afflictions are behind us there. Those conflicting dispositions of ignorance, greed, senseless aggression, and false assumptions about each other have evaporated, leaving only a true sense of purpose and unity.

It's a world with a happy ending – as hard as that is to conceive of for most of you. It took a major alteration in reality. It took the ScreenMasters. Most of all, it took one who was willing to gamble everything.

Looking back from that world, I am writing this for you. This is the first chronicle of the ScreenMasters. In another way though, it is also the final story of all that they were not and never could be. Think of the ScreenMasters who came to Earth as discoverers. They came here, like Columbus in the past, and saw a savage people living in a savage world. They came here to solve a problem, but, in the end, they were confronted with a terrible choice: them or us.

Little did they know.

BOOK I

The Parting

"First say to yourself what you would be;
and then do what you have to do."

– *Epictetus (55 A.D.-135 A.D.)*

Chapter One[1]

Earth, and a Few Other Things, as They Were

1. Coming to an End

They had been traveling in the ovaloid vessel for what they considered to be a relatively short time, but to others may have seemed like years, perhaps even decades.

Distances on The Screen were calculated in gridframes, which were measured in multiples of light-years depending on the many variables applicable in their equations. Or, as we might say, "We'll be there in no time."

There were just two of them on board. It was a starship that, at its equator, had a circumference of approximately 8,000 miles along the major axis, and a third longer the other way. It was bigger than the Moon.

The tall, avian-appearing ScreenMaster was clearly in charge. First, because the ship was his, and second, because the other ScreenMaster had joined underway.

The two of them had been traveling together for the extended time, but had spent little of it with each other.

There was plenty of room.

One of them liked to fly in the vast spaces inside the ship.

One of them preferred – or better put, longed – to sleep for protracted periods.

---

[1] *At the conclusion of this book is a section entitled, "Front and Back Matter with Appendices," which contains a dramatis personae, a glossary, a chronology, and other information for you.*

In fact, these were the two activities going on right now.

The ship flew itself. Its great engines humming along as though set for perpetual motion. There were no operational vibrations. The ship was fueled by space itself. It was casting distant telemetries, inquiring in all directions.

It was the perfect vessel for them.

In the daunting vastness of space, even this enormous starship, or "barge," as they called it, seemed insignificant, almost unnoticeable: a speck in the nothingness.

The avian's great wings had been sustaining him in flight for many days, and the resultant, deep meditative state was rejuvenating and revivifying in its rhythmic waves of hard exertion and soaring rest. The vibration of the alert took awhile to get through. Finally, he realized that something was happening.

The other ScreenMaster was deep in a sleep that few races could emulate. Total sensory deprivation, profound in its solitude, surrounded him with the soothing chill and dryness he cherished. For him, too, the alert took time to penetrate and arouse him to its urgency. It was like climbing out of a precious darkness, a treasured estrangement from involvement, into the brightness and annoying colors of a world he never wanted.

In due course, they met in the forwardmost area of the ship. Instrumentations were everywhere, processing and reporting, as the two of them found their way to the stations in front of the great oval, convex window built into the bow of the starship. Only the blackness of space presented itself. The barge seemed, to the eye, not to be moving at all, but they both knew that they were still traveling at a tremendous speed toward their destination, now coming within range.

"We are beginning approach maneuvers."

"So it would seem."

"Do you see it yet?"

The other ScreenMaster was surrounded by a green light momentarily. He waved his scaly arms, and it disappeared.

"Yes. It's a small planet, bright blue, and very ugly looking to me."

"How much time do we have before we get there?"

The forward window seemed to be just a black patch, without color or light, pasted on the front of the ship. Its starkness made the avian ScreenMaster ache for his own beautiful world.

"At this speed, we should begin to prepare. It won't be long now."

Like all travelers, they were happy to be reaching their destination, but a little sad that the relaxation of travel's routines would soon be coming to an end.

2. Introduction

The station moved through the etchless black like a shadow. Onboard, the people of SkyKing worked with the purpose and the urgency of a ship's crew sailing for a distant, unknown shore. It was 2091.

Below them, the planet teemed with frenetic light.

The history of the Second International Collaborative Scientific Research Laboratory and Space Station is well known.

It had begun slowly, and inexorably became humanity's crown jewel. Eventually home to over 350,000 carefully selected people, SkyKing, as it was quickly deemed, evolved into a complex society of men, women, and children with the myriad permutations of normal human activity, free from the bonds, and the safety, of Earth.

Orbiting the Earth seven times a day, it became as ubiquitous as the Moon, visible in the sky, day and night.

In the beginning, the idea of a space station had been conceived out of the shuttle program in the late 1980s. What had once been 25-foot canisters delivered laboriously one at a time to a space station with a planned obsolescence of only twenty years had now, with the much invigorated second postwar effort, reached a point of technical and human elaboration only dimly envisioned in those early days. This one was built to last.

Travel to and from the new station became as routine as commercial atmospheric air travel had been in its heyday.

With the evolution of SkyKing, the Earth itself had changed. Governments, previously contentious, began to realize the station's overwhelming power and importance, and they either became peacefully involved with the station and its activities or ultimately became isolated from the wealth of connected nations.

In the end, everyone joined in. Sadly, the late preceding decades of the twenty-first century had become an internecine period in Earth's history, and what emerged from those vicious regional and sectarian battles determined much about what was to come. Beyond all doubt or argument, SkyKing was the preeminent feature of the new unity in the postwar pantheon of human accomplishments. It was an unmistakable and unavoidable symbol of the new day.

During this time, three important things happened: First, the short-lived and limited laso-nuclear exchanges of the late 2070s had frightened everyone with their ferocity. Second, the human realization of such vast destruction in real rather than abstract terms caused Earth's people to develop a new doctrine of cooperation which became known as Earth Pact. Third, and perhaps most importantly, the damage of the war had slightly enlarged a preexisting "ScreenRent" in the gridframes surrounding the Earth's area of The Screen. This was detected by the ScreenMasters.

They estimated that the damage to The Screen near the Earth could potentially become the dreaded VentSyndrome. They determined that there was an immediate need for action to prevent this. This decision led to their arrival, search for, and timely discovery of Farson Uiost, whom they declared to be ScreenMaster of Earth.

That all of this happened after the destructive wars had ceased and during a time of new hope and reconstruction caused a sense of disbelief among the Earth's people. Things were going so well. Everyone, every nation was working reasonably together for the first time in human history. There were still religious zealots and some extremists, but for the most part world peace had finally been achieved.

There were still armies and there was still hunger and poverty and crime, but the governments of the world had opened the channels of communication. Politicians dedicated to building peace had achieved ascendancy. Things were getting better. It is not hard to see why the ScreenMasters' massive vessel appearing in the skies over Earth was not as overawing as depicted in innumerable science fiction novels in our past. Fear on the planet had generally gone way down. People were not huddling in conspiratorial groups, or hiding from discrimination and fear, or waiting for opportunities to take advantage of disasters. The global world was working. This period was filled with wonder and hope. Science had predicted that contact was coming. No one knew when, of course. Aliens in a spaceship caused intense interest, but not panic, curiosity not fear. After all, they had named one of our own as the newest ScreenMaster. Farson Uiost. The world was suddenly very interested in him. Even as the world began to learn more about Farson, the ScreenMasters were quietly doing their work.

Before this sudden unprecedented notoriety, the life of Farson Uiost was unnotable and he was – by no means – an obvious or a predictable candidate for fame.

The world press headlines were unanimous: Farson who?

2. Genesis

The Uiosts lived in rural Ohio and were part of a deeply religious and purposely isolated sect. Their rudimentary eco-farm barely scratched out a living for Farson's father, David. Mary, his mother, was a beautiful, intelligent woman whose life had slowly ebbed away with Farson's approaching birth.

The doctor had put it plainly, "Mr. Uiost, if your wife lives another two days, the child will be born. If not, you'll lose them both unless you come with me right now to the hospital."

David's response to this dichotomy was to firmly take the doctor by the lapels of his suit coat and encourage him roughly out of the house and without ceremony into the snowy night. Then he threw the doctor's bag and the other items he had brought into the house with him out into the snow as well. "You get out of here! Go back where you came from!"

For David Uiost, all things were in the hands of his God.

Alone and with no assistance, in the early morning hours of February 4, 2063, David Uiost awkwardly delivered a baby boy and lost his beloved wife, fulfilling the doctor's prediction. The boy was extremely frail and ghostly thin, as though a meager crop from a fallow field.

As she died, Mary asked her husband, "Was there enough time?" Her last vision was her husband nodding his head. She may have also noticed the first tears he had shed in the twenty-three years of their marriage.

David was not a man to understand emotions, or to deeply dwell on them. In his hour of confusion and joy, he naturally turned to religion and the third chapter of Ecclesiastes, which begins:

> To every thing there is a season and
> A time to every purpose under the heaven:
> A time to be born, and a time to die;
> A time to plant, and a time to pluck up that which is
> planted.
> A time to kill, and a time to heal;
> A time to break down, and a time to build up;
> A time to weep, and a time to laugh;
> A time to mourn, and a time to dance;
> A time to cast away stones, and a time to gather stones
> together;
> A time to embrace … .

As David Uiost thought through this last verse, he was actually hugging his newborn son, with the umbilical cord still attached. Mary was dead, but the boy was still being nourished by her. As he gently cut the cord with his pocketknife and tied it off, David held his son tightly. The father's tears fell on the boy's wet body, mixing with the afterbirth and blood. Where the tears fell, there were little circles of clarity.

For the only time in his life, the boy was together with his family.

In his own way, David tried desperately to understand the moment. Had anyone been within earshot, they would have heard his praying words: "Farther I cannot go. Take my son."

Perhaps it was the winter's deadly cold, his broken heart, or something else, but when the neighbors came several days later, David Uiost was dead. They could see that the father had done what he could. The boy was cradled in a wooden box with a primitive carving scratched into its slated side:

FAR SON

Beside the cradle, on that dark and cold winter night, David Uiost had died with his exhausted broken heart, his prayers, his thoughts on life, his limited understanding, and his anguish. He died with his feelings and a final firsthand knowledge of sad sorrow and unrelenting suffering. What he did not understand had overcome him. His weakness and his faith had set a course for his son from which there was now no turning back.

Farson was on his own.

There were mysteries that confronted the neighbors – in addition to the death of the mother and father. When they opened the door of the small house, there was a waning fire, embers still glowing in the hearth. David Uiost's body was covered with a soft blue blanket, and the cradle seemed to be rocking slightly as though someone had just been there.

The exigencies of saving the boy's fragile life carried the moment. These mysteries of what exactly happened were left for some other day.

The boy's life was saved, but in the desperate beginnings of his life he had already lost everything. Farson, who ultimately was to teach humanity so much, was granted almost nothing for himself. The sad circumstances of his birth foreshadowed what was to follow. Despite all the odds against him: a dead mother, a misguided and dying father, desperate isolation in an empty, cold wilderness cabin for days, only one clear, incontrovertible fact could be truly ascertained: Farson had survived.

What happened after that is history.

3. Hattie

For the next eighteen years of his life, Farson Uiost traveled through time as any other boy would have. He was unusual perhaps in the fact that he was immediately adopted after the death of his biological parents. His new parents were William and Mary Chamberlain. Both were highly skilled mathematicians working at Indiana University. They were obviously thrilled to have the boy.

As it turned out, his adoption was a great stroke of luck for Farson.

In stark contrast to Farson's deeply religious parents, the Chamberlains were scientists, and had no interest whatsoever in any religion. They were patient and caring, if somewhat distant. Their renowned skill in mathematics gave them an immunity from American homogeneity, allowing them to stand apart, and it provided them with a lifestyle in which all their material needs were easily met, leaving the Chamberlains free to move in the higher orbit of ideas.

Farson thrived in the freedom of the Chamberlains' home, partially because of the Chamberlains' generosity, but, really, it was because of Hattie.

The Chamberlains, before adopting Farson, had hired Hattie. At first, she came to them as a domestic helper, but in the years they had been together, that initial relationship had completely dissolved into what could only be described as "family." Hattie and her husband Sam were much more a part of Farson's formative years than were William and Mary Chamberlain. It was Hattie who truly cared for him as a small boy. It was Hattie's large plump arms that held him, it was her affable face that he most often stared up into, and it was her enormous brown eyes that taught him about love. The friendship that developed between Hattie and Farson became far more important to both of them than their circumstances might have predicted. In truth, Hattie became Farson's mother.

"Farseeey?" That deep alto voice he knew so well echoed through the front hall, up the spiraling, polished stairway. "You get yourself over here right now!" The last words were spoken from a rapidly increasing proximity. Farson knew that Hattie was on the march. He could now easily hear her talking to herself, "Good God, where is that boy? You'd think he'd come a runnin' when I call him after all I've done for him. FARSEEEY! You get down here, boy!"

Farson knew it was inevitable. Hattie knew the old house as well as he did. She knew all the little hideaway places, and she knew about the secret staircase. Even worse, she knew him. Hattie knew exactly where he was; it was just a matter of time until she got him.

In the meantime, Farson was using his time well. The old house had several gables, and a very special one faced the eastern night sky perfectly for viewing his favorite constellation. Since just before Christmas a year ago he had stared at the constellation Canis Major through the surprisingly capable telescope William and Mary had given him. The telescope's magnification, though excellent, was greatly exceeded by Farson's imagination.

In his mind, Farson stood on the planet that circled the Dog Star, Sirius. The cloudless violet sky filled his vision. There was a soft breeze, somewhat chilled, mussing his scruffy brown hair. He was on a verdant hill overlooking the rust-colored, grain-waved flatlands that stretched to the far horizon. He felt as if he towered over the universe, invincible. Through the black expanse of endless space he had traveled effortlessly to Serenity, this planet he had created. The planet itself had awaited Farson's creative mental touch and agile imagination in whatever whim he expressed it. Serenity was a rich tableau on which Farson was brush stroking as only a seven-year-old's imagination could. Through the illimitable light-years of space, this child of Earth (sitting in his attic) had stretched his consciousness to establish residence and reality on a far speck of the heavens. He resolutely stood here (and there) ready to ward off all dangers and to cause the birth of an entire civilization. The brilliant light of the remote star of this planet pasteled through the planet's sky and caused Farson to bring his hand up to shade his eyes. Then he began to really concentrate. Suddenly, a city appeared on the plains just before the slope of the hills. Roads, vehicles, and lights sprang up. Life began to spread outwardly from the newly forming urban mosaic. Structures began to leap upward, and – as "time" passed – the city became congested and constricted squeezing out its vertical growth by sheer necessity. A thousand years of expanding civilization passed in the blink of his mind's eye. It was a virtuoso performance. Farson's dreams were complex and intricate. The planet, Serenity, had no moon, but, slowly, a shadowed presence spread across its surface ...

"GOTCHA!! You little rascal!"

Hattie's big hands suddenly grabbed Farson from behind and lifted him off the floor and out of his star-crossed reverie. He was suddenly airborne and spiraling up to face his captor.

signaled for her to sit down in the chair beside the desk. As she sat down, he thought that he could not remember when he had last met alone with someone without his top advisor in that chair. She seemed perfectly comfortable and at ease. She adjusted her position and looked around. Her attention seemed to fasten on the small statue on his desk. It was of a cowboy riding a wildly bucking bronco. President Sortt laughed softly and said, "It's done in Moon rocks. I think they were saying something about bucking broncos and my job." Karina nodded pleasantly. She seemed to be distracted as if waiting for something.

There was a low whooshing noise in the Oval Office, accompanied by a soft purple light that filled the room like a thin mist. Then it began to centralize near an outside window into a large gracefully slender shape. The president had been expecting this. Karina was smiling. A friend had arrived.

"Mr. President, I'd like you to meet ZZ<<Arkol."

A large golden robot, slightly over seven feet tall, had materialized out of the mist. It stood next to a window that looked out onto Pennsylvania Avenue.

Karina went on, "Mr. President, please consider him a friend, as I do. Don't be alarmed. He is from the ScreenMasters' barge, and he is very powerful in his own right. He is programmed only to protect me. As long as he thinks I am safe, he is no threat to anyone."

<<Karina, this man is an extremely complex manipulator of human beings; you are not really safe here.>>[2]

Karina was getting used to ZZ<<'s telepathic programs, although she didn't really enjoy the mental intrusions all that much.

<<Please, ZZ.>> She switched to audible. "The president and I need to talk. I am safe."

---

[2] *This is the first instance of ScreenCommunication. The glossary has more information.*

<<*No. This is contradicting my protocols.*>>

<<*Yes. Let us be.*>> Her forcefulness registered with the robot.

"Mr. President, he won't interfere."

The president had remained standing, wondering if he should move or not. He decided to walk over to the robot.

"Can you speak?" the president asked.

"Yes," the robot answered.

"Why are you here?"

ZZ<< seemed to think the question over, and the purple light that surrounded him strobed slightly, almost imperceptibly, and seemed to deepen in color and intensity.

"I am not 'here.' So it is impossible to answer your question."

The president looked at Karina, "What does that mean?"

"It's very difficult to explain, Mr. President. I don't fully understand it, yet, but ZZ<<'s correct. Although he really is here, he may also be in other places as well. It's some sort of a power that has to do with what they call The Screen."

The president reached out, into the purple glow. His hand passed through the thin hue and came to rest on the warm, golden hardness beneath.

"Feels real enough." The president withdrew his hand and rubbed it together with his other. His fingertips and palm were tingling. The power within the robot was obvious. The president shrugged, resigned to never getting a real answer and walked back toward his desk. As he sat down, he asked Karina, "Do you know why I've asked you to come here this morning?"

"You're hoping I can tell you about my brother Farson."

"Correct."

Karina felt ZZ<<Arkol request that she move closer. She stood up and walked nearer to the robot.

<<What are you going to tell him, Karina? Farson has so much to do. All that can happen here is the creation of confusion.>>

Ignoring the robot's warning, Karina turned to Sortt. "Well, first, Mr. President, Farson's a good person. He's not going to hurt anyone. He's a very thoughtful person. Right now, he is probably trying to figure out what is going on even more than you are. The truth is, all we can do is wait."

"Wait for what?"

"To find out why Farson has been selected by them. To find out what the ScreenMasters want."

"Do you know?"

"I know some things, but not everything," Karina said, playing her fingers through her ponytail. "I know that what Farson is doing is absolutely crucial to all the inhabitants of Earth, and he has asked me to reassure you and ask for your patience. We need time." She seemed distracted for a moment. The president noticed ZZ<<'s visor was strobing more quickly. He wondered if they were communicating somehow. She turned to the president and said, "I must go, but don't worry. We will be in touch again soon."

The president stood watching her as a purple light seemed to reach out from the robot and surround her.

The robot and Karina Chamberlain silently disappeared, fading from view. It seemed like it happened slowly, but in truth they were gone in an instant. Their images remained ghosted on the president's eyes for a few seconds.

That was really beautiful, the president thought as he was left alone in his office. He recalled an aide's descriptive report of the ScreenMaster situation during this morning's briefing. "From their 'Be Not Afraid' speech at the outset, the ScreenMasters have proven to be fully capable of communicating effectively whenever they want to, and, to be fair, they have tried to constantly reassure us. That's about all we know." The aide's report went on, "We cannot break their cordon in New Hampshire, that's for sure. They have been completely nonviolent by all accounts. They've simply neutralized our forces and stood their ground." The report concluded, "We are unharmed, unchanged, and completely powerless to affect this situation in any positive way. "

The president turned to the window. *It could be worse. Much worse.*

5. Jealous

"Farsy, you've GOT to eat more. You're too skinny!!"

"Is it true, Hattie?" Farson would not be deterred.

"Eat!"

"Is it true?"

"Eat!"

"Is it TRUE?"

"Yes, it's true, Farson. Now EAT!!"

But Farson Uiost could not eat. Especially now that he knew it WAS true. He was upset and worried. For seven-plus years of his life he had been the only child. Just him and Hattie, and the Chamberlains who had provided whatever was needed. It was heaven on Earth. Now SHE was coming. Time had run out for him, and he just couldn't believe it.

"Hattie, how could this happen? How could they do this to me?"

"Listen, boy, they adopted you, and now they adopted her. What's the matter with you anyway? Jealous?" Farson faked the laughter of the carefree, the confident. It was a clearly failed attempt to cover his true emotion.

"Humphh! Why should I be jealous? She won't get in my room, I'll tell you that! And she better stay out of The Ship."

Farson was already mapping out his territory. "The Ship" was a portion of the attic where he kept his telescopes. The Ship was the center of his galactic travels and the sacred repository for all of his games and plans. It was "his" and only Hattie was allowed to enter, and then only for calling him to dinner, or during their hide-and-seek games.

"Oh, boy, she'd better stay out of The Ship!"

6. Karina

Karina Chamberlain did not comply. Ultimately, she became so familiar with Farson's room that at times it seemed to be "their" room. Of course, she also became copilot of The Ship.

But when she first arrived in Indiana, she was vastly different from the confident little girl she became after a year with Farson. In the beginning she was frightened and withdrawn, choosing the isolation of her room to facing what had happened to her life. This suited Farson perfectly because he had decided to take on the posture that she did not exist. Hattie, on the other hand, upon first seeing Karina, had fallen head-over-heels in love with her.

Karina slept. Hattie had carefully prepared the spare bedroom in advance at the Chamberlains' request. All the festive patterns of wallpaper and bright colors seemed wasted, for Karina had simply gone to bed, wordlessly, and stayed right there. Farson continued his star trek in the attic and his other activities throughout the rather large and sprawling house. It did seem, however, that after a week of nothing at all being heard or seen from Karina's room, other than Hattie coming and going, shaking her head and looking sad, he found many things to do that required his presence near or directly outside the door of that very room.

"Well, where is she, Hattie? She's been in there for a week. Is she dead? I hope so. Has she said anything?"

"Why don't you go in and see for yourself, boy?"

"Nothing doing! What do you think I am, crazy? If she wants to stay in there, I think that's great. Just great! The heck with her!"

Hattie watched him as he waved his hands as though dismissing everything. "Well, then get yourself along, boy. Mind your own business. Go fly The Ship somewhere. Don't hang around here no more."

Farson began to wander down the hall toward his own room. Then there was a sound, the first one, from inside Karina's room. Before he knew it, he was rushing down the hall with Hattie. The two of them jammed through the door together, just barely squeezing in, and not without much extra jostling hip effort. Farson was crushed against the door jamb by Hattie's soft bulk. The squeeze left him gasping to regain his breath. Like a comedy team falling onto stage, they stumbled to the side of Karina's bed.

She had been crying. Hearing Hattie and Farson stumbling in, she looked up. Farson lost his breath a second time. *She's pretty.*

Suddenly, for Farson everything had changed.

7. Sam

In the ensuing three years, Farson traversed the ages of eight, nine, and ten. Karina traveled with him through the ages of six, seven, and eight. Hattie continued along agelessly being Hattie.

The household worked well in providing a stable home and the semblance of family: two orphans from separate and horrific tragedies who had become fast friends, two domestic workers, steadfast and hardworking, and, two distant, brilliant, childless adult mathematicians toiling at their craft.

For Farson, Hattie's husband Sam suddenly came into being around this time. Perhaps it was because Hattie's attentions were now diverted part of the time to Karina, or maybe it was because a boy of eight found that what Sam liked to do when he wasn't working around the estate was very interesting. In any case, Sam and Farson finally noticed one another.

The only sounds were the spring peepers or the lonely call of the occasional loon. The sky was bright and clear. Farson was slightly bored waiting for the fishing trip to begin. What Sam was doing was mystifying Farson. He crinkled his forehead and tipped his head slightly to get a closer look at Sam's endeavor. Perhaps too abruptly in the quiet of the morning – but probably any noise would have startled Sam in such deep concentration – Farson blurted, "*What* are you doing?"

Sam's hands were wrist deep in dark brown earth. His undivided attention had been focused on feeling for the worm. Farson's sudden interrogatory came just as Sam's hands had found the worm and were slowly and skillfully pulling its slimy length out of the soil. Farson's question made Sam jump, and he yanked the worm in half.

"JESUS H. CHRIST, BOY! Why'd ya sneak up on a body like that? I done ripped this sucker plum in half now." He threw the torn half worm into a small bucket of dirt and other captured worms and turned stern-faced to address the boy directly. "Don't sneak up on a body like that, Farson. You might scare the life out of them. Whistle or something first." Farson whistled softly through exaggeratedly pursed lips, eyes wide, feigning an apologetic look. Sam went back to feeling around in the earth.

Farson whistled again. This time a little louder.

Sam kept digging and feeling around, obviously ignoring Farson.

Suddenly, the air was filled with an ear-piercing whistle that caused Sam to jump to his feet.

Farson stood there, holding a small silver police whistle in his right hand.

For a moment they stared aggressively at each other.

Then Sam started to laugh, and Farson laughed, too. Then they were both laughing so hard that they had to sit down. As they caught their breaths, Sam held out his large, calloused hand, saying, "Where the heck did you get that?" Farson quickly put the whistle in Sam's hand. Sam turned it over inquisitively and gave it back, shaking his head. They were friends from that time on.

"OK, boy, I'm diggin' worms 'cause I feel like fishin'. This is your lucky day. Ya might just learn somethin'." He had found another worm in the ground and threw it whole into the bucket with the others. Farson watched it fly. As it landed, the worm continued its journey by squirming into the loose soil. Farson looked up at Sam and encountered something he thought belonged only to his beloved Hattie: those big brown, loving eyes. Sam was watching Farson watching the worm. Sam and Farson smiled at each other as though some secret had been shared.

Farson said, "OK, Sam, let's go."

8. Fishing with Sam

Sam loved to fish. It didn't seem to bother him in any way if he caught nothing at all. It was fishing he loved. Sitting by the little lake, feeling the quiet and the warm air was enough for him. Sam *loved* to fish.

He started off toward the fishing hole with a long, loping stride that Farson couldn't match without running to keep up. They stopped by the shed behind the Chamberlains' house to pick up some extra fishing gear. It was the first time Farson had ever been in the shed. He knew Sam spent much of his time in there, and that all the utensils and tools Sam used to keep up the Chamberlains' grounds were in there. As Farson looked in, he realized, his eyes and awareness widening, that more than anything else, the shed was Sam's place. There was a little potbellied stove, a stack of wood, and a chair at one end. There were many, many books. There was a little rug under the chair, and the whole place looked comfortable and cozy. As Farson was taking all of this in, Sam urged him backwards out of the shed, with two gentle pushes, closed the door quickly and said, "All right, all right, let's go fishin'. Stop daydreamin'."

Sam took hold of Farson's little hand with his big one, and they walked off like father and son toward the fishing.

They were walking down to the little brook that wandered around behind the estate. They had to cross the five-foot-wide stream bed on a one-plank bridge that was precariously balanced over rocks and stones with water rushing underneath. Sam, although a big man, swept across effortlessly and stood on the other side beckoning for Farson to join him. Farson was hesitating.

"Just go right across, boy. Don't even think about it, or you'll never make it. Don't think. Just go."

Thinking all the way, Farson went. The boards moved, the rocks shifted, the water rushed by faster and faster, and everything went upside down. Farson found himself sitting in the cold water of the little brook as a strong hand grabbed him, lifted him, and set him back on his feet on the far bank. He was dripping wet and embarrassed.

"I told you not to think, boy. Sometimes, it's better not to think too much. Just go with your instincts. Let them take over. Remember God gave us brains and feet. You're going to have to learn when to use what."

It was a warm day, so Farson dried out quickly. By the time they got to what Sam called the "Fishin' Hole," he had almost gotten over the indignity of his failed crossing.

"You think too much," Sam said as he settled in and baited up his hook. Sam's fingers glistened with worm juice as he threaded the little creature onto the hook. The impaling seemed to cause some nervous disruption because the worm wiggled crazily as it was cast out over the water on the end of the line attached to Sam's rod and reel. Plop! Ripples spread out as the hooked worm sank into the water to a hopefully imminent doom in the mouth of an unsuspecting, yet-to-come-along fish.

"Now you, boy." Sam pulled out a ball of string with a bobber and a specially bent safety pin from his pocket. He cut a worm in half and repeated the procedure as before. Once both lines were in the water, Sam rinsed off his hands, dried them on his jeans. Then he took a bite out of something from his other pocket.

"What's that?" asked Farson.

"Tobacco, boy. Now fish."

9. Sam Reads a Poem to Farson

They fished all afternoon, and for Farson it was one of the most wonderful afternoons of his young life. He caught his first fish ever and then his second. He helped Sam catch six more. They "cleaned" them together while Sam tried to explain to Farson why people called it cleaning a fish, when you were really killing it by scraping out its insides while it was still alive. Sam shook his head and told Farson to stop thinking so much. Farson tried, but to no avail. Then they walked home together carrying the "clean" fish. Farson made it across the little one-plank bridge, but only because Sam grabbed him before he splashed down again. Back on the Chamberlains' property, Sam went into the shed and started a cooking fire in the stove while Farson roamed around looking at everything, asking way too many questions. Sam answered none of them. Not the one about the old plow. Not the one about the shovels and rakes. Not even the one about the books of poetry that filled Sam's corner by his chair. When Farson asked if he could sit in a little chair – way in the back of the shed that looked about the right size for a boy his age – it took Sam by surprise. Suddenly, there they were again, Sam and Farson, staring at each other in another contest of egos. The question had upset Sam. That only made Farson want an answer even more.

Finally, in resignation, Sam said, "Well, I guess you could use it. Just this once."

Farson went scrambling over garden tools and baskets and boxes to retrieve the chair, and he dragged it to the front. Sam reached into his pocket for a rag. Farson didn't see it, but if he had, he might have thought Sam was wiping his forehead, when, in truth, he was secretly wiping tears from his eyes. Then he spat tobacco juice into a bucket by the stove and said something to himself that sounded like "Goddamn it all." Farson got the chair into position and sat in it as Sam was cooking up a few fish with some thin potato slices. They sat and ate together. Farson thought it was the most delicious food he had ever tasted. After lunch, Sam sat down in his old worn, leather chair and opened a small book on his lap. Farson was still in the little chair.

"What's that?"

"It's a book. Just listen, boy. I'll read you a poem. Ever heard of poetry?" Farson made a face. "It might just do you some good."

Then Sam started to read. As he read, Farson realized that there was more to Sam than appearances and circumstances had indicated. What Sam was reading was an old poem by Carl Sandburg. Not the popular children's poetry Farson had been bored by in school.

Sam's reading of the poem, although not a polished performance, had the strength of Sam's raw emotion and experience to deepen its impact. To Farson, Sam almost seemed to be singing it:

I wish to God I never saw you, Mag,
I wish you never quit your job and came along with me.
I wish we never bought a license and a white dress
For you to get married in the day we ran off to a minister
And told him we would love each other and take care of each other
Always and always long as the sun and rain lasts anywhere.
Yes, I'm wishing now you lived somewhere away from here
And I was a bum on the bumpers a thousand miles away dead broke.
I wish the kids had never come
And rent and coal and clothes to pay for
And a grocery man calling for cash,
Every day cash for beans and prunes.
I wish to God I never saw you, Mag.
I wish to God the kids had never come.

When Sam read the last line, he put the book down, and put his hands in his lap and leaned back in his chair, still chewing his tobacco, in a world all his own, rocking back and forth in his chair, lost in thought.

Soon after that, Farson left the shed, with Sam alone by the stove. Sam would remain alone with his thoughts for a while. The remaining fish they had caught were still in the sink. There were some dishes to do. All in due time.

The coals in the stove clinked as they adjusted to the fire's ever changing heat.

10. Hattie and Farson

"Hattie," Farson asked, "did you and Sam ever have children of your own?"

"Farsy! What kind of a question is that? What's got into you, boy?"

"Well, did you?" Those large gentle arms swooped down like an avalanche and pulled him into the warm mountains of her embrace.

"Well, now, there ain't no kids around here but you and Kari. And me and Sam got you both. What's past is past, Farsy. What's here and now is what's important." Her embrace was so intense that Farson gasped for breath. But still Hattie hugged him a while longer. Then there was a silence in the hug they shared. Farson thought of Sam and his poem. Hattie and her hugs. One was lost in memories; the other was lost in love for Farson and Karina. Both Sam and Hattie carried a similar essence that unmistakably connected them to some great single event. Somehow Farson knew what it was. Hattie and Sam had had a boy themselves. The child had died. It had devastated them. *And it still hurts like crazy.* He found himself thinking about his own family, and he found himself hugging

Hattie tighter and tighter in a hug that was taking on a life of its own. Farson hoped it would never end. Hattie knew better.

Sam was still alone in the shed.

The three of them were together, passing through time: Sam into the past, Hattie into the near future, and Farson through all times.

The single thread of love wove them together into a family needing no explanation, no formalities, but with a great strength. Each of them was clinging to this thread with all their might.

11. Farson in His Cabin

Farson was looking at his dead father's old smoking pipe. The Chamberlains had acquired it in the package of tattered possessions that accompanied Farson at the time of his arrival in their home. After all these years, he still had it. It was an old pipe that looked crudely handmade. Farson knew his father had made it. He closed his eyes and smelled the pipe. It still had a sweet aroma from the tobacco. He imagined his father sitting by the window and smoking in the evenings after working all day. His father and mother were long dead now. Still in his mind, and imagination, Farson could see it all, and most of all, he could feel it all as if he had been there.

Farson noticed that the snowstorm outside was building. He looked around the inside of his cabin. His papers were spread on the desk, and the room was not particularly well-lighted, except where he was sitting. Even there the light was only just bright enough to read by. Farson always moved his papers and books around to get the visibility he needed. The room was somewhat crowded with furniture, including a very comfortable-looking sofa and a large rough-hewn wooden table. There was a potbellied stove at one end that warmed the room with its radiating heat.

In the corner, opposite the door, there was a tall, golden robot standing stock-still as only a robot can. For three days now, the thing had been there. Farson was getting used to it. *Three days. It seems longer than that.* The robot would do whatever he asked it to do. It accompanied Farson wherever he went like a silent disconnected shadow. The robot was very adroit, and it moved in ghostlike silence. Farson couldn't figure out how such a large piece of machinery could be so quiet. It was a little bit irritating sometimes, like a person who appears suddenly. He found himself now always looking to be sure the robot was coming along or at least to ascertain where it was. Not that he needed to know. He no longer doubted the thing's devotion to proximity with him. Farson did doubt, however, that there would ever come a time when he would really get used to it.

Farson was thinking over all the facts that had become known since they had arrived.

The ScreenMasters are a group of individuals who have each been selected to guard all things regarding what they refer so reverently to as "The Screen." Apparently something important has happened in Earth's sector of this Screen. Part of the problem were the nuclear explosions of the past few years, which seemed to have exacerbated an existing problem but were not apparently the root cause of it. The ScreenMasters had detected the possibility of what they called a "VentSyndrome." This situation required their immediate and continuing presence until the solution was reached. "One way or the other," as they had put it. The completion of this syndrome, and its effects, must be avoided at all costs.

Farson knew that there were ScreenMasters in the vicinity of Earth now and that this was extraordinarily unusual. Their "barge," a spacecraft of enormous size and mysterious capabilities, was easily visible in the skies over the Earth, dwarfing even the Moon itself.

The ScreenMasters believe that all of space is made up of an intricate, fabric-like mosaic. Each of the basic components, or GridFrames, are too large and complex to be truly understood by anyone other than a ScreenMaster. ScreenMasters are rare in the extreme. It was the coincidence of the investigation of a possible VentSyndrome near Earth, and the subsequent discovery of Farson, that brought them here. They refer to him as the "ScreenMaster of Earth." He had no idea why he was chosen.

Farson had learned that a VentSyndrome is like a giant wound in The Screen. It must be repaired, or big things will fall apart. Earth would be destroyed, of course. Far more was involved than just Earth's survival. The presence of so many ScreenMasters bore that out. There is a flashpoint somewhere in The Screen around Earth to be found and repaired. That spot is so infinitesimal that it may never be found. The effort must be made. It is a point in space *and* time. Which makes the search even more complicated. This search had been occupying the ScreenMasters' full time and attention. They had been unsuccessful in finding it despite extensive and continuing efforts. Then they realized that they would never find it. They were deeply troubled by this failure.

This despair led them to the conclusion that only a ScreenMaster from Earth could find it. That led them to Farson. *And now, I am a ScreenMaster?*

For all practical purposes Farson knew that he now controlled the fate of the Earth, the space around it, and really far, far more than that. <<*There are few ScreenMasters, and The Screen is large.*>> That was how they had put it to him during their first, secret telepathic contact with him. It took him awhile to figure out what was happening, where these strange thoughts were coming from.

They expected him to help them. In fact, they insisted on it. He was given no choice.

Farson strolled over to the table and rubbed his fingers over its gnarled, scratched surface. He knew each scratch, each imperfection. He ran his fingers over a series of short, sharp holes in the old wood. *This was when Karina came to the table and stabbed her fork into it over and over.* He remembered her tears and her anger and his confusion. Had he done something to hurt her or anger her? He remembered how it had affected him, seeing her that upset. There were other scratches and dents and fading stains that marbled the surface like a mad design.

He put the old pipe on the table. It balanced easily, nestling into a crack running through the center. He smoothed his hand over one particular area on the table, almost caressing it. *That, I will never forget.* He could still feel the emotions of that day. He could still see her face, her eyes closed. The table seemed to grow warm under his hand as he relived the moment she first said she loved him. He remembered the confusion, the suspicion after so many years of child's play and horsing around. His best friend. His sister. Those feelings so long sublimated in teasing and goofy competitions, running all over the house, laughing, pushing, falling and getting up, and running more. He remembered her eyes that day. So different. Better. He remembered the relief that he was not alone. He remembered her fearlessness in the truth.

His hand moved over the small waves of grain. He was like a blind man reading: the surface transmitting a world to him. *Will I ever see that world again?* That brought a smile to his face. The answer was obvious.

Suddenly, the robot was moving.

12. Ascension

The president sat in the ornate and historic chair beside the fireplace in the Oval Office absentmindedly gazing out the window. He was lost in thought. His so-called campaign for reelection was now a joke. The enormous events that had just occurred had changed everything.

He was also thinking about MoonBase and its great potential of natural resources and strategic position.

He was thinking about SkyKing and its amazing technology and emerging cultural diversity. How unlike it was to anything Earth had ever seen in its history. How near to perfection it was.

There was a large grandfather clock in the office, and he could hear each laborious tick, tick, tick of the second hand and then the ponderous tock of the minute passing. With each notching of the clock's gears he felt drawn deeper into the decisions that were becoming unavoidable. Not that President Sortt was one to avoid decisions. Far from that. He was one who could make decisions, and had made many important ones. But – as only those in his position had learned in the hardest way possible – some important decisions were far more important than others.

In quiet procrastination in his office, the president found himself thinking about his own family and what all of this would mean to them: his wife, his son, and his daughter. Their lives would be changed forever. Their wonderful, hopeful plans, which even now, they still believed to be possible, would be cast aside. His own personal dreams never included even one element of what was now before him.

The world was just getting to know Farson Uiost, but President Andrew Sortt already knew too much. He knew without a doubt that Farson was going to change the world. Not the way a new, amazing technology could change the world. Not like a new stylish star in Hollywood. Not like an election. That made him laugh. *Elections never change anything.*

Farson was the change that changed everything. Not in that Madison Avenue way, but in the way that was beyond all calculation. Farson was the fundamental change. He also knew that Farson's quiet life in education and research in North Conway was over as well. *No one is immune.* The moment the ScreenMasters identified him as ScreenMaster of Earth, Farson went from unknown to the name on the lips of every living soul on the planet.

The president knew all of this so vividly; it was as though he had already seen it all happen. As though he had already lived it.

The president walked over to the window and looked out at Pennsylvania Avenue. He could see the people out there walking around, bundled up against the cold. He saw a plane taking off in the distance, heading up from the city. He noticed a squirrel on the lawn, its movements this way and that as though uncertain of which way to go. Its twitchy tail made him laugh. He thought about the four-inch bulletproof glass that he was looking through. *All of this is going to change. All of this is becoming unnecessary. No, it is unnecessary already. The Earth as we have known it is over. It has to be. It's the only way.*

John Andrew McKinley Sortt had always been a thoughtful person, given to long moments lost in thought while people and events just had to wait for him. The first and last president of the United States of Earth stood in his office just gazing out of the window like a boy at home. He was looking at a squirrel on the grounds.

After a while he turned to his desk and went back to work. There was another tick and then a lower tock as the hands on the clock moved, inching toward the hour. He sat down in the chair again and felt the hand-stitched cushion under his arm. He pondered the thousands of decisions that had been made in this room. In this very chair. He heard the police sirens somewhere in the district. The city rushing to its own aid. He stood up again. This decision had been made a long ago. *Farson has seen to that.* Outside the window the snow was just beginning to fall. The clock struck noon.

The squirrel was gone.

Farson was thinking, too.

The ScreenMasters had told him that time, not distance, is the consideration. <<*In space,*>> they said, <<*Time is the frontier, and time is what matters.*>> Right now, Farson was thinking of home. Not in North Conway, but in his treasured childhood home with Hattie, Sam, and Karina. He was thinking of things that were in many ways unrelated to time: love and family. <<*No, Farson, love IS time. Time is The Screen. All these things are related. You must think more deeply.*>> Farson had become accustomed to the invasion of his thoughts by the ScreenMaster, Uvo. He scarcely noticed that no words had been spoken or that Uvo was hundreds of miles away in high orbit above the Earth. <<*Uvo, why do I resist that notion? Why do I long for my life as it was? Why do I resist the responsibility? I don't care about being a ScreenMaster. I wish only to be the me I was.*>> The response came within the next heartbeat; it was soft and reassuring. <<*Because to be yourself – what you are – IS the only answer. That is why, ScreenMaster Uiost, you have been chosen. You know The Screen, and you always have. You are unusual in that your imagination and your intelligence have always been directed to the larger and larger things, more and more complex ideas. Yet you love so deeply, and you have known love of the purest kind. You have no choice in this. Not by our power, but solely by your own free will are you compelled.*>>

Farson persisted for the hundredth time in arguing with himself to regain what he had lost. He remembered the look in Karina's eyes when she first realized what Farson was to her, not just her brother. He remembered the relief. He remembered that look. It was a moment seared into his being. There were more moments.

<<*I am no longer free, Uvo. If I must be what and who you say I am, then I cannot choose for myself. I have no free will.*>>

Farson remembered her laughter. Her abandon was so complete; he could not resist joining her. Her life force so much a part of his, he had no choice. He wanted that and nothing else.

Uvo began again for the hundredth time without hesitation and without impatience to make his case that things are as they must be. <<*You can choose. You have chosen. Not because I say so, but because you feel it. You see it. It's not because of me, or us. You must be a ScreenMaster, Farson Uiost, because it is yours to be. We know from eons of doing this that there is not another individual in a billion ScreenGrids who can do what you can do. There is only you. Only you can ScreenMend this segment.*>>

Farson felt the surrender cascading within him and over him. He felt it wash over him like a shiver chill in the night. As though a lurking shadow had passed him unseen in the dark. It reminded him of when Hattie had stood over his bed, watching him. When she pulled off the covers and there he was, reading by flashlight long after he had been told to go to sleep. That sudden chill of surprise discovery invading his warm contentment. The memory of Hattie's sudden appearance, her hands yanking away his self-delusion in unavoidable surrender was still crystal clear. That memory was a happy one. The one facing him now was a cold unknown.

He was smiling even now at Hattie's attack. His flashlight had been whipped out of his hand. The book went flying. "Give it up, boy. Tomorrow's another day." Then she tucked him in, patted him on the head, and turned off the light. He saw her shaking her head as she left the room. The flashlight in her hand casting light around the room as she moved away.

Was the ScreenMasters' invasion so different? They had taken everything, and given him ... what? Like Hattie, Uvo promised another tomorrow, but Hattie's promise had been honest. Uvo's? *Perhaps not.*

Farson knew that with the ScreenMasters there was no tomorrow as today had been. Suddenly, into Farson's worried mind came the thought of Sam's words as they had stood at the bridge over the brook: "Sometimes, boy, don't think. Just go." He smiled at the thought. He remembered the little bridge and Sam's helping hand and his loud, quick laugh. Farson knew that the ScreenMasters were far, far different from Sam, and the bridge they wanted him to cross was much bigger than the one on the way to the fishing hole.

<<OK, Uvo, you have me cornered. I have no other option. I accept The Screen as Master. Let us begin.>>

With those words, and the affirming thoughts behind them, the cabin room was instantly filled with a thin but bright, purple light. Farson was gone in the flash. The robot followed, although its purple light was a weaker hue, just a thin halo that surrounded its golden shape. It was almost unnoticeable in comparison to the bright, fierce lightning bolt of Farson's departure.

Then the room was empty.

During transit Farson noticed his blurring arms were covered in what appeared to be goose bumps. There was a tingling sensation as though he was horripilating in a soft warm breeze. He looked around and was genuinely surprised at what he saw.

<<*Welcome to ScreenPassage, Farson. You are on your way.*>> Farson found that message somehow comforting.

13. ScreenPatch

In the exact moment when Farson and the robot disappeared, the ScreenMasters' barge began to emit small bronze-colored globes that sped off one after the other in all directions. In time they completely encircled the planet as close as a hundred miles apart. Then they began to blanket the planet with a pulsing field, surrounding it with thin purple bands like longitudes and latitudes. *Like the bending bars of a circular cage.* Once the bands were all in place, they made a screen-like structure around the Earth. Then in a vast, soft flash everything changed for mankind.

On board SkyKing, the dog watch was just beginning. Gerald Antonoff had just assumed his station in front of the wall-sized monitor. He was surveying the final construction of the new sixth whorl. He was dialing up a higher magnification when he noticed out of the corner of his eye that the Earth Monitor had gone blank. Shifting in his chair, he pushed the reset button calling for a re-initialization of the monitor's surveillance system. When the monitor came on again, it showed nothing but empty space. He checked it again. Still nothing. Just the stars of space appeared. He called for another camera to cycle to where the Earth would be visible. That camera showed the same thing: nothing there. Then he called for the entire Alpha Command module to shift around to Earth phasing. As the porthole slowly entered a segment where Earth would be directly visible to Antonoff's direct line of sight, it filled with only empty, starry space.

The lieutenant bolted upright in his chair all the way to a standing position. The chair slid backward hard against the wall. What he was seeing was unthinkable and yet unmistakable. He gazed unbelievingly at the emptiness where Earth absolutely, positively should have been. His hand slammed down onto the alarm console, and he shouted into it with a loud shaking voice. "Get me Commander Peterson! Right now!"

Chapter Two

"Earth Is Gone!"

14. Out of Armageddon and MoonBase

Commander James Peterson was reclining in bed with a morning glass of orange juice. It was 4:00 a.m. The steward had awakened him gently but, still, Peterson – staring at the eight-ounce glass of ice-cold, fresh-squeezed orange juice – was thinking that a stiffer drink might suit his current mood a whole lot better.

UESS SkyKing (ES-1) was the most sought-after command in Earth Navy. Flag rank was assured after a successful tour, and worldwide fame and lifelong celebrity was *de rigueur.*

Commander Peterson was not the sort of man to care much for fame; he was, however, very interested in having a successful command tour of SkyKing. To him, commanding the station was the crowning achievement of his career. It was the one thing he always wanted; he knew it was what he was born to do.

The orbiting space station was a city of over three hundred thousand souls now. People were born there, died there, and buried there. SkyKing had none of the street gangs, violence, and crime that Earth cities had known so well. The station was also a very freewheeling society that challenged him and his authority constantly in every way imaginable. SkyKing contained all the knowns and unknowns of human life. Isolated and insulated as it was, it was still a society of human beings after all.

In spades, he thought to himself.

To his credit, Commander Peterson had few illusions about the ultimate value of military rule over civilians. He was from a family of military veterans and heroes of every conflict in which the United States had ever participated. His family history in the military extended all the way back to the American Revolution. Now, as Commander of Earth Station One, affectionately known as SkyKing, he understood perfectly the role he was playing for the world below and for the new United States of Earth.

Out of centuries of conflict and carnage the democratic representative form of government had inexorably emerged as universal. Out of desperation it had gained increasing preeminence among all contesting countries as the only possible way out of Armageddon. The Constitution was still the same one written in 1787, but the number of players had increased to over ten billion people. In fact, many of the old countries and nations of the world still existed, but the overall notions of compromise and universal equality had spread like wildfire out of the ashes of conflict. The world was a much more civilized and democratic place in part because of the disastrous conflicts and in part because of the influence and power of SkyKing.

SkyKing was developing its own independent customs, traditions, and realities. For example, people of SkyKing had developed a new form of football that became an increasingly popular commercial telecast. The people of SkyKing routinely lived much longer than the "Earthers," as Earth-bound human beings were known. The people of SkyKing tended to think of Earthers as strange and dirty, as well they might, since SkyKing had always been effectively disinfected, with no diseases. Earth-bound humans visiting the station were tolerated, not genuinely welcomed. Unless, of course, they wanted to stay.

Then there were the inscrutable Skers (they pronounced it like "highers" with an "Sk" first). These are the SkyKing-born people who formed the special class of crew members who lived by the teachings of Ban Jonsn. They were austere, rigorous, severe in their self-disciplines, modest, plain in their dress and customs, unadorned, and reclusive in their personal lives and social customs. They were also very clannish, working with other crew members daily, but never socially assimilating with non-Skers in any real way. To a Sker, the only real people in their personal lives were other Skers. But the Skers sometimes made exceptions. Jim Peterson was one. His irresistible, eight-year-old daughter was absolutely another one.

The Commander of SkyKing touched his wrist pad, and a holographic control panel appeared. He touched a floating laser button and responded to the insistent incoming alarm. "Peterson here." The holographic screen clearly displayed the incoming caller's anxiety-strained face. Jim knew something was definitely up.

"Lieutenant Antonoff here, Commander. We have lost contact with the planet, sir." In the silence, he repeated himself, "We've lost it, sir. The Earth is gone." As Jim Peterson processed this information, he noticed that Brittany was standing in the doorway, listening to every word.

On the Moon, 238,875 miles away, Viera Nichols gently moved her hips, and her lover moved enthusiastically along beneath her. Together they had climbed a mountain of ecstasy. In the temporarily reduced gravity, their combined effort pleased her greatly.

Each with their own thoughts, they ascended a rising conclusion of passion and then rested, exhausted in each other's arms. In a moment, Commander Nichols released the young ensign with a soft contraction, and he fell away blissfully in the low Moon gravity. Their fun was over.

"To work," she said rising and moving to her dressing room. Her hand waved dismissively to the ensign, indicating he should go. He obediently began packing up his things and getting dressed. On the way to the bathroom Viera dialed the gravity back to Earth-normal. As she stepped into the shower, she could feel her weight returning.

She washed and dressed, and when she finished, the room was empty. She was alone.

That boy has potential, she thought. Then she noticed that the muted intercom was flashing red. The responder display was within easy reach.

"Commander Nichols," she said.

"Commander, this is Yeoman Chin on the bridge. The Commander of SkyKing would like to talk to you on the red link."

"Thank you, Yeoman. Patch him through."

Viera brushed her hair absentmindedly away from her forehead as she waited. The red link meant trouble. As she waited, she looked out her window to the black emptiness of space over the cold gray curve of the Moon.

15. The ScreenMasters' Barge

Uvo and Farson were locked in concentration. <<*Can you feel the Rent? Can you, ScreenMaster Uiost?*>>

Farson could feel something, but it took awhile before he realized what it was. It was a worm. It was almost on the hook but not quite. There's a little hard thing up in the end of a good worm, and the hook has to go through it or the worm will probably not stay on the hook. This is especially true if there's a smart fish in the area. So you have to get it through right there to be sure it stays on in that crucial moment.

"Ain't you got that thing on there yet?" A giant figure loomed over Farson.

"Sure, I got it. I got it." Farson then threw the hook and tiny sinker out as far as he could.

"Goddamn thing come off already, boy. I seen it fly." Farson knew he had a good chance that something had stayed on and now he was happy just to get Sam off his back, as the line relaxed into the still water, beneath the red and white bobber and the deep blue summer sky.

"Where's *your* hook, Sam?"

"It's out there, boy. It's out there."

The two sat and fished.

<<*You are going to change history, ScreenMaster, not us. We've carried out our duty. Until the ScreenRent is adjusted and mended, time cannot be allowed to continue for Earth. If nothing is done, the Rent will soon begin to collapse, and The Screen will be affected. This segment first, but then the Rent could become a ScreenTear, and this cannot be allowed under any circumstances.*>>

Uvo knew, of course, that Farson was listening. But the old ScreenMaster also knew a virtuoso when he saw one.

Farson Uiost offered a thought, <<*If they must never live again, then that is how it will be.*>>

<<*Yes, Farson, that is how it will be. But you, as an Earth-born ScreenMaster at his moment of Ascension, have a great advantage that is very unusual. Be not afraid, little one. Time is on your side.*>>

And the fishing had been good. Farson caught eight, Sam two. "Best damn two for sure," he'd said defiantly.

"What do you mean? After cleaning? You can't mean after cleaning," Farson asked incredulously.

"So your knife's sharper than mine. I still know a damn good fish when I see one, and I don't see no good ones on your string."

"Wanna swap?"

"Sure." As Sam reached for Farson's fish, Farson ran ahead.

"Let's ask Hattie to cook 'em up as usual."

"Now you're talkin', boy."

16. Farson Begins to Search The Screen

He looked into Karina's clear eyes and said, "I love you, you know."

"You don't love me. You love Sitwory. You love the game. You love the excitement. Who are you kidding, Routier!"

Still the Earth circled in stasis. Farson knew what that meant.

<<*It's my planet, Uvo.*>>

<<*Exactly, ScreenMaster, and only you can save it.*>>

"Mr. Uiost, are you with us?"

The question came from a professor. Farson was in a classroom.

"Mr. Uiost, need I ask you again?"

"No, just give me a second."

"Are you sick, Mr. Uiost?"

"No."

"May I continue, then?"

"Yes, of course, Professor. Please, I'm sorry."

The professor turned and walked to the podium in front of plus or minus three hundred students depending on illness, tardiness, amorous preoccupation, or whatever else determined the attendance of the class on any day. "Now, where was I? I believe I was discussing (Farson felt the stare) the character of the balance between nature and unnature. It's simple, really. Nature is what man has not changed, and unnature is what he has changed. It's an interesting field of study really, because nothing is out of bounds. I am a specialist in unnature, as you know, and as such, I hope for its triumph, eventually. 'Eventually' in this discussion is an important concept because the methods of delay and opposition are interestingly reduced when we discuss the actual timetables of eventuality. Well they should be because, let's face it, mankind is a great and fantastic success. Are we not?"

<<*Uvo!*>>
<<*Yes, Little One?*>>
<<*How deep am I?*>>
<<*You've only scratched the surface.*>> Farson felt relief. Then he felt the power again surging within him.
<<*Uvo ...* >> Farson realized he was shouting.

"That concludes my lecture for today. I would like you to take the rest of the period to discuss this topic, and only this topic, among yourselves. "Would Mr. Uiost be so kind as to join me in my office?"

<<*Uvo, it's here somewhere.*>>
<<*Why?*>>
Why.

Farson was looking at Sitwory. *Et tu*? She smiled at him and took his hand, laughing.

17. Life in North Conway

"Come on, Farson, have a drink!"

"OK, I'll have a glass of white wine. "

"Should I ask for the list?"

"No, just white will do."

"That's what I'll have, too then."

Farson noticed they were sitting in a pub. It was warm and there was music. Facts were pouring in.

<<*I'm close, Uvo.*>>

<<*Why?*>>

<<*I can feel it.*>>

<<*What does it feel like?*>>

<<*It's a spiral. It's hard to tell sometimes if I'm getting closer or farther away. If you threw a football, but it was a little off-center, that wobbling would best approximate the sense of motion I'm feeling. There is, however, a center of greatest strength. That is my destination.*>>

Uvo was contemplating the word "football."

<<*ScreenMaster! Are you sure?*>>

<<*No. Absolutely not.*>>

"Do you want to dance?" she asked. Some people in the pub were dancing. "Come on." Karina took Farson's hand and led him to the floor. "Just try. You'll like it." They began to dance. Farson actually did like it, and the feel of his sister's warm body next to his was more than enough to keep him interested.

They began to move with the music, now fast, now slow. Farson could feel her heart beating sometimes. So close to his. She could certainly feel his. Closer. Longer. A fast dance. Then, they were dancing slowly, together again.

Walking to their table. "Thanks, big guy. That was super," she said.

18. ZZ<<Arkol and the President

The glow of the robot's metallic skin still caused a sense of wonder and secret confusion. It was now standing as still as a cabinet in the corner of the office. No sign of life, other than the slow red liquid-like strobing across his faceplate. The president was studying the tall, metallic structure of the robot's body. It was well over seven feet, but it did not seem overly heavy. When the robot moved, it moved easily and nimbly. Always silently. Sortt knew that the robot was very aware of its surroundings. He could sense its telemetry and sentience. Consciousness? *No doubt about it.* On the two other occasions that the robot and the president had been in the same room, he had noticed that the robot always seemed to choose the most strategic location in the room to stand, as it had again today. It had a clear view of the room, its back to a wall where nothing could approach without a clear purpose. One never had to excuse oneself to move around the robot. It was always out of the way, but somehow the center of attention.

"Good day, Mr. President." The audible greeting was in a soft, male voice. Even though the room had been as quiet as a tomb, the interruption seemed natural without startling or surprise. The president spoke to ZZ<<Arkol25609 as though a conversation had already been in progress.

"What are the numbers in your name?"

"It is an ancestral matter, of no concern here."

"What do they mean?"

"Why do you ask?

"Just curious." The robot seemed to be thinking this over.

"My name is an interstitial abbreviation of a much more complex nomenclature that indicates the history of my origin and other important categorical information which is available with the proper protocols." There was a silence for a few seconds. Then the robot added, "To answer your question, the numbers are indicative of a date of origin. "ZZ" is a sort of version designation. "Arkol" is my family name. The symbol is a function indicator, like an emblem of rank. In aggregate my name is also a location. The organization of the elements is a directional historical statement if one knows the context." The president was shaking his head in wonder. He didn't know much about these robots – or ScreenKeepers as they were also called – that came to Earth with the ScreenMasters and the rise of Farson Uiost, but he did know that when they spoke, if they spoke at all, they spoke sparingly and exactly. He thought about what this robot had just said. "Indicative of a date of origin" not "the" date of origin. "Like" an emblem of rank, but not an actual rank. It had said overall its name was a location in the sense that that does not change, but clearly the robot was highly mobile. Finally, "a directional historical statement," again not an actual history. The robot had just given much information, but it had also raised many questions. Sortt had a feeling that academicians might be studying that statement for years in hopes of deciphering it. A question popped into Sortt's head.

"Family? You have a family?" The robot's strobing was steady. The president felt there was little chance that the robot's part of this conversation was going to continue, so he added one more question that he felt had a better chance of elucidation. "Do the ScreenMasters trust you?"

The strobing accelerated slightly.

"Not entirely."

"Does Farson trust you?"

"Yes."

19. Changing History

<<What are you doing, Farson?>>

<<Changing history, as you instructed.>>

<<ZZ<<Arkol talking with President Sortt? That's an unusual use of the robot, to say the least.>>

<<ZZ<< plainly permitted it. That is significant, I believe.>>

<<If you say so, Farson, but why did ZZ<<Arkol indicate that he was not fully trusted?>>

<<Uvo, why do you ask questions to which you already know the answers?>>

<<To hear the answers I expect, of course.>>

<<Sorry to disappoint.>>

20. Hattie (2)

"I'll tell you about that boy. He was the nicest, kindest, most knowing child I ever laid eyes on. He was like my family. He could have been my son. He could have been a little bit my father and darned if he didn't remind me a little bit of my own brother. Even some Granddaddy in there, too.

"Jees...usss! I loved that child."

21. Farson Gets Close

Farson was getting close, and he knew it.

"Farsy! What are you doing?"

"Darn it, Kari. You know exactly what I'm doing."

"I do not. Tell me."

"Why? We're both here. We're both doing it." Karina shifted beneath him.

"Doing what?" Farson caught a glimpse of her eyes.

"Making love."

"Just making love?"

Farson knew exactly what she meant. "No, Karina. Making love together."

"Pay attention then." Farson felt a soft mental touch pulling him closer and closer to her.

22. Exogenesis

The president stood looking at Uvo. The president took a seat with the thought: *That's the goddamndest thing I've ever seen.* What the president was looking at was a fairly familiar, if an unusual sight. The ScreenMaster, Uvo, was the classic image of an angel. Not that Sortt had ever seen an angel, but he knew one when he saw it.

<<Are you uncomfortable, Mr. President?>>

"Yes." The president knew that Uvo was communicating mentally with him. The president was speaking audibly in response. It seemed to be working. Uvo's next mental intrusion came faster than he expected, much faster.

<<Can I offer you anything that would make you more comfortable?>>

"Not really." It was all happening a little too fast. Again the intrusion came almost instantly, and in some strange way it was pleasant to him. Perhaps because of the amazing clarity of the thought that Uvo offered.

<<*Do you realize where we are?*>>

The president stood up and smoothed and buttoned his jacket. He took a deep breath. He knew the ScreenMaster was discussing the situation Earth was now in. "I have some idea. But do you know where you are? That is the question."

<<*Do you speak of your puny missiles? You can't be serious.*>>

The president turned to face Uvo, "No. I speak of my people. They are my sacred duty, and they are in my keeping. I request from you a promise that they will survive whatever you do here. That and only that will satisfy me."

<<*You think you can threaten us? You are defenseless.*>> The president stood his ground.

"Remember, Uvo. Farson Uiost is from here. He is one of us."

<<*Really? Is that what you think?*>>

"So, Sam, what's with the chair?"

"Chair? You mean that chair? The one you're sitting in, boy?"

"Yeah."

"Well, that chair belonged to a fine young person, younger than you and finer than you, too. He and me, we never really got to know each other, though, but when he was gone, I was very sad. So sad that one night I took a block of wood. I started hackin' at it. Worked all night. In the middle of the night I had a perfect likeness of him. So perfect it really looked ... well, it started to get to me so I started hackin' away again, and before the sun come up, I had that chair put together. The one you're in." Farson and Sam both knew that this was not a true story.

Sam got up and walked to the small bin on the floor. He took a scoop of coal, and then with a short step to the fire, he opened the little door and threw it into the potbellied stove. The embers flared, and then the fire darkened as the new coal spread out on top. "Go home, Farson."

"OK, Sam. See you tomorrow."

"OK, Insect. See you tomorrow."

23. Not to Me

<<*Uvo, I've found it. You're not going to like it, but this planet is very important. Very important. The cause of the instability is obvious after a while if you look hard enough. The planet, with its creations – many of which are seemingly unworthy, is a vital link. We must adjust the imbalance, the Rent, as you call it, without destroying the planet and the people here. Otherwise things will get much worse.*>>

<<*ScreenMaster Uiost, how can we agree with this proposal? You are asking for the truly unknown, perhaps the impossible. You know very well the direction things are going now. What you are asking is unreasonable.*>>

Farson looked into the ScreenMaster's mind and sent his next thought deep into it, with force. Deep into Uvo's mind, where the ScreenMaster could be left with no doubt whatsoever.

<<*Really? Are you sure, Uvo?*>>

24. Space-Going Vessels

"Hi Jim. You called?" James Peterson was not happy. He had just had confirming reports that his orbit was deteriorating, and that he had little choice but to try to establish an orbit around the Moon.

"Viera, I think I'm going to need some help here. The Earth really is gone."

Commander Nichols of MoonBase had been aware of the problem, of course, and was faced with an even more challenging situation, being far less independent than SkyKing. She said, "We are also adrift, we're in the same boat."

"So it would seem." They both were faced with a reality that no one could truly cope with. Earth gone. What did that mean? The people? The history? It was such an unknowable unknown. There was a long silence in the transmission.

Jim Peterson, knowing the high rivalry and deep suspicions that had always existed between the MoonBase and SkyKing, was relieved that they were being honest with each other, without the usual and annoying posturing banter. "Is there any way we can synchronize? It should offer some stability for the moment."

"We're working on it, Jim, but there will be problems."

"Nothing compared to just drifting around." Peterson knew well the differences. MoonBase people are rough pioneers. They work in a harsh environment, and they live hard and crudely. The Skers are religious. Their environment was pristine and controlled. They live strict lives of self-denial. They called it "unselfishness." The regular, non-Sker, SkyKing crew members were an unpredictable mix of the two. The lives of MoonBasers were wild and unpredictable to the Skers. The Skers were ordered and structured. The crew members were in the middle. With the Moon on its own in what had been a normal Earth orbit, things had been stable and regular; a sort of routine symbiosis had evolved. This new role of becoming the anchor planet was inconceivable to MoonBasers, and the role of becoming a satellite to the

Moon, locked in dependency with MoonBasers, was equally alien to SkyKing and its crew.

For both, the other had always been anathema, or at best, the butt of jokes and derision. Something known but ignored. Now they had to find common ground for action. They had to do it quickly. Peterson knew instinctively that his SkyKing crew would be the bridge to cooperation.

"Viera, you know you can count on my full cooperation. You have the raw materials and the production facilities. We have the food. We also have three hundred thousand-plus people to your eight thousand. So, let's get together." Viera sensed something behind his words.

"Was there a threat in there somewhere, Commander Peterson?"

"No, Viera, but neither of us have a choice right now. We need each other more than ever. Crew members of SkyKing are coming over to offer you all the help we can. Work with them and we might just all survive."

"Then what, Jim? This is starting to sound like an invasion." Commander Nichols was suspicious as she stared into the holographic visage of her friend Jim Peterson hovering in front of her. "Is that what it is, Jim? Are you sending your troops over?"

Peterson heard his daughter Brittany, stirring in her sleep in the next room. He glanced in that direction. Brittany was waking up. "No. It may look like that, but you will see. It'll be okay."

"Maybe we both will have to 'see,' Jim. Tit for tat, as they say."

The two commanders signed off with unanswered questions hanging in the air.

The two holographic images faded slowly. Ghosting images remained briefly on the screens and perhaps more than briefly in each of the two commanders' minds.

The blackness of space where Earth had been loomed as large as the planet ever had. It was suddenly so empty out there. People knew it could not be true. But the emptiness also was not to be denied. Like the fading images on the monitor screens, the planet's reality, as if it was still there, lingered in their minds, even as they got back to work. Even as they began the fight for survival.

25. How Can That Be?

"Come on, Handy, tell us true. Did the purple really cover the sun?"

"It did."

"Had you ever seen that before?"

"No. Absolutely not."

"How old are you, Handy?" Handy was thinking about this, but did not answer. "Has anyone else ever mentioned this happening before?"

"One passerby."

"What did he say?"

He said, "Be not afraid."

"Are you saying you saw Farson?"

"Yep. I saw him: Farson Uiost. Never forget that day, long as I live."

"How can that be, Handy? It was thousands and thousands of years ago."

"Yeah." Handy was nodding his head. "How *can* that be?"

26. Mrs. Chamberlain and the Headmaster

"Mrs. Chamberlain, how are you?" The headmaster was not feeling all that friendly, really.

"Very well, sir, thank you. Do you know why I am here?"

"Yes, Mrs. Chamberlain. Farson has been suspended for stealing."

"And what did he steal?" the mother asked.

"A telescope, I'm afraid, Mrs. Chamberlain."

"Has it been returned?"

"No."

"Is he on campus?"

"No. He's gone."

"Why is he off campus? Wasn't that your responsibility?"

"Yes."

"So. Are you at fault in this matter?"

"I suppose you could say that."

"Well then … " Her reply was not friendly.

"What are you going to do?"

"Exactly what you would do." Mrs. Chamberlain walked toward the headmaster and touched him gently on the shoulder and stepped back. The headmaster dematerialized, and was quickly replaced by another, an exact duplicate. Mrs. Chamberlain continued to work briefly on the new version, using powerful holographic tendrils and working swiftly, very expertly. She waited as the robot came fully online. "There," she said, "that should do it." She stepped back, and the new headmaster, looking very human, spoke to her.

"Mrs. Chamberlain, how are you?" The new headmaster was very friendly.

"Very well, sir, thank you. Do you know why I am here?"

"I have no idea, Mrs. Chamberlain. Farson is doing very well, and he is continuing exactly as our best plans could have predicted."

"He is on campus, of course?"

"Of course."

"Very well. My husband and I have another donation for the school's new hospital project."

"That is wonderful and very generous of you." Mrs. Chamberlain left the school in less than twenty minutes. On the way, she felt a familiar mental touch.

<<*Only he who aims at nothing always hits his mark.*>> To her, this held an element of humor.

<<*Only you would come up with that comment, Farson. I hope the telescope makes you happy.*>>

<<*I love it.*>>

27. Karina's Right

"I have a right to see him, ZZ." <<*Don't you agree?*>> Her mental contact was far more forceful than her verbal one, and ZZ<<Arkol25609 knew it right away.

<<*Karina, I'm not sure what you mean? You have 'seen' him.*>>

"I know when I see my brother and when I don't, ZZ? I can tell when I really see him and when I really don't." She suddenly turned threatening, angry. <<*How would you like it if I never actually 'saw' you again?*>> The rapid shifting back and forth from verbal to mental communication was bothersome to the robot. Her growing acumen with her new powers was unsettling. *How could she have learned so much so quickly?*

<<*Your brother is always with you now. He is constantly reliving the moment he learned to love, the moment he learned to really think, the moment he first saw you. You are always there with him now.*>>

"I'm talking about **him**, ZZ<<, **his body**. I want to see him. I want *him*."

<<*Karina, why are you badgering the robot? He can't defend himself; all you're doing is gumming up his circuits. They are very gentle creatures, you know.*>>

<<*Farson! Where are you? Why won't you come to me?*>>

There was a silence, then half a silence, then less, but still it was there, a separation. <<*Karina, I know. I feel it, too. But I'm so deep now. I'm almost lost out here. Time is confusing and vast. I'm changing complicated things, and I don't really want to. I can't always see the way back, and I thought I would. But I can always sense you and somehow always know where you are.*>> Karina could feel the separation increasing, and then the contact was gone, as though Farson had been pulled violently into a world without a sound or thought.

<< *Farson!*>>

Karina felt her tears welling up. Her sadness seemed to physically deflate her, like life ebbing from her. It was like grief. Some time passed and still she felt alone. And then … a faint whisper as though a billion miles away ...

<<*Karina! I am still here. It's changing now. I'm changing. Listen, I have things to tell you …* >>

She sat up as though waking, like a flower turning to the morning sun seeking its warmth. She listened as Farson's thoughts filled her mind with wonder and dread.

28. Sitwory Gazing

Sitwory was gazing. *It's not difficult*, she thought, looking out the window. *You just release your mind and fly The Ship.* But The Ship is not what one might have expected. It went wherever you thought, and it always, always, always came home in time for dinner. The planet they were approaching ("they" included the drunken Routier) was known throughout the omniverse for its unusual dress code. Most planets conformed to tradition and wore something, although in wildly different ways in both quantity and quality. Beach, as this planet was known, was completely nude. Clothing was considered to be the most perverse nature of civil disobedience known on the planet and was not present, nor permitted, in a phenomenally consistent way. Ever. People who came to Beach always followed local customs, no matter where they were from. In some ways it made perfect sense. Most people loved it. Once they got used to it.

"Routier, wake up, little guy. We're here." Routier opened his eyes. Sitwory was undressing in preparation for their arrival at Beach. "Come on, Routier. Get with it. We're almost there." Routier watched her throw off her blouse. Then she took off her pants and slippers. Then she removed her bra and underpants. She stood before him completely nude. *Perfect,* he thought. *She's perfect.* He was thinking about that first time he saw her. Nothing had changed. "Come on, Routier! Get with it!" Routier stood and removed his pants, then his shirt, then his undershirt, then his underwear. She looked him over admiringly. "Good, Routier! It took you long enough. Now, man the navigator's station."

<<*That is not the way it happened, Farson.*>>

<<*Are you sure, Karina?*>> She replayed the memory in her mind. She was sure. *Still,* she thought, *it's not a bad version.*

29. Another Day In Paradise

Farson and Karina
Moving through all time
Touching place to place
Touching face to face
Farson and Karina
Love's best purity
Farson and Karina
Oh, sincerity ...

"Oh, come on, Handy. Get to bed." Always the first in bed, Mrs. Handy knew exactly what was going on. She had seen it all a hundred times over the past two years. "Get to bed, Handy!" She was repeating herself.

Handy put down his guitar and looked out the window. It was a quiet night, a still night. The sky was so dark.

Handy was thinking and poetically planning back right here again tomorrow night. He looked around: an empty glass, a full ashtray, some magazines, and the pages of poetry he had written. He turned and walked into the bedroom and made his way over to the bed.

Mrs. Handy let him nestle in beside her. As he was dozing off, beneath a soft comforter, he opened his eyes lazily and licked his dry lips. Through the open window he could see that stark blackness he had grown accustomed to, like a void but not a void. Like a night sky, but not at all like a night sky at all. Everything had changed. He dozed off in the quiet of a starless sky as motionless as a painting.

In the morning he was up very early as though to get a jump on a busy schedule he did not have.

He looked around at his home in the "bottle" as he called it. *Another day in paradise.* His thoughts were like those trees that fell in the woods, but no one heard them.

30. We'll See

<<*ScreenMaster Uiost! That is way, way too many.*>>

<<*By whose standards?*>>

<<*What do you mean by that?*>>

<<*You said I have an advantage. I'm taking it.*>>

<<*We'll see, ScreenMaster. We'll see.*>>

31. *What If I'm Crazy?*

Let America be America again.
Let it be the dream it used to be.
Let it be the pioneer on the plain
A home where we roam free.

(America never was America to me.)

Let America be the dream the dreamers dream
Let it be that great strong land of love
Where no kings connive nor tyrants scheme
Where no one is crushed from above.

(America never was America to me.)

Handy stopped writing. He looked around. There was a nearing-empty glass of gin and melting ice to the right. There was a scratched-out poem to the left. There were self-rolled stubbed-out cigarettes in an ashtray. There was a song in the air. "Let it be the dream it used to be. Let it be the pioneer on the plain ... " Handy thought it through again. *That's a new verse. I didn't write it.*

What if I'm just going crazy?

A thought of regret came to Handy. *It's too bad really. There was a lot going for Earth before this all happened. We were really great.* He thought of all that those people had done and said. All those years of being free and stupid. Those years when what was said never seemed to matter. How it was all the written and recorded for history. How it seemed as though it would go on forever. *The world without limits,* he thought. Then another thought came to him. *Where are we now?*

Chapter Three

"Where Are We Now?"

32. Nearing Beach, Sitwory

"Farson, where are we now?"

"Nearing Beach, Sitwory. Where the "H"-"E"- double two sticks do you think we are?" Sitwory slowly sat up and looked around, languid from "landing The Ship." Routier was lying beside her, naked, and covered with perspiration and exhausted. "That's a tradition other planets could use." They had learned from experience that navigation and landing on Beach was always accompanied with creative and amative expression. It was just one of those things that Beach demanded. It sort of went with the dress code. She looked over at Farson. He was looking at her. He was on the verge of laughing out loud.

<<*You are here, Farson. That's amazing.*>>
<<*Are you happy?*>>
<<*Yes.*>>
<<*I told you, you would know.*>>

Farson sat up and pressed his lips against her cheek and then, a deeper kiss on her mouth, a much more intimate kiss. The conversation could have gone on, even with all the distractions. Karina knew what Farson was doing, using their memories to stay in touch, taking her with him to those moments they had lived so intensely together. Living them again in every way, but with subtle changes that only she would know. The way their lips touched, how she closed her eyes, what happened next. They both knew that he was playing in time, changing things, but it didn't really matter. It was so real. "Time again," he called these moments. She smiled to herself, knowing that the small changes were how she knew he was with her: messages from The Screen. An unreality that told her it was real. A secret communication code, indecipherable to anyone not just the two of them. She thought of his phrase "Time again." *Time again*, she thought. *And again. Please. Again.*

33. What Are You?

<<*Farson, you are getting carried away!*>>

<<*Uvo. Listen. Let's think deeper. This is my Ascension. Can't you feel the power? Let it go, Uvo! Awake! Come with me. 'Be not afraid.'*>>

<<*Farson, remember, you are a ScreenMaster, not the messiah.*>>

<<*And what are you, Uvo?*>>

34. Twill

Farson knocked on the office door.

"Come in, Mr. Uiost." The professor was seated deeply and comfortably in a black leather chair that leaned backward and to one side, which some might have thought defective, but Farson knew that the angle indicated a very advanced free-gimbaled mechanism. That impression was confirmed as Farson moved across the office, and the chair automatically adjusted to a new position, always keeping the professor facing Farson.

<<*So, who are you?*>> The professor paused abruptly. Not taken aback, just amused. He had been expecting it. The clarity of power of the thought, its authority, did surprise him slightly. Upon reflection he knew it was to be expected. But still, from a FirstLevel ScreenMaster it was unusual.

The chair shifted nimbly, and, suddenly, they were now close together.

<<*I am Twill, Farson.*>> The professor arose from the chair and walked to the blackboard. He began speaking. "There is a theory, Mr. Uiost, that unnature has gained an irreversible advantage over nature. What do you theorize?"

Farson felt the gaze again. "Well, Professor, there does seem to be an imbalance." Twill knew he was trying to be funny. Almost dismissive of Twill's true meaning.

The professor walked to the window and looked out on a playing field full of children of many different ages all playing together. He spoke to Farson as though they were friends. "So, what? What does that matter? Nature. Unnature. It's all ours anyway." The professor returned to his chair, which quickly gimbaled him into the most advantageous position to face Farson. Slightly higher, slightly too close. Twill was waiting for his answer like an outfielder waiting for a high fly ball to fall into his mitt. His sense of impatience was in the air.

"Because, *Professor* Twill, it is of great importance."

"Be more specific."

"Professor, you remember the *Monitor*?"

"Yes, the first metal ship? It sank as I recall, Mr. Uiost."

"Yes. It sank because it weighed too much. Even though scientists of that day thought they knew exactly what they were doing. They didn't. The *Monitor* sank suddenly and unfortunately in its first combat situation. It was a spectacular failure."

"So?" The professor stood up, and the chair retracted itself. The professor was studying Farson's face. "What has that got to do with anything?"

"Professor Twill, when a society is over encumbered with just one idea to a distraction, it often falls short in the human mix of things, which always requires ingenuity and extreme flexibility. It is one thing to put a few men at risk with a fashionable new technology, but it is altogether another when one considers this sort of folly in an environment where there is a power capable of destroying everything if you misjudge. Where entire species can be at risk. Have you considered that, Twill? That you could be wrong?"

<<*Farson, I am worried about you. You have learned much. You are certainly a virtuoso. Perhaps to a fault. Your theories are wild, far from what ScreenMasters consider to be true. It makes it very costly to be persuaded by you in even the slightest way.*>>

<<*More to the opposite, I would say.*>> Farson's thoughts were like arrows striking the dead center of their target.

<<*But, Farson, there is order here, and you can see why. We've worked hard at it, and now you want to completely disregard it.*>>

<<*For a time.*>>

<<*Not for always?*>>

<<*For a time, Twill. Be not of so little faith. Watch. Listen. Come with me if you want. Counsel me. Twill, counsel me. Don't oppose me.*>>

"Mr. Uiost, it seems to me you are out on an indefensible limb. That is the biggest cock-and-bull idea I've heard in years. But you do interest me. You are articulate and persuasive up to a point. Then it stops. Your logic fails. Would you be willing to show me a real-life example of what you are describing? Some observable corroboration, if you will?"

<<Be careful what you ask for, Twill. You might just get it.>>

35. Marooned

<<Uvo, I am not alone now. You said I would be. You probably won't believe me yet, with so much in the balance. Read this epistle. See how I work it out as I go. See how the words rush and then stumble. You'll know it's me; you will know. You will ask, "How can that be? Written so many years ago?" If you know the way, 'ago' is closer than you think.>>

To the Skers

Your world is beyond a dream. It is The Epi-Dream. Your people are so beautiful that none can compare. You are healthy in body and spirit. You are both here together, and here with The Father and His Son, and, yes, with The Holy Ghost. It is with the deepest love and brotherhood that I write these unworthy passages to you.

I, Farson, was with Him in Bethlehem, and again in Calvary. I was on the Mount and ate the loaves and the fishes. I was with Paul when he healed the blind man. As told in Acts, I was there as devils leapt to the unknown. I drank the wine that was the water, and I have walked on the waves.

More, I have seen death many times. It is nothing compared to the promise of The Kingdom within your city.

I write to you because it was foretold that I would.

I am unfit to do this.

I walk away from the work and despair. I was instructed to do it thus. I cannot resist that. I was there in America. I saw the sign. I know them. And I know you.

The people of your city in the sky shall live long in prosperity. They shall explore new worlds and seek out new inventions. They shall be children of God among the stars as you have all prayed and as it has been foretold. The comforting words and The Book shall be with them. *For this*, I thank you for The Others.

And more.

I would presume to warn you.

Because even as The Son toppled the money-lenders' table, I must also act.

There is an enemy. He comes with no notice. But I will give you guidance to know him, before he knows you.

As the dead child fell from the rafters, so too can you fall.

Keep the mind that was in Him in you. Walk in the direction of your treasure. Forgive the prodigal son. Remember, the meekest among you will inherit. Always remember, "Be not afraid," for I am with you.

God bless you and keep your fortunes as you sail free in destiny as has been foretold, beneath stars of your most cherished dreams.

Even as I pass from this life, I will come again. There is no death, but there is life. You must live. Your world must live. The kingdom which is given freely still requires much. As you sail into your destiny, remember that The Others are the kingdom, they are the power, and they are the glory forever. Without them, you are lost.

May the peace of the love which flows in your people, and the sacrifice which you cherish, keep your hearts and minds in the knowledge which you have learned and I have taught. Not for me have I done all this, but for you. You are the children. You are chosen. You are my people, in whom all love and grace is bestowed. You shall see Him as he is. As I have. Trust in that knowledge which cannot be known except by faith. Hold to your hearts the substance of things unseen.

Forever in grace and love. – Farson Uiost

<<Well, Farson, you have achieved a level of religiosity that I certainly did not foresee. It seems out of place to me. To us.>>

<<Why would you say that? The Screen itself satisfies the definition, not to mention what is actually beyond The Screen. You cannot blame them for what you yourself have seen and believed without question. You cannot blame them for doing what you knew from the start they would do. Your words and phrases are different, but they are the same. Perhaps the first inklings of a pattern is now occurring to you, but I doubt it. Do you doubt it, Uvo?>>

<<Doubt, Farson? How novel of you.>>

Uvo's thoughts were preoccupied now with Farson's thoughts. "Beyond The Screen?" Even Uvo's wondrous mind was stumbling over that phrase.

<<Better if you think of it as poetic, Uvo. 'Novel' could mean something new, something unusual and this ... this is far, far from 'new' or 'unusual.' Only those who cannot see what I see feel that way. There are many, though silent and apart, who now see the truth as I do.>>

36. SkyKing

Jim Peterson was addressing the fifty shuttle pilots assigned to his command in the shuttle hanger. Ten were navy regulars, ten were reservists doing their tour, and the remaining thirty were Skers.

They were all good people. He knew each and every one. He spoke into a public address system from an elevated stage. Each pilot could easily see their commander. He was alone on the platform.

"Stay strong, troops. We are called to a mighty duty today. This is not a religious operation, but it is perhaps a chance to save a lot of people.

"Skers, you will have to act as part of the team today. So, let me remind you that ordinary people struggle, each on his or her own, throughout their lives. Most of us have no script or guide, no scripture to follow. Each person is unique and surprisingly individual. But all of us are equal. There are no good or bad people here on SkyKing, or on MoonBase. There are just people: people who are in a lot of trouble, people who can help each other, and who really need each other right now. We all have to put those facts first, ahead of all others, including our religious beliefs. If you can't do that, then stay here. If you can, let's go to the Moon and save what's left of humanity."

Those last words filled the room: "What's left of humanity."

Addressing the Skers again, he said, "As much as some of you might not be looking forward to the prospect of living and working among the 'unenlightened,' we must all prepare for extended operations on the Moon." Even though this was intended for the Skers, everyone was listening because everyone knew how important the Skers were to this operation and to everything. Many SkyKing crew members also had reservations about the scrappy and apparently disorganized mining community on the Moon. The space station was highly organized and sterile by comparison. The Moon, to a Sker, was a mess of quixotic elements, illogically arranged with filthy working conditions, and a social situation that bordered on chaos. In truth, most of the occupants of SkyKing looked down on the MoonBasers both figuratively and literally from their lofty home. But things had drastically changed, and the two disparate communities were rising to the occasion, each in its own way.

The Sker captain advanced a step forward. Voul Jonsn was regal in his erect bearing. He was handsome and intelligent. Standing there in his pure white uniform, in front of thirty other Skers, Voul appeared larger than life. Much larger. Jim Peterson walked to stand beside him, a contrast in his rumpled dark-blue working uniform. He was feeling a little sheepish, despite the reality of his command position. Peterson was not yet quite sure exactly how Voul would respond to the new mission and to the new circumstances. Voul's face, as Peterson surveyed it, was even more inscrutable than usual. The Skers were careful planners, and this situation was definitely not in their plan. But when Voul spoke, he spoke so simply and clearly that Commander Peterson knew he was worrying for nothing. Voul's words rang true throughout the hangar.

"Commander, what are your orders? We are ready to serve."

Peterson scratched his stubble. Three days' growth; there was no disguising that. Next to the immaculate Voul and Sker pilots, he felt disheveled and dirty. It had not been an easy three days. But, Commander Peterson continued on.

"Voul, once you arrive, get everything set up and ready to go. Then meet with Viera Nichols and agree on the privacy issues and the other conditions we have discussed. Make peace, not war. It's a vast cold void that surrounds us now, and we need all the friends we can get."

The commander felt a familiar presence behind him. His daughter Brittany had come up on stage. He hugged her, a brunette and blithe child who immediately hugged herself to her dad. Commander Peterson peered over Brittany and through her hug to the assembled men and women. He smiled and said, "Good luck, Voul. We have no choice now. And good luck to us all." He watched as the pilots were dismissed and began climbing into the shuttles, preparing for launch. It would not be long before the bay doors would open and the fleet would be on its way. He took Brittany's hand, and walked through the hatch which led back to the bridge. Just before it closed behind him, he turned and looked one more time into the hangar. Voul was about to enter his shuttle, but he had also turned for one more look back. He waved and Peterson waved back. But Brittany was waving far more enthusiastically and also shouting Voul's name and saying, "I love you, Voul. Be careful!" Peterson saw the Sker leader smile broadly and nod his head. Jim Peterson thought to himself, *those two*.

The Sker captain turned from the commander and his daughter and entered his shuttle. He spoke to his first officer. "Is the fleet ready?" The first officer nodded.

"Yes, sir." Voul, despite his confident appearance, was having second thoughts. SkyKing would soon be a vessel in space, not a space station. As such, in the order of naval command only the ranking officer of the line could technically be in command of a vessel. Commander Peterson was a logistics officer, and a damn good one. And while SkyKing had been a station, he had always been in command. But now, things were, at least technically, very different. Commander Peterson knew he was now number two, because Voul outranked him as an officer of the line. They both knew it, of course. They knew something else as well: that SkyKing was in deep trouble. Voul Jonsn knew that the moment they achieved orbit around the moon, command would technically transfer back to Commander Peterson and that again the sacred dream of his people to "sail free" would be out of their hands. Right now, right here they were free of the Earth, free of the encumbering orbit, and free of being ruled by others. The scriptures were crying out to him to seize the moment. He could feel the anticipation in the other Skers around him. The moment they had been waiting for for generations was at hand.

But things were not yet ready. Things were not as they had been planned.

Captain Jonsn looked into the eyes of his shuttle pilot, also a Sker, of course. "Then, send the shuttles, Lieutenant. Let's go to the Moon!" With a soft click of the heels of his polished boots, he came to attention, turned and moved to the pilot's command chair. The other officers and crew assumed their positions as well. The shuttle came alive.

In ten minutes, fifty space shuttles, in perfect formation, fully loaded with troops, arms, and vehicles, were flying toward the Moon with serious intent.

37. The Chamberlains

<<*Karina, did you know about the Chamberlains?*>>

<<*No, Farson.*>>

<<*They were ScreenKeepers. Do you agree?*>>

<<*The evidence is accumulating.*>>

<<*Have you thought about Hattie and Sam?*>>

<<*I am so confused, Farson. Sometimes I wonder if I ever really knew anything.*>>

<<*They are real.*>>

<<*Even now?*>>

<<*Even now.*>>

38. An Interim Arrangement

"Viera?"

"Yes, Jim?" Commander Nichols had just received the information about the shuttles and was considering the situation and the possible defense of MoonBase. Men and women were running to battle station assignments all over the Moon that, up until this moment, they had all heard of but had never actually manned. Seventy-five years of colonization had set certain patterns. Repelling an attack was one contingency that had been originally provided for in some detail but never practiced. It was an option that everyone knew would never happen. The written protocols were filed away somewhere deep in the archives and while the administrative staff searched for them, Viera had ordered the defensive operations to begin, but she was, in every sense of the word, just winging it. Jim Peterson's voice, as always, seemed to have a soothing and organizing effect on her thoughts.

"Voul Jonsn and his pilots are en route. Please welcome them and help them. Their interests are only in completing their systemization mission and then to get out of your hair as soon as possible; they want to help you steady up the Moon and to get us into a stable orbit. They know that now, without the Moon, SkyKing systems will falter. We were not ready for all of this either, and we certainly were not prepared for independent flight under any conditions. Their instructions from me are to work out an interim arrangement for synchronization and stabilization. Then to get off the Moon as fast as possible."

"Are you coming over, Jim?"

"Not yet, maybe later. I'll let you know." He could see her face, of course, and her concern. He smiled. Her eyes widened a little, and her eyebrows moved upwardly ever so slightly. She couldn't help herself. They were old friends. She smiled back. "Peterson out." It was a matter-of-fact conversation, but there was also a little tenderness and Viera appreciated Jim Peterson's predictable friendliness. Viera reached for the monitor switch and flipped it down, signing off without saying goodbye. She had always liked Jim Peterson, and the thought of seeing him and his daughter was a pleasing thought. The thought of all these Skers and troops heading her way was far less pleasing, but these were crazy times. *If we're not all killed, it might be fun*, she thought on her way to MoonBase Central. She had also always liked the fresh, crisp white uniforms that the Skers wore. *Sexy*, she thought, smiling. *They really look sexy in those uniforms.*

39. Girlie Mags, a Glass of Gin, No Ice

Handy looked around, and he didn't like what he saw: girlie mags and a glass of gin with no ice. He took a drink. *My guitar.* The quick thought came in a rush. *Where is it?* In a brief befuddled panic, Handy jerked his head to look. *There it is.* As if emerging from a deep dream where things were going all wrong, he realized things were still as they were. Relieved for no reason other than those he attributed to his usual overindulgence *(if that is the correct phrase)*, he shook off his sense of trepidation and reached, unsteadily, to pick the instrument up. He played a song. His stubby fingers felt a little sluggish on the frets. But he soldiered on.

As he played, Handy looked around and took a wheezy breath. He stopped for moment, raised the laserlite to his stogie, and took a puff. *The tobacco's still good,* he thought. He took another drink from the room temperature glass, ice long ago melted away. He unmuted the room's monitor. It was tuned to a news channel, and people were talking. Handy knew he should have gone to bed a long time ago. *But sometimes you just keep drinkin' and smokin' till God brings tomorrow.* He knew that tomorrow is no proof of God. That unexpected events intervene when you're not looking and that people mess things up when you least expect it is the only true creed. He knew full well that if you follow rather than lead, you will be presented with some interesting and perhaps unwelcome realities. Handy was still alone, and that was a fact he knew well. *Fair enough. I am one of the most powerful ScreenMasters there is, and I have to drink all alone.* That made him laugh.

<<*Farson, is this what you wanted? Me sitting here all alone night after night?*>>

<<*I apologize, but things are what they are, and you know it.*>>

<<*Farson, where are you going?*>>

<<*To hell, Handy, to hell.*>> Handy looked down at the magazines on the sofa, too many of them for a casual explanation.

<<*Oh, great. Where does that leave me?*>>

40. Noumenon

<<*How high should I go?*>> Handy was trying to estimate his capacity. *It's one thing to write poetry, he thought. It's another to be a ScreenMaster. Farson's a damn good kid. Best I've ever seen. There is the other question, and I'm not ready to answer that.*

Farson was suddenly beside Handy.

<<*And what's that, Handy?*>>

<<*Farson.*>> Handy was not surprised. <<*Whatever you think, there are still some things you don't know.*>>

<<*How can that be, Handy?*>>

<<*Farson, why are you so sure? How could you have missed it?* >>

<<*The noumenon?*>>

<<*So you do know it. What of charity, Farson? Don't forget that.*>>

<<*"For now we see through a glass, darkly; but then face to face: now I know in part; but then shall I know even as also I am known. And now abideth faith, hope, charity, these three; but the greatest of these is charity."*>>

<<*The boy knows his scripture.*>>

<<*Handy, it's not really scripture; it's more like common sense, if you know what I mean.*>> Farson laughed.

Handy quaffed down his drink, a good four ounces of gin and vermouth and took a big pull on the waning cigar, inhaling deeply and with disregard. <<*Who do you think you're talking to, boy? I wasn't born yesterday, you know.*>> This made Handy laugh even more than Farson had.

Farson was gone. Handy was on his way to gone in another sense. "It's a little boring here, just me and missus, you know," he said out loud to no one.

Outside a storm was forming off in the East. Handy stared at it and laughed again. "I better be gettin' ready to batten down the hatches." *It ought to be here in another thousand years or so.*

41. The Man Who Knew Too Much

Handy opened his eyes, looked up, and then fell asleep. He was flat on his back. When he finally awoke again, he felt refreshed. He looked around and turned on the VT. Alfred Hitchcock's *The Man Who Knew Too Much* was playing in black and white. Handy watched it for a while. He was thinking about his own life. *I know too much, too.* Handy was not born on Earth, but like Earth's people, he was there.

The planet was becoming a utopia of sorts, even its name was changing. Everyone had pretty much everything they needed. People took their time and did things right.

The people of Emerald Earth, as Farson had renamed it, were farmers and technicians. Someone had said they were now all working in the new Garden of Eden. They were generally happy gardeners, to be sure. They had no politics; only people that were dedicated to wisely working the planet. The planet was very, very productive. Technology to the people of Emerald Earth was everything and they put all of their considerable technical skills into agriculture, research, and improving and maintaining the environment. Hunger was now unheard of. Money was long gone and unneeded. The only currency of exchange was helping each other, and, of course, there was exporting food and raw materials.

Travel was easy on the transcontinental shuttle-ways and transporter arches that were nonpolluting and located conveniently around the planet. Education was universal and continuous, and the people of Emerald Earth had evolved into a very ingenious and inventive people, known as the Emers. Their government was informal and mostly unneeded, very egalitarian, much, much smaller than what had gone before. Elections were never held. There were no campaigns. In many ways – perhaps in every way – the planet had achieved what every philosopher and social activist had always dreamed of: unceasing fairness, peace, and prosperity. The people of Emerald Earth had eventually come to the inescapable conclusion that their planet was really all they had. Finally, they were making the most of it. Emerald Earth was perhaps the most beautiful place in all of space. Emerald Earth, where Handy Townsend was not born at all. He had been born on a planet torn by war and pollution, greed and avarice. His planet had destroyed itself and everything around it. His planet had been a disaster. Handy was a child of that planet and always would be.

Now, sitting in front of the VT, watching an antique movie, Handy had a well-earned sense of peace, although it was a troubled peace. He was worried about the changes going on now. *Things are changing that shouldn't be changing. Thank God for Farson. Maybe he can fix it.*

<<Handy, I'm causing it. I'm trying to accelerate it.>> In a purple glow Farson Uiost appeared on the sofa beside Handy. Handy pushed the bowl of popcorn over to him, and Farson took a handful. "Good movie?" Farson asked.

"You ought to know," Handy answered, chuckling to himself without looking at Farson.

The two of them sat there for another hour, watching the movie, eating popcorn. At the end of the movie Handy was asleep. Farson stood up and looked at him. His rough shirt was open to the waist. He had a potbelly. The stogie was cold in the ashtray. The glass was empty, of course, and moistly staining the table. There were a few kernels of popcorn in his lap and on the sofa. Farson extended his arm, and a purple streak swept like lightning toward Handy, only to be turned back, suddenly, on Farson. In a purple flash, Farson disappeared. He was laughing as he went.

<<Farson, he is way too powerful for that sort of thing.>>
<<Only testing, Uvo, only testing.>>

Handy drowsily adjusted his posture on the sofa, brushing popcorn off himself and looking over at his empty glass.

He glanced at the movie, now nearing its dramatic conclusion. The heroine, a skilled sharpshooter, was just placing her rifle's crosshairs on the man who had captured and held her daughter hostage. As she pulled the trigger, Handy closed his eyes and fell asleep.

Chapter Four
The Skers

42. They Were Innocents

They were innocents, and, in the beginning, they were few. They were born on SkyKing one by one, and one after the other. They were men and women who looked to the sky as if they could have it. In truth, they were always dreamers. But SkyKing needed, and ultimately demanded, a hardworking people to fill it, a driven people with a mission. Slowly, their numbers grew and grew.

The first people of the station were astronauts, but after that, the teachers and the bakers and all the others came. They kept coming for fifty years. Then they began to multiply among themselves. Of course, Earth kept sending more. But the Skers, those born on SkyKing, had always been special, and everyone knew it. SkyKing was their home. They became SkyKing's people. They were different in their thinking and their ways. Ultimately, they became a naturally religious and an infinitely disciplined people. They were clean, clear-headed, dedicated, and industrious, like the little world they reinvented. That they eventually took over all the important and vital functions on SkyKing was an inevitability. Their destiny. That they were so consistently good at running the station was the catalyst for their success and, ultimately, for the success of SkyKing.

Importantly, the Skers were also scrupulously fair and exquisitely trustworthy. They genuinely liked to help. The Skers perfected SkyKing. They managed the gardens and made agriculture an important success on the space station, and an export of great importance to the Moon and its people. They pioneered the cherished Right of Privacy. They made their children the building blocks of their world. They helped to bring peace to Earth. Like the Native American Indians, and other aborigines, before them, the Skers worked to preserve their own world by living in peace with all around them. Preserve it they did, by their peaceful and healthy productive lives. Through loyalty and tradition, they sought only their highest goal of peace and understanding. On SkyKing, circling the Earth in high orbit, they found it.

Captain Voul Jonsn was their leader since the great Ban Jonsn, his revered father, died. The high rank of captain came later. He was the son of Ban Jonsn, whom the Skers honored above all others. Now Voul was captain of SkyKing, a space-traveling vessel, recently independent of Earth. To him the heavy responsibilities of leadership came naturally, if uneasily.

Now it was Voul to whom had fallen the sad abandoning of all the Sker principles to fight a battle off their world. If he didn't do it, SkyKing would perish. If he did do it, he would have tarnished forever his father's legacy. Unthinkable that he would be the one to break the sacred vows and fight another's battle. Voul knew there was no other choice.

He was sitting before the flagship shuttle's console of the SkyKing fleet as he thought these things over. His rumination was interrupted by an incoming communication.

"Commander MoonBase to SkyKing Captain, over."

He recognized the uncertainty in her voice. He had spoken to Viera Nichols only once or twice in the past, but he had never met her. He remembered that she had called him by his first name despite their lack of actual familiarity. "Yes,

Commander?" he replied, intoning a calm receptiveness. He could tell that Viera Nichols's complete undivided attention was fastened on him. The holographic images were always crystal clear. They knew of each other, of course, but their first face-to-face meeting was coming soon and they both knew it. Viera thought of Voul as an ascetic who moved around on SkyKing. A man she would never meet. Their worlds were so different and so far apart in every way. She considered him incredibly aloof and afar. When his name came up in correspondence or in meetings, it was like a reference to a person in an encyclopedia, a paragraph somewhere about someone in history but not really an actual person. *It's weird that he is commanding the incoming shuttle crews. It's weird that I will finally meet him like this.*

He knew of her as the leader of the raucous and unruly world of MoonBase where discipline and structure did not exist, at least in any way Skers understood. The stories from MoonBase were vivid and unbelievable, but he had been assured that they were all true.

43. Can We Help?

The male voice on the communicator was unaffected and direct. She liked it. *His tone is perfect*, she thought.

"Commander Peterson has briefed me on your conversation with him, Commander Nichols. We are en route to your location, ETA about 30 minutes." *Short and sweet.*

"Yes, I know, Voul." Viera was more than aware of the approaching fleet and of its capabilities. Even though the Moon's ancient defense protocols were in the process of being implemented – *sorted out,* she mentally corrected herself – she knew that the Moon was virtually defenseless if it came to a fight. *At least for now.* "Is there anything we can do?" Captain

Jonsn was listening to her intonation for any signs of trouble. He knew that if the MoonBase interfered with their mission, SkyKing's existence could be threatened. No one thought that would happen, but Voul, after all, was a Sker, and Skers left no contingency to chance. All possibilities were automatically considered in depth. So he knew it was not beyond the realm of imagination for MoonBase to react badly. For SkyKing, however, MoonBase was the only solution. SkyKing could not long survive without the Moon, so for now he was attentive as only a Sker could be, and projecting a genuine feeling of friendship and cooperation to Commander Nichols.

"Well then, Commander, with your permission, we will be landing soon, and I should be at your office within an hour."

"It's strange that you now ask for permission to land after launching every shuttle in the fleet without notification." Viera and the entire crew of MoonBase had always kept their distance from SkyKing and especially from the lofty and remote Skers. She and the entire Moon operation had historically wanted nothing to do with any of them. She certainly didn't relish the idea of hundreds of them marching all over MoonBase telling her what to do. They were religious zealots for God's sake! The Skers were the antipathy of MoonBasers, who lived freewheeling, undisciplined, hedonistic lives, and their raucous activities in the off-duty hours, were, to say the least, not to the taste of the antiseptic Skers. *And I am their leader.* She smiled to herself.

"Commander, do we have your permission?" Voul was listening intently now, both to his own thoughts and to the thoughts of the MoonBase commander. He said a silent prayer of thanks for this ability. Skers had developed mild telepathic capabilities over the years, probably due to their strictures of procreation and reproduction, possibly also due in part to their reluctance to speak unnecessarily, but certainly because of the rigorous mental disciplines of their religion. The quietude of thought was a realm where the Skers thrived. Voul, like all Skers, was perfectly comfortable in long periods of silence. They prayed in solitude. One of these long silences was now occurring, somewhat awkwardly. Viera was not comfortable at all. In the silence, Voul listened intently for any sign of hesitation or deception. Hesitation, yes, that was there; but there was no deception. In fact, he noticed in her simplicity of thought a clarity of purpose that surprised him and that he found oddly beautiful. *That is inappropriate,* he thought as he continued to investigate her mind. He was unable to stop his curiosity. He searched again in his own mind through her phrasing and through the thoughts behind her thoughts. To buffer himself, he attempted to program a mental shield against dwelling on the new findings in Viera Nichols's thoughts, but, again he found he kept returning to them. She was compelling. She is so unSker-like, in every way. When he shook his head to clear his focus, he found it still did not work. He was still in her mind. *Or she is in mine?*

Skers at best were mild telepaths, but they were highly empathic in areas of truth and honesty. They could easily detect patterns of thought that were too complex or convoluted for the moment. It was not widely known outside their own race, but it was entirely impossible to lie to a Sker without them knowing it immediately. *She's not lying, but there is something back there in her mind, something like a hedge on a bet.* While Viera was somewhat uncomfortable in the silence, she was using the time to resolve a struggle in her own thoughts, trying to find a proper response. Voul decided to try to reestablish verbal contact again.

"Commander Nichols?"

"Yes, Voul."

"Do we have your permission?" Viera was slightly surprised at this repeating of the question. From what she knew of Skers, it was very unusual to repeat anything already stated clearly. Even this slight show of impatience was out of character.

"It's a little unsettling, Voul." With fifty shuttles bearing down, full of men and women who really knew very little about her and MoonBase, and who perhaps couldn't care less, on a mission of their own, involving the survival of their race and their world, she felt her sense of hesitation was entirely proper for the circumstance.

"Is there anything I can do to make it easier for you?" He said this to her openly and he meant it, but he was actually thinking about his crew, mostly Skers, and what they would be experiencing on the Moon. This sort of close encounter with the decadent MoonBasers was never contemplated in the high councils. The idea that the Skers would be able to work together within the unmade bed of MoonBase, the crew members of which were almost universally agnostic and who did whatever they wanted regarding morals and lurid behavior of all descriptions, was an idea that really had not occurred to anyone in the inner Sker world. "Make peace, not war," was what Commander Peterson had said. Viera was speaking again.

"Captain Jonsn" – Voul found he was disappointed that she did not use his first name this time – "you are requested to land your command shuttle at the airlock of New Chicago, and to instruct the remainder of your force to remain in low orbit around the Moon. We are granting permission for only you to land your shuttle at this time. Please come to my location in about sixty minutes, say 1200 hours." Viera hoped this would be agreeable. If it was not, there was very little she could do about it.

Voul was thinking about his father, as he nodded in agreement and relayed the information to MoonBase and to the other forty-nine shuttles. His father would have known exactly what to do. Viera saw the nod and the disappointment at the forced change in his plans – something else Skers did not abide well. Voul watched carefully as Viera acknowledged his acquiescence. There was no revealing expression on her face as she turned to the left and signed off with a flick of her wrist, her fading image still present in his mind well after the connection was severed.

Back on SkyKing, Commander Peterson, who had been monitoring the audio of this exchange, was also nodding in agreement. He realized that there was now one chance and one chance only to avoid unpleasantness: that, upon meeting each other, Viera Nichols and Voul Jonsn would get along and trust one another. *That may be a real long shot*, he thought.

44. Viera Gets Dressed

Viera Nichols always began every day with intense exercise, usually in the nude, of course. Her body was that of a youthful athlete. She stood before the mirror in her compartment's exercise room. *Absolutely perfect*, she thought. Her tawny hair was shoulder length, soft and shiny. Her skin was smooth. Her breasts, her thighs, her buttocks, and her legs were trim and firm with subtle and defined musculature. *Low gravity helps.*

Viera had never had a cavity, never really been sick. Her life had been a long string of success after success, and as commander of MoonBase, she was now at the pinnacle of her career and of her life. For nine years in space she had happily observed the aging process slowing down to an almost imperceptible pace. She liked that. *Spacers have all the advantages.*

Her daily exercise program could include running, swimming, cycling, weight lifting, calisthenics, yoga, meditation, stretching, and a large serving of martial arts with Ensign Reginald Chambois at the end of her workout. MoonBase had it all.

Here in her compartment she had weights, a treadmill, mats for yoga and calisthenics, and a sophisticated lighting, gravitational, and circulation systems. It was all perfect for the quiet times she loved and for exercising with a certain young ensign.

Today was no different. As the exercise session ended with a wrestling match, Viera locked the ensign's shoulders to the mat with her knees, facing toward his feet. She noticed that he had an excellent erection. She found that having his body so near to her was comforting, and she relaxed somewhat. She reached out for him. She slowly stroked the stiffness as she turned to kiss him. She continued, and he continued too. In the end, they settled down to rest for a while. It had all been so deeply satisfying to her. The two of them soon fell asleep, intertwined and nude, unfettered and free in the world of MoonBase.

Acting on his commander's very specific and emphatic instructions to show Captain Voul Jonsn to her quarters immediately at the appointed time, the orderly standing guard outside of the commander's suite of rooms opened the door and led the leader of the Skers into the room just as Viera and the ensign were waking up. Voul stood still for a moment in the doorway, looking at them, embarrassed and a little confused. He had been forewarned. Now he was disarmed at the reality of the Moon's ways staring him in the face.

"Come in, Voul. Don't act like such a priss." She had barely moved, only to get a better view of SkyKing's captain, standing at her door. "You're the one who launched the shuttles. You're the one who came rushing over here. At least follow your own religious dogma: 'Judge not, lest ye be judged.'"

More disarming than her raw nudity and obvious lasciviousness was Commander Nichols's awareness of Voul's religious scriptures. Standing there before a scene of sin and debauchery the like of which no Sker had come across in almost a hundred years aboard SkyKing, Voul Jonsn was scrambling mentally to practice the religion he had preached his whole life. There were disturbing stirrings that made the task difficult, but not impossible. Voul sat down in the Spartan chair near the edge of the mat, and looking at the young man, he asked, "Viera, are you going to introduce us, or is such rudeness now just another barbarous tradition here on MoonBase?"

45. Commander Peterson and His Daughter Brittany

Jim Peterson was watching his daughter Brittany walk down the beach. She reached the water's edge and suddenly turned to her father and announced, "No waves today, Dad." Peterson ruefully acknowledged his daughter's insight. Normally there were waves, little ones to be sure, but there were always waves. It was the pull of the planet on SkyKing's reservoir that caused the phenomenon. Now the waves were gone because the planet was gone.

"Don't worry, honey. They'll be back." Brittany, believed what her father had said and began to tiptoe in the water. She seemed contented there on the shore of SkyLake.

The commander of SkyKing took out a small wrist device from his pocket and snapped it on. He touched it as though quickly typing with one hand. A small holographic monitor appeared. He asked softly, "Status?"

"They appear to be in consultation, sir. The other shuttles are orbiting, and Captain Jonsn's craft is at New Chicago's primary landing pad. Reports from his copilot indicate that nothing is out of the ordinary. Voul has gone alone to see the commander of MoonBase, as she requested. Shall we inquire?" Peterson looked through the projection of the yeoman's face to see his daughter walking on the beach. He remembered how, as a child, she would lie on her back with her legs straight up in the air, kicking wildly as she laughed and splashed in the shallow, warm water of SkyLake.

"No, yeoman, keep up surveillance and keep me informed of any status changes immediately. Commander out." He touched his wrist device once, and the projected screen disappeared. He looked again out over the lake.

What an incredible achievement it was. Through conservation, importing, manufacturing, and recovery SkyKing had accumulated enough excess water over the years to live. *The ancient pyramids were smaller in their footprint.* He knew what the water represented: life in the stars and nothing less. SkyLake, as it was known, was the source of food, health, atmosphere, basically everything to SkyKing and its inhabitants.

Jim could remember when Brittany was five years old and, splashing in eight inches of water, would turn to him and shout, "Daddy, look. I'm swimming," kicking her feet and thrashing her arms. She was growing up. Now she was almost fifteen. She looked back and waved to him.

Peterson thought of the depth of over one hundred feet in the middle with an average depth of over thirty feet overall. He thought of the fish now swimming in SkyLake. *Another species of Sker.*

To Jim Peterson, the Skers were an amazing people. Much like the Native American Indians in their ability to live at peace and in harmony with their world, and very much unlike the Indians in that the Skers had been able to keep control of their land despite the long odds against them. *Religious or not, if there were no Skers up here, we'd have to invent them.*

Jim remembered once when Brittany came running up the beach to him, wet and sandy, and jumped into his lap. “Ugh! Brittany, you're all wet and gross,” he had said. This only made her squirm around more, grinding sand and spreading wetness all over her father's clothing. Soon enough, though, they were nestled together again, resting on the beach, enjoying the unusual time alone. The memory made him smile.

And then, Jim was thinking of Brittany's mother, his wife.

She was killed in the saddest moment of his life during construction of the sixth whorl, and she had left him a strange legacy. Perhaps the most popular woman on the space station, Joanie Peterson's death created a huge emptiness. Brittany helped fill his life to be sure, and he loved her dearly, and Jim knew there could never be another woman after Joanie.

Fortunately, Joanie had built a strong family and raised a strong child. Brittany was able, just barely, at the age of six to cope with the loss of her mother because of her father's love and his devotion to her. It had been a tough time nine years ago, but life had gone on.

Peterson had decided that as full-time commander of SkyKing and as the full-time parent of Brittany he could not separate the two responsibilities so he joined the two roles. Brittany had benefited from this decision tremendously. She was a staple in the wardroom, on the bridge, in communications, and throughout all the areas and compartments of the station. Many times she had been with her father during command emergencies. She was a source of support and equilibrium for him, and now he could not think of having it any other way. Brittany had accompanied her father on Earth missions too, and she had been to the Moon several times. Probably no child in history had had her experiences, and as her father watched the young woman walking on the beach, he knew she was none the worse for wear.

Commander Peterson felt a slight vibration at his wrist. He touched the device, and the monitor appeared again. "Commander, Captain Jonsn would like to talk with you."

Peterson adjusted the volume to low, hoping Brittany would not notice. "I'll take his call now."

46. Karina's Idea

"Sitwory?" Farson felt around in the dark until he touched his sister's hand. He held it gently. "What do you think?"

"Routier, I think you're a rogue." She moved a little closer and put her arm around Farson. "When I think of all those years we were together and for some reason I sublimated these feelings for you, I wonder why."

"Brothers and sisters do that." Farson could feel the gentle warmth of his desire increasing.

"It does add to the pleasure, doesn't it, Routier?"

"All those years of waiting? Is that what you mean, Sitwory?"

<<Oh, Farson, sometimes you are just plain goofy.>>

<<What do you mean, Kari?>>

<<I mean that I was really nineteen before I realized that my love for you was OK.>>

<<We went to Beach many times before that.>>
<<I know, Farson, I know, but that was your idea.>>

Farson looked up from his telescope and turned away from the window. He was thinking of Kari and how much fun she was. How together they had conquered space in The Ship. How much he had grown to depend on her companionship and her friendship. *I really love her.* "That can't be." The loud voice was Farson's denying reality to the empty attic room. Then he settled back and leaned against the wall, thinking how much she laughed when he told her about the new planet he had recently encountered. She really laughed when he said they'd be going to Beach soon.

47. Twill Keeps Smiling

ScreenMaster Uiost was suddenly staring at a smiling Twill, who had just made another attempt at restricting Farson's activities during his Ascension. Level after level this had persisted.

Farson turned to Twill with a surprising amount of anger at his unyielding and inconvenient animosity. Twill had been watching him, and his countenance now carried a new awareness and, still, that smile, now enhanced by his new discovery. He had noticed Farson's ire.

<<What, Farson? You think I should surrender? After all that has happened? All that we have built? We came here to settle matters, not play your little games. Yes, you are powerful, but can you keep it up? Can you do the other things you are doing and still keep up this struggle with me? If you falter for an instant, I will crush you and you know it.>> Twill's smile increased as he stated his case.

<<You are the way things were, Twill, not like the way things will be. You are like the unnature you love. You go past all reason and rhyme, and then you tell us it rhymes and that insanity is reason. Even as The Screen is being torn apart, you are still arguing that up is down and wrong is right.>>

<<And you, Farson, you are so different? You have taken everything we know and turned it upside down. What did you expect? That we would say, 'Okay. No problem?' Your 'nature' is going to destroy everything, and I am fighting you every inch of the way.>>

Farson watched as Twill tried to inhibit his movements. He could tell Twill was having trouble keeping up. *<<Twill, we are still in the lower levels. What will you do when I go higher? You have already lost. Your efforts are annoying in their lack of knowledge, not in any sense of effectiveness or danger for me.>>* With this Farson accelerated his passage leaving Twill standing still, left with only the option of looking where Farson had been. He smiled again.

That bothered Farson. *Why is he still smiling?*

48. The Solar Sails

Material was very precious on SkyKing, so the thought of building a structure many times larger than the size of the station itself was bold indeed. But that they were going to do it in secret multiplied the boldness astronomically. And they were going to do it using only the excess materials found around the station.

Over the years things began to take shape.

One of the most difficult circumstances to overcome was the total freedom of movement that had evolved on SkyKing. People lived and moved around wherever they wanted. The transporter system on SkyKing was a function of its environment, a near vacuum. The transport distance was restricted to one hundred miles or so, but travel around SkyKing was as easy as walking into a unit, selecting a destination, and stepping out, immediately there. So people were everywhere, coming and going. It was difficult to operate in secret. The Skers felt compelled to keep the secret of the solar sails. They didn't want to do it, but they felt it was crucial to their success. The disappearance of Earth had created confusion among the Skers about this, but, for the sake of conservatism about something so vital to them, they continued to maintain the secrecy. The deception had never been easy for them.

The solar sails were constructed of a material so light and thin that the slightest impact or pressure during handling could rip them to shreds like a howling nor'easter through badly trimmed canvas sails. But once unfurled and inflated, the sails became surprisingly strong and resilient. They were meant to fly.

The Skers had five whorls sails-equipped, and the sails for the sixth whorl were ready with couplings and rings attached. As soon as the sixth whorl sails were completed, SkyKing would be eventually capable of interstellar flight at speeds no one could predict. It would be near the speed of light, but possibly infinitely accelerating. All the theories aside, what the Skers were so boldly dreaming of had never been attempted: SkyKing in independent flight.

In the process of building the mainsail, as the sail for the sixth whorl was called, all of their resources had been exhausted. The Skers had simplified their lives down to just the fundamental essentials. They had given everything to the effort. Virtually an unknown to the other crew members socially, the Skers were considered puritanical and stark. Most often they were referred to as religious zealots. The Skers had paid dearly for all of their secrets and their efforts. Sacrifices of every kind had been made. Interestingly, as the Skers deepened their "simplification," they became more devoted to the station's work and more valuable than ever to SkyKing. Probably out of guilt for what they were taking, they gave unceasingly of themselves. Eventually, the Skers were essentially in operational control of the station, certainly in all practical, day-to-day ways, if not in the official organization. All of this also developed for good reasons. They were sober, vigilant, and always ready to find the solution to whatever challenges came up. This attitude had saved many lives and possibly saved the station itself over the years. This presence of a stable, dependable, and knowledgeable personnel base certainly made SkyKing the success it was. Everyone knew it. The Skers were responsible, dependable, and in their own way, a very admirable people. They were complex and confusing to the others, but the others liked having them around. The Skers were like part of the station itself, almost unnoticed in their growing importance. They were always there, always working and planning, always keeping things going. They were driven and motivated by a calling higher than just manning the station. They were planning things way beyond what the average crew member was thinking of: Their secrets plans were entirely unknown outside of the Sker nation.

For the Skers, the solar sails were essential for their purposes; "holy" would be the description they would use. The Skers considered the solar sails to be the first chapter of the new book of Genesis they were writing. Where they were going was not clear, but it had everything to do with exploration. The Skers were explorers of the first magnitude, and they meant to get going.

"Captain Jonsn here, Commander."

"Report, Voul, if you would, please."

"Thank you, Commander. My report is difficult." Peterson had a premonition of what was coming, knowing Viera Nichols's way of doing business.

"Did she shock you, Voul? That's the way she does it." Voul's image remained unwavering.

"No, sir, but she tried. In the end, after the departure of the ensign, she agreed with me." Peterson was attentive.

"What exactly did she agree to?"

"She agreed that SkyKing must move into orbit around the Moon."

"Did she also agree to continue the mining contracts?"

"Yes, sir." Voul blinked, waiting for the next question.

"Very good, Voul. Are you coming back right away?"

"No, sir, I'm to remain at MoonBase as liaison for SkyKing." Peterson noticed his daughter was awake and looking up at him. Voul was watching the two of them. Peterson could feel Voul's affection for his daughter.

"That's fine, Voul. Excellent. You'll soon be within transporter range, so we can get you in and out easily." He could tell Voul had thought about all of this, and it didn't make him feel any better about Voul being away from SkyKing. "It'll be OK. Commander out." Brittany was listening.

"Is Voul in trouble, Dad?" Brittany was watching his face for an answer.

He could see her concern. "Not yet."

"Commander to control." Peterson was hailing the bridge.

"Control here, Commander."

"Move the station into lunar orbit, Lieutenant."

"It will take some time, Commander."

"Begin the process. Voul has set up the agreement. We have work to do."

49. Farson on the Plane

Farson was sitting down. It was real time for him at this point, which meant he was only in one place and one time. *For now.* He had left his cabin in North Conway, and traveled to the New Logan Airport for a shuttle flight to Washington. He was alone, except for the robots standing in the aisle. When he traveled, he had two. He was on his way to see the president.

<<*Why are you traveling like this, Farson?*>>

<<*Uvo, sometimes people do things for no reason, other than that is the way they want to do it.*>>

<<*'People?' Farson? What are you doing?*>>

The flight attendant handed Farson a cup of coffee with cream and double sugar. He thanked her. He was thinking about how relaxing a plane ride could be. He was remembering once when he was on leave from boot camp, how he had hitchhiked across America, waiting in military airports for sympathetic pilots to offer him a lift. He made it from San Diego to Boston on military aircraft in six days. One leg was on a very old transport, and he slept the whole way. He could still remember the droning of the engines for hours after hours, wondering how they kept going.

Despite the coffee, Farson began to doze off. In a dream, he reached for his fishing pole and cast the line into the lake. He settled back to wait for the inevitable tugs.

At first very softly, "Mr. Uiost?" Then more assertively, "Mr. *Uiost.* You have a phone call." Farson awoke, groggy and somewhat unsettled. The flight attendant handed him a handset.

It was Karina.

"Farson, the president is agitated. He wants to know."

"Know what, Karina?" Farson knew he was being evasive, but, since the president's office was his next stop, he didn't want to deal with President Sortt's worries before it was time. Farson was well aware that the president knew some important things he really should not know, and he was wondering how much Sortt actually did know, and how did he know it. First, obviously, he knew that Earth was not perfectly safe, defenseless really. The people of Earth had no idea what was going on, and certainly the ScreenKeepers themselves did not advertise it. Second, was Sortt hoping to take advantage of this "penumbra" period? Had he acquired any new facts from other ScreenMasters? Farson doubted that, but there was Twill. Even if President Sortt did know more, given the status of Earth and his own isolation on the planet, what difference would it make? He asked Karina's opinion.

"He might know more than he is letting on."

"That's what I was thinking."

"Who would help him, and why?" Karina asked.

Farson again thought of Twill.

<<*Uvo, why is he bothering me?*>>

<<*Because he has taken it upon himself to oppose you.*>>

<<*Is Twill the adversary?*>>

<<*At this time, I would say he is.*>>

"Time will tell, Kari. See you soon." Karina put down the phone and looked out the window into the North Conway winter and woods surrounding the cabin. *I wish.* The phone call was unnecessary, but they both knew why she had called. *I could hear him breathing.*

Farson hung up, and the flight attendant took the secure phone away. *Sometimes I just love to hear the sound of her voice.* He leaned back and thought about Twill. Two ScreenMasters in opposition: That was very unusual. Farson knew Twill was capable and very possibly the stronger of the two in some ways. *At this point.*

Farson was starting to fall asleep again, but not before the thought reoccurred ... *at this point. Not for long.* Farson bolted upright in his airline seat. He was suddenly struck with the question of whose thought that last one was. He heard Twill laughing in his mind.

<<*You are all the same: humans, so limited, so weak and so confused.*>>

<<*Twill, are you really listening or just tagging along now? Time flies, Twill. Are you keeping up?*>>

<<*We will see, Farson.*>>

<<*Yes, we will, Twill. Yes, we will.*>> Farson knew that Twill was posturing with a ScreenMaster version of bravado. Sure, he could interrupt a thought, but that was about it. <<*Bluffing never pays off, Twill.*>>

<<*You should know, Farson.*>> Farson had no response for once. He knew that there was some truth in Twill's words.

50. Frission

Voul looked at Viera. She was standing before him. She was flaunting her nudity, and he knew it. She knew he knew it. Her brown hair was still slightly disheveled. The ensign had made a quick exit. Voul's eyes traveled over her involuntarily. Her body was beautiful to him. He tried to look away. But now they were alone. *How old is she?* She seemed so smooth and beautiful to him. He was confused with all these thoughts. He continued to look at her. He was intensely excited. He felt a low shudder way inside. It made him uncomfortable and confused. He was outside of his norm here; he was on uncertain ground. Oddly, he was enjoying himself, undeniably, which confused him even more deeply.

"Come on, Voul, relax," She moved closer. "Haven't you ever seen a woman before?" Voul could smell her. He sensed that this was very exciting for her as well. He could almost hear his heart beating. His mind's eye still held the image of her with the ensign on the exercise mat: She had been the prodigal epitome of pure physical pleasure, anathema to Sker ways. These were very difficult things for the self-abnegating Sker. He had spent his life devoted to asceticism and to cherishing the simplicities of life, to comprehending life as pure without venality. That, here and now, he was enjoying the very emotions he had worked so long to extirpate seemed perverse and unsettling to Voul. He was walking through the Valley. His senses were on flaming high, as though suddenly in a high oxygen atmosphere. She was very close now. Voul seemed to be frozen in place: unable to back off. That would be a show of fear and weakness. He knew to stand his ground would mean worse to come, perhaps.

Viera put her arms around his neck and pressed near to him in an embrace. "Voul, we are just people out in space; we're not all that different from the people of SkyKing. We all have the same urges, the same wants." Voul was experiencing the vivid feeling of her breasts through his crisp, white uniform, and her body pressing in. He disentangled himself gently but with renewed resolution and walked to the wall monitor. "How do I get a visual from here, Viera?" He was acting as if nothing had happened. Viera moved next to him and input a code. The screen came to life, and the panorama of the Moon's surface outside the base appeared as though through a window. Voul began speaking in a calm, warm voice.

"Viera, to you all is sensual and physical. To us all is spiritual and metaphysical. It will be difficult to work together without some concessions on your part." Viera moved across the room to a hard chair and sat down, her slender legs casually apart, leaning forward, ready to listen intently. She was smiling slightly, eyebrows up. Voul stared at her. *A Sker woman would never do that.* Sker women, although usually beautiful, cultivated matings of the spirit which manifested themselves in a high-quality relationship of productivity, peace, and privacy. Sker women were not sexual partners for their men in the usual sense. Over the years the Skers had had no divorces. Skers mated for "Life," as they put it, meaning for children only, when they mated at all. Voul was still unmated. Viera leaned back and stretched voluptuously.

"Concessions on both sides, Voul? Or just me?" Voul stood before the monitor a while longer, avoiding the images in the room behind him. The lunar vista from this angle was pleasing to him: the crisp craters, the distant mountains, and the deep black sky. He was wondering about what concessions a Sker could make that would satisfy Viera. He had stripped his life to the bone already. All he had left was his way of life and his Spartan system of beliefs. Innocuous, hardworking, without the usual daily guile, the Skers, by their own account, had achieved "a sinless existence of promise unending." The solar sails, their dreams of freedom, were their one exception. What concessions could they make at this point to the MoonBasers, and, perhaps more immediately, what concessions could Voul make to Viera to win her confidence?

"Are you offering suggestions, Viera?" The naked MoonBase commander stood up and moved lithely to the closet. Voul watched her. She took out a one-piece MoonBase uniform and removed the wrapper. She laid it on the small bed near the wall. She turned to Voul again.

"Well, you could begin by telling me what you want us to do. But first I'm going to take a shower. Care to join me?" Voul watched her walk, laughing, into the bathroom, leaving the door open. He heard the steam spray, and through the door, behind the steamy shower closet, he saw her blurry image washing. He turned away, back into his thoughts. His father, Ban Jonsn, had done so much for the Skers. He had shown them the way, really. His sacrifices set the pace of change. So much good had been done. The Skers had grown powerful, but only because of the good they did. Their power was real and unassailable because it was welcomed and then supported. What concessions could he make now? He could hear Viera in the dryer. He looked around as she came back into the room. Her hair was combed and dry and clean. She reached for the uniform and began to put it on, but turned to him again first. "Well, Voul?"

"We want to insert SkyKing into lunar orbit and continue our commercial and other relationships concerning the mines. We'd like everything else to remain exactly the same. Perhaps no concessions are necessary on either side." Viera had moved closer to Voul. The difference in their heights was only a few inches so they were looking directly into each other's eyes. That was exactly what Viera had intended.

"Perhaps, but now you are going to be a satellite of MoonBase. First, we didn't know you could move the station so easily, Voul. That is a surprise we are still evaluating. Second, we don't really want a satellite. We liked you when you were much farther away. This close means you are well within transporter range, and that could be a problem. And third, our mining arrangements were supported, in major part, by Earth commerce and by your access to things we needed on Earth. Now what?" Voul could sense the strength of her words and the truth of them. Would she believe him? They both knew SkyKing's position was weakened and vulnerable without the planet.

"We can support your people agriculturally and in other ways. We want to make this a peaceful transition and to limit the implications. We'd like to maintain the status quo as much as possible. You must see your responsibility here. MoonBase and SkyKing may be all there is. The need for an alliance is obvious."

Viera moved even closer to Voul. He again could sense the warmth of her body. *Why am I so attracted to him? He is irresistible.* Perhaps it was his unapproachable reputation over all the years. Everyone knew of Voul Jonsn. The fact that he was right here in front of her was arousing to Viera. Ordinarily, Skers never left SkyKing, and MoonBasers never went there. So, while there was interaction, it was minimal. Viera Nichols had actually spoken with Voul many times, but she had never been in the same room with him before. The attraction she was feeling to him was beginning to overwhelm her. Voul could sense her intensifying thoughts. She could tell he was noticing, and she wanted him to. In the vortex of Viera's passion Voul saw himself in her thoughts engaging sexually with her. He saw himself in the act of making love with her. He saw things that heretofore he had not even dreamed of. His attention lingered there, allowing the thoughts to run their course. Viera was very close to him now, he could feel her soft breathing on his face. Voul was transfixed and unable to break away. Voul's mind had instinctively linked with hers, Viera was suddenly experiencing an ecstasy beyond any she had previously known, and Voul was diving deeper and deeper into her mind. Her eyes widened looking at him. He found something deep inside her mind: something remote and untouched, something warm and private. Her eyes were boring into his. She knew exactly where his mental touch was and what it had found so easily. She relaxed and let him have it. "Viera," he whispered after a time. She put her arms around him and held on tight. He didn't move at first, and then he reached out with his hands to her face and gently began to push her slightly away. Looking into her eyes, still gently holding her, he said again, "Viera." She continued to hold him without answering, willing the moment to go on.

"Is Voul all right?" Brittany was concerned.

Jim Peterson, realizing that this was the first time he did not know exactly what Voul Jonsn would do or what he would be confronted with, said softly to his daughter, "I'm sure he is, Brit. I'm sure he is." *I'm sure he is.*

51. "I Am a Sker"

Then Voul did something that was beyond explanation, something neither he nor anyone who knew him could have predicted. Something he would have said was impossible moments before he did it. He kissed her. It was no ordinary kiss. In his passage through her mind he had slowly gotten the idea from her. The entire process was in her mind so vividly that it came to life in his. It surprised him. The concept involved his tongue and reaching into and around her mouth and teeth. Even as he was doing it, his mind was racing with the knowledge that he was enjoying it: this almost unspeakable act. Her teeth were smooth, and her mouth was clean. Her tongue rushed up and embraced his as if in reward. He continued and the reward improved and the sensations enriched. Soon he was so deep into kissing Viera Nichols that time was standing still.

"Viera, we must stop." He whispered to her.

"Why, Voul?"

"Because I am a Sker."

Voul disengaged and walked to the porthole. He took his own head in his hands.

"What's the matter with you, Voul? Am I too much for you?" Voul turned to Viera. She was there, standing before him in all her beauty and attractiveness. He was looking at her.

"Yes, I think you are." Voul went back to the monitor and stared at the landscape. He was lost in a deep personal conflict: struggling to break free and yet remain with her at the same time. The thoughts of procrastination appeared. Tomorrow, they said. Tomorrow you will be stronger. Voul knew that today was all there was. Tomorrow never comes. He turned to face her.

"We have a job to do together, Viera. Help me." Then, he stiffened up, in the proper posture for a Sker, and said, "Oppose us and we will resist you." She walked up to where he was standing with his back turned to her, his stern words still hanging in the air. She put her hand on his shoulder, and he turned around to face her. She looked Voul Jonsn in the eyes, and said, "How can you stand there and threaten me?"

She finished dressing quickly and left him alone in her compartment. He was back staring at the monitor again. The view outside seemed cold and dark to him.

52. Commander Peterson Gets a Call

"Jim, what in the name of God is really going on? Why all the shuttles and skypeople?" Viera was perturbed. He was at home. Brittany was napping in front of the VT. A program was playing about an adventure on the Moon, two teenagers and what appeared to be an enormous dog.

Viera was demanding his attention. There was a knock at the door. It was the duty yeoman. Peterson touched his wrist lightly, putting Viera on hold. He looked up at the yeoman.

"Status?" Peterson asked.

"Commander, Voul has reported to his copilot that everything is normal. He is staying on the Moon for now. There are no signs of conflict."

"Including principal contact?"

"Of course, sir."

Peterson touched his wrist again, returning to Viera Nichols. She had noticed the brief interruption.

"Viera, my daughter asked about Voul this afternoon. She asked, 'Is he all right?' Can you answer that question for me?"

"Voul is currently in my compartment. He is fine."

"Are the agreements in place?"

"Yes, Jim." Commander Peterson knew everything was on track, but he wanted to hear her say it.

"SkyKing will move into a close lunar orbit within a day or two. During transit, Voul is in full command of the shuttles and the operation." Peterson readied himself for the next exchange.

"How close are you coming, Jim?"

"That's up to Voul, but certainly within transporter range."

"99.9 miles, Jim?" One hundred miles was the outside range of SkyKing's system.

"Sorry, Viera. A stable orbit will have to be closer than that." Viera calculated for a moment. She knew the apoapsis would be in the seventy-five mile range, and the final periapsis would be around sixty-two miles. A low lunar orbit was much better for SkyKing. The farther away the better for the MoonBasers.

"That's bad, Jim." At this moment Voul walked into the transmission behind Viera. Jim Peterson could see him. Voul put his arm around Viera in full view of the monitor. After a second it went blank. Peterson knew Voul had turned the communication device off.

Voul's thoughts were direct now. *No, Viera. That's good.* At the touch of his thought Viera turned and looked at Voul in astonishment. How clear it was. He was smiling at her.

"Commander, we've lost the transmission."
"Yeoman, it was cut off on the Moon. Not your fault."
"Aye, aye, sir."

53. Here We Go Again

Moving SkyKing into lunar orbit was, physically, not a difficult thing to do, but it tore the station apart emotionally. The debate raged furiously in the week or so before the shuttle fleet departure. The science of the shift was easy, but the emotional detachment from Earth was rending, even though the planet was missing. There were furious debates.

The acceleration needed was minimal and even though the transorbital maneuvering system had never been used that way before, in the end it functioned exactly as the design engineers had intended. Moving into Earth orbit for SkyKing had been very stable and smooth. In the 122 years of its existence, no orbital deterioration had ever been allowed. That long stability and the unshakeable confidence of the population had both been cast aside. Perhaps bravely, perhaps out of inescapable necessity, the change was effected with flawless execution.

SkyKing moved out of its position very easily, using just a small fraction of the power the station had available. In another sense the move drained the station's power in ways no one could have predicted. Moving into low lunar orbit changed everything.

The struggle among the crew was the largest impediment. The Skers wanted to move quickly into orbit; the other non-

Sker crew members basically did not want to abandon their high Earth orbit position. They felt certain that the Earth would reappear. The Skers felt that they had no choice but to move to the Moon. Mars and Venus were too far away, and just drifting around would go against the Skers' carefully planned and purposed existence, and it would disrupt systems and routines, not to mention timetables. Without a strict structural framework, and a dependable orbit, the Skers would be like birds forced to swim. They might do it, but it wasn't their first choice. Moon itself was slowly moving away, so something had to be done. It was too soon and the wrong destination, but it was the right thing to do.

Ultimately, the non-Sker crew agreed to the predictably minimalist Sker approach. They made the case that the Moon was vital in every way to the plans of the future. "We must not let it get away!" That common-sense rallying cry won the day. The discussion occupied the intellectual energies of the station for a while. A long lost report had come to light. It was submitted at the time of the original station commission hearings, well over a hundred years ago. It deliberated on the pros and cons of whether or not improving and hardening SkyKing should even be attempted at all. The document also carefully outlined the quotas of who would come and go. Much of the press coverage in those days, and nearly the entire public debate, was about who should go to SkyKing and who should not. In the beginning there was a plethora of volunteers, and most of them had little loyalty to Earth or were so disillusioned with their lives that their real motive for wanting to go to SkyKing was simply to escape the maddening contradictions of life on the planet. The sachems of press and politics noticed this trend and began a "campaign for balance" as they called it. The thought behind The Balance Decree, which finally emerged from the debate, was that SkyKing, however big and populous it was to become, should, and would, always reflect the population of Earth as much as possible, based on the station's needs and the levels of experience available. The document had set up the station's emigration for balance. That commitment to balance had nearly caused the station's destruction.

Naturally, most of the early crew members came from the United States of America. The language of SkyKing became English, because the education percentages in the United States were still much higher than any other country at that time. And, of course, SkyKing was originally an American idea.

Ultimately, every country was represented, many times over. But in the beginning, to get the needed people to construct the enormous space station, conscripts were taken. Volunteers were given priority and taught the needed skills, but after the beginning rush of volunteers, the second wave of people who went to SkyKing were selected and told to go there. They had no choice. Conscription was a major factor in the populating of the station. In time, though, the system evolved, tied to the global educational system, into something that no one had ever really thought of in advance. Earth schools deliberately began to provide a pool of qualified people that SkyKing could choose from. Eventually, the selection system changed again, and assignment to a maturing and diversifying (and more comfortable) SkyKing became a coveted billet. This was especially true after the benefits of living in space became apparent. SkyKing's early history, like that of all colonies, was difficult and factional.

A key period speech by a young politician in those early days made the selection system palatable to the population and thereby played a key role in the success of SkyKing.

Ironically, the very same words that concluded that rousing and pivotal speech were the very words used by the

Skers, a hundred years later in their winning arguments to move SkyKing immediately into lunar orbit.

"People of the United States of Earth, you are called to a great adventure. Space. The opportunity presents itself and while each of you didn't ask for it, each of you must accept it.

"Because up above in the black void lies our future. Up above lies our hope. Up above in space awaits peace and prosperity. It's an opportunity you did not create, but it's an opportunity you must accept.

"Already the historic opportunity is at risk of getting away. People are quarreling. People are complaining. People are obstructing. But others are working. Others are building. Others are planning. In space we will enrich the Earth and stop its social and economic decline. We will create new generations of explorers, and new generations of pioneers.

"This future hangs starkly before us like the full moon in the sky. All around the world it's clear what must be done, and the people know it. Let us be the first to commit our lives to it. Let us be the ones who said, 'We must not let it get away!'"

"Don't let it get away!" became the motto of the station program, and those words inspired the first decade of renewed effort and the movement of thousands and thousands of people to SkyKing.

Many years later, those very words, spoken so long ago by young John Andrew McKinley Sortt, saved the station again.

There was a beeping in the room. The crew member on watch touched the console. "Aft watch here," he said swiveling to the monitor.

"Ship's away, sir. Rotation has stopped. We are en route to the Moon."

SkyKing, the station, was now a ship in space.

The crew member staffing the aft watch closed the logbook. He was thinking of a professor he had in college, who taught the changeability of history and how it can bend and alter before your very eyes, changing the past and future as the present becomes like a rudder for all the ages. *How right he was.* He turned the scanners to maximum and activated the running lights on SkyKing. The space station lit up like a Christmas tree and started moving toward the Moon. *How right he was.*

54. Farson and the President

President Sortt knew a decision was soon to be made. He could feel it. With EarthStasis deepening, interaction was becoming more and more difficult. Something had to be done about the ScreenMasters and the threat they posed to the people of Earth. Everything was variable and tenuous. He didn't even feel like the president anymore. *Those damn ScreenMasters.* He looked over at the robot standing there. *And you!*

Farson Uiost was shown into the president's private office. "Good morning, Mr. President." They shook hands. "As you are probably aware, the ScreenMasters are in control of Earth now, and they are here to decide our planet's fate. Whether you like it or not, nothing you do can change whatever they have decided to do. If Earth does not survive, it will be its past that killed it, not its present. And, if Earth does survive, it will never be the same again." Farson said these words as though on autopilot. As if he didn't really feel them, as if they were what the ScreenMasters had told him to say, and he just said them without agreement or dissent.

Farson, after a brief pause, asked a question. "Why did you attempt to engage ZZ<<Arkol25609, Mr. Sortt?"

The president found the young man's first words annoying in their finality and pronouncement, almost inhuman, but the second part, the question, was easier to take, more human in their curiosity. The robot in question stood near the door like a statue, unmoving, but Sortt knew how intelligent and observant it really was. *How powerful it is. How quickly it can move when it wants to.* The president did not want to answer the question but found that he could not resist. He also found that he could not help being completely honest with Farson, and that was a little surprising given the president's history in politics.

"Twill told me I could. After the transportation to Uvo's barge and then returning here, I was exceptionally nervous with all that he told me. I do regret questioning the robot now that I realize how painful it can be. Oddly enough, I find that I want to have a good relationship with ZZ<<Arkol, although that may be impossible now."

"He is stronger than you or Twill thinks, Mr. President. It'll be okay." The robot seemed to be watching this exchange. Farson walked to behind the president's desk, and indicating the presidential chair, said, "May I?" The president stood up and moved aside. Farson sat down in the president's chair with a mischievous look on his face. Pulling the chair up and adjusting himself at the desk. "Why are you listening to Twill, Mr. Sortt? What good can possibly come of that?"

"He's a ScreenMaster. Isn't that enough of a reason?" Farson swiveled in the chair and moved closer. He leaned forward on the desk.

"That's oversimplified, Mr. President. I am the ScreenMaster of Earth. Any other ScreenMaster besides me should not be talking to you. That he did talk to you should tell you something. Did meeting with him help?"

"No. It confused me, and it hurt some other things."

"Of course, it did. Do you know why?"

"No, I don't, Farson."

"Because that's exactly what Twill wanted. You played right into his plan. You will see, if you don't already, that you should listen to ZZ<<Arkol, because he speaks for me, to Karina because she is my sister and I trust her, and to me, no others. We'll save the planet and our people. We'll save SkyKing and MoonBase. We need your cooperation and patience. Twill opposes me. He will try to destroy everything. Why would you want to be involved with him?" It was obvious that these words were sinking in.

"I've got to do *something*, Farson. What Twill said about stasis being just a long death, an eternal death, that's a hard fate to face, Farson. I have to do something."

"Death, Mr. Sortt, is a theoretical question, not a fact. All that the human race has achieved in art and science and in human relations is perhaps one of the greatest treasures in the omniverse. I know because now I really get around. Trust me when I say, that stasis, however seemingly impossible to endure when thinking about it in advance, will be just more days, weeks, months, and years for the people. Handy Townsend will be there. It won't seem all that different to those of you actually going through it. In the meantime, you will see things that now you can't even imagine. In the end all will be well."

"How can we be sure? Aren't you new to this ScreenMaster thing? Twill said you were an idiot."

"Did he? Well, we shall see. Even Twill has his place, if only he knew it."

Farson signaled the robot to begin transportation protocols. They both began to glow. Farson was now fully outlined in the purple shimmers of a forming ScreenLite. The president was watching Farson with interest, and he wasn't sure he wanted Farson to go.

"Wait a minute, Farson. How can I know who to listen to? Twill said the same things you just said."

Farson laughed and said, "Judge for yourself."

An increasing hue of purple filled the Oval Office and spilled through the windows and out into the hall. The president remained bathed in light as Farson and his ScreenKeeper robot dematerialized almost instantly, but the images disappeared very slowly, lingering in the room like reflections. Sortt continued looking. The bright light was still shining in his eyes. He sensed a great slowing down.

55. Twill and Farson

Farson was down in Sam's shed stoking the fire. Looking into the fire chamber of the potbellied stove, he just barely cracked the door. The embers were burning brightly. There was a slight cake of ash on top. He took out a little handle from under the stove as Sam had taught him. It was tapered at one end. He opened another, smaller, door near the bottom of the stove and inserted the handle in the crude slot provided and gently moved the handle back and forth a few times. The ash sifted through the grate with a slight cloud that was sucked up the draft. A few of the smaller clinkers fell through as well. He emptied the catch pan outside onto a large pile of cold ash and clinkers that had accumulated there over the passing weeks of winter. It would eventually be mixed as enrichment into the soil of Sam's garden once spring finally arrived.

Now the fire was flaring with a new surge of flame and heat. Quickly, Farson put a shovelful of coal on top, then another, then just about half another and closed the door on top, leaving the bottom door open. Then he began to scan the books of poetry on Sam's bookshelf. The room was warm and cozy. *Nothing like the warmth of a well-tended coal fire,* Farson thought as he picked a book out and slowly flipped through the pages.

Farson was very happy that Sam let him come here. A few minutes passed. He was contentedly reading the book. He looked at the fire and got up to close the bottom door of the stove. He opened the small iron vents in the lower door just about halfway. Then he went back to reading.

<<*What are you doing, Farson?*>>

<<*Reading a good book and tending the stove, Twill.*>>

<<*Stove? What's that, Farson?*>>

<<*Corroboration, Twill. You asked for corroboration.*>>

<<*Farson, you've lost me entirely. I don't see any corroboration for your wild theories in your stove or in anything else you are doing. What I do see is a ScreenMaster spiraling out of control.*>> Farson was aware of Twill's tedious arguments. Arguments he had been polemically making to all the other ScreenMasters.

<<*Look deeper, Twill. In tending the stove I'm able to keep it burning long after it would have gone out on its own, based merely on the laws of consumption and combustion.*>>

<<*Is this a miracle, Farson, keeping a crude fossil fuel device burning?*>>

<<*No, Twill, but the knowledge of how it's done is.*>>

<<*Is this your corroboration? Your justification? Is this really the best you can do, Farson?*>> Twill was laughing. It was a strange gurgling sound.

<<*If you could accept this and turn from your current course of opposition, it could end here.*>>

<<*Why would I do that, Farson?*>> The ScreenMaster of Earth stood up and walked to the fire and peered in. The fire was flaming slightly. Flames were licking at the new coal.

Farson closed the lower doors just a little more. Twill repeated his question. <<*Tell me why would I do that?*>>

Farson shoveled in two big shovelfuls and closed the doors and vents. He walked to the door, opened it, and turned off the lights. As the door closed, Twill heard Farson's thoughts. <<*It'll still be burning in the morning, Twill.*>>

<<*Uvo, I'm worried about Twill.*>> Having said that, Farson now witnessed something few had ever seen or heard. Uvo started to laugh. His wings expanded to their full span, and he leaned back and expelled a shrill whistle that went from long to short and back to long again. It reminded Farson of an SOS message sent in ancient Morse code. Then Uvo did it again.

<<*I'm glad you find it so amusing, Uvo. Do you understand why I'm worried?*>>

<<*Yes, I do, Farson. I do. I'm only hoping that you understand.*>>

56. A Blue Light, Almost White

Handy looked up. He was on St. Maarten, an island in the Caribbean. He was in a grass shack, but it had plenty of power. A holographic monitor hung in the air in front of him. He took a drink of gin, of course. He glanced at the monitor. He took a puff on his cigar. Then he took another puff and started to type on a keyboard that followed his hands wherever they went:

Farson you are so near...
Farson you are so near...
Farson, Farson.

Farson, you are so dear...
Farson, you are so dear...
Farson, Farson. You are the One.

But it's just begun...
It's only just begun.

A bluish purple interrupted him and filled the room, and then there he was, Farson Uiost, Ascending ScreenMaster of Earth. <<*How high should I go, Handy?*>> Farson began to move through the room, such as it was. He seemed nervous about something. The shack's primitive appearance was deceptive. Like all things Handy, it was not exactly what it appeared to be. Handy Townsend stood up groggily, went to the refrigerator, the monitor still following him, took out a cold glass, and filled it with gin. "That's more like it," he said to himself, looking at the full glass, ignoring his visitor. Farson sat down on the couch. There were several magazines around with photographs of naked women. Farson picked one up. The cover showed a young woman, a brunette, hugging her breasts. There was a sheer curtain running down her body and going between her legs, somewhat tautly. She seemed a perfect specimen.

<<*Handy, why do you have this stuff around?*>> Handy was slowly working his way back to the couch and pushed Farson aside to make room, resuming his former position more or less exactly.

Still ignoring Farson, Handy picked up the guitar and started to play a song. Farson nodded to himself. *This is so predictable.*

With one hand, Handy scrolled the computer back to the poem he had just written, and adjusted the guitar on his knee and continued playing. The music was very interesting and complicated. After about five minutes of Handy's gentle and surprisingly adept instrumental performance, be began to sing the poem. It was beautiful, as always, to Farson, who was now relaxed and calm. The music was typical Handy: rhythmic, melodic, and varied in intensity throughout. <<*Farson, are you going to sing along or make me do this all alone?*>> Farson laughed out loud and began to sing the words on the monitor. Their voices harmonized easily, as usual.

Farson looked up. Handy was heading back to the fridge. <<*Handy, my question was how high should I go?*>> Handy stopped. He turned around and looked at Farson.

"I would say that's up to you, Farson." Handy resumed, in an affected leisurely manner – as if he didn't have a care in the world – his trek to the bottle of gin, stopping only to relight his cigar on the way back to the couch.

<<*There's something out there, Handy. I know it, but no one has mentioned it.*>> Handy came back to the couch, puffing profusely, a big cloud of smoke forming around him, and then trying to find a place on the cluttered table to put his cold and perspiring, already half-empty glass of gin and ice.

"You mean the Phanta, right, Farson? They're just ghosts." Handy reached for his computer pad and at the same time for his cigar, and began to type. A few minutes later he stopped to smoke a little and take a big drink again.

<<*Don't do that, Handy.*>>

"Every time I relight it tastes better and better, Farson."

Farson began to localize, and purple light filled the room once more. As he disappeared, Handy witnessed his Ascension request.

<<*Level33, Handy.*>>

The room filled with a bright blue light, almost white, and the shed exploded into nothingness. As the grass roofing and splinters of teak wood fell to the ground, Farson and

Handy were far away, speeding along together faster than either of them thought they could ever go.

<<*That's pretty high, Farson. I can only help you partway, and then you're on your own.*>>

<<*What else is new, Handy?*>> Handy laughed as he fell behind. Farson heard the faint response to his request as he sped into a distance unknown.

<<*Granted.*>>

And then, Farson was alone. Very alone.

57. Levels

The levels of ScreenMasters were well known, up to Ten. In fact, until Farson's Ascension, ScreenMaster theory held that Ten was as high as the levels went. To be honest, not much was known about LevelTen, other than that it was very lonely for the one ScreenMaster who achieved it. It seemed to involve deep concentration, for want of a better word. Perhaps supplication would be another way to describe it. LevelTen was also very difficult to step out of, as ScreenMasters always did from levels they have mastered. Levels one through nine are basic transpositions, moving on the same plane but at different places along the plane. Most ScreenMasters never get through even these initial levels. One through six are achieved on average by most, some make it to seven, eight, and a few to nine. Handy, the first ScreenMaster, eventually got to Ten, but not with any real distinction, other than being the only one to ever do it in ScreenMaster history. In the end, he also became an excellent ScreenMaster and a great teacher, but while he was there on LevelTen, he became so engaged and enmeshed that he stopped even trying to advance further. As a result of his LevelTen experiences, its lessons, if not its access pathway, became known to the

ScreenMasters. It remained impossible for them to achieve despite all of Handy's work and records. Most ScreenMasters start at Level1 and work their whole careers to reach five or six more. Only Handy had gotten to Ten's secrets. Some say he never actually returned, or that he could never do it again, but there he was, waiting on LevelTen, as Farson stopped briefly with him.

Farson then traveled on and on until, eventually, he stopped again, at Level23.

No one had ever heard of such an Ascension. The entire Screen was agitated and excited by Farson's achievement. Discussions among the ScreenMasters showed an almost total rejection of the first report as pure fabrication, but Handy stuck to his guns. When Farson announced Level33 as his destination, the other ScreenMasters were dumbfounded at such ambition. They dismissed it as beyond impossible; it was unthinkable. Then Farson announced, "Level24."

The Screen buzzed with amazement. There was much negativity, but there was also a universal awareness that future announcements would probably only go higher. The ScreenMasters knew they would have to acquiesce. Temerity was the better part of discretion because valor held no meaning for them. A consensus was forming. Farson could not be denied, but could he be believed? If not believed, could he be stopped? Didn't the other ScreenMasters, after all, have rights? Why not ask him to prove mastery of one of these advanced levels he claimed to be racing through? The discussion continued. This would require an explanation so thorough that all others could easily achieve that level, but which level? For reasons that could only be called self-serving, the ScreenMasters called on Handy for help; they wanted LevelTen. Handy would know if it was true, and the others would gain what had been unattainable to them. Farson realized that he had no choice. He turned back at Level32, heading for Ten. He was not looking forward to it, for he remembered the chosen level all too well.

It was totally dark, totally silent, and virtually sensationless. But Farson noticed something in the nothing. Rather, he noticed the nothing. That was the key. Suddenly, he had no memory. Like a baby in a darkened room, in the middle of the night, he was totally alone. He could sense no others. He was like a baby; he did the only thing he could do. He cried. And cried. And cried. In the darkness, things began to form. He was everywhere at once. And he was nowhere. <<*This is the defining level, ScreenMasters. Here is where our powers are truly demonstrated to us and greater ones given. Here we become true ScreenMasters. Until this level is achieved, the ScreenMaster is still tied to old things, to the old knowledge. Here, you are born again. Before this level, you could see in different times, hear others in different places, as we all do. With the achievement of this level you become capable of being in other times, being others in those times. Being you in other times. This level began to teach me how to change things to protect other things without disruption. Handy knows all of this. This is the level that gave him preeminence. Here a ScreenMaster is truly free to live many lives and to be many different things in many different places.*>>

<<*And what else, Farson?*>> Handy's question hung in the air. Farson knew there was more. He also knew that he would be unable to explain it to them: deciphering, discerning, and discovering this level was the first great test of a ScreenMaster. He truly wanted them to know. But he knew they would each have to earn it for themselves. Some might, but most never would. They all wanted it. There was a clamoring on The Screen.

<<*Handy, the answer to your question, as you know, is conundrumatic. It is within. For now, here is one thing to tide you all over. At first LevelTen is so overwhelming in all the new*

things you can do here that you sort of black out. It feels sensationless yet is so sensation rich it can become sensual overload. The freedom to go and do whatever you want with impunity creates a counterintuitive sense of loss and loneliness. These are all just deceptions – in a way – to divert you from the truth.>>

<<*And what is the 'truth,' Farson?*>> Handy's interrogative came swiftly, almost urgently. He knew the ScreenMasters were impatient.

<<*The 'truth,' Handy, is that LevelTen is not LevelTen.*>> All ScreenMasters were now fully attentive throughout The Screen. LevelTen had been the ultimate quest for them all, the final step that none but Handy, and now Farson, so easily, had accomplished. They were waiting. <<*It is the final step of the first set of levels. It is the last gate in a labyrinth that ultimately leads to here.*>>

<<*Where is 'here,' Farson?*>> The question was an aggregate inquiry from all those listening so intently. The Screen itself was demanding an answer.

<<*'Here' is where what is required is more than ability and acumen. Here what is needed comes from before, when we all were what we were. For me, the solution comes from my humanity. From that place where I learned – and all of you must learn – to leap into the unknown without a self-referential regard. This is where you leave all behind and leap into the deeply unknown without fear. Fear will defeat you at LevelTen every time.*>>

<<*A leap of faith, Farson? Is that really what you're talking about?*>>

<<*Exactly, Handy. A leap of faith. Without it, LevelTen is a barrier, a protection from weakness and a duplicity of purpose. 'Lasciate ogni speranza, voi ch'entrate.'*>>[3] His Italian seemed

[3] *Abandon all hope, ye who enter here.*

perfect to Handy's ear. <<*Far from instilling fear, though, this level asks that you abandon the 'hope' you have known and cherished for so long, and recognize, in this case, a truer reality. Here, you must put fear behind you.*>> The ScreenMasters all knew that Farson had met their demand for an explanation and yet had left them to their own devices about how to act on it. It was an inflection point, and they all knew it. In the cloud of their collective revelations, Farson had succeeded when they had all expected him to fail. Their conclusion that his Ascension was mere form without true substance and without the understanding of years of work evaporated as quickly as he left LevelTen, now redefined, to complete his transition to the first true and complete ScreenMaster. Farson had changed everything and now, even though they knew that every ScreenMaster was important, they also knew that there was only one who really mattered.

<<*For now, Farson, but not for always.*>> Twill's thoughts were still reaching Farson, as he traveled still farther away.

<<*I'm impressed, Twill. You are strong, but, really, you've got some serious catching up to do.*>>

Twill felt something he had thought was long gone. Something akin to Farson's vaunted "humanity." Something that he knew came from his long-forgotten biology forged in a faraway place. Seething with rage and feelings of vengeance and malevolence, he was verging on ferociousness. *Not ferocity. Wrath. That's what it is.*

<<*You see, Twill. You just don't get it. That's your 'unnature' again. Nature has no anger. The farther you go down that road, the farther from me you will be. When you are on the wrong road, you should always turn back.*>>

Perfect. Twill's own thoughts were filling him with anger and resentment even as Farson emerged right beside him.

<<*Twill, you are like the man in the thorns who is trying to kick his way out. It won't work.*>> Twill looked at Farson, the roiling storm of animus beginning to consume him. How could this human know what he was feeling? The centuries of ancestry came streaming back from the deep places of denial where Twill had kept them hidden, and for the first time in ages he was feeling his essential being again, the essence of the creature that had become a ScreenMaster. <<*You insisted, Twill, that I explain LevelTen. Now you don't like it?*>> Twill's talons struck at Farson as he passed by. Again he struck out: no contact. <<*Shame on you, Twill. That will achieve nothing.*>> Twill straightened up from his attack posture and settled back on scaled legs, shell enclosing him again, exhausted from the effort. Farson saw the professor coming into his mind. <<*That's better. Study things, Twill. Forget the old ways. It's a new day. I've given you LevelTen. You should be happy after all these years. The fire rages in the stove, but is harnessed and controlled. Instead of destruction, it brings comfort and protection. Build your trust.*>> Twill, the professor, was now writing in his grade book.

"Mr. Uiost, your conclusions are irresistible and compelling, but to a fault."

"To a fault, Professor? What do you mean?"

"You have forgotten two essential things: unpredictability, for one."

"And the other?" The professor stood, and, suddenly, there was Twill again, a huge, menacing figure showing the dreadful countenance of fierce dominance that had subsumed a thousand races so viciously in ancient times. Even Farson was taken aback by the mighty creature's intensely angry visage. The Screen was watching. Farson interrupted, answering his own question. "That there have always been despots, oppressors, and dictators? Is that it, Twill? That tyrants have always fallen before the onslaught of a willingness to sacrifice everything, to give up one's life to overcome tyranny? That tyrants have always been defeated in the end by forces far inferior in appearance but in the end superior by determination and desire? This time, Twill, will be no different, of course." Twill appeared strangely satisfied with Farson's answer.

<<*You took the words right out of my mouth, Farson.*>>

Farson's thoughts echoed in Twill's awareness. <<*We are all going together, Twill. One way or the other.*>>

<<*Of course, Farson. I would have it no other way.*>>

<<*Do you really understand the implications of Earth?*>>

<<*Do you understand its vulnerability?*>>

<<*Oh, I see, Twill. You don't really get it, do you? When you say, 'vulnerability,' you really mean to threaten me, don't you?*>>

<<*Exactly, Farson. Exactly.*>> Farson felt something imbedded in Twill's final thoughts but then dismissed it. Then he looked back again and found it. Twill had thought Farson had moved on and dropped his guard a little. Farson was surprised at what he saw.

Earth is too complicated and intricate for Twill, that's clear. He may know something about the people and what they may become, but he doesn't see it all yet. In the end he may actually discover it.

Could I have underestimated him?

58. Karina Screams

Karina screamed out loud. She was on a shuttle en route from Earth to SkyKing. The ScreenMasters had allowed it because Farson wanted her to go. In her compartment, she screamed again. Her agony was obvious. Her cabin monitor came on, and the shuttle pilot's young face appeared. "Miss Chamberlain, are you all right?" Karina staggered toward the bunk. Suddenly falling to the floor, she screamed again. "Miss Chamberlain! Give me a sign." Karina waved her hand as though swatting at an insect over and over, like she was trying to shoo something away. The pilot's image remained on the monitor. "Say something, Miss Chamberlain! Give me something." The pilot was on the verge of dispatching a security crew to her cabin. He was also thinking of turning around and heading back toward Earth.

Karina shouted out, "K … k … keep going!" The pilot nodded in acknowledgement, and the monitor blinked back to standby mode. Karina screamed again, and then she started to cry, large, racking sobs, and she was gasping for breath.

The shuttle continued on its way.

59. Eagles

Handy decided that the time had come again to shoot some eagles.

They were everywhere. *And that ain't good.* He continued along this train of thought. He remembered the times when eagles were an endangered species. He could recall the arguments for the magnificence of the eagle, and how they must be saved. In those days, the eagle was the symbol of freedom and national strength. Now Handy knew the truth. Eagles were predators and in a rare class of survivors: the sharks, the cockroach, and, of course, man.

In the changing of Emerald Earth, the environment in which eagles could thrive had spread across the planet. It was also the environment in which crops and humanity also thrived. Cockroaches did not. Most insects did not; some made it, but not many. It didn't matter, because they weren't needed on the new Emerald Earth as the Emers recreated it.

Many more surprises awaited on Emerald Earth. Humanity had truly and finally inherited the Garden of Eden again. To say the least.

The Emers worked in the fields and in the city. The Emers had few concerns and much happiness.

Earth was finally at peace, and nothing could change that.

Handy took the shot. There was a scattering in the sky: a sharp interruption in the eagle's leisurely and graceful flight. In a flurry of feathers and screeching, the bird fell to the ground with a distant thud.

That's one. Handy's thought was accompanied by the sound of the gun bolt being jacked back, a smoking round removed and another one being injected into the firing chamber. Handy snapped the single barreled shotgun closed, aimed carefully again, and smoothly squeezed the trigger.

As the gun fired again, Handy was smiling as he reached for another round in his pocket. *That's two.* The prairies around seemed to rustle with the wind.

60. The Cradle

Farson stood beside the cradle.

<<*Farson, what are you doing?*>>

Uvo was alarmed.

<<*Moving things along, Uvo. Just moving things along.*>>

61. Level24

<<*Mrs. Chamberlain, caution is advised in these matters.*>> The robot was strobing very brightly as though mildly agitated. A bolt of yellow light shot out from Mrs. Chamberlain and engulfed the robot, who was unaffected.

Another bolt shot out, this time a shade of blue mixed with the yellow, becoming almost green. Still unaffected. Then another, this time a pure bright, white light blasted through the air. The robot began to glow in a richly purple light and calmly spoke again, <<*Mrs. Chamberlain, remember, I Am Who I Am.*>>

Mrs. Chamberlain seemed confused for a moment, then she spoke out loud, "Farson?"

<<*Uvo! Level24!*>>

62. CT<<Dinsil2371

CT<<Dinsil2371 looked at the woman. She had a very friendly face.

The woman returned the look, stare for stare, sensing its thoughts, thinking how beautiful and complicated the robot looked. She could see some of its facial mechanisms moving.

<<*You are called to great adventure. If you can do it, a ScreenMaster will be your son. It will be surprisingly easy, but we wanted you to know. It is the way of The Screen.*>>

Hattie looked around at her room. It was nothing special. But it was home. She nodded, mostly because she was tired. Partly because she hoped it was true.

A son, she thought, *another chance*; she was surprised and frightened all at once.

Hattie was nodding, as CT<<Dinsil2371 gently disappeared. *I must be going crazy.* She looked down at the newspaper the robot had given her. It was opened to the classifieds.

63. "Not Quite, Viera."

Viera was sitting at her desk, signing the document Voul had given her. It was a temporary treaty between SkyKing and MoonBase, written as though they were both space-traveling vessels. "That way," Voul had said, "if Earth should ever reappear, all could go back to normal operations without defaulting on any of the interim provisions." It hadn't been easy and had taken several days. What the treaty said was that they would help each other, and not interfere with each other. Honesty was the thread that would hold them together.

Viera finished signing. Voul had already signed.

"That's about it, Voul." Viera was looking at him.

"Not quite, Viera." Voul took her hand and guided her gently into his arms. "Not quite."

Later, Voul sat reading his books, still in Viera's compartment. The contemplative transfixion that generally occurred during this meditation period naturally created a sense of peaceful self-examination. Honestly looking into his motives and actions over the past days, he began to question his judgement. *Am I swept away with physical pleasure? Is it just human love that makes me sign documents and then delay?* He thought of Viera and her ways. He thought of the Skers and their ways.

Voul closed his books, stood, and began to gather his belongings. He had been on the Moon with Viera for several days. In a few minutes he walked into the suit closet, donned his spacesuit, and left the building.

MoonBase monitors picked up the opening hatch, and Commander Nichols was immediately notified in her office where she was conducting a department heads' meeting. She moved quickly to open a link. Before she could get through, Voul's shuttle was already lifting off. She did get through.

"Voul, where are you going?" There was a long silence and then some static, and then Voul came on the link.

"I'll be back, Viera. But, I can't stay here any longer now." After a few minutes, she returned to the meeting, but the people in the room noticed a sadness in her they had not seen before. "Well," she said, "where were we? Let's take another look at that idea of using our gurney technology to access a surface structure. Exactly what were those vertical construction parameters again?"

The discussion resumed dealing with logistics, some surprising possibilities of transportation back and forth to the space station, and building a timetable to get farms operating on the Moon's surface and other issues of their changing world. Viera was obviously interested, but everyone in the room could sense her emotions were a little frayed, and that she seemed somewhat distracted.

64. Voul Rejoins the Fleet

A lieutenant was sitting in the pilot's chair when Voul came aboard. He moved to the copilot seat and as Voul swung into the command chair, he said, "Let's go, Barny." Voul began giving commands to the other distant shuttles. The fleet began to move toward the Moon. Voul met them in Moon orbit. As he rejoined the fleet, they immediately headed to the new base camp in the foothills around the main Moon compound.

In less than thirteen hours the SkyKing base camp was set up. All shuttles were down except for six that remained in a geosynchronous orbit directly overhead. Modular buildings, connected by surface tunnels, were beginning to appear, and all was exactly as MoonBase had agreed. Communications were being established within the base camp, and people were already moving around in the tunnels from building to building.

Things were starting to happen very quickly.

As SkyKing moved within range, the crew had begun to transport everything they would need to the Skers' new base on the Moon. It had all been arranged ahead of time, and Voul was still immersed in the details of logistics, organization, and deployment.

In two days, there were over five hundred Skers on the Moon, and there were several Sker substations set up at perimeter points around Bravo Base and some in strategic remote locations around the Moon. Skers were fanning out in separate units, each self-contained and with specifically prearranged objectives, preparing for things and events to come. The mining operations were continuing, relations between the Moon and SkyKing seemed right on track, and everything was going smoothly, as planned.

In time the "orbit secure" report was made. SkyKing's running lights were turned off. The station was clearly visible in its geosynchronous orbit over the Moon.

Viera was well aware of the new situation's implications for her command. With its transporting systems now within easy range, MoonBase was a virtual prisoner to the Skers' higher technology. SkyKing was living up to its name again.

None of this was particularly upsetting to Viera. It was what it had to be, given the circumstances.

What was upsetting, was how deeply she was missing Voul.

MoonBase and SkyKing, now locked together and planetless, flew on through the blackness of space. All the teeming permutations of human life, nestled in their little confines and compartments, went on as if nothing had changed.

Everyone was adapting seamlessly to new circumstances, new opportunities.

An odd report came in. Another shuttle had suddenly appeared out of nowhere on SkyKing's remote scanners. Commander Nichols was alerted, and inquiries were made. On her way to command central, she was notified, "Commander, it's Karina Chamberlain on a shuttle from Earth; at least that's what she says."

The MoonBase commander asked, "From Earth? Are you sure?"

"The shuttle pilot has just confirmed the flight plan from takeoff in Hawaii on a course to the Moon. We are guiding him through the final phases for landing. They should arrive on the Moon in about an hour or so."

Viera was thinking, *This is not good timing*. "Well, that confirms Earth is still there, doesn't it?" She knew the answer to her question, but what effect this revelation would have on the current joint operations was anything but clear.

Commander Peterson, listening to these transmissions onboard SkyKing, looked out into the void, as if into the mouth of a cave's dark interior. SkyKing had confirmed the shuttle's calculated point of origin, but there was absolutely no sign of Earth. He listened to Viera's next order.

"Have Miss Chamberlain brought to me when they land. With her permission, of course."

On a private frequency he called Viera. "Viera, there is no guarantee that this means anything except that Farson wants his sister here. We should be careful changing plans or drawing conclusions until we speak with her." Viera agreed. She instructed the duty staff accordingly.

65. Karina Arrives on SkyKing

Karina focused. She looked around the entry port. A guard was in the room, standing by. "Are you a Sker?" Karina asked, a little too abruptly as she gathered herself. The guard seemed unperturbed.

"No. I'm MoonBase." She looked him over.

"Take me to Voul Jonsn."

"I'll see what I can do," he said, and left the room to speak to the chain of command. Karina heard the keying of a transmission and a few garbled phrases. The last thing she could remember on Earth was that terrible thought that Farson was gone, or worse. She could always feel him in her mind as though he might appear at any moment. She could always sense the purple light about to appear, and she always knew that he was watching over her and loving her just out of mind's reach, but never out of mind's touch.

When she first screamed, it had been because it seemed as though a guillotine had cut her off from Farson suddenly, sharply, decisively. Their mental communication channel that had been open since Farson's Ascension shut down suddenly with a finality that frightened her as nothing else ever had.

<<*Farson,*>> she thought, <<*where are you?*>> She walked to the porthole of the compartment. The Moon that no longer circled Earth now filled its windows with black space. She had just come from Earth, but Earth was nowhere to be seen. *The ScreenMasters and their satellites.* Then she thought again, *How could that be? We were alive and moving on the Earth. Yet, from here, it's gone. Utterly gone. Can the ScreenMasters do such a thing? A planet gone, but somehow it's still there? Why let me leave? How can I get back in? Is there still a "back in" to get to?* She was confused, and it wasn't getting any better. She was very concerned about her brother's absence.

Space sprawled silently by, a slow black river in eternal night. She imagined she could feel the station moving through a soft, steady wind. "The rhythm of The Screen," Farson had said. She opened her mind and reached out for him as he had taught her to do. She strained to sense any inkling, any hint of him.

Then she strained her mind again, harder.

Her thoughts were met with only space flowing by the porthole like currents on their way to who knows where. A vast echoless emptiness.

There was a gentle knock on the door of the compartment. The guard had returned. "Miss Chamberlain, Captain Jonsn is waiting to see you as you requested. I can have you there in about two minutes. Both commanders would also like to see you."

"Let's go," she said. She left her compartment following the guard's crisp pace down the hallway.

Karina's mind refused to focus on walking or on the guard as they went through the corridors. Instead, almost in a daze – perhaps like an old-time sailor's wife watching the horizon from a widow's walk – Karina was mentally squinting for a glimpse, a glimmer of Farson somewhere, anywhere on The Screen's horizon. Her mind stretched itself to its limit for Farson, but still returned without result. Her efforts were just empty tendrils of doubt drifting aimlessly in space. There was nothing, no trace of Farson.

She was walking faster now. The guard could feel her closing in on him and stepped up his pace.

66. Farson, Are You Coming?

Voul looked around the "Tent," as the Skers were calling his command module, to find the communicator. SkyKing's crew had carefully planned and executed the establishment of a remote base camp and substations on the Moon. Their contingency plans had worked perfectly. So, Voul was comfortable in his headquarters and well supplied. The securing of the Moon as an orbital "anchor" for SkyKing, until other, more permanent, arrangements could be made, was well on the way to successful completion. "Other arrangements" included the long-planned unfurling of SkyKing's solar sails and the harnessing of the solar wind for a journey into the Skers' self-proclaimed and long-dreamed-of destiny, which was now, sadly and controversially on hold, but certainly not forgotten.

The Skers' agricultural productivity had tied them to the needs of the Moon, and the MoonBasers' mining resources had completed the circle of trade. With the disappearance of Earth, and the implications of that event, one thing had changed inevitably: The Skers' timetable was now accelerated from the relaxed, orderly, almost leisurely approach followed so concisely for so many years. Now in Sker terms, an almost all-out panic existed. The reasons for this situation were many, but fear of MoonBase, and its influences, was a factor. Since the Skers did not know what was going to happen, they decided to be ready for anything. That meant everything was changed. As their leader, Voul was responsible for decisions no Sker wanted to make. *We don't even know why all of this is happening.* Voul's thoughts about the uncertainty of the situation, and the options in front of him were interrupted by Karina Chamberlain's knock on the door of his new sparse and utilitarian headquarters still settling into the dust of the gray and barren dark side of the Moon. He opened the door.

She was a beautiful young woman whose face and figure were immediately recognizable, and who came with an awesome and obvious intelligence and power. *So this is Farson's sister.*

He found himself indulging in a momentary thought of Viera. In the seconds between seeing Karina and saying hello, he lingered in those new and confounding, disturbing emotions that had nearly overwhelmed him lately: love and longing for Viera. He was daydreaming about her as Karina walked toward him. In the midst of so much change and with so much hard work before him, he was thinking of her kiss, her embrace. Mentally shaking off the thoughts, Voul realized that the person standing before him, offering him her hand in greeting, was a far more important human being than any he had ever met, including his own father. As he relished Viera's last whisper in his ear, "Hurry back," he could feel Karina's intelligent mind probing his as their hands met. She was smiling. <<*If you are in awe of me, Voul, wait until you meet Farson.*>> Voul was reeling from this mental "touch," as he shook her hand mechanically. He could not focus for a moment. Then he asked, "Will I be meeting Farson?" Karina was thinking about Viera's attachment to this Sker that she had noticed in his thoughts. "Will I be meeting Viera?" Voul was surprised. Karina laughed at him. "You should get used to it, Voul. Your secrets are all open now." The two of them looked at each other. They were still shaking hands.

A powerful tendril thought touched Karina's mind at this moment with a harmonic familiarity, like the scent of a long-forgotten garden. She knew it was Farson without a doubt. <<*Farson, where are you? Are you coming?*>>

Then she faced Voul, with a new smile of anticipation. His question about Farson had just been answered. "If we're lucky, Voul, you just might."

Voul spoke through his wrist communicator as they left the Sker's base camp and headed off to MoonBase headquarters. "Jim, she has arrived."

67. Tally-Ho!

Farson was traversing Level13, 14, 15, and 16 again like a child playing hopscotch. The ScreenMasters were astounded. Uvo and Twill were just watching and witnessing. Twill expressed his opinion first. <<*I've got to hand it to him. This is highly unusual. I think of the troubles I had with Level9 and what he's doing now, I really have to wonder, Uvo, if this isn't a truly different kind of ScreenMaster, as you have so often said.*>>

Uvo was particularly reflective in his opinion. Twill grew irritated at the delay in Uvo's response. Uvo was intractable in his formulations, as usual. Level20 came into Farson's view and with a ScreenMaster's equivalent of a loud "Tally-Ho!" Farson pressed on and on.

<<*I'm glad to hear you say that, Twill.*>> Finally, Uvo had articulated. <<*Quite glad, actually.*>>

68. Sad to Say

Handy staggered drunkenly to the refrigerator. *Can't really walk straight.* He poured himself a large shot of ice-cold vodka this time. Some old friend of Russian extraction had once told him to keep the vodka in the freezer until its viscosity increased to that of a syrup. "This," his Russian friend had said, "is the true Russian way to drink vodka." Handy did exactly what he remembered his friend had done on that occasion. He took the frosted, frozen bottle, twisted off its cap, and immediately tipped it to his lips for a long, slow pull. As his head went back, his Adam's apple went slowly up and down, allowing the beverage to proceed down at its own pace. Handy humorously remembered his friend's surprising gulp-capacity.

He hesitated for a moment, letting the cold in his throat warm up a little bit. Then Handy tipped his head way back, slugged down more large gulps, lost his balance, and fell over backwards, smashing his head on the table. It tipped over as he crashed with a sound of a sack of potatoes hitting the floor. Suddenly and painfully supine, rubbing his head dizzily, he became nauseated and vomited violently, the cold of the vodka passing his lips a second time, now in the opposite direction. In this depressing and disgusting circumstance, The Screen's first Master had only one thought. *Farson will not like this at all.* The shattered bottle lay beside him in pieces, slushy vodka melting into pools.

Handy's friend from a thousand years ago would have shaken his head and said, "Nyet. Nyet, Nyet!" Farson would shake his head in dismay and disappointment at Handy's excessive abuse of everything. His Russian friend would also certainly have reprimanded him. "Wasting good vodka is the worst sin of all."

Handy, at this point, agreed with them both.

He tried to get up but slipped in the mess of his own making, a despicable scene in a world at a dead stop. *Who'll ever know around here?* Handy's last thoughts before he blacked out.

In the morning, he awoke in his bed. Everything was neat and tidy. There was a handwritten note from Farson by the coffee pot when Handy went for a cup: "I know, Handy." Handy poured some coffee and walked out to the porch and sat down. He sipped the coffee and watched a world that never moved.

69. A New Definition

Farson was in a strange place. He was still alone but now in the full immersion of his own worst fears. He was rethinking everything. It was a place where he was undiscovered. He was still himself, but there were no restraints, and he was wandering as though looking for an exit where there could be no exit. He knew that things were bad. He knew he was so unworthy. He knew in his heart that this power had come to the wrong person. He was experiencing discouragement. He was disillusioned. His protections were fleeing. Worse, he had nothing with which to replace them. The ideas that usually flowed enthusiastically from his mind like water naturally coursing down a smooth mountain stream had dried up. He was lying down on his back; he was unable to move. He was pinned.

Some things reminded him of dark images. People he loved whom he could never love again. Things he had loved that were gone forever. His deepest longings were empty things with no meaning. He was flattened. Like a patient going under ether, he was losing control.

<<*Uvo!*>> No answer came. *I'm beyond that.* He tried to stand up and yet felt no movement. Paralysis: There was no color, no inspiration, and way in the back of his consciousness there was a sense of regret for things that could not be undone, and there was dread of things to come. Time was passing with no accomplishments. It was as though he was waiting for a bad thing to run its course to worse, and then to much worse. A small chair presented itself. He moved toward it but could not reach it. In the gloom he heard a voice calling for him. <<*Farson ... Farson ...* >>

He saw himself surpassing level after level. How high am I now? Still there was no respite. Like a falling man watching skyscraper windows fly by, Farson was going faster and faster, toward something, an ending perhaps. Something was beginning to present itself.

There was a crowd of people, well dressed, standing around him, and he noticed the purple of a fading ScreenGlow and the emptiness where someone had just been. *I made him disappear.* Farson was emerging into a distant time within a heartbeat of when he had just been traversing level after level. It was "the planet of troubles." *Why did I do that?* Now he remembered. *It seems so long ago.*

One of the dignitaries standing beside him began to kneel. He seemed fearful. Then the whole crowd was kneeling. Farson stood there in the purple shimmering. A voice began to speak. It was his.

"I am Farson Uiost, ScreenMaster of Earth. Your planet will soon resume a peaceful transit of time, but first I must speak to you of the ways of The Screen."

The crowd was very quiet. Farson could see men and women, and he could hear the ever-restless children, impatient with their parents. A little way off a woman who looked remarkably like Karina picked up her small son and cradled him gently in her arms.

"Peacefulness is required of all civilized planets. It is mandated by the ScreenMasters. Your leaders have been unfaithful, and you should have thrown them over. Peace is from within a world and from within a people. It has to come from within. You must work to make peace your goal. Love, unselfish giving, hard work, joy and sorrow, laws of freedom: reason, good over evil, beauty, and faith are all part of peace. Without peace you are alone. Without peace you shall perish.

"I am here to explain this to you."

Farson began to move within the crowd. He walked among the kneeling thousands. He touched their heads, told them all to stand, and their children looked up at him. He lifted up a young girl and hugged her. "I have removed your leader," he said, "to another level of existence where he will learn his lessons. You will remain here." As he said the word "here," he reached out a hand, and a small globe of the planet appeared above his palm; it was hovering there. "This is your fragile world, which has been given to you." He gently moved his arms and hands to hold the planet above his head, above theirs, too. "This is a great gift. Sometimes worlds must be destroyed, and sometimes they can be saved. My home planet, Earth, was a world such as yours. Full of derision and strife, full of hatred and war, we too were assaulted by the results of our own actions, but we are learning our lesson. The ScreenMasters came to us. Now, I have come to you."

There was a snapping sound, like a rubber band breaking, and the color around Farson began to fade. Suddenly, his ScreenLite disappeared.

He was a man among men.

For several moments people were silent and uncertain. Farson then began to walk among them and toward a far field, just outside the city limits. The people followed him. "Come," he said. "I will show you."

Farson knelt by a stream perhaps a mile from where he had entered this world. There was clear water drifting by. He bent to take a drink from the palms of his hands. Small fishes moved away as his face neared the surface. He could sense the intelligence in the little creatures swimming. He could feel the water grasses moving under the surface. The water was life-full and cold. He scooped up a little more to drink in, and then washed his hands and face. It was refreshing. The multitude had followed him, and he could hear them murmuring among themselves. They were coming closer. Someone touched him. "Who are you? Why are you here? Why did you kill the prefect? He was our leader." Farson could feel their anger. He wiped his hands on his corduroys. He adjusted his shirt and cardigan sweater. The crowd moved closer. Suddenly, a rock hit him in the face and filled his eyes with blood. Another rock came flying in and more blood, more pain. He remained standing somehow. He raised his hands over his head. The crowd moved back. Then, when nothing happened, they rushed forward, tearing at Farson, taking him down. He could feel himself being torn apart. Little pieces of his being were taken from him. His strength sapped. He was being kicked and stomped. His head was being crushed and then his body and his bones. He was being crushed to death by their anger and their hatred. The fury of the crowd was terrible. It was unabashed fear, released. Farson felt his consciousness pressed and stamped into the soil beside the little stream. Finally, the crowd moved back, sated. Farson could feel the transmission of the scene of carnage to a worldwide audience, and he could sense the global arousal and excitement. Farson knew that his arrival and actions had been seen by everyone, and he knew that his death had also been seen by everyone. People were still rushing forward to stamp and spit on the ground and run away. Now, where he had been, there was only redness and scattered fibers from his cardigan sweater and corduroys. Where once the great Farson Uiost had stood, nothing remained. The pain of his physical destruction left Farson feeling sad. In the blood and torn cloth a small tenuous glimmer of purple slowly appeared. People screamed when they saw it and moved backward, afraid. The crowd split up as people fled. Farson's ScreenMaster purple was reforming.

The purple grew and formed again into the shape of Farson Uiost dressed in a cardigan sweater and corduroys, exactly as before, but now it surrounded Farson in a pulsating light.

Farson, again, stood before the crowd. He was again holding their globe floating over his hand, extended over his palm.

"I wish I were sure that you really know what you have just done. I pray that you know not. Are you really so unrelenting in the errors of your ways? Do my words not cause you to rethink your actions? Are your hearts so hardened?" The globe began to turn slightly faster, and a dark cloud spread around it. The sky overhead grew ominous, and the air grew colder. The people looked up into the sky, to the horizons, and then at each other. Then they looked at Farson. "I came among you to teach and to show you the way. You know who I am. You know what I represent. Yet, you scorn me and trample me the moment you think I am weak. You cannot do these things and escape the results. Not because it is I who would destroy and punish, but rather because it is you yourselves who threaten. The Screen demands so much more than that."

The skies overhead were dark now, and the wind was cold. People of this world were used to the warm weather of a tropical climate. The world was green and lush. Life had been easy. Now what? They were worried and wondering.

Farson's purple glow intensified, the warmth of it spread among the people, and they moved in closer, as to a fire's hearth. Farson spoke again. "Things are going to be very different for you and your world now. Make the most of it. Many of you will not adapt. To those who do, I leave these words. Be peaceful and be kind. Return to your old ways and you will perish."

"I shall return."

A brilliant flash of white and then purple, soundless and unforgettable, engulfed the people. Slowly it abated leaving a palpable emptiness where Farson had been, and a world growing colder.

In the aftermath, people huddled together in the coldness and looked for shelter. Shelter, they knew, that would be woefully inadequate if the current weather persisted. With fearful countenances and dread in their hearts, the crowd of people walked off to their homes, each person with his or her own thoughts about what had occurred and about the painful changes which events had given them.

In time, the little stream slowed to a crawl, and the cold winds whipped the green grasses of the fields to a dry brown. Throughout the world, things warm and green turned to gray and cold, and people worried about their children. With society disrupted by catastrophic climate changes, people stayed home and planned for their families' survival.

Politics and cruelty quickly gave way to the exigencies of a dark, intractable, undeniable future that they were all now inexorably facing together.

Farson anticipated Uvo's voice, but it did not come. Now, he was again racing along the level-to-level-continuum: higher and higher; faster and faster.

<<*Twill, I've lost him.*>>

<<*Well, Uvo, you stayed with him longer than I could. You are still a Great One.*>>

<<*Compared to what, Twill? I've never seen anything like what Farson is doing.*>>

<<*A new definition of ScreenMaster, Uvo?*>>

<<*A new dictionary, Twill, a whole new dictionary.*>>

70. Things Are Getting Out of Control

Karina's question to Farson, "Are you coming?" hung in her thoughts unanswered. She searched her memory. Yes, there had been a touch, but it seemed so distant and remote that she barely recognized it. But it had been there.

She turned back to Voul.

"Mr. Jonsn, why do you think I am here?" The Sker captain was surprised at the passive tone of her question. He was expecting something more demanding and perhaps more authoritative.

"I was going to ask you the same thing. All I know is that you have just come out of nowhere really. Our people say you came from Earth, which we are not even sure still exists." Voul looked Karina Chamberlain over. She was very attractive, and her soft brown hair, and statuesque appearance, made her all the more so. Her connection to Farson made her powerful and an uncertain element in the current uncertain equation. The disappearance of Earth had generated a series of events that were still unfolding. Voul's mission was an open-ended one, because with Earth gone, the Skers' plan of sailing for the stars in a self-contained world of their own had been greatly accelerated, perhaps too much to control. In his tent on the Moon, Voul had been assessing this. Now on their way to MoonBase he had an answer to her question, but he wasn't sure if it was true, or if he was just hoping it was true.

"Karina, I think Farson sent you here to help us. Did you come from Earth?"

"Yes, I did, Voul."

"What has happened there?"

Karina knew that it would take a lot more to fully answer Voul's question than he imagined in asking it. How could she explain it? Stasis was a harsh thing, but she knew it was far better than the ScreenMasters' original plan. She also knew what the Skers were planning, and she knew their new base on the Moon was, on the one hand, an attempt to deal with the disappearance of Earth and, on the other, it was a duplicitous act that was advancing their plans to assume full control of SkyKing. Truthfully, at this point, Karina was much more interested in Farson's predicament than in anything the Skers or the MoonBasers were doing. Yet here she was because Farson wanted her to be here. So, she knew that the perspicacious Sker walking with her was entirely correct in his assessment of who sent her to SkyKing, but he was far from knowing the whole truth.

Again, she called out with her thought to Farson. Waiting for a response, she felt a void coursing through her. Was it really a void? Was it something that her mind had never come across before? Was it something new, some new phenomenon? She again spoke to Voul.

"I might be able to help explain to you what has happened to Earth, but you will not like it, even if you can understand it."

"Give me a chance," Voul encouraged her to continue.

"Can we have something to eat first?" She was hungry, and a little delay would help her collect her thoughts.

She began her explanation as their lunch was winding down over coffee. "When the ScreenMasters came to Earth, they selected my brother to be what they call 'ScreenMaster of Earth.' Some other planets have ScreenMasters as well. Farson is now ours. There is a problem in The Screen caused by something that is happening here now or that happened here at some time in our past, or both. Farson is charged with finding it. In that process he is going through what they call Ascension, or, in other words, official confirmation as a ScreenMaster. Farson didn't need their confirmation, and he has ascended higher, by far, than any other ScreenMaster in

Screen history. In fact he is still out on The Screen ascending now. No one really knows where he is or what he is doing, including me. So, we are all waiting for him to rejoin us. At this point, he may be dead for all anyone knows." She said this with a hesitation in her voice, and Voul noticed the emotion in the words. She knew Farson was alive and regretted misleading Voul. *I did say, "For all anyone knows."*

"Without Farson, can The Screen be fixed?" Voul asked.

"Apparently not completely, and not without drastic measures. For now, the ScreenMasters have put a bandage on the situation. We all watched their satellites being deployed. The Earth is still there, but it is no longer passing through the ordinary space-time algorithms. That buys us all time to find the problem and hopefully to repair it. Only Farson can do that."

Voul was thinking this over. Earth in stasis. The Moon and SkyKing have been cut loose. Time seemed to be running out. *When will the Earth come back?* He asked Karina the question he was thinking.

"It might never come back. For SkyKing and MoonBase it is gone now. I would say you are doing exactly the right thing here, attempting to stabilize the situation and survive." Voul had another question.

"Can we really do that?" Karina laughed a small laugh at his nervousness.

"I believe you can. So does Farson. I think that he sent me here to be off of Earth. He may also have sent me here to help you, but I'm not sure about that."

"You mentioned more drastic measures than stasis. Are the ScreenMasters so powerful?"

"Oh, yes, Voul. The ScreenMasters are very powerful. Much more than we could have guessed. They are masters of The Screen. The Screen is everything."

"You think Farson can repair the problem, if he is still alive?"

She nodded, her ponytail confirming it. She watched Voul's open face and looked into his clear eyes. She was sending him a message. *He's alive.*

Voul stood up and walked to the porthole, to gaze out at the moonscape.

He thought of the solar sails being prepared for so many years. Of the crew of MoonBase and the decades of their work mining there. He thought of his recent experiences with Viera and the changes happening on SkyKing. He knew that from the way things were just a week ago, to the way things were now was way out of his control. Probably out of anyone's control. *Well, hopefully not anyone.* He shivered at the prospect of a totally unknown future. He turned to Karina and said, "Everything is so unknown, so uncertain. It's not the Sker way. I hope we are doing the right thing, Karina. I wish Farson were here to tell us."

"That makes two of us, Voul." *That makes a lot more than just two of us. That makes ALL of us.*

Voul was looking into her eyes. Lunch was over.

71. I Think I've Got It

Farson's progress stopped softly. He was standing in a bright light. There was something with him. He heard his name spoken not thought: "Farson Uiost." The sound was strange but in a reassuring way. Distant and near at the same time. Soft and clear, but strong and irresistible too. New and intimate. Friendly and commanding. A statement, not a question. His name seemed to echo in this level's resonance.

"Yes." Farson felt compelled to answer. "Is that you, Handy?"

Farson knew instantly it was not Handy. Farson knew he had reached his highest level. There were questions forming in his mind: What has happened? Why?

Thoughts of his planet filled his mind. Its mistakes now threatening The Screen. How he was fighting to save his people, his planet. How the ScreenMasters considered it a lost cause. The thought came to him how difficult it would be to repair the situation, changing Earth completely, the survival of its people in question. Emerald Earth would survive. Thoughts of the others filled his mind. He knew that Emerald Earth would be a new place. But, memories would be gone. People gone, but forever? History would be gone in a new history.

Farson knew that the decisions made there on old Earth disrupted everything because of the way those people were. He knew that his planet itself would pay. In the history of Earth the Rent was slowly created; it can only be repaired with a ScreenMend, and that requires a *tabula rasa*: a blank slate. *It's a factor of time. To change history means the people who did those things can never have lived.* He knew there would have to be a radical procedure to insure an effective thoroughness. His idea seemed tenuous, but worth trying. *Delaying the inevitable?* That's what the ScreenMasters say.

Being there, alone but not alone, at this level, Farson thought to himself of an ancient nursery rhyme. *All the King's horses, and all the King's men couldn't put Humpty Dumpty together again.* Farson asked a question.

"What of Handy? He lives on Emerald Earth." There was no answer. Farson knew that he had made the decision to leave Handy there. There was no one else. He had a sense that whoever or whatever was with him on this level could not help him now, that he was all alone.

Then, Farson was moving again. The troubling, pseudo-mental contact dissipating slowly as the darkness resumed.

Suddenly he knew that what he had thought was his "highest level" was really only just the beginning.

Farson was sitting before the old computer he had rebuilt in the attic. He was only seventeen. Karina was beside him. There was a cursor lock on the screen.

"Damn it, Karina, look at that! The damn thing locked up."

"You've been saving as you went, right?" Karina knew that saving as you go will save the keystrokes of work done if a cursor lock occurs.

"Yeah, right." Farson had not been saving because when he wrote, he forgot about everything else. Concentration was his strong suit.

The locked cursor rigidly stayed there on the screen, unblinking; it looked dead. It was dead. All those ideas and images behind it. They were right there. But gone forever.

"I hate this. I hate this." Farson was beginning to lose his temper. Karina saw it coming.

"Come with me," she said. Farson's angry face stared at her. "Just leave it right there, Farson, and come with me. Right now."

Farson stood up but refused her offered hand; he was too mad for that. They were in the little "Library," as they called it, just off the main area of The Ship. There was a desk, a couch, and a reading lamp. They went to the couch. Karina had him sit on it. She began to massage the sides of his head, facing him. Farson put his arms around her waist. As always, she was soft and warm. He drew her to him and buried his face in her middle. The warmth soothed him. He hugged her closer, her hands moving on his neck and shoulders, their love warming and comforting. She gently pushed him into a lying position, and she lay down beside him and kissed him on his lips. "I can feel your silly anger flowing away, Farson. Let it go. Let love have its way."

Farson kissed her, losing himself in the growing tender fervor of the deep love he felt for her. Her soft hair flowed over him, engulfing him in relief. Farson felt himself sliding into that other consciousness that they had together. It was like coming home. He felt the release, and the feeling of being one with Karina.

When Karina opened her eyes, Farson was back at the machine.

"Farson, what are you doing?" She noticed he had taken the computer partially apart, and now he was working on the keyboard.

"I think I've got it," he said, not stopping for a second.

"Karina, Karina … " Farson sang her name as Hattie always did, but he was mocking her. When Hattie sang it, the sonorous intonation was full of love. It hurt Karina to hear Farson sing her name in the same tune and taunting her so maddeningly. Like fingers on a chalkboard his words grated unbearably. Hattie's song had always been fun and soothing. He always mixed it with another more annoying song.

"My Mother, your Mother lives across the street
Sixteen, seventeen Blueberry Street.
Every time they have a fight this is what they say:
Boys are made out of cotton;
Girls are made out of Pepsi,
Boys go to college to get more knowledge,
Girls go to Jupiter to get more stupider."

"Karina, Karina …"

Karina looked through the cracked-open door at the boy who lived in the Chamberlains' house. He was in the hall, trying to make her mad. He kept repeating the same stupid rhymes over and over. She thought of her parents and of how much she missed them. Her father's joy of life, her mother's dependable love and companionship, up to the moment of their death. These things were everything to her. Now she had nothing. She felt so lonely, so isolated. She felt the tears welling up. How could they have done this to her? How could they have left her in this situation, with this stupid, stupid boy tormenting her when no one was looking? She slammed the door and ran to the bed. She buried her head in the pillow and cried and cried. She could still hear him out there, taunting her.

<<*You know I feel bad about that, Karina. You know that, don't you?*>>

<<*Of course, I know that. I learned all about you while I was on Jupiter, Farson.*>>

Despite the distance and time involved they still enjoyed the joke together. Karina pointed at a wire in the back of the computer. "Was that hooked up, Farson? It might be important."

<<*Karina, you never said that.*>>

<<*I know, but I wanted you to see how far I've come.*>>

<<*So, all of that was just you showing off your ScreenMaster abilities?*>>

<<*Of course. I learned it from the great master himself.*>>

Farson pushed the loose wire back into its socket.

Chapter Five

Destiny

72. Farson, Voul, and Karina

The purple light of The Screen preceded Farson as he materialized. Karina knew immediately what was happening, and her heart leapt in anticipation. Voul looked confused. He looked at her inquiringly.

Karina said, "It's my brother."

Then, there was Farson. Karina was in his arms. She was happy, sobbing, crying, angry, and talking all at once. "Karina, Karina," Farson said softly in the way he had made fun of her as a boy; only now it was the height of endearment between them, "everything is all right." They just held each other for a long moment, and then another. They were lingering in the comfort of being together and in their mutual memories. ScreenMaster or not, Farson loved this young woman. Their relationship was a very simple one, and for Farson it held the strength of the universe. For Karina, there were no words or thoughts to express her feelings. She simply held on tight. Voul was shifting his feet around. Farson and Karina noticed him again and moved slowly away from their embrace. Slightly out of breath, Karina spoke first. She knew that Farson knew everything that was going on, and that he had had more to do with things as they now were than anyone could possibly know. She knew everything, of course. As she began to introduce him to Voul, she noticed that

Farson seemed a little surprised since he already knew everything there was to know about Voul. <<*Try not to laugh, Farson. People need their little formalities.*>>

<<*Karina, I know that. In fact there are a few formalities I want to discuss with you.*>>

<<*Funny. Especially from someone who has been missing and who has a lot of explaining to do.*>>

<<*That sounds like fun.*>> They were both laughing and smiling at this private exchange. It was great to be together. Voul was watching and catching glimpses of what was being said. <<*Interesting,*>> Farson said to Karina. <<*He can hear us a little.*>>

<<*Yes, he can, Farson. The Skers are an interesting people. They are, human, after all.*>> That made Farson laugh out loud.

<<*Only you, Karina, would say something like that.*>>

"Farson, this is Voul Jonsn, Captain of SkyKing. He is also the leader of the Skers. Voul, this is my brother, Farson Uiost, ScreenMaster of Earth." Farson and Voul exchanged an intense eye contact. Voul sensed that he was being probed, but the feeling passed quickly. He knew that this was no ordinary man. Voul didn't really know what to make of Farson, who had suddenly appeared on the Moon out of nowhere. No ship, no nothing, just Farson standing there in his usual brown cardigan sweater, loose shirt, corduroy slacks, and loafers. He had noticed some mental activity, but at a level he was not used to. It seemed to Voul that Farson and Karina were sharing something humorous, but something also sensual. He picked up on the former emotions more than the latter, but the latter were strangely more intensely intriguing. Voul was in the white uniform of the SkyKing captain, crisp and military in appearance, and he was very neatly groomed. Anyone walking into the room and seeing the three people there would have readily assumed that Voul was in command.

Anyone thinking that, however, would have been vastly mistaken. Farson turned mentally to Karina and said, <<*I think I've got it, Karina. I think I know what to do.*>> Karina looked at Farson.

<<*Is that good?*>> She knew too much about what was going on not to understand that solutions involved in repairing The Screen might not take the Earth's welfare fully into account. Especially since she knew that the ScreenRent occurred at Earth because of something the people of Earth had done. Her mental question hung in the air like a seabird hovering over the spindrift off turbulent seas.

<<*Good and bad, Karina. Like all things. Emerald Earth is the answer. It's the only way out.*>>

"Emerald Earth." She thought she noticed a special intonation in Farson's use of the phrase. It was not the first time she had heard the two words together, it was, however, the first time she knew the reality in the phrase. She turned to the SkyKing captain. "Well, Voul, here's your answer about Earth. Now, it's called Emerald Earth: green and amber, pastoral, and deeply valuable. It is also gone, and it will stay that way."

"Gone? But not dead. True?" Voul said it like it was a statement, not a question. Farson moved in a little closer.

"Voul, Earth is dead for all intents and purposes. Someday – a far, far distant day from here – that may change. And, it could change for the better, so let's not be impatient. What we do here, right now, determines much. Green and amber are important colors in the ScreenMasters' palette. Emerald stands for pastoral things, sustenance, growing, and Earth stands for the amber for the harvests, and rich, fertile growings again. Emerald Earth means generosity and peace and science and agriculture. Nothing else." Farson was looking at his sister. She was thinking of Earth's dirty but promising technology, its quarreling nations, and its imbalanced cities with vastly unequal populations. Her mind was focusing on the vision of Emerald Earth that Farson had painted so vividly in her thoughts.

Voul asked, "Will this happen slowly? Or will it happen all at once?" Farson just continued to look at him. Karina was fidgeting. Voul continued, "Will this transition be something Earth's people will support, or is it compulsory, Farson?" Farson continued looking at him, unblinkingly. Karina already knew. <<*It's already done, isn't it, Farson?*>>

"As I said, Voul, Earth is gone. Now. SkyKing and MoonBase must get on with things. They have their own destinies, separate from Earth. Your long-planned agendas mean nothing now. If I were you, I'd get moving as soon as possible. Events are already underway that will very soon make this segment of space far less attractive in which to linger.

"How soon?"

"That's not the question, Voul. It's too late for that. Things are irrevocably underway right now. There's no time to lose. If you step on it, you'll be okay." Voul looked down, and then looked up again. Farson was watching him. Voul realized that what Farson had just suggested had nothing to do with his perfectly shined shoes.

73. Farson Releases the Skers

Karina had gone looking for Viera. When they were alone, Farson said to Voul, "Tell me about the solar sails." Voul was shocked. Through all the years of Sker history no non-Sker had ever spoken the words, "solar sails" let alone actually known of the existence of them. Farson noticed Voul's visceral reaction. "Voul, I know a lot more than you think I do, and I'm a friend of the Skers, so don't worry." Voul continued his silence. He was thinking of his pledge to never speak of the sails to any non-Sker. He was thinking of his hopes for his people. Many, many thoughts were swirling in his mind. Farson was waiting.

"ScreenMaster Uiost, if you know of our sails, then you must also know of their importance to my people. Some things, so long secret, are not easily spoken of."

"I know," said Farson, "but now you must."

Voul walked to a chair and sat down. Until Farson Uiost got here he was in charge, and the Skers were moving by their own scriptural destiny to a point where decisions could, and would, be made. Now that point was suddenly thrust upon them, and volition was slipping away. Voul found himself extremely uneasy, and he was so reluctant to speak that he was verging on being physically unable to speak. So many sacrifices; so much effort; so much hope; so many prayers had all gone into the secret sails. Now the secret was a secret no more. What were the implications? Voul was conflicted and confused.

"Who else knows?" asked Voul.

"No one."

"How can that be, ScreenMaster? How could you be the only one? Someone must have shown you. Someone must have told you. Someone must have confirmed it." Voul was very near to anger, but Skers never angered.

"No one told me, Voul. I just knew. I know the Skers, and I know how much they value adventure and exploration. I have read your father's book, *The Sky Within*." Voul was astonished. This man knew of the solar sails, and he knew the Skers' sacred book.

"If you know these things," Voul said, "then you know the answers concerning the sails that you seek." Breaking no law, Voul had responded to the ScreenMaster's question. Farson moved closer still. Now at whispering range.

"They are ready." Farson unblinkingly watched the Sker's eyes for confirmation. Closely, his concentration stared into the Sker's mind. Farson had known the fact of the sails, but what he wanted was to see recognition in Voul's mind that Farson was right about what the Skers needed to do now. *There it is.* Before Voul could object or question, Farson disappeared, leaving a telltale hue of purple hanging in the air like the scintillations on a lake as the sun was setting. Voul was left alone with excruciating knowledge he did not want. Farson's voice appeared in his thought. <<*Fear not, faithful Voul. I come not to kill the Skers, but to save them and to set them free. Tell your people to prepare.*>>

Voul called Commander Peterson in his office on SkyKing and said, "We must talk, Jim. I'm coming up." Commander Peterson nodded and informed the bridge to anticipate Voul's arrival from the surface of the Moon. He thought to himself, *Farson, Karina, and now Voul is returning. The gang's all here.*

74. It All Comes Down to This

When Voul's call came in, Commander Peterson was sitting on the couch in his office, looking into his holographic control panel, thinking about the visual display floating in front of him. It showed an interesting thing. Although SkyKing was orbiting the Moon, the Moon was still exhibiting a faint but undefined trace of orbital influence from the point in space where the Earth had been. The effect was very marginal at best, but the Sker engineers had noticed it right away and they had requested instructions from Peterson. *So, it must still be there.* He touched another button and searched through the data from before the Earth disappeared. The information showed drastic changes in both the spatial data and the orbital influence data. There was no doubt: Earth was gone, for all intents and purposes. There was also no doubt that Earth was still there, very, very faintly. *It's as though all of the evidence of life and activity is totally gone, but the spatial balances are slower to adjust.* He had a thought, "Are the measurements diminishing or maintaining?" The Skers began some programming and testing sequences, and they checked the data gathered since the planet disappeared.

"It seems to be fading, sir, but by increasingly smaller and smaller increments. So the answer is that it is both diminishing and maintaining. Plus, there is no calculation that results in a final equational solution, other than an infinitely predictable progression approaching zero but never actually reaching it."

Commander Peterson thought of something else: a finely focused and powerful communications beam targeted at the Earth's deduced location. He issued the order, and crew arranged the equipment and began the high-frequency, forceful transmission. It took only a second, and immediately the communications room was bombarded with sound so intense that everyone covered their ears, trying to soften the painful impact. *It bounced. With force.* For a while, Peterson continued to study the visual display. His next action was to begin a pattern of low-level emissions fired off at regular intervals. He set the program to run for twelve continuous hours, creating a sort of time-lapse photography with sound. "That should do it," he said out loud to what he thought was an empty room.

"Should do what, Dad?" asked Brittany. His daughter had come into the Communications Station while her father was engrossed in his calculations. Her father turned to her, smiling at her uncanny ability to find him whenever she wanted to, wherever he was on SkyKing. She knew that station the way every child knows her home. After all, she was born there.

"Just a test I'm running, honey. You'll be glad to know that Voul is coming."

"When?" she asked. The thought was pleasant to her.

"He's on his way, right now." Transportation was easy between the Moon and SkyKing, given their close proximity. Peterson remembered that Voul had insisted on a tight, close orbit for that very reason.

Commander Peterson reviewed the status of the mining operation. The Skers had motivated MoonBase somehow to be way ahead of schedule – probably by concentrating on just what the Skers wanted. The agricultural transfer from SkyKing to MoonBase was already complete. *Voul wastes no time.*

He pressed a series of holographic keys on his display. After a moment Viera Nichols appeared on the floating screen.

"Hi, Jim." Viera looked radiant. Jim felt the familiar wave of pleasant desire whenever he looked at her. Becoming involved with someone was a luxury he had not allowed, and would never allow himself since his wife's death, but he was a man after all. Viera was a woman. *A lot of woman.* For her part, Viera had always been interested in Jim Peterson and he knew it, but given Viera's passionate proclivities, he didn't make too much of her interest. Still, every once in a while, in his loneliness, he did think about it. Looking at her now he could see that her interests had gone elsewhere. He took notice of this change with mixed emotions.

Brittany had moved onto the couch next to her father. Peterson casually put his arm around her and pulled her to his side. Viera noticed the familiarity of the fatherly gesture and found that she was admiring the two of them. She thought about the steady contentment they must draw from such a solid and mutual relationship. "And, hello there, Brittany," Viera said. Brittany smiled brightly.

"Hi, Commander Nichols." Viera thought about what a beautiful thing a fifteen-year-old girl's smile can be. She and Brittany were exchanging looks with eyebrow movements, probably toying with the idea of starting their usual joking; around routines. But, Commander Peterson had other things on his mind.

"Viera, how are things really going down there?" Viera could be seen shifting papers around on her desk. She looked at Peterson through the monitor, and he could tell there was something on her mind. Her expression seemed happier than one might have expected under the circumstances, but she also had a look of someone under pressure.

"Estimates are that the completion of all phases will occur by noon tomorrow. A day and a half ahead of schedule." Peterson nodded. "It's because of the Skers. They work around the clock, like machines." Jim knew the Sker work ethic all too well.

"Has Voul been pushing them?"

"Well, not really. He has seemed very relaxed. The Skers just have no wasted efforts, and they are very efficient, as you know. Everyone on the Moon tells me they are easier to work with than even the regular miners. They join in, no arguments, solve every problem, are very accommodating, and offer suggestions and seem to actually be enjoying themselves. I have to say that my crew is working harder and smarter because of them. Voul has really done a great job of coordination. He's just like the rest of them; he is working hard, and he's getting it done. "

"So, Voul's just like the rest of them, Viera? Just another Sker?" Peterson asked with a little smile, his arm on Brittany's shoulder, her soft brunette hair cascading. Viera felt a little pang of sublimated envy watching Jim and Brittany sitting together. She wondered if that daughter-to-parent bond would ever happen for her.

"Very funny," she said and moved on to another topic. Peterson let it pass, noting that ordinarily a comment like that from him would have required a strong response. *Interesting. She is keeping it to herself.* Then Viera went on, "Once Karina Chamberlain arrived, things did change. We first detected something on our scanners. Something barely noticeable, just a sort of spike in energy readings, like a window being thrown open and then closed. The whole thing lasted just a few seconds. Then Karina's shuttle appeared clear as a bell.

"After meeting briefly with Voul, she came to my office. I have to say that she is really quite nice. She has requested a full tour of the Moon."

"Has she told you anything about what's happening?"

"Voul went to the Sker area before she arrived. So, we have not discussed this subject. I know that she and Voul and Farson had a conversation and that Voul is en route to SkyKing now. I don't know the details, Jim. Karina seems happy, I can tell you that. It's as if she hasn't got a care in the world. It's nice having her here." Viera was smiling and clearly shrugging off the incredible details of how Karina could have appeared out of nowhere. "When it comes to all of this ScreenMaster stuff, I've sort of decided that 'mine is not to question why.' "

"That's not a bad thought right now, Viera. Keep up the good work. Let's stay in communication." He signed off. Viera saw Brittany's hand waving as the transmission ended.

There was a chime at the Petersons' door. Commander Peterson opened it, and Voul walked in. He was agitated, for a Sker. Still calm, dressed in a flawlessly white uniform, but Jim recognized the pattern from years of working with Voul. It took a lot for emotions to show, but it did happen. Without a word to Brittany – even though she was looking at him, waiting for the usual warmness they shared – Voul started right in on the topic of the day. "Commander," he said in a formal tone, "Farson Uiost appeared in my MoonBase tent a half hour ago while I was meeting with Karina Chamberlain." Peterson already knew of the meeting. "He discussed a sequence of events that involve the greatest secret in Sker history, and then he left. The implications for Skers are enormous. Unfortunately, there are some things coming to light now that have been kept secret for many years. I am sorry about this, Jim, but Sker ways are what they are, and sometimes I am what I am." He paused. Peterson was looking at him.

"What events, Voul? What secrets have been kept?"

Voul knew he had arrived at the moment of truth. So many years of clandestine planning and sacrifice had all come down to this.

75. "My Mother, Your Mother"

My mother, your mother lives across the street
Sixteen, seventeen Blueberry Street.
When they get into a fight, this is what they say:
"Girls are made out of Pepsi.
Boys are made out of cotton.
Girls go to college to get more knowledge.
Boys go to Jupiter to get more stupider."

Farson stood looking at Karina. She had her hands on her hips, and her tongue was out, pointing it right at him. "That's the dumbest thing I've ever heard you say, Kari."

"You're a jerk, Farson." She was very mad. Farson was mad, too. Just when he had started to like her and let her come into The Ship, she starts bringing dolls and girls' stuff in with her. It wasn't enough to travel through the stars, and just to be here in The Ship. Oh, no. She had to bring girls' stuff in.

"Kari, sticks and stones will break my bones, but names will never hurt me." He turned and started to walk out, when something hit him in the head, and other things started to shower upon him and land noisily on the floor around him. Kari had thrown her doll at him, and now was catapulting all of its clothing at him as well. He looked at her. She was reaching for the telescope. Her tear-filled face was twisted with hurt and anger. He was surprised at the intensity of her emotions. "NO! Not that!" He rushed at her. She now had the telescope in her hands and was ready to throw it. He caught her arm in mid-toss with one hand and held onto the telescope with the other. They were standing, muscles tensed, angry very close.

"Jerk! Jerk! Jerk!" He could feel her breath and how mad she was.

"Calm down. I'm sorry. I'm sorry. Don't wreck the telescope!" She was still twisting and trying to get away. He held her arms and prevented her from getting away. At first, he was trying to save the telescope, but now something else was happening. He actually was sorry. She let go of the telescope, looking him right in the eye, and jerked her other arm out of his grasp.

"Jerk!" She spit out the word and ran from the attic, leaving him alone. She turned out the light at the bottom of the stairs, leaving him in the dark as well.

"Why is she so mad, Hattie?"

"Because you took something away from her that was very important." Hattie was mixing up a batch of peanut butter cookies. Kari and Farson always helped her. Farson reflexively looked over at Kari's stool near the counter. It was empty.

"What?" Farson was fidgeting. Hattie knew he was also upset. "What did I take away from her?"

"Her comfort. She relaxed with you. You must have hurt her good." Hattie continued mixing. Farson was still fidgeting.

"I just don't like dolls in The Ship." Hattie's brown eyes were softly looking at him.

"She does, Farson. She's a little girl."

Farson spent a lot of time thinking about that. It took him a few days before he realized that it was he who had broken the trust. Hattie was right.

It took him a few more days to really get mentally prepared, but once he made up his mind, he went looking for her.

He looked everywhere. In the kitchen, in the basement, in the garage, in the yard, in the neighbors' yard, her room, his room ... everywhere. Finally, he gave up and went to The Ship.

There she was, doll and all. The two of them looked at each other and laughed. Karina knew that Farson had missed her. She had known he was looking everywhere. She had spoken to Hattie. Suddenly, they were happy again. Not forgotten, but the incident had taught them something. Farson sat down beside her. She told him of an imaginary man who had come into her life while he was gone and who loved to play with her dolls and do whatever she wanted him to do. He was a wonderful, handsome man who taught her more about space and everything than Farson had ever done. Farson wanted to know more about this guy. "What's his name?" he asked.

"Routier," she replied.

76. Farson and Harry

Farson stood looking at Harry S. Truman. He seemed like a nice enough guy, Farson thought. And yet his decision to drop the first bomb on Hiroshima in Japan on August 6, 1945, and then, impactfully, a second and bigger bomb on Nagasaki on August 9, 1945, had reaped a world-changing whirlwind. It was the Nagasaki plutonium bomb that caused the ultimate damage to The Screen.

The logic of the horror was so predictable. The cause and the effect were equally bad. As Farson watched President Truman move around his office, he sadly knew there were reasons, embedded in human history and psychology, that made those decisions inevitable. *Inevitability does not pardon what happened.* Farson knew his thoughts on this decision were harsh because he now understood its implications. But watching the man before him, he knew – as no other ScreenMaster could ever know – that Harry Truman was not a horrible man, despite the horror he wrought. He was just a man.

Harry Truman died on December 26, 1972, the day after Christmas.

While all the kids were enjoying their presents, the thirty-third president of the United States, who had ultimately caused more damage than any other human being who had ever lived, died quietly after a lingering illness and a stubborn fight for his life. He fought so hard against his own death, it was as though his life meant more to him than all those others who died in a blink of an eye at his command. Farson was watching the funeral proceedings as Truman's casket was lowered slowly into the earth. His thoughts were understanding, and filled with the clarity of events in 1945 and now. *Had only he cared as much for them, and the lives of all those who followed, as he did for his own life, we would not be here now. Everything he thought to save, he destroyed. So human.*

<<Farson, you're getting carried away here. Truman was just the straw that broke the camel's back. He was just another piece of a bloody spiral. He didn't actually cause it. It took a lot of death and a lot of physics to create the Rent. It's an old story. Truman was one of many in a long, long endless line.>>

<<No, Uvo, you're wrong. I've traced it directly to him. He is where it happened. Right here. Everything else, horrible as it all was, is explainable. This was his decision, and he should have known better. More importantly, he could have known better.>>

<<You want to believe that, I'm sure, Farson, but you can't blame him for everything. This is a history of a vicious people doing vicious things that make no sense from our point of view. They killed each other throughout their history and always for 'the greater good,' from their point of view. We must have a larger view.>>

<<Nagasaki was a special case, Uvo. It is unique. It may have been the culmination of some sad stage of human insanity, but it cannot be explained away like other human acts. When that bomb went off, and all of the knowing fear and hopeless terror of the victims that exploded with it, it caused the Rent. It's plain to see. If Truman had said no to that second bomb, we would not be here. The wrong man, at the wrong time, in the wrong place. It was an inflection point in the destiny of humanity. The elevating point where we could have turned upward was passed without the all-important evolutionary impulses that should have, and could have ignited the fuse of our success. What Truman did to the people of Nagasaki was almost an involuntary and unthinking reflex like an early human jumping to lash out at a rustling branch in the jungle. Or a boy stomping on ants because he could. There were plenty of highly evolved and intelligent people advising and watching President

Truman who knew better, but they did nothing, or at least, in the end, they had no effect. I was there, Uvo. I saw it all. So, yes, one thing did lead to another; you are correct. But, thought about in another way, one thing did not lead to the other, and it could have.>>

<<*It would have happened eventually anyway, Farson. We all knew it. Humanity's evolution was corrupted. There was no changing that.*>>

<<*Who can say, Uvo? We are still here, are we not?*>>

Farson stood, again, looking down at the old man who had just died. His last breath still hung in the air. Bess Truman and a doctor were there, but they were quiet in the knowledge of Harry's passing. Farson thought of what he would have to do to repair the Rent. He found Uvo in his thoughts. The winged ScreenMaster was on the barge going through his morning routines. Farson could sense his bewilderment at the way he was lingering, over and over, in the room, unseen, looking at Truman's body. He sent a thought in Uvo's direction. <<*Sorry, Uvo, I'm only human.*>>

<<*No, my friend, you are not. You are much more than that now.*>>

77. Twill Retires

"You see, Mr. Uiost, I was right. Natural things get out of control. 'Nature' just doesn't work as a concept. People are extremely smart, and they've learned that the simple rearrangement of matter can positively alter the reality of things as they know them. It's too easy to build around, build over. Nature supplies all the materials for its own undoing. Things as they are can be very hard to accept. People know this, and they ask, 'Why not?' 'If we can change things, why not do it?' Mr. Uiost, these people haven't even dreamt of something so elemental, something so essentially powerful as The Screen, let alone try to marshal the forces it represents. They have taken the forces of 'unnature' and used them to deeply affect their immediate lives. At the same time, they have affected forces that could devastate their existence. They have affected things out of which the omniverse, as you call it, is made. Ignorance, that is their problem. What are the options? Nature offers only enslavement to them. Unnature is the essence of their glory. Clearly, mankind was bound for 'glory' from the beginning. Right, Mr. Uiost? Why not just let them have what they've earned?"

Farson looked at Twill. He was dressed like a college professor sitting in his gimbaled chair. Farson was a student in this timeline. Twill was a NinthLevel ScreenMaster and the author of the only Ascension Challenge in the history of The Screen. He hated Farson. He wanted to stop him. Humanity was the problem. That much was perfectly clear to Twill.

Ascensions had always been exciting events but never a contest of wills between ScreenMasters. Twill, however, had achieved some notoriety because of his repeated attempts of LevelTen and his unprecedented documentation of his approach to that level. Except for Handy Townsend, and now Farson, of course, Twill was considered one of the top ScreenMasters of all time. His devoted and assiduous attention to LevelTen's approach was a sort of academic highlight in ScreenMaster history. It had evolved into a caretaking system similar to a curatorship. Twill had taken ownership of LevelTen even though he had never successfully achieved it. His knowledge of LevelTen was second only to Handy's. In his opinion, Handy's successful entry and completion of LevelTen was a fluke; his status among ScreenMasters, a sham. Twill's best explanation of this "achievement" was that Handy was "dumb lucky." This made Handy laugh hysterically every time he heard it.

Now, because of Farson's far-reaching Ascension, Twill was having some doubts about his assumptions of the nature of The Screen. He was testing. The academic discussion of unnature was a metaphor. The intrusion of humanity, and the problems it had caused "in the fabric of The Screen," as he had it, was now a wild card in Twill's theories, throwing much of what he had hypothesized into confusion. Other ScreenMasters were questioning him now. In many ways, Farson's Ascension had become Twill's downfall.

<<*Farson, I wouldn't want to be in your shoes. But, then I'm not really sure that I even comprehend what you are doing anymore. When I discovered The ScreenMoiré at 9.96, it indicated a possible GateWay, but after the dust settled, I have to admit that I was a little too pleased with the first discovery to take the second discovery possibility all the way to its logical conclusion. Then you blasted through so many levels on your first Ascension Day that when you got there, the GateWay was obvious. You proved it all, and went on to full exploration. You were so fearless that it really looked like confidence and ability, but it was sheer foolishness and you know it.*>> Farson thought about Twill's "discovery." It was a pattern in The Screen that allowed for the slewing, or a sideways acceleration of a ScreenMaster's Ascension. The truth of Twill's discovery, which he completely missed, was that there was a way to pass from level to level faster than could be done inside of the moiré. What Twill thought was a "gate" was really a vastly accelerated shuttle system that removed all the barriers. What Farson now knew of The Screen's basic features would astound Twill into silence and reverence for the beauty of what it truly was, if he knew the truth.

Farson was the first ScreenMaster to reach this part of The Screen's structure.

<<*Twill, there is so much to the TrueScreen I wouldn't know where to begin. I do know that we have now entered the next phase of discovery, and that it's no longer levels that we should be concerned with ... it's layers.*>> Twill's chair rocked back and forth in the stillness of the moment.

<<*Layers?*>>

<<*Yes, Twill, ScreenLayers. Plus, there is something in the area between the Layers that is rather shocking and amazing.*>> Twill was very attentive. He felt as though an omniscience was bestowing sacred knowledge upon him. As much as he hated Farson, the truth of the information now coming to his consciousness was beyond doubt. Twill's being seemed to pulse and expand with every word, each new thought. After all, Twill was a diligent ScreenMaster. This was ScreenTruth. It was unbelievable, and unavoidably believable, at the same time. Twill was struggling in this moment. In his own way, Twill felt the humbling presence of revelation.

Farson continued unaffected by the change coming over Twill. <<*There is a gatekeeper of some kind. Non-visual, but very strong and aware. I was traveling along our known level-continuum and was stopped abruptly at Level100.*>> Twill was reeling.

<<*How ... ?*>> he started to ask. Farson smiled, knowing his question.

<<*The Moiré creates a sort of centripetal thrust which ultimately lifted me on a shaft of aligned grids going up or down, but always toward the center of something. It took awhile to master the stepping patterns, but once I did, I started to Ascend without impediment, as though in an elevator, if you can imagine that. At One Hundred, I was stopped. I could go no further.*>>

Twill stretched his arms over his head and looked out of his office window. He leaned back in the chair. The sky was blue and crisp. It was an autumn afternoon. A small, white cloud was working its way across the sky. He thought how closely it resembled the pleasing shape of a small child on his birth planet. Farson was watching it too, except to him it looked like half a worm bound for a fishhook. <<*Twill, it's time to end this conflict. You have to say the words.*>> Twill knew it was coming all along, but that didn't make it any easier. He had long since lost any feeling of surrender or concession. He had known for a while that this moment was inevitable: the unthinkable surrender to a human. There was also the incontrovertible fact of how wrong he had been, even if he still held the unshakeable conviction that Farson was wrong as well. Farson held the moment, and he was convincing to the other ScreenMasters. Now Twill's punishment for failure in his unprecedented contest was all that lay ahead. He looked back at the little cloud. It was dissipating. There was a sense of relief as Twill spoke the words.

<<*I concede.*>> *For now.*

A purple hue with a blackening edge surrounded Twill instantly and with great force. In the moment before disappearing, Twill assumed the shape of his birth world race. Farson saw the tender eyes, and the long slender body, the figure-eight coiling, and intelligent face of ScreenMaster Twill, now retired, smiling softly back at Farson. Farson sensed that Twill would miss traveling The Screen.

Goodbye, my friend, he thought as Twill was gone. At the last second, the softness in Twill's eyes darkened into a knowing malevolence. Farson saw it. <<*Will you never learn, Twill?*>>

78. SkyKing's Destiny

"Commander, SkyKing has a destiny of its own, and the Skers are ready to accept it." Voul was standing in Commander Peterson's office in the Alpha Command module. People called it "the office." In this office there was a very large picture window, and people loved to look out of it. Sometimes Peterson would come back to his office, and a person would be in there peering out into space. Brittany loved it. Jim walked over to the window and looked out. Only the quiet black of space looked back.

Jim sat down again in his high-backed, red chair. His wife had thought it was not the right chair for him at all: It was too big, a bad color, awkward looking. There was nothing about it that she liked. He had told her that since it was the chair the government had sent to him, it was the chair he would use. That was the way he was back then, and it was still the way he was. In that willingness to take whatever was sent his way and make the most of it, he was very much like the Skers. They took the life that came to them, and then they made the most of it. So did Jim Peterson.

Speaking to Voul, Jim asked, "Can you be more specific? I'm not following you yet." Voul shifted slightly. This was obviously uncomfortable for him. He took a big breath and began.

"Commander, we have been building a means of escape since the first days of Sker birth on SkyKing. It was a long and arduous, ambitious undertaking. We felt that by sacrificing our needs and energies we could save enough raw materials to succeed. We used every scrap of wasted and unwanted material, and we developed a system of elemental reduction so that we could alter almost any material into the material we needed. We rewrote hundreds of specifications slightly so that Earth sent more of everything than was actually needed. In time we completed what has now come to be called in our history and in our spiritual lives "the solar sails."

Peterson was listening, but he wasn't sure what he was hearing. Voul continued. "We determined that once SkyKing was free of the Earth's gravity, sails of an enormous size and configuration could capture enough of the solar wind to begin, slowly at first, moving away from the sun. Then, as our speed increased, so would maneuverability. Ultimately, we could turn and sail almost directly into the sun, 'pointing,' if you will, and even slingshot around it to increase speed further. In time we will be traveling at least at the speed of light, and some calculations indicate that we could go even faster. In any case, we would be free at last." Voul ended this speech with a look of trepidation on his face, as if he were afraid that forgiveness for this egregious breach of trust was out of reach. Unforgivable. Jim understood. Deception was totally foreign to the enigmatic Skers, but this level of deception would be painful to them at a high degree. "Voul, what in the hell are you talking about?" Unfathomability was stretching credulity so thin that even Commander Peterson knew his question was inadequately couched. The more intensely he listened to Voul, the less he understood.

It wasn't easy. Voul took a deep breath. "Commander, we have built sails with which we had hoped to propel SkyKing out of Earth orbit. We were preparing to commandeer the station. We could have done it. Now without Earth's presence, we face an irreconcilable dilemma."

"Mutiny? You were planning mutiny, Voul? That's hard to believe." The Skers planning to mutiny? Jim didn't think he could believe that. Voul and Jim Peterson looked at each other across a vast space of incomprehensibility and agitation.

"It's all changed now, Jim. Farson Uiost has told me it was all part of a plan and for us to prepare to depart as soon as possible. It is essential that we all stay together. We are the last of humanity now. So, now we are preparing a planned deployment of the sails and to move away with the Moon, and speaking for every Sker on SkyKing, we want you to command. There is no other way."

Brittany came into the office and headed straight for Voul. He hugged her, but distractedly, which was unusual. Jim came around from behind the desk and walked to the door of the office. He opened it for Voul to leave. "You'd better give me some time to think this over." Voul was shaking his head.

"The sail handlers are unfurling now on whorls One through Five. We need to coordinate it. There is no time."

"Give me a few minutes, Voul."

"The work must begin, Commander. It's involved and time-consuming. It must begin immediately." Jim held the door again indicating that Voul should leave. Brittany didn't understand what was going on, entirely. Voul turned and walked through the door and into the corridor where he stopped and turned to Jim Peterson just about to close the door. "I am sorry, Commander. It was a plan that was begun by my father. It was a myth and a ritual, a legend. In many ways, I never thought it would ever come to this. None of us did. It was just part of being a Sker." Voul's head dropped slightly as he turned and walked down the passageway.

Jim Peterson closed the door gently and walked to the porthole. He felt alone. The black expanse of space stared back at him. Brittany was standing beside him.

79. A Lover in June

Viera Nichols sat alone in her cabin. She had completed her exhaustive exercise regimen, and in the afterglow of exertion she was musing her fate. Typically, she exercised in the nude, but this morning she was wearing a suit of a very light, breathable, latex-based material that fit her like a second skin but was a little more modest than being naked, a little. *It must be Voul's influence. I'm covering up.*

She lay back on the mat and felt a complete sense of relaxation wash over her, like the cool of a clean, fresh sheet spreading its soothing gentleness during an afternoon nap. It wasn't long before she dozed off.

When Farson appeared in the room, he found her in that position: on her back, totally relaxed, and sound asleep. Karina appeared beside him. The two of them stood over Viera watching her sleep. Karina whispered, "I'm glad I came with you, Farson. This may have been too much for the old wandering soul of the ScreenMaster of Earth." Farson realized that Karina was looking at Viera's arresting figure and beauty.

"Not when you're around, Kari."

"Exactly, Farson. Exactly. That's why I said I'm glad I'm here."

Farson and Karina were having a good laugh over this little exchange. They both knew how far from possible was the liaison between either one of them and anyone else. It was emotionally impossible, but there was much more to it than that. Farson looked down at his sister's hand in his. *There's my love for her.*

Karina's thought invaded his. <<*Plus, I'd know whatever you did. And you know it.*>>

<<*You also know what I think. So you know what I know.*>>

"Farson, don't give me that. If I knew what you know, I'd be ScreenMaster of Earth." Her whispered response made them both laugh again. Apparently, it was a new joke between them.

Viera was stirring. She had heard them whispering and laughing. Her eyes languished in sleep, then they opened lazily, and closed sleepily again. Then her eyes snapped open. She jumped nimbly to her feet. Having seen Farson's picture, she knew exactly who he was, but she was surprised to see him in her private room nonetheless. "You?" she asked. Then she saw Karina. Farson and Karina were both looking right at her. Viera noticed the purple hue surrounding them each. It was really two separate traces of color: one around Farson, and one around Karina. At their hands the colors blended and were a deeper hue. Viera noticed this, but had no idea of its tremendous significance. Her question hung in the air. It was Farson who answered.

"Well, Viera," he began as if speaking to an old friend, "we've finally come to the consideration of the Moon. You know, of course, that something has happened to Earth, and, therefore, her Moon is also in some sort of situation. Right?"

Viera nodded.

"Therefore what to do with the Moon? That's the question." Viera had a vague sense of dread at this statement. For nine years the fate of the Moon had been hers to manage and command. Farson's casual tone, and the deep import of his intent, registered in her mind. *This guy is in charge and I'm not.* Her thought was troubled. Farson went on, breaking more new ground. "We have placed the Earth in stasis, which means time has changed down there, but it's a little more than just a change." He understated the situation and then partially elaborated. "Earth to you is gone. To return *that* Earth to life would mean a return of the timeline that Earth created and that involved the potentially irreparable damage to The Screen. So we're creating a ScreenPatch, which is just that, a patch, not a repair. The damage is done and cannot be undone, but just like a patched tube on a bicycle tire will never be as good as it was before it was punctured, The Screen is damaged but, with this adjustment, it's almost good as new. I'm here to watch over it. Now, for all intents and purposes,

Earth, and its people, do not exist, except for SkyKing and MoonBase, of course."

Viera was fidgeting. She was feeling uneasy. She knew most of this, but to hear him say it so offhand-like was a little chilling. Farson started to continue, but Viera interrupted him. "Are they dead?" Surprisingly, it was Karina who answered.

"Viera, Emerald Earth, as Earth is now called, will be all right in time. It will take thousands and thousands of their years. That's what stasis is. So, no; they are not dead. But they are gone for now, and changing in important ways. We're ready to begin something new with SkyKing and MoonBase, but there can be, and there will be, no physical contact between Emerald Earth and your people. You and your miners, the Moon, and the Skers and the crew of SkyKing, must leave this area. Right now." Farson took up the narrative again.

"SkyKing is going to try to sail under its own power, which will make things easier. In a few days you will see something of which few have ever dreamed of. Enormous solar sails will unfurl. The original Sker plan was to slowly begin to move away from the Sun and the Moon and begin their scriptural 'Walk Among The Stars.' Things have changed. They still want that independence and freedom, but they know it is impossible for either of you to survive alone. You must go together." Viera had listened with a growing numbness. "You must get the Moon underway. First, because the station is already leaving, and, second, because without the Moon all could be lost."

"Does Voul know all of this?" She was thinking about the nature of her crew and the nature of SkyKing and the Skers: Like oil and water, they just don't mix. She suddenly felt Farson's mind in hers. <<*Viera, you and Voul are doing fine.*>> There was an irony in his thoughts. Viera realized he was not only communicating telepathically with her, he had also read her thoughts. Farson knew her first thought was for Voul, not the Moon. She shuddered with the thought of Farson's knowledge.

"He does now," Farson said. "I just told him. When you two first met in your compartment, he was under orders to assist you in helping the station achieve orbit. Your support will be needed even more now but for different reasons. Right now, he is very busy readying the sails and working with greatly accelerated schedules, but he knows what you know.

"The issues of stasis and Emerald Earth, and the realities of that situation are slowly becoming known on both MoonBase and SkyKing. There is no reason to hide it. You are the first on MoonBase to learn of the solar sails and what the Skers have been up to."

"As of now," Karina added. She could imagine what her crew would think when they knew.

"Correct," agreed Farson. "Viera," he looked at Karina as he said this, "I've got to go, but SkyKing and the Moon need each other now more than ever. Your two organizations are the only remaining groups of the human race still free to decide their own fate. The others have had their fates decided for them. So, do what you think is right. You should ally with SkyKing and enthusiastically work for success in getting away from here as soon as possible. There are really very few options right now, but that will change in the future. Voul will fill you in on all the details very soon."

"Will we survive, Farson? It all seems so implausible and farfetched and it's all happening so fast." Her concerns were fired at him like lasers. Farson smiled.

"'Farfetched' is not a bad way to put it, Viera. Yes, it is highly likely that you will survive if you cooperate with each other. You and Voul are off to a very good start." Farson smiled at her, and his purple glow began to intensify, but

Karina's remained steady. "I will return when you've made more progress." Then another thought appeared in Viera's mind. <<*Go forth and multiply.*>> In a purple light he was gone. Viera could feel his confidence, and it made her happier. Karina had remained.

"Viera, let's take a walk," Karina said. She started to walk toward the compartment door. It opened as she approached. She waited for Viera, who had not moved. "Show me around the Moon," she said. "I want a tour." Like the door, Viera seemed to move without volition of her own. She walked out followed by Karina Chamberlain.

After walking together through the base's main operations for about an hour, Viera had come to feel more comfortable with Karina. They had been talking together and speaking with crew members on the operation decks and then on into the living compartments.

Karina was surprised at the clutter and had blushed at the decorations: Pictures of nudes, coupling nudes, and all sorts of erotica were pretty much everywhere. She was confronted with naked men and women walking around casually in the housing quarters, some openly affectionate; in fact, there was a mixed group sitting in a circle watching as two women made love in front of them. All of this was very common on MoonBase, nothing out of the ordinary, but Viera was watching Karina for some sign of disapproval.

"Is it always like this?" Karina asked.

Viera was lost in her own familiar thoughts about the open and free-ranging nature of MoonBase and its people, when the question was so softly articulated. She knew some things about Karina from her biography: She was brought up in the conservative Midwest of the United States with close ties to old-fashioned New England. She had had only one relationship with a man in her life. Viera knew that the openness of MoonBase would be surprising. "Yes, it is. On off-shifts people do whatever they want. Sex is a lot of what people want, as you may know." Their eyes briefly touched. Viera felt the intensity. "Our culture is based on a casual, routine openness in front of each other. We really hide nothing and bow to no generalized code of personal moral conduct other than our motto, 'Hurt no one.' Plus, we only have one penalty here on the Moon: banishment. So, if someone is doing something that hurts no one, they may do it. But once that 'Hurt no one' law is broken, punishment is swift and certain. Remember, this group is no bunch of … angels." She almost said, "Skers," but had caught herself at the last second.

"Where would you banish them to now?" Viera smiled.

"It hasn't come up in a long, long time."

Karina did know something about MoonBasers. They were generally troublemakers from Earth who were given two choices: prison or the Moon. She also knew that the Moon was considered to be excellent duty, and although difficult, it paid very well. The food was great because of the SkyKing connection, and it was generally felt that the MoonBase people were among the most fun-loving and hardworking anywhere. Karina looked back over her shoulder toward the circle of MoonBasers, her eyes reluctant to either move on or believe what they were seeing.

"Want to go back, Karina? They won't mind at all." Karina blushed.

"No," she quickly said to the never nonplussed Viera. Karina could still feel the burning of her blush, and she wondered why she was so embarrassed, and so curious.

They walked out of the personnel quarters and on into the mines themselves, or rather into the shafts that led to the mines. There was a map of the Moon at the first junction; it was covered with streaks and lines. The entire globe, both hemispheres, was covered with indications of activity and daily laser markings.

"Have you explored and excavated the entire subsurface of the Moon?" Karina asked Viera.

"Not really, although it looks like it on this map, doesn't it? But we have fully explored the surface with vehicular travel and now have some extensive and remote settlements, but there's much more to the Moon than the surface. In that regard we haven't even scratched the rich areas below. This hunk of rock is one of the richest concentrations of heavy and precious metals you can imagine. It's tough to dig it out, but it's worth the effort. It'll take forever to mine it dry. There is so much per square inch, and we waste nothing." There was much pride in her voice.

"You really love the Moon, don't you, Viera?"

"Like a lover in June," she answered quickly but Karina felt the depth of feeling behind the flippancy. Viera walked ahead a little. Karina watched her solid, confident stride and heard her say it again, almost to herself. "Like a lover in June. I was born for this."

They inspected the airlocks and tool garages and watched a group of on-duty miners playing cards while the robots worked. They walked together right through a shower corral, with about thirty miners between shifts showering together with great enthusiasm (which was heightened heartily by the sight of their commander and her beautiful companion). Then they finally came to what Viera had wanted to show Karina from the moment the tour had begun.

In one of the major junctions of the tunnels of the Moon, there was what appeared to be a quiet oasis with picnic tables and sunlamps. There were luxurious plants growing under the lights, and to Karina's surprise the place had the feeling of being outside, deep in the caverns of the Moon. "We call this the 'Rest Area,'" Viera said.

Karina looked around the extensive space. She estimated that it was over an acre. She saw the unmistakable main feature of the area: a broad and clear-as-air picture window at least twenty-five feet wide and just as high. It took a few seconds for Karina to realize that it was a large monitor. The surface of the Moon filled the window. There were people in the area, but there was plenty of room. Viera asked Karina if she'd like to sit down and have a cup of coffee.

"Sure," answered Karina, and they found a table off to the side and sat down together. It wasn't long before a waiter appeared to take their order. Not long after that they were having coffee and a small plate of Sker cakes, as Viera called them. They were little sweet cakes that melted in your mouth but were actually very good for you and had virtually no effect on one's figure other than a very nutritious one, no matter how many one ate.

"These are delicious," said Karina, loving every bite.

"The Skers won't tell us what they're made of, but they are very popular."

Karina smiled through what looked like powdered sugar-covered lips, "I know why they're so popular," she said lifting another one to her mouth.

Viera looked out on the moonscape and took a sip of the coffee. The vapor rising from the cup curled into her nostrils causing them to flare slightly with the pleasure of the aroma. It was a nice moment for the two women, each with her own thoughts allowing the moment to stretch out, enjoying the unexpected relaxation they had found together.

"Before the Earth disappeared, the monitor was perfectly positioned for a full view of the planet. We all loved it here. Every crew member enjoys this area of the Moon, and each year we have improved and enlarged it." The other people were clearly reflecting the universal appreciation of the rest area. They were doing what people throughout history have done in parks: walking, talking, holding hands, exercising, and just sitting quietly, contemplating their lives. Viera was especially content. "I can't bear losing this, Karina. It's just too perfect for me. I wasn't born here, but I came to life here. I was born biologically in Denver, but many years later I was reborn here in the Moon's dust and Earthrises, in the one-sixth gravity, and the incredible freedom of this wonderful, wonderful place. Earth never held any promise for me with all of its stereotypical thinking and moralistic dogma. Every time I turned around, I was being condemned, criticized, and complained about, or being told to do it to someone else. No one appreciated what I was really good at, but they found myriad ways to judge me on the things I was not good at. In the military I found a code of ethics that was at least dependable and predictable as long as I stayed within its strictures. In the military, we wear our status on our sleeves, and our rules are there for all to see. I was comfortable in Earth service, but not really happy.

"Here, I am happy." She continued to look at the picture window monitor as a robot rover drove by dragging ten little courier bins behind it. "I don't want to lose this. There is no other place for someone like me, Karina." She took a sip of coffee and looked directly into Karina's eyes. "There isn't enough 'room' on SkyKing for all of us. And the Skers will never come here and leave their precious station. We will never willingly go there. Voul's plan to sail away together is the only one that makes sense."

Karina looked back into Viera's dark brown eyes. The swirls of brown and other rich colors there seemed like a whirlpool. She felt the gentle thoughts pulling her there. She found that her affection for this woman was growing. *She is a wonderful woman, so warm, so loving, so intelligent, beautiful, happy, and very courageous.*

Viera's mind was thinking about new solutions, ways to improve, upgrade, and make MoonBase better and better in every way. "You know, Karina, I think we can connect SkyKing with a wide tether using gurney technology. It won't be easy, but it's possible. That would help a lot, wouldn't it?"

Karina saw Viera's vision of a Moon tunnel connecting SkyKing and MoonBase with a high-speed transit system shuttling back and forth.

"Well, Viera, first we have to see if the two of you can survive what is coming next." Karina's halo of purple intensified and she began to dissipate. Viera saw it and felt a sadness, knowing that Karina was leaving and wishing she would stay. Karina felt it.

"What *is* coming next, Karina?" There was an urgency in her voice. She was worried. Karina knew there was also an uncertainty in Viera's confidence. She knew that Viera's world had been a shelter for her, but that now, sadly, her own loneliness would be returning. She sent two final thoughts to Viera – one also for herself – as she departed: The first, to answer her question, and the second, as reassurance for them both. << *You'll know soon enough, Viera.*>> And then, <<*I'll be back.*>>

Then she was gone. Viera sat still for a moment, thinking things over. Then she stood up and headed for the nearby gurney entrance at a brisk walk. Her rest period was over.

80. Farson Throws a Rock

Farson was sitting by the stream where he and Sam had fished so many times. It was now about a week since Sam had died, and Farson was still fighting the feelings of loss and guilt. Wondering if there wasn't something he could have done. Wondering if he had said all he had wanted to say.

Wondering if the last time he had hugged the big man, had he hugged him with all of his might? Had he held anything back? Did he tell Sam how much he really loved him? Did he tell him how much he absolutely loved to go fishing with him? Wondering how he would ever get along without Sam. There were tears forming in his eyes, tears of love and sorrow, love and joy, and then tears of love, pure and simple.

Farson was still sitting there by the side of the stream wondering about Sam and how he could ever get by each day without seeing him, without talking to him, without holding up his stringer of fish, comparing them to his, and saying things like, "Seems a bit paltry there, Sam-o!" How could he get by without hearing that big-chested laugh and the usual comment, "Next to yours they look like zeppelins plucked from the sky" or "Next to yours they look like the *Queen Mary*, the *Bismarck*, and the *Titanic*," or some such hyperbole. Farson could not see a way without Sam.

He took a small but very round river rock and rolled it around in the palm of his hand.

He was thinking of Sam sitting by the potbellied stove reading from one of his many books of poetry. Farson could feel the warmth of the coal filling the room. He could remember the feeling of belonging. He liked that feeling.

After a while Farson stood up and threw the little round rock with all his might into the air out over the stream. The rock flew straight and true and seemed to float in the air and then arc downward to the water. A small splash, no skips and then it was gone.

There was a small outcropping of the opposite shore that had high cattails. The rock fell well short of that. *I never could reach that. It's just too far*. Sam used to make fun of him as he threw rocks well across the river, deep into the cattails. "Takes a real man to throw 'em like that, Farsy." Then he would heave off another one. "Yep, a real man, not some scrawny kid what can't even fish right."

81. Did You Notice, Uvo?

<<Did you notice, Uvo? He elevated Karina as well. Now that's power. Who would have ever thought that was possible?>>

<<I'm not sure 'elevated' is the correct word, Twill.>>

82. We Need Boys

Handy was touched, if badly drunk. Babies always did that to him. They were so little, so wide-eyed; babies held a special fascination for Handy. This little one was a boy baby. *Good, we need boys.*

"So what're ya gonna call this one, Farson?" Handy said over his shoulder in Farson's direction absentmindedly. He was more interested in refilling his glass from the bottle by the fridge. Farson was cradling the boy in his arms.

"How about 'Ian'?" Farson looked to Handy for a reaction. "Do you like that?"

"Better than Adam." Handy now had the drink in hand and was returning to the sofa with the bottle as well, thereby avoiding unnecessary interruptions in the future.

"You never liked that idea."

"It was too cute, really, Farson. Who do you think you are, anyway?"

"So what about 'Ian'?" Farson was a little impatient with Handy's posturing.

"It's short. That's good. What does it mean? All your names have a meaning." Handy had already consumed the new drink and was pouring again from the bottle into his glass. He was a little irritated that things concerning the contents of his glass were taking up so much of his time.

Farson carried the baby to just in front of Handy. He knelt down to give his old friend a better view. "God is gracious." He said. "Ian means 'God is gracious.'" Farson seemed pleased with this.

"God, Farson? Aren't you reaching?"

"Come on, Handy. It seemed like a good name. Kari liked it, too."

"Shit, Farson, she'd like any name you came up with. She's in love with you. I wouldn't bring her in as part of a vast majority backing you up."

Farson smiled at that. Handy burst into a ribald belly laugh. Farson just shook his head as Handy's loud obnoxious laughter filled the room.

"Well, anyway, 'Ian' it is."

83. Farmer Jordan Moves Across the Wheat

When Ian's father heard of the choice, he was elated. What a beautiful name for his new son: Ian. *Oh, yes. Life is good.*

Word had reached him on the vast expanse of the central plain. He was in the second day of his third row. The satellite transmission had been clear as a bell. As always, his work could be seen from orbit on a clear day. His tour involved four hundred robotractors and combines, with accompanying auto-units. His entire convoy would remain on its assignment indefinitely, harvesting and replanting two full segments, thousands of square miles.

"Strapper" Jordan took great comfort in his family as he walked from the control room of the field rover where he lived. The entire harvester unit moved in carefully planned synchronization across the fertile prairies. It's footprint covered almost five acres, not including the ancillary attachments. Some moved the crop onto conveyors that then packaged it, ready to send it to the transport locations. Some planted and fertilized after the main vehicles had harvested. It was all robotic, all mechanized, all flawless in performance. The equipment was totally solar and wind powered, not a single element of pollution. Strapper's harvester was typical. It had eleven rooms and was completely furnished and self-contained. There was a SkyCar slip at the far end for visits from other farmers, but it was very easy for Strapper to spend the entire tour quite happy on the enormous craft. Like freighter captains of old, Emerald Earth farmers lived on seas of amber waves, leaving their other world behind for a world of work, family, and dedication.

Not only was the farming of Emerald Earth synchronized and beautifully engineered, it was an immense privilege to be a Green Emer, as they were called, but even more to be an active hand.

The Good Earth. He watched the endless amber pass the windows of his control room and relaxed inside the harvester. The sounds of the blades and vacuums were hushed through the insulated construction and highly advanced technology of the vehicle. The soft, quiet droning soothed him. As a sailor of old might have, he loved the sound of his craft moving through its element. He knew it was under control and going properly on its way. *Steady as she goes.*

From high above it could have appeared as if a small finger were drawing a line across the vastness of the fields: Strapper's unit moving across the enormous expanse of the wheat in the central plains of an area once known as North America, now part of the vast and continuous lands of Emerald Earth.

He was thinking of his newborn son, Ian, now named properly by ScreenMaster Uiost. He was proud it was a boy. Another man has joined the Jordan clan, another hand in the longest line of farmers on Emerald Earth. *This is our planet, and now another takes his place in the line. It is all exactly as Farson promised it would be.*

84. The Cat's Out of the Bag

Karina was back. She looked at her companion. "Tell me about the mines, Viera." Karina was asking a serious question and Viera knew it, but it seemed humorous to her. Explaining the mines wasn't a casual conversation over coffee. To really explain the mines would take hours, detailed computer simulations, and the expertise of at least fifteen senior people. The intricate nature of the structures of the mines, the tunneling technology, and the gurney tech were complex and mathematical. The science of the Moon was daunting, even to the experts who devised it. The search for ore lodes and the extraction and recycling techniques was a discipline of its own. The pattern of trade they had established with SkyKing and Earth, and how all of that would change now, was another complex topic. The scheduling of the mines would take more hours of explanation. The discovery of how rich and essentially inexhaustible were the Moon's natural resources, dense with its multitude of riches far beyond any research or expectations recorded when they were planning the process, was a history in itself. Then there was the water. Only when MoonBase was firmly established were the deeper treasures unlocked. Only then did the truth of the Moon become known. Explaining the Moon was an enterprise of intellectual effort and depiction that would challenge the best. MoonBasers had learned it all by doing.

Viera knew that, like her brother, Karina was very serious in these matters, and it would not serve anything to underestimate her curiosity for details. She was clearly a ScreenMaster herself now, although her transformation was never announced. *It just happened.* Farson made it happen, Viera knew. So, she mentally hitched herself up and, still struggling with a mild and ill-defined sense of nervousness at being alone with Karina Chamberlain again, she began to tell the story of the Moon.

"Well, in truth, Karina, they are far more than just mines really. They are really underground highways that honeycomb the Moon just beneath the surface, and some much deeper now. We are mining the Moon, but we are not hollowing her out. At least not yet. On the surface, the Moon appears to be populated somewhat, but when you go just beneath the surface, things really show themselves for what they are. MoonBase is not a surface installation, although we are quite proud of New Chicago.

"We've been here for almost a hundred years, working in the low gravity with very efficient systems and robot machines that do not require any rest. Most people think of the MoonBasers as dirty miners, but that is very far from the truth. Better to think of us as participants, owners really, of vast plantations that produce great wealth. Our real workers are robotics, and for every miner there are at least two hundred separate mechanical entities that serve him, or her, in multifaceted capacities that would leave most Earthers' heads spinning, both for the scope of activity we achieve and for the capabilities this place has developed." Viera was up and walking toward the map near one of the tables. "This map is really very misleading."

The discussion went on through the day and into the night. Finally, Karina asked what seemed like a final question. "Have you developed fighting abilities or mobility?"

Viera's eyes were wide open, and her eyebrows flared unevenly, one higher than the other. "Yes, we have, but not perhaps in the way most people would think." She hesitated.

Karina was looking directly at Viera; they were unblinkingly eye-to-eye as she stated, "So, it is exactly as Farson said it would be. 'They shall move off together in search of the future, and then Emerald Earth herself will be free.'"

"Farson said that?" Karina smiled.

"Yes he did, Viera. Much more than that, as well." Viera was obviously surprised at the turn their conversation had taken. Karina seldom spoke of Farson. As the purple spreading over Karina's body began to concentrate, she was smiling. "Be not afraid. We come to save, not to injure or judge." As she dissipated, Viera saw Karina's smile increase radiantly, and she also saw that she was like a little girl leaving on a trip waving to her best friend. <<*Got to go, now, Viera. I enjoyed our visit, and I will see you soon.*>> Then she was gone.

Viera thought about the last many hours with Karina, and she knew it was as enjoyable for her as it apparently had been for Karina. It had been as if they were becoming close friends. Viera was concerned that vital secrets were now openly known, but she was not all that concerned. It was almost as if it were all inevitable and meant to be; no reason to worry. Secrets were starting to matter less, and trusting was starting to matter more. Viera smiled to herself. She knew that what had just happened was good, and that it was no accident. So many things were changing, and it all felt like change for the better.

Viera turned and walked over to the map and pressed a combination of sensor pads that marked places around the Moon. Then she touched the resulting frame with both hands, and it moved out of the way, revealing a hallway behind the wall. Viera walked into it, and the panel closed behind her. Within minutes, she was in her command center. It was filled with instruments and robots moving around like employees in a well-oiled company. She walked to the center console and pushed a few buttons. A familiar face appeared. "The cat's out of the bag, Voul."

"In more ways than one," he said.

85. Level100

Farson stood looking at it. It now seemed larger than he thought it was when he first saw it. It was enormous actually. *It's viscous looking, almost gluey.* Farson's only thought was to flee. He knew it was too much for him; extraneous thoughts were filling him with irrelevant fear. He wondered why. *My thoughts are not usually like this. What is going on?*

The vision before him, if that's what it really was, had already stopped him twice, causing minor crowding in this portion of The Screen. Farson was trying to communicate with it. He knew that its movements must be overcome and, unfortunately, he was getting nowhere, as if it didn't even notice him.

Farson now tried to retreat. He ran back down through the layers and levels, but it was still there. The blockings were becoming more and more effective. He was relentlessly being backed into a corner where there would be nowhere to go and no retreat. Too late, Farson realized he had already passed the point of no return. Then something attacked in a blur.

"Ouch!" Farson said more out of surprise than pain, knowing that nothing should be able to hurt him at this point. Farson had a brief thought of his own death and a vision of fangs and claws coming at him with no impediment, tearing him apart, when suddenly, in fighting the feeling off, he struck something hard. There was a pinging metallic sound to the collision. Farson was recoiling from the impact. The blurry, gluey thing was just as surprised as Farson at the impact and seemed to hesitate. Farson saw an opportunity and maneuvered past the frozen barrier.

Farson reached out. <<*What are they?*>> Farson was still breathing hard and shaken from the chase and from the struggle with the thing. It was Uvo who answered.

<<*We call it Phanta. It is part of everything. They apparently want to keep a balance somewhere. What you saw here was a very old one. Twill said it was inevitable. He was right directionally, of course. And he was wrong, as usual, about the details. We are not sure what this encounter means. They are like ghosts to us; many felt they were unreal, imagined. Your passage and ascendancy is new territory for us. You should go on, Farson.*>>

Farson leaned back in his chair and looked at the fire. His hand smoothed his corduroys. Ten light centuries away he watched the ScreenKeeper, ZZ<<Arkol move closer to protect him. Farson, in North Conway, rubbed his hand across the front of his chest. He could still feel the contact. *In two places at once*, he thought, *and that thing affected me in both.* <<*Am I going too far?*>> ZZ<<Arkol was listening as Uvo answered.

<<*We can watch, but only you can know.*>>

Farson continued looking at the fire, suddenly uncertain. *That encounter was unexpected.* Then another's thought forced its way into his mind. <<*The way is narrow and few there are who find it.*>> Farson had a question.

<<*What was that? It tried to stop me. It didn't hurt me. What role can it have? What should I do now?*>> There was no answer. Just a small clinking sound as the embers in the fire shifted in the flames. Farson suddenly knew. These blurry entities were important only when threatened. *Their power may be part of the solution.* He felt an echo of assent.

<<ZZ, how high should I go?>>

The robot strobed, and Farson felt his gentle, mechanical thoughts repeating in his mind, clear as a bell. *<<Only you can know.>>* Suddenly, Farson was ascending again. The robot turned his head to watch briefly, almost out of reflex, but Farson was already out of sight, moving upward through The Screen. Ascending took his full effort, full focus. ZZ<<Arkol25609 resumed his station on The Screen, and, together with all the others, did his best to monitor Farson's travels.

When Karina got to the cabin, Farson was gone. The fire was still burning; the rocker was barely moving. She sat smoothly into the chair and, in a few moments, began to rock gently while she waited.

86. Voul and Viera, Together Again

"Change is going to do us good, you know," he said. Viera looked at Voul in disbelief.

"You've got to be kidding, Voul. Change is the last thing we need. You're certainly not ready, and we're really not ready. Change could destroy everything. We're going to have to work hard at it if this whole thing is to have any chance at all." Voul was watching her splendid face contort with earnestness and sincerity. He loved her so much.

"Viera, Farson said it, and it's going to happen." Viera studied him: Voul Jonsn, Captain of SkyKing and the hereditary leader of the Skers. The man who had the highest religious morals of any she had ever known. *Who am I kidding? He's the only one I've ever known that had high moral standards of any kind.* He was a law unto himself. He was pure, free, and loving. Not at all like her. *I am like an animal compared to him. He is perfect in every way. I am not perfect in any way.*

She continued her thoughts, reviewing coming events. *MoonBase will begin to move away. SkyKing insists on coming along. How could this have happened? The miners and their robots have developed an inertial system of energy impulses using the Moon's nukes as thrusters and as directional propellant. The Skers have their solar sails. So many pieces to this puzzle.* She was troubled with the changes rushing toward her world. She moved closer to Voul.

"Well, we're going to have to synchronize the movements because I'm not going anywhere without you, Voul. If we are going to do this, it has to be done right. Together."

"I agree, Viera. I'm not going without you either." He was looking into her eyes in the way only he could. He was deep in there. He was thinking something to her. No, he was thinking about her and she could hear it. He was thinking about them. She could feel him. She could smell him. They were close. She wanted him in her arms, and he knew it. "Viera," Voul whispered softly. Viera felt a warm sensation spreading through her, and something frozen for a long time began to melt. A little more trust began to inch its way out, like a sprout seeking the spring sun after a long cold winter; she was feeling love. She liked the feeling.

"Yes, Voul?" She was suddenly on fire for this man. Not like the others she had known, her feelings now were beyond mere passion.

"We have a few minutes," he said. She was in his arms. His own thoughts were hard for him to fully comprehend, but dread and shame were part of it, as though he was about to do something he knew was wrong, but it didn't matter. The Sker philosophies were very inclusive and the Skers were an understanding people, but what was going on between Voul and Viera would be a shock to them, to say the least. It would be a shock to the system.

I can control this. Viera's warmth engulfed him, and he experienced the feeling of her hair next to his face and her body pressing in. *I can control this.* Viera heard it.

"Why bother, Voul? Some things should not be controlled. Sometimes you have to just let go."

Just about an hour later, Voul was walking along the corridor that led to the Petersons' compartment. He was still thinking of her, and the thoughts were pleasant. His training and history aside, Voul was happy and unquestioning of that happiness. He was just walking along, like any other young man in love. He was thinking about her and enjoying every second of it. His thoughts of controlling the situation with Viera were now being filled in with thoughts of love and the realization that now he only really wanted uncontrolled love. He was thinking of their most recent interlude and the sheer enjoyment of it. As he arrived at the door, he was wondering if her interest in him was monogamous, and he concluded that it must be.

He rang for entry. As he was waiting for a response, he thought to himself about seeing Viera with the young ensign. *I'll have to ask her about that.* The door slid open. There was Commander Peterson and behind him, his daughter, the wonderful Brittany, full of curiosity and obvious intelligence, sitting in the kitchen, having her dinner.

"Hi, Voul," said Peterson.

"Hi, Uncle Voul!" said Brittany.

Voul stood there for a minute, wondering if he was interrupting anything.

"Come in," said the commander, "have a seat. We're just finishing up. Can we get you anything?" Voul moved into the room, but from his hesitation Commander Peterson knew he hadn't come for dinner. Now Brittany was up and coming over, as she always did, for a hug. Clearly, she had missed him. *There has always been something special between those two,* Commander Peterson thought. He liked it, and always had. After greeting Brittany, Voul walked toward the table with her in hand and tentatively sat down.

"No thank you, sir. I have come on official business. Commander, I am requesting permission to begin the unfurling of the solar sails and at the same time to coordinate the Moon course plotting, with the goal of an immediate departure, or at least as soon as possible. This is also Farson's wish, as I believe you know."

Brittany was watching Voul, listening to his words. She was just happy he was there. Peterson recognized her look of contentedness. *What would she say if she knew what irrevocable steps we are taking and what it all really means?* Shrugging off such thoughts of dread, thoughts of impending disaster, he pressed on. "Permission granted. Keep me informed." He was nodding his head, but there were a few more things that needed to be discussed.

"As SkyKing begins to transit, we will share command, Voul, and I expect you to keep your end of the bargain."

"I will, Commander."

"Have the MoonBasers bought in?"

"Absolutely, Commander. They have a full realization that the Moon and SkyKing are for now irrevocably linked in Farson's plans."

"Is your crew assembled and ready?" Peterson was referring to the three hundred Skers who would be the sailing crew for SkyKing: the trimmers, the helmsmen, the deck hands, the fore deck, and the navigators/tacticians. It was an impressive array of talent, trained and assembled without ever actually seeing the sails rigged or having never sailed anything.

After Voul nodded assent, Peterson add another question. "Can they do it?"

"Without a doubt, Commander. When the sails are unfurled, SkyKing will begin to move in the solar wind in the direction we have determined. It will be as planned. There will be no trouble matching speed and course with the Moon, using our orbital thrusters and the sails. It will take time. They will take off much faster at first, but then we will catch up. They will be well out of shuttle range for a time. The scale of moving the Moon is colossal, but in its own way, it's amazing how subtly they can control their speed and direction. The MoonBasers are surprisingly technical and adroit in their capabilities. Ultimately, we will both be traveling together at great speeds."

"Stopping will be a problem, correct?"

"Affirmative. But planning ahead is a Sker trait." Voul smiled at his own comment; it was very unusual for Voul to make a joke, but that's exactly what he had just done. Peterson took a subtle double take. It was a reference to the secrecy of the sails and the Skers' duplicity. Peterson, knowing all that he now knew, realized Voul's comment actually was a little humorous.

"What's gotten into you, Voul? Jokes are not, shall we say, your strong suit."

"Was it funny, Commander?"

"Sort of, Voul. It wasn't a knee-slapper. Let's hope that when it does come to stopping, that your Sker skills at 'planning' are better than your attempts at comedy. We'll have to deal with decelerating when the time comes. It'll be awhile, right, Voul?"

"The navigators tell me it'll be a problem for Brittany sometime in her early twenties."

Peterson thought about that for a while. It was peaceful here in the commander's cabin. Black space outside the portal, a quiet drifting sensation: This was his way of life now. He was thinking about Earth gone, and how only those people left here on SkyKing and on the Moon were actually going on, according to Farson. Peterson's mind recoiled at the thought. All those people on Earth in stasis. *The living dead.* Voul knew what he was thinking.

"Commander, my father once said, 'Give no thought for yesterday; today is sufficient unto itself.' This is a time such as he was discussing. We are fortunate to have the opportunities we have. We are the arrow shot into the air. We know not where. But we must proceed. You know that. We must succeed.

"Our old lives are over, and our new lives are just beginning. We have much to be grateful for. I thought the biggest obstacle would be the MoonBasers and their ways, but I no longer think that. I am deeply troubled by them, and by the feelings they stir in me. It is very unsettling, but I am learning to trust, and to change. So must we all.

"As my Council learns the full implications of these changes, I am going to need your help, Jim. For now, things are as they must be."

Brittany was back at the table, eating her salad, grown in the greenhouses of the station and in the soil of the Moon. She was enjoying the meal. Voul was watching her, and his eyes were fighting back tears. Jim Peterson had never seen that before. Voul sensed his scrutiny, and before Peterson could ask, Voul volunteered, "I apologize, Jim. It's a lot to assimilate. Viera. The sails. Earth. I was watching you two and feeling very much at home here. I hope it will always be so. Now I have to go. There are so many things to do," he said. But before he could leave, Brittany came over to him and held open her arms for a goodbye hug. Voul complied.

Commander Peterson was watching. Then Voul went to the door.

Peterson said, "Give my regards to Viera."

After he had gone, they went back to dinner. Brittany commented. "I think Voul was about to cry, Dad."

"I know, honey. It's just that a lot is happening." She reached for the dressing, adding a little extra to her next bite, a bright red tomato. Jim could see new concern in her eyes as she ate quietly. *Everything is changing.*

87. Farson Suddenly Knew

It was 9:00 a.m., August 8, 1945. In the secrecy and safety of the Oval Office, Truman had just said the fateful words to his aide. "Proceed as planned."

At 11:02 a.m. the next morning, the bomb bay doors of the adapted B-29 bomber, *Bock's Car,* opened at 1,650 feet above the city of Nagasaki and the bombardier, Kermit Beahan, skillfully acquired his target through an opening in the blanketing clouds and pressed the release. "Bomb away," he said. It was also Kermit's birthday. He was twenty-seven years old.

Farson was falling with the bomb through the late morning air over Nagasaki. He felt the rip, and he saw the ScreenTear begin. He was surprised that it occurred before detonation, but it was right there. His long search had brought him to this exact moment. *It's a combination of the destructive intent and the victims' innocent unknowing. Too much all at once.* The ScreenFabric was brittle in this area from so many impactful things occurring in its history. He could see them all. *What a coincidence*, he thought, *that there should be two fateful decisions made here, in so short a time, killing so many with so little regard. All in an area of tenuous weakness to begin with. It's remarkable, really.*

<<*It's not remarkable at all, Farson. Especially, if you know the history.*>> The voice was too clear for there to be any doubt.

<<*You?*>>

The glass of gin fell to the floor, slipping from Handy's hand, crashing into pieces. "Goddamn it!" He slurred. "Shit. Shit. Shit." He went to the refrigerator and took out the bottle. It was empty. "Oh, great," he said. "That's just great."

Much later, Handy, sober and vigilant, stood watching the eagles soaring overhead through the notch of his gun's sight. The gun went off with a loud report. There was a distant flurry of feathers, a twisting in the air, and a falling bird. *Damn varmints. You've got to stay right after them.*

"That's three," he said out loud, reloading. The bird hit the soft ground with a muted thud.

88. The Earth Is Still

Farson watched the whole thing unfold in the barge's timescape projectors. Uvo was beside him. The beautiful floating holographic images foretold the story in seconds. Under its enshroudment, Earth slowed in its orbit, and leveled slightly. The ice caps melted, and the oceans grew and then were absorbed. The giant land masses smoothed and combined, green and amber hues spread across the globe, as the blue dissipated. Then the planet disappeared in an instant, a disturbance spreading outwardly in the space all around.

Farson knew that for the people inside, stasis was timeless and imperceptible as it took its hold on their lives. But watching from outside, he also knew that the implications were immediate and profoundly existential.

<<*You've made your selections from SkyKing, Farson?*>>

<<*Yes. They were not happy. But they will adjust. It is a great calling.*>>

<<*And the Moon?*>>

<<*As I said, they are moving off together.*>>

<<*Then all is as it should be?*>>

<<*No, Uvo, all is as it must be.*>>

Farson reappeared in the cabin to find Karina still sitting in the rocking chair. The fire was embering along, in need of attendance. She looked up. "Hello, dear," she said humorously. She stood up and came into his arms. "Is it done?"

"Yes."

They stood there together, holding each other for a while, and then Karina returned to the chair. Farson pulled up a little wooden stool and sat in front of the fire, staring into the glowing charcoal and weak flames still licking.

"It's done, Karina. Earth is in stasis. Emerald Earth is established. SkyKing and the Moon are moving off into the unknown. The Screen is partially repaired, and my Ascension is complete. I wonder what comes next."

Farson felt his sister's eyes on him. She had quietly moved from her chair to behind him at the fire. She knew Farson's mind was wandering on The Screen, looking for clues, for some hint of what was coming.

Rubbing his warm shoulders, her mind was focusing only on having him so close. Using the word he used, but thinking her own thoughts, she said, "Keep wondering, Farson. You might just get lost." He could sense her moving closer as he reached for another log.

BOOK II

The Beyond

"Beware of those who flourish
with hereditary honors."

– *Latin Proverb (Date unknown)*

"All is flux, nothing stays still."

– *Heraclitus (535 B.C. – 475 B.C.)*

Chapter Six
SkyKing
and MoonBase

89. Moonwake

Lieutenant Gerald Antonoff, on board SkyKing, was staring into a sight that few people had ever seen: a space station with huge golden sails unfurled, following in the wake of the Moon. To him, the view looking back through the remote cameras on the aft end of the Moon, the station looked like a child's jack toy attached to five full-blown golden spinnakers.

It had taken many weeks of hard effort for the Skers to set and trim the sails, to begin to catch up with the Moon, and then to ultimately match velocity and course. Finally, now they were in position, and on top of their sailing game.

The Skers had proven their skill a hundred times over during the past months, and they had learned much. As Antonoff sat before the camera consoles, monitoring the approaching rendezvous, he was finding himself absolutely amazed at what was happening around him.

Lieutenant Antonoff had pretty much seen it all since coming to SkyKing from Moscow. He had been selected because of his navigational skills and his command of English. His mother and father had both been in the Russian army, so the military life was normal to him. It had been six years since he had first come aboard. He had seen the increasing power and influence of the Skers, and, of course, it had been on his watch when the Earth had disappeared. He was still single and only turning thirty in the coming spring. *What does that mean now?* He had planned a return to his homeland and a small celebration with friends. *That'll never happen.*

He was still looking out at the station through the Moon monitors. In the weeks following the departure of the Moon and SkyKing, things had certainly happened quickly. The Moon had taken off like a shot, and SkyKing had started off after her, very slowly at first. There were detailed discussions for the first two days about whether they were actually moving or not. Then it became clear that the Skers' mathematics and designs were all correct, brilliant really. The sails that had been so secret were out in the open and working gloriously for all to see. They were now the biggest thing in everyone's sky.

The constant acceleration of the Moon by particle catapult and the directed nuclear fusion thrusters, plus the gathering of velocity by SkyKing with her magnificent sails had created far-reaching and remarkable changes. Earth was just a collective memory. The Moon was darkened by the bellowing sails of SkyKing as they approached from behind.

For the people of SkyKing, little had changed: Their day-to-day lives went on as before but now with a significant difference. Unlike an Earth sailing vessel hard on the wind, heeling and surging, SkyKing was steady as ever, silently, inexorably moving through space ever faster. However, in the minds and attitude of the Skers, everything was vastly different. It was as if a bright light had been cast into their abyss, to uncover a people who loved the light, but had been afraid to admit that it could be theirs. So deep had been their caverns of secrecy and so far from the light were they then, that now released and free, the Skers had definitely come to life. Then, they had been a quiet race which had lived on the edge of Earth glory. Now, they were in their own element. Now they were free. SkyKing was moving through space, racing to catch up and join the formerly unwanted but now essential Moon, with its people so different in every way from them. One might have expected discontent among the Skers. One might have expected a wary unfriendliness to develop. Far from that, they were apparently enjoying every minute of it. When asked about it in debriefings, the Skers to a person said, and with a smile, "All is well."

The Moon solved all of their problems for minerals and raw materials, and took very little in the way of crops and air and water. The Moon's presence ahead now shielded them and would shield them from the coming realities of space.

As time had passed, the Skers had come to respect the MoonBasers more and more. It was as Voul had said, "We are the same family, different parents."

The lieutenant knew the end of his watch was coming soon, and he began to complete his logs and reports for the day. The Ops Center was calm and routine, very comforting. The cameras scanned the whorls, all six of them now, and he could turn the lenses to the Moon's surface. He did this. He could see where the first "city" of the Moon was being built. It was a joint effort between the Skers and the MoonBasers. Voul had called it "The Gift of the Magi," but Viera had said, "We'll just call it New Chicago." That was that.

Antonoff could see the immense dome under construction; he could imagine the farms being planned. "They'll have no trouble working the farms," he thought, "with all those robots."

On one of the monitors, he could see his relief crew coming up from AlphaCommand. He checked the gauges and dials one more time: *All is well.*

"Amazing," he thought as the hatch opened and the pure white uniforms of his Sker replacement and crew appeared brightly in the room. The young man in charge walked briskly to the helm console, took in the dials with a business-like appraisal, and turned to Antonoff and smiled.

"You are relieved, Lieutenant." Antonoff took his gear and left the operations center to the crew of the new shift. He was thinking to himself as he left, *They are all like that, sort of stiff. But they are efficient.* He was wondering what they do to relax when they are not working. But then he remembered. *They are always working.*

In twenty minutes Lieutenant Antonoff was nestling into his bunk for a well-deserved rest.

Back in the center, the nimble hands and fingers of Midshipman Repoul Bensn flew over the dials and controls making minute adjustments to the sail trim. Like a fine musician playing his instrument, Repoul knew precisely what he was doing. He stopped for a minute and referred to a book he had put on the desk. The gold binding flashed momentarily in the starlight from the porthole of the chamber. He quickly returned to the adjustments, his hands moving constantly, gently coaxing a little more here, a little more there. Tighten this, loosen that. Almost imperceptibly SkyKing increased its speed. The change was infinitesimal, but Repoul's thoughts were large and grateful. The change registered on the delicate instruments. The midshipman knew its meaning only too well. A smile crept into his eyes. He touched the com dial on the side of the navigator's station.

"Yes, Midshipman?" It was Voul Jonsn.

"Did you see it, Captain?"

"Yes, Repoul, we saw it. It was as you theorized, was it not?" The young man beamed.

"Yes, Captain, exactly. We were right. It takes a great risk, but the risk is rewarded."

"Daily effort. Daily reward." Voul quoted a famous Sker scripture. The young man nodded.

"As your father foretold." Voul smiled at the midshipman's respect.

"As have others before and after him, Midshipman Bensn." They both were enjoying the moment in a deeply Sker way.

90. Righteousness

Viera was in her quarters on the Moon, reading. Surprisingly, she had become interested in an old historical atlas from Earth. Her interests were always impossible to predict. Yoga, swimming, poetry, sexual extremities ... almost anything could catch her fancy. Now she was reading up on the expansion of the Rus' people throughout what later became the Russian Empire. She was on her bed, naked, of course.

The intent look on her face illustrated the concentration of which she was capable. The light in the room was concentrated on the book she was reading and cast a soft light across her figure. To anyone watching, she might have seemed a work of art: a complex and beautiful woman. Leaving Earth orbit hadn't been as hard for her as for other members of the MoonBase crew. She really had no interest in returning to the old ways. She would do it, of course, if need be, but this new situation of endless adventure and of traveling into the unknown – the beyond – suited her perfectly. It was in her nature.

Now life itself had become a grand experiment.

She looked up from the history book and thought of Karina. She loved Karina. She missed her. Their friendship had blossomed as Karina came in and out of her life on the Moon. Although Viera knew Karina must miss her brother, she always seemed happy and content when the two women were together. Viera noted happily that Karina had now made the Moon her second home. Not always present, but she was around more often than not. That was good. The crew of MoonBase loved her, and she had many friends, but Viera's friendship with Karina was special. Its deepening had come to mean a lot to both of them.

Viera began to let her mind wander. She was a dreamer when there was time. Although a pragmatic and experienced commander of men and women, inside her mind, she was highly explorative, and she loved that aspect of her personality. She leaned back and let her imagination go. Many of her male companions had at first been surprised at her adaptive sensuality; others had enthusiastically joined in and discovered that where Viera's sensuality could take them was enrapturing and sometimes left them in a much different place at the end. For her, normality involved intense and unpredictable sexual interludes of all kinds and right now, she was having one of these. Sweat glistening, and short of breath, in her private element: She appreciated sensuality for its own sake. No explanations needed.

The only article of clothing she wore was the small and newly acquired com link on her wrist. Since departing the orbital area of Earth, the Skers had distributed these devices to all hands.

As her hand slowly moved along its usual and predictable path, the device beeped. She reached over and touched a button on the side, and a holographic screen appeared in the air over her. Another touch and Voul's face appeared in high resolution. It was a two-way connection. He looked at her and for a moment hesitated, shaking his head, knowing full well what she was doing. Her beauty and abandon always took him by surprise.

"Viera, am I interrupting anything? Do you have a moment?" She squirmed a little, but didn't change anything;

rather, something seemed to intensify as she saw Voul's handsome face. Her tongue touched her lips playfully, and now Voul began to squirm a little. He waited patiently and watched. She accelerated and twisted softly on the bed. Soon in obvious orgasm, she simply gasped and then after a moment, quietly turned face-to-face with a recuperative gesture of brushing her hair back from her slightly damp forehead. Voul continued, "I really need to talk with you." Viera looked up through half-opened eyelids still slightly adream with pleasure from performing in front of Voul. Nonetheless, she knew why Voul had called.

"Where are you guys going, Voul? Keep it up and we won't be able to maintain position without more nukes."

Voul just looked at her. How could she have noticed? How could she have known? He had thought she was preoccupied. "Hey, we're no fools over here, Voul," she continued, "Where do you think you're going?"

It had been less than an hour since Midshipman Repoul Bensn's theories had proven what Voul's father had predicted, and already Viera was clearly aware of the minute, but significant, change of speed. Was there a threatening element in her words? "What do you mean, Viera?"

"Voul, any uncoordinated change in the relative predicted positions of our two 'vessels' sets off alarms all over the place. What are you doing? What are you thinking? We've got a deal, right?" The threat was definitely there, but it was friendly. Her eyebrows, he noticed, told the story.

"Testing our sail trim, of course, and improving it as you would expect us to," he said. Viera stood up. Voul's eyes watched and followed her. She stepped into her one-piece jumpsuit, an orange one, and seam sealed it up around her with a flip of her wrist. It fit her perfectly. She knew he was watching. Again her eyebrows said much.

"Voul, you know we have laser stream capability and if we ever thought you were trying to abandon us, we know how to disable SkyKing and take her in tow without a hell of a big effort. There is nothing you can do about that. We're together. Period." She smiled sweetly at him, taking the edge off.

Voul blinked. It was true. SkyKing could accelerate, but it would take time to get away. They would not have that time if the Moon objected. He tried to change the subject.

"How's New Chicago coming?"

"The city will take about six years to finish, as you well know. In some areas we now have air integrity, and for the first time we now 'walk among the stars' without suits."

Voul recognized the phrase, "Walk among the stars," as sacred Sker scripture, and marveled at this woman, who one moment was in the throes of self-induced ecstasy, then a threatening adversary, then quoting scripture. "Viera, you are being irreverent."

"You love it. Don't you, Voul? When are you coming back over here?" Viera saw his eyes dance with a little smile, and she felt his mental gaze touch her mind in the Skers' way. A quiet thought formed in her mind. It was warm, clean, soothing. She was surrounded with the feeling of soft white linen, and the smells of warm spring days. She was quieting, and then restful. Her edge disappeared as though in a deep, healing breath. She knew it was Voul. He was so strong and so assured. "You've grown, Voul."

"Yes, Viera, but you are the same. I don't think I'll be coming over anytime soon, sorry to say." Viera looked at her wrist, and Voul thought she was going to end the transmission on the note of that rejection. Her fingers moved quickly on the device, and he thought to stop her and then changed his mind. Suddenly, she was playfully staring right at him. She saw his sadness at the thought of her turning it off. She laughed out loud at him.

"Oh, yes, you will, Voul. You know you will." Then she disconnected.

Voul looked up from his desk on SkyKing. He thought of all the responsibility, and of all the danger ahead of them. Those thoughts were crowded aside with the thought of Viera and of holding her again. *You might be right.* He wrestled with his humanness, and for a moment he indulged himself with further thoughts of her. For him, the path he walked was one of drifting thoughts and memories that rose like little freshets off a strong current, eddying to the side while the main surge continued on toward the falls. His thought enraptured on the memory of her lips when they were wet with his own, when they were together and her breath tangled itself around his consciousness like strong, growing vines. *You might just be right.* Then the thought clearly came to him that this indulgence would have to stop, for, like an addictive personality toying with substances, he was not the one to play with this fire. It would have to stop. Another thought came quickly on the heels of the first one: *Not just yet.*

Voul, paradoxically, was now feeling refreshed from his encounter with Viera. He glanced around his stateroom. It was, as all things Sker, in perfect order, clean and practical. His bed was made to a taut, white smoothness. The floor was shiny with a gleam that he was very proud of. Everything was so intentional. Others would walk in and notice nothing, but another Sker would see it all at first glance. There were other hints of Voul's high standing. His father's books, their well-used appearance, and the obvious fact that they were still in perfect condition after all these years. The Skers had a definite thing for perfection, and some things in a Sker's possession were far more important than other things. To Voul, his father's books had always been the most important of all things for which he was responsible.

Shaking himself into renewed activity, he began his morning stretching routine, and while he was in it, the stateroom's door chimed. Someone wanted to come in.

"Enter," he said. It was Midshipman Bensn. "Yes, Repoul?" He came in and spoke, glancing around the room.

"Captain, we have attained the position at which you wanted me to notify you before proceeding. There is no doubt about the fact that we could, as sailing ships have always done, exceed the wind velocity on this tack. Probably within a year, if my calculations are correct."

"You have no doubt that they are."

"None at all, Captain, it is a *fait accompli*, to use an Earth expression. A fact achieved. We will eventually exceed, by some margin, the speed of light. At that point we will have achieved all of our goals, including freedom from the encumbrances of Earth, MoonBase, and the sun. They will have no way to stop us. With the new genoa unfurled we will pull smartly away."

Voul looked at his midshipman and saw the cockiness that sinks ships and destroys empires. He shook his head.

"You are wrong, Mr. Bensn. They already know. I order you to stand fast and keep the genoa stowed away until such time as I say to use it. Return to original course and speed." Repoul's eyes narrowed down to razor slits. He stared at Voul in disbelief. He saw the steel in Voul's determination. But he still pressed his argument, laced with incredulity.

"It is scripture you are playing with here, Captain. It is our time. It has been foretold. We must go on alone." Voul softened somewhat in the light of this naiveté. He smiled. He almost laughed, but restrained himself.

"You are right, of course, Repoul, but tell it to Viera Nichols. She just threatened to start shooting holes in the solar sails if we don't desist. They noticed the acceleration within a few moments of your achievement and have followed our activities every step of the way. No, Mr. Bensn, keep the new genoa stowed for another day. For now we remain encumbered. There's no getting away in this circumstance. Steady as she goes." He was thinking of Viera when he said it. *She's steady, all right. Like a beautiful freight train.* His brief distraction was noticed by Bensn who took it as a sign of internal struggle. He was worried.

They stood there for a moment, eye to eye. Bensn knew he could not win. Voul knew he didn't want to fight. In a quiet Sker mind touch, agreement was reached. *For now.*

On MoonBase, Viera noticed the mental atmosphere soften. Surprised at the insight, she looked down at her wrist. The com link had a very faint purple hue, and she knew why. "All is as it must be," Karina had said. *So it is. She is rubbing off on me.*

Later that day a message came through. "The station has steadied up, Commander. Just as you said they would." She nodded and secretly smiled. "Very well," she said.

SkyKing and MoonBase sailed on into the black ink of space together full of irony, full of need, writing a new story, a new history, now all their own.

91. Dead Wings

Handy picked up the fourth bird and broke its neck with his bare hands. He stretched out the nearly eight-foot wings and laid them flat on the grassy earth. He stood back a little and looked at his arrangement. He had all four birds in a formation on the ground, flying together, in death. Somehow this made him very happy. It was a warm afternoon; the grass was soft and fluttering, the ground moving slightly beneath him. He lay down, and soon he was sound asleep beside the dead birds. A strange addition to the flock. He was curled up among them, gently snoring as the grass rustled beneath him like feathers flying in the wind.

A thousand miles away Strapper Jordan was jarred awake. An abrupt break in the gentle rocking of the moving tractor fleet had caused it. As he arose, his moving world had become quiet and still. Knowing the subroutines as well as he did, Strapper realized all was not well outside. Everything had come to a stop.

Upon disembarking the harvester complex, he was puzzled. His lead tractor had stopped at the far end of a wheat field. It had stopped and shut itself down and would go no farther. Something was barring the way. He hiked to the front of the tractor and reached out to touch what he could not see, but what he knew must be there. It was invisible, but also cold and hard like metal. A barrier of some kind. His intuition told him it was not still; it was moving in some infinitesimal way.

Jordan was at a loss of what to do next and that was a first. Standing beside the tractor amid vast waves of amber grain beneath a blue sky and bright sun, Strapper took a big, deep breath. It almost became a sigh. He reached down, picked a fresh stem of wheat to put in his mouth, and spitting out the old one first. He scratched his head, pushing his hat to one side. He went back into to the tractor and entered the cabin. After all the years of farming, nothing like this had ever happened. It was mystifying. He picked up a communicator, invoking the emergency-only provision. "Central, this is Strapper. Come in." He waited awhile and then repeated the message. The return call he wanted eventually came back from the occasionally manned central com station.

"Strapper, this is Central. Go ahead." Jordan was wondering how to explain what was happening.

Handy and the birds were all "flying" together on the warm ground. He was still asleep. The birds were still dead. He suddenly was awake. Something was up. Something new. Something unexpected. He was hungover, as usual.

Handy shrugged like a repair worker roused to solve other people's problems. <<*Remember, Handy, you live on Emerald Earth too, now.*>>

He looked up into the sky; the eagles were circling again, like buzzards overhead. He shook his head and frowned at them. Now he had to go to work.

<<*You live among them, and move in all times, and now you have some decisions to make. As we foresaw, they would eventually realize their situation. This is just the beginning. Remember, you have an important assignment here. A vital assignment.*>> Rubbing his eyes, Handy was moving.

<<*You think I don't know, Farson? Have you forgotten?*>> Even as he shared the thought, Handy knew it was unnecessary. Farson had forgotten nothing.

92. Commander Peterson, Retired

For James Peterson the recent months had been a rare period of relief from the pressures of command mixed with the joy of freedom to spend virtually all of his time with his daughter Brittany. She was an auburn brunette now almost sixteen years old. She had responded to this enriched relationship by taking it for granted over the years, as children do, and settling in to the relaxed, secure atmosphere of a normal childhood. Every morning her dad had prepared her breakfast so she would awake to the smell of omelets, or fresh bread, or warm cereal or whatever they were to have that morning. She would come out, padding on bare feet, to the table where her dad was sitting and reading the morning transmissions. He would absentmindedly hand her a glass of juice – most often fresh orange juice – and the day would begin to unfold in the easy predictable fashion of life at its best. James Peterson had come to see that a solid routine had added greatly to the emotional well-being of his daughter, and that she had flourished in it. He had seen her move away from constantly questioning him about when she would see him next, to a situation where she never even gave it a thought. At first, he worried that something had happened to her devotion to him, but in time he had come to see that her devotion had deepened into a trust and a full acceptance of her one-parent reality.

He knew now what really had happened when his wife had died. He had picked up the pieces, and he and Brittany had gone on. Until SkyKing had unfurled its sails and Voul Jonsn had taken command, he had had no time to really consider these things too deeply or to put his own new life in order. In a way he had gone on as if nothing had happened. As a military man, he had always put his career, mission, and duty first. Now he was sort of off-duty. He had to adjust to it. He found himself enjoying it. He lived in a six-room suite on SkyKing, and he retained certain powers and prerequisites which would eventually return to him again anyway, when the plan to have SkyKing orbit the Moon was realized. He had full run of the space station. *Such a beautiful place.* He looked out the large view-port in the kitchen and saw the motionless stars and a small portion of the Moon up ahead.

What a view.

He knew that, as the Skers were chosen, so, too, was he. This was a blessing for him because to return to Earth in a desk billet was purgatorial at best and destructive to his healthy psychology at worst. He had always felt the pressure from Earth Command to return to Earth and make way for younger officers on their way up, but he had resisted it, and now, he was really glad about that.

Standing there cooking omelets, Jim Peterson and his daughter were sailing off into the unknown. They were part of an adventure the like of which no one could have predicted, and of which no one had even conceived. They were going where no others had ever gone. They were still together despite all that had happened.

"Hey," he said, "these omelets are ready."

Brittany was already at the table.

93. Handy and Uvo

Handy stood casually leaning on an invisible wall. The harvester's forwardmost bumper was frozen in time, buried in the anomaly. *That is so strange. Hard to get used to.* Strapper Jordan was standing beside the craft. Handy was thinking. He was also traveling faster than thought out onto The Screen. He was "sorting," as the ScreenMasters put it.

<<*Uvo?*>>

<<*Yes, Handy. What can I do for you?*>>

<<*The shock wave is causing problems.*>>

<<*To be expected.*>>

<<*It's so different on our end. Kind of weird, really. We wouldn't have noticed it except for Strapper's tractor. It bumped it. Then it became slightly embedded. He can't back it out.*>>

<<*Come on, Handy. You've been there too long. You know very well what's happening.*>>

<<*I was hoping you wouldn't say that.*>>

<<*We've tried, Handy. We've tried. Things are out of control. We can't delay it, and we can't stop it. We can only hope that Farson knows what he's doing. To us, the planet shouldn't be there*

at all. A tractor hitting the expansion effect is ridiculous, really. What did you tell them?>>

<<*I'm still thinking that over.*>>

Strapper Jordan reentered the tractor to program his next row and arrange for a new bumper. He thought about the old one and went out to see. It was sliced off, as were the front fenders and part of the cooling system where the barrier had touched. He looked at the damaged parts and shrugged. To Jordan it was just another problem to be overcome and then back to business. Then he noticed the barrier was gone.

Commander Peterson noticed something. He was sitting at the breakfast table watching Brittany finishing her ChainFoods eggs and juice, when he saw it over her shoulder. The far distant space where Earth had been seemed to brighten slightly; then a white line shot straight up followed by a pulse of energy. Then, like a vague star going nova, it briefly filled the sky and settled back to a black emptiness, where nothing was again. Stunned momentarily, he began to sort through the facts. The space where Earth wasn't had flared and then disappeared. There was something else: the flaring pulse. It seemed to be an expanding ring. A shock wave? Peterson wondered as his hand touched his wrist and he said, "Voul, call me right now." Within seconds, Voul was on the communicator.

"Yes, Jim, we saw it."

"What do you think it was?"

"We don't know, but we surmise that it may have something to do with what the ScreenMasters are doing. Perhaps it was the Patch they are always talking about."

"I don't mean to interfere, Voul," he said with such clear sincerity in his voice that was impossible to ignore, "but what does it mean to us?" There was a long pause that worried

Commander Peterson before Voul gave an answer that worried him even more.

"It may mean many things, Commander, but for now I think we should prepare for what the sailors of old would have called 'rough seas.' In our preliminary evaluation, it's a shock wave, and it will be an enormous one. If that proves to be true, then we must move very quickly. As Farson told us, 'There is an enemy. It comes with no notice. I will give you guidance to know it, before it knows you.' We are ready, Jim, but it's not going to be easy. We are moving away as Farson instructed, but it may still hit us with force. Farson also said, 'That which you fear most comes upon you.' If it is a shock wave, then we may have to evacuate SkyKing, except for the working crew."

"Get them onto the Moon, you mean?" Peterson knew the implications of that.

"Yes, you can join me here now, and help with the main contingency plan. We think we might be able to duck in front of the Moon."

"I'll be right there." Brittany was still eating, but she was watching her dad, too.

"Is everything okay, Dad?"

"I'm going to the Moon, honey. Want to come? You can see Viera."

"Really?" she asked, excited. "That'll be fun. When are we going?" Peterson was already on his way to the door. Brittany had to run to keep up.

94. Viera Decides

Viera was sitting at her desk as Voul returned. She looked up and knew something was wrong. She stood up and walked over to him. She could smell his clean scent. His hair was soft-looking and languished across his face as he moved. *Is he letting it grow?* His skin was smooth and firm, yet it looked warm to her. *He looks like an athlete at his peak.* He was looking at her, quite intensely. "Hi, Voul," she said. "I told you, you'd come." Voul couldn't help but smile. Here she was in deep danger, and she was still joking around. Then she surprised him again. "I saw what happened, Voul. We know."

"We are ready to send the families and nonessentials to you," he said. "We will still need a lot of help from your people." She slumped slightly and harrumphed.

"Well," she said, "there are 3,700 of us here. With quarters for about 4,000 tops. You've got how many? 305,000 or so? I don't know what the hell we can do." Viera had one other question that was pounding in her brain, but she was afraid to ask it. He answered it.

"I'm not staying, Viera. I have duties on SkyKing. Our people can shelter in the mines. We'll bring our own provisions and services. It shouldn't be for more than a week."

They stood there for a moment or two, looking at each other, taking it all in. Voul Jonsn, leader and captain of the Skers, and Viera Nichols, commander of MoonBase: so different, and yet not so different at all. "You'll be there when it hits, Voul?" He nodded.

"If we move quickly, it should be all right."

"Voul, I know we can't be sure." They moved together, closer. Then, once again, she was in the arms of the man she loved most of all the men she had ever known. He was experiencing a passionate shuddering, in the arms of the only woman he had never known. Viera looked into his eyes and saw her man there, struggling. She leaned into him more, and kissed him. He couldn't even think. It was overwhelming him. His heart was pounding. He loved it. He wanted it to go on and on. Viera held on and kissed on. They could feel each other so closely, so passionately. They couldn't step away.

Finally, she did, she had to, and the heat seemed to dissipate a little as the distance increased. "Let's get to work, buddy. We haven't got that long. There'll be time for us. Right?" Voul was like a man stepping into the cold from a hot steam bath. He took a moment to get his thermal bearings. Her breath was still on his face. They were still very close. As his head cleared, they moved a little farther apart. He felt an extreme emptiness and wanted her fill it again. She laughed and headed for the door. He collected himself and walked alone to the transporter and then back to SkyKing.

In his office, waiting for the arrival of his officers, Voul was thinking to himself of what she had said. *Buddy?*

MoonBase and SkyKing accomplished the seemingly impossible, but not without a great cost. In eighteen hours, all the "nonessentials," including all the children, had been evacuated from the station. Just before the last contingent departed, he had called Viera again. The SkyKing crew was going to need help in the maneuvering, and the Moon's men and women were disciplined in teamwork, if unruly under command. He asked if Long John Hanson Silver, her second-in-command, could come over with a group of about one hundred others to assist. He asked that they all be volunteers, because the odds were against complete success. She laughed at Voul and said, "Indeed. Volunteers? That's all we've got here." She was, however, wondering what it would be like without the ever-dependable sergeant around for a while, especially during a crisis.

Silver was a burly man, with rippling muscles and a will to match his physique. He and Viera had never really been close friends, and certainly not lovers, but there was enormous mutual respect. Viera knew that she would have to talk it over with John Silver. There would be no ordering him off his beloved MoonBase. He had always been there for her and for the crew. Over the years, she had come to see that while he tolerated SkyKing and its eccentric Skers, he was not their most enthusiastic fan. She knew if he went to the station in this crisis, it would not be easy for him. His quick acceptance of the assignment surprised her. She explained the mission again and the innumerable uncertainties surrounding it.

"John, you know there's a real possibility that you'll be dead soon if you go there."

"Don't count on it, Viera." His big shoulders were tall and straight. His arms were gently folded in front of him, but the strength in them was more than obvious. The steady look in his eyes, again, calmed her and reassured her.

"We can't get along without you, John. So, be very careful."

"Well, Farson promised us all a future." *He wasn't all that specific.* John Silver was all business. "So here it is. We all have jobs to do. I was wondering when mine would come along. It's simple. The Skers have a major problem. We can help. They have requested my help. What else can I do?"

"OK, John, but you know I'm not all that happy about this." He nodded, and she continued. "We need SkyKing as much as they do. Without Earth AND without SkyKing, we just can't make it. At least with SkyKing, we have a chance. So, SkyKing wants your help, but you are saving the Moon as well."

"Earth?" he laughed. "It's a goner, Commander. We have what we have, and that's the end of it. We can't lose the station. We're not going to lose the station." She looked at him. He was so certain. He was so confident. Did he really understand the ragtag plan, the enormous number of variables? Did he know how high the odds were stacked against them? Did he know how fast the shock wave was coming? How powerful it was?

"It's good that you're ready to help, John. It is going to make a big difference."

John Hanson Silver looked at his commander. She was one of the prettiest women he'd ever seen. Standing there in her tight jumpsuit, she was too good to be true. Smart, tough, durable, charismatic. And she was usually right. "You're a lousy liar, Viera."

She moved to shake his hand, but he took her in his arms and kissed her right on the mouth, pressing their bodies together with his miner's strength, in a miner's way. She did not resist.

"You waited long enough," she said as she pushed him away after a moment or two. "Eight years and now you get a hard-on." They both laughed. Then they shook hands, and he stepped onto the platform. "Good luck, John. Good luck to your team. Tell them I love them all, and we want them all back in one piece. We'll have a party to end all parties when this is over."

"You got that right."

"Tell them, John."

"I'll tell them, Commander. I'll tell them what you said."

As John Hanson Silver stepped off the transport platform onto SkyKing, he was followed by one hundred, hand-picked MoonBasers with all their gear and equipment. They were met by Voul's lieutenants and immediately taken to their stations to begin emergency preparations for the mission ahead.

Back on the Moon, two perfectly timed explosions shook the small planet. Viera looked at the controls, confirmed the accuracy, and then touched her wrist monitor. Voul appeared holographically before her. "That's it, Voul. Velocity is corrected exactly to your specifications, and we are turning our backs on the wave. One more burn, and all is ready on this end."

"Excellent." he said. "Well done." *Now the hard part begins.*

95. Jim Peterson Remembers

Commander Peterson enjoyed remembering her. He knew that it might be healthier if he didn't indulge himself in this way, but he was a prisoner of his memories. He was currently reclining in his stateroom doing it again. He was remembering when he and his wife were young, before they were married, and how they would go for trips in the car back on Earth. It was an electric and quiet, but they would be chattering and enjoying themselves all the way. A smile appeared on his face. *Those were happy days.* He would sometimes drive with his arm around her. Sometimes they would stop and make out for a while, just kissing and holding each other close.

He could even remember how, after they were married, he would become irritated with her sometimes over some stupid little everyday thing. He remembered how mad they could get at each other when they argued. The arguments never lasted, and soon they were back in each other's arms again. He knew he would give anything for just one of those arguments again, for just one of those make-up kisses again. He knew they were gone forever now.

His wife had died during station construction of the sixth whorl. She had died trying to save another crew member, and when she died, a lot of things that Jim had really loved died with her. He knew those things would never come again, except in his memories. In his mind he was still free to experience Joanie's humor and her silliness. In his mind he could still smell her scent, her perfume. He could still remember the feeling of her, of being inside her, and of feeling her move in love with him. He missed it all, and more, he missed her. He missed her like crazy. He knew that for him the marriage had gone on. There was no turning back. Joanie had been his wife in life, and still she was his wife after death. "Until death do us part." *Until both of us die.*

He let his memories linger for a while. He just leaned back and let his mind relax in the warmth of his memories about her, indulging the clarity of the moment, enjoying having her with him.

Now SkyKing was sailing faster and faster and with one hundred new crew members aboard and working hard, she racing toward a distant point where Voul hoped the station would be safe. "Repoul, have you got this new course under control? My original calculations showed that we should have tacked at least twice by now, and you have only done it once. What's up?"

"Captain Jonsn, I believe that our original calculations were overly conservative in two ways: First, in speed, we are much faster at this point than we thought we would be, and second, on pointing, we are able to go higher into the solar wind than we thought. The genoa is much better than the sailmakers predicted, and Commander Peterson's amazing 'boom-rail' has allowed a closer trimming of the horizontal staysails than the original specifications anticipated. However, I will continue to recalculate continuously and notify you of any variation from the new formulas and projections. We are in position, and the Moon remains in perfect formation ahead." Bensn was very matter-of-fact about this, and Voul detected no guile or emotional uncertainty. Repoul Bensn was stating the truth as he knew it. Voul knew he was lucky to have such a fine navigator working on this project, just when SkyKing needed it the most.

"There's a lot riding on this, Midshipman."

"I know, Captain."

Voul considered what they were about to do. He was rethinking everything: Earth disappearing, SkyKing and MoonBase flying off together, Viera, and the MoonBasers. He tried to put Viera out of his mind, without success, of course. Now the Skers and everyone else deserved his undivided attention, but still she was on his mind. Part of him now? The crew of SkyKing had changed their mission radically and had rolled with the punches. They had demonstrated a dedication and versatility that Voul's father had always foreseen and foretold, but those foretellings were now reality. He looked over at Repoul Bensn working hard at the helm station. He strolled to the porthole and looked out into space. By all accounts the Skers had achieved their scriptural destiny with a magnificence that should have filled him with joy. So, why was he filled with foreboding? Why did he feel like something was sneaking up behind him?

Because that's exactly what IS happening. Voul looked over at Repoul Bensn. Repoul was looking at him. They shared a moment of mutual thoughts and then returned to their respective assignments.

96. Jim Peterson, Alone with His Thoughts

The shock wave was getting nearer and nearer, coming up from behind like a somber, spectral dread, a fear overtaking them.

Jim Peterson was savoring the last few minutes of privacy before going back on duty. He was still in his stateroom chair, lounging along with thoughts from the past. He was remembering how much Brittany loved the water. Even though most of her life was spent in space, she still loved to swim and exercise in the water. He was recalling the first time she had tried a whirlpool at the recreational area. The attendant had said, "No one under twelve is allowed in the whirlpool." Jim had looked at the attendant and then at his daughter who was obviously no more than seven and said to the monitoring adult with a perfectly straight face, "She is twelve." Everyone laughed heartily, but Brittany had to get out, nonetheless. Jim was smiling with his memories. Brittany was asleep in her room. All was well with her world.

Somewhat refreshed, he got up and made his way to AlphaCommand to assume his station next to Voul on the bridge.

The Moon was getting closer, and the golden sails of SkyKing were reaching for the stars.

John Hanson Silver and his crew were working hard, well into their long shift. Together with the crew of SkyKing, they were sailing the largest vessel ever propelled by wind of any kind. They were in a desperate race against the coming shock wave, and all hands were bearing to with determination and skill that captains and crews of the brigs of old would have admired. Racing before the storm, SkyKing stretched for a distant waypoint in the black void. A point that represented far more than was told on the charts and in the calculations. It was a point where safety waited. If only they could get there in time.

Everything was now readying for a final tack that would bring them to a heading that would allow them to cross in front of the Moon just as the shock wave washed over them all. The plan was simple but technically intricate and difficult. As they entered into the penumbra of the Moon, the sails would be furled and stowed after a final maneuver to match courses. Then the wave would pass, and sheltering in front of the Moon, they would be safe, to a degree. Silver looked at the schematic of the sail plan. He was not sure all the sails could be furled before the wave struck. *It's not going to be as clean as they think. There will be trouble.*

97. Farson Watching

Farson was sitting in his old rocking chair in the North Conway cabin. It was as if he were really there. He could feel the chair and the warmth from the fire. He enjoyed wearing his old cardigan sweater. He enjoyed being in North Conway. He knew there was a lot more to it than that.

He watched time pass and pieced things together. Earth in stasis – a long stasis – but not a complete one. The Moon and SkyKing, off to the stars. Then all the people: Voul Jonsn and the Skers, Viera Nichols and the MoonBasers, Jim Peterson and Brittany, John Hanson Silver, and many, many more, including, of course, the ScreenMasters: Uvo, Twill, himself, and Karina.

Then, there were the farmers and urbanites on Emerald Earth, and the Rent, which would not go away. There were decisions that he must make, and soon. The ScreenMasters were coming back, and this time a resolution would be reached. Farson could sense Uvo's thoughts.

<<*Your compromise solution may not be enough, Farson. We're coming back to see. Prepare.*>>

Farson knew he was ready for them. He had always been, but it had taken time to realize all of that. The Rent could be repaired, and Earth could survive. There were uncertainties. Then, of course, there was Handy Townsend.

Karina appeared in the room beside Farson. She was wearing a ScreenMaster's robe. It was beautiful on her; she was outlined in shimmering purple. The ScreenKeeper robot, ZZ<<Arkol, appeared along with her but remained dark and unmoving; only its eyes quietly strobing hinted at the power there. She spoke, "Yes, Farson. The Earth may survive, but what about us? What will become of you and me? What will become of us?"

"We'll be all right, Karina. Earth and I are connected. That's why I'm a ScreenMaster. That's why this has all happened to us. You and I are forever." Farson found he was deep in contact with her and with so many memories, his head was spinning.

"Now listen, Farsy. This is no joke. If you're going to fish with me, ya gotta fish right. Ya gotta put the worm on the hook. Ya gotta clean the fish. Ya gotta do everything for you, and I gotta do everything for me. The way you're goin' it looks like I'm doin' everything and you're doing nothin'. Fishin' is more than that. It's a whole big thing from start to finish. Start to finish, Farson. All or nothin'."

Farson was sitting with his back against an old, knotty oak tree. The sky was blue as a baby's eyes, and the water was moving past like a smooth, brown blanket. Their two lines were in the water, suspended down from little red-and-white bobbers that leaned into the gentle current. Sam was beside Farson, to his left. It was a scene that outwardly was very tranquil, but inwardly was anything but.

"Farsy?"

"What?" The reply was not all that friendly in tone.

"You gotta do it. It ain't gonna work any other way."

"Why not? We've been happy 'til now."

"Well now, that's what you say, but what would I say if you asked me that question?"

"What question?"

"You know what question." Sam's face made an expression of exasperation that only he could make. Farson had tried it a few times on Karina but with mixed results. Mostly she tilted her head and looked at him quizzically, saying, "What's that supposed to mean?" Farson had a theory that whenever women were out-emotioned or outwitted in eye-to-eye stare-downs they always did that quizzical look and tried to confuse you. It usually worked. Sam was continuing his train of thought. "Now just grab that worm and stick it on the hook. You're not going to catch anything until you get some worm out there. Fish won't bite on a bare hook." Just then Farson's rod dipped about twelve inches down, almost touching the water. It stayed down, wiggling hard. He started to fight with it, while Sam's eyes got a little bigger. Farson's full attention was suddenly focused on the struggle with the rod and he was definitely winning. Sam couldn't believe what was going on. It was a little while until Farson was confident that the fish was hooked and certain to be landed. Sam would have played with it a little, but Farson brought it right in. It was flipping at Sam's feet, and there was a tension in the air. Sam said, "Go ahead and do it." But Farson was resolute.

"You do it. Same as always."

"No." Sam was equally resolute.

"The fish will die."

"Then he will die." They both just stared out at the river like statues. This went on for a few minutes. The fish was still flopping around but with less enthusiasm, then even less. "Goddamn it, boy! You're a piece of work!" Sam picked up the fish, yanked out the hook, and sailed the fish back into the water with an underarm pitch that could easily have struck out a batter. The fish skipped once, twice, and then skidded to a stop on the water and sank with a twitching splash. "What the … ?" Sam was looking at the hook. There was a small piece of worm on it. "How'd that get there, Farson? When did you …" Farson was smiling at Sam, but then suddenly and disingenuously frowned at him.

"Your throw probably killed the fish anyway, Sam."

"No way, Farson. No way."

"Farson, come back." Karina was annoyed at Farson's obvious distraction. "You and I need to talk about what you're going to do." Farson could still see the clammy worm flesh in his mind as he turned to answer Karina. His attention refocused on the room in North Conway and on the woman the world knew as his sister.

"I will do what I will do."

"Don't give me that messianic crap, Farson. This is Karina, not one of your devoted followers. I need to know what you're going to do."

Farson had seldom seen her like this. She generally enjoyed the more mystical aspects of their life together. "What's the matter, Karina? You seem to be a little out of your usual sorts. These things are pretty much all worked out in advance at this point, and you know it. The Rent still exists. There isn't much left to do until it's repaired. You know that, too."

Karina looked at Farson. She wasn't looking at her brother, but at the only man she had ever loved. She was looking at her reason for living. Karina loved Farson with all of her heart and soul. Farson had told her that she should keep her soul for herself, but that had not had any effect. The feelings were too deep, too passionate, too much a part of her. Her eyes were filling with tears.

"Farson, you can't do it all alone." Farson looked at her. In the back of his changing mind there was a place where he and his sister were lovers. Where they could sleep together and touch and love one another. That place had been dormant for a while, but it was active again right now. He stood up. He took her in his arms and kissed her.

Karina pushed him away slightly and looked into his eyes. "Farson," she whispered his name and hugged him to her. They kissed. They kissed again. His hands touched her. Hers touched him. They lay down in front of the fire and undressed each other slowly and made love deeply, sincerely. The fires inside and out were warm and deepening. Farson stayed inside her gently after their lovemaking had consummated. As time passed and he relaxed, she remained warm and close. It was one of those moments they would both long remember. She looked at him and half asked, half stated, "Handy?" Farson looked at her through the avenues of time and the mosaics of space that only ScreenMasters can understand and navigate. In the levels upon levels and circles within circles that are The Screen, he returned her gaze. He nodded his head in agreement.

With that one gesture many important things were exchanged.

"Of course," she said. "There's always Handy."

98. Voul Gives In

Something was bothering Voul. He was the commanding officer of the first independent Sker space vessel, which was a heavy burden, and it was causing him to have recurring reservations about becoming formally involved, openly, with a non-Sker. He did love her. *Really.*

It was clear that the Sker philosophy of abstinence and austerity was at odds with Viera's view of human normality. Skers were simple people who denied the body and its dominion over them. Viera indulged her body and enjoyed every minute of it. She reveled in it, and she was teaching Voul. He was, as things were turning out, a very good student.

Skers did mate for procreation but, as a rule, did not cohabitate. Viera "mated" for fun and demanded constant cohabitation. Viera was also widely known to be highly promiscuous, and Voul was the exemplification of chastity and of the highest standards of Sker decorum. He was all of that, and so was his father before him. The purity of Viera's lineage was dubious at best and had been the subject of many jokes. Not among the Skers, of course. Voul loved the Sker Way, and understood it. Viera did not understand it at all. Viera, nude and beautiful, moved in his mind like a siren calling him to her island.

What are we going to do? She had felt his mind pressing into hers; it was warm and safe. She had felt him embrace her and she responded. There had been no touch, but no touch had ever been more intimate, her senses rose with her heartbeat, and she flushed with passion. In her mind they made love in a way she had never experienced. They touched each other and caressed each other with a tender, intimate intensity that lifted her beyond the mere physical responses she had experienced so many times before.

She was in the throes of deep orgasms that went on and on. They were truly one; he was with her and sharing it all.

We'll think of something. He knew that while this was enough for today, things would still need resolution. *It can wait.* He saw his hand brushing her face, her shoulders, her breasts beneath her clothing. He knew things were accelerating.

SkyKing sailed on into deep space. While none of them knew it, at the precise moment SkyKing had completed its final tact back toward the Moon, they had all crossed the point of no return.

All over the station, Skers knew that the prophecy, "We shall depart," had come true.

The Moon was slowly growing larger and larger on the monitors of SkyKing as the shock wave and the future cascaded inexorably toward them all.

Chapter Seven
Emerald Earth

99. Handy and the Bottle (1)

Handy was moving toward another bad time, and he knew it. The too-many bad habits he had cultivated over the years were coming back to haunt him in his idleness. Handy had a job to do on Emerald Earth, but he was only now starting to actually do it.

If you've got a hundred years between breaths, a body has to find something to do with his time.

Handy was not alone on Emerald Earth, but he constantly experienced a vastness of solitude unknown in the long history of the planet.

In stasis, the Earth moved through its own time, but Handy, being himself, was immune. He moved around like an interloper in a department store full of living manikins. While the planet was in the custody of the ScreenMasters, it was Handy, the caretaker, who swept the floors and took out the trash.

There were others, he knew, obviously, who moved around in real time, but this freedom was very controlled and very limited. The harvesters trekked across the vast amber fields while the Emers manned the transports. They were producing crop after crop in the normal growing seasons, but at the other end, in real time, the output was fantastic and rich, enough to feed a solar system. The monitors at the transport station managed the flow of crop exports. And, then there was Emerald City.

Handy stood, now, on a hill overlooking it. He shook his head. It was odd, by any definition, that Farson would have set up this little growing warren in Earth's now pristine environs. Like a strange experiment: the last remains.

<<*Farson, you move in mysterious ways.*>>

Handy walked on, down the low hill. On the way he came across a snake. It appeared dead, of course, but it was very much alive and would be for an eternity. Handy bent down and looked at it. The snake was well over three feet long. Handy took out his knife, which he knew was exactly twelve and a half inches long and marked off lengths in the soft brown earth beside the creature. *Almost four. So, probably forty-seven inches or so. A full-grown rattler.* Handy touched the snake's skin. It was cold even though the sun was hot.

How do they do that?

He continued on his walk. The snake did not move as Handy passed. It's sidewinding position held like a sculpture, the graceful appearance of movement toward a destination more instinctual in thought than in the moment's reality.

Handy could see the huge discontinuity in the distance, from horizon to horizon, encircling the entire Earth, like a curvature. *This is like the Land of Oz.* It was clearly a separating entity from the surrounding space, and seemingly solid and barrier-like, although beautiful, too, in its way. Reality's termination.

Handy had thought to approach the city for years now but had put it off while he tended to other things. *No hurry.* In a very long life, Handy had learned the values of patience and he practiced that virtue well. He had seen the city at night, and sometimes he could smell it when it "farted," as he called it. Apparently, periodically, it would need to replenish or expel something, and the field would shimmer as it expanded and contracted. Once, when he was close to it, he thought he heard it make a sound. It had made him laugh. "It farted again," he had said out loud to no one.

Handy decided that with several miles of clear desert to go, he might as well camp for the night and then figure out what he was going to do in the morning. He set about pitching the tent and building a fire, which was easy with his tools. Another thing Handy had learned in his life was to never throw anything away. He had quite a collection of tools. A laser streaked briefly into the scrub he had collected and made a roaring fire in seconds. The tent inflated and before long he was sitting there having a sandwich, a small glass of whiskey, a smoke, and soon playing his guitar, as usual. A new song formed with the crackling of the fire.

I've never been that perfect.
I've never been as wonderful.
But I've seen a lot of times
And I still sing in rhymes.

Those people in the bottle
Need to meet me over a drink.
They'll never expect it,
Won't know what to think.

A man who moves in real time,
While the world crawls home.
A man who can see them and
Tell them they're not alone.

Handy kept playing and singing until he grew tired and just a little drunk. He rolled over a little closer to the fire and fell asleep.

About fifteen feet to his left a mountain lion crouched in an attack posture. Somewhere in the back of its mind a thought was forming, but it would be hundreds of years before anything happened.

Handy slept on, oblivious and contented, just like a happy baby.

100. Stasis

Stasis was strange for those in the bottle. It was like sleeping in a dream they knew. There's no waking, though because it's real. They clearly knew something had happened. No contact with the outside world was unsettling. The slowness of reality was known to them now. It was fairly easy, really, for them. Biding one's time is, after all, human nature.

101. The Gurney

Viera knew something about miners. She knew that they loved fresh air and light. This knowledge made all the difference on MoonBase. She had insisted that the air of the mines should always be rich with oxygen, clean, and aggressively ventilated, as if a mild breeze was consistently coursing along through the miles and miles of shafts and tunnels. The mines themselves were more like giant hallways than mines. The floors were fused rock, smoothed and polished, the walls were of the same material but had been colored off-white, and the entire complex had an antiseptically clean appearance. Viera also knew that the miners wanted, to travel freely and swiftly. Transporter technology was beyond the capabilities of the Moon, but the gurney, as the frictionless pneumatic tube system was known, was almost as good.

102. There Is One Thing

"They can take the light away out there, but they can't take the light away in here." President Sortt tapped his chest, indicating his heart. He walked to the window and looked out. In the distance he knew was the stasis field where the wide-open horizon should have been. "They have stopped us, but they haven't killed us. We still live, albeit in a prison. We still have Farson." The two people in the room with him sat motionless, listening. The term "president" had taken on a different meaning. Once a political title, now it was more like a tribal chiefdom. With no trappings of power, Andrew Sortt presided over the sepulcher of humanity. By the simple fact that he was contented with his new role, he proved his worthiness. During the preceding era of politics and infighting, he had been the supreme master. He rose to the presidency through extreme guile and manipulation, but never power for its own sake. Andrew Sortt was a man who truly cared about his fellow men and women, and while he had done whatever was required to get there, once in power, he was benevolent, liberal, and always watching out for the little guy and for the general good.

This situation now was altogether different from anything that had ever happened before. The president clearly knew, especially after recent conversations with Handy Townsend, what was going on. He knew that time was vastly different for him now. He knew that as things now stood, his world, Emerald Earth as Handy was calling it, was speeding up. He kept feeling that there was a thought just on the edge of his consciousness trying to get out that would show him what to do, but it stayed put like a diver hesitating on the board or a thief about to run. He knew Earth was moving slowly in one way, but fast in another: They were advancing into the far and distant future beyond their wildest dreams. And yet, they were still tethered tightly together.

"So, Handy," he said, "it's hard for me to be real happy about this." Handy was sitting in the elegant Harvard chair in front of the president's desk, dressed like a cowboy: boots, belt, stringed shirt, even a fully loaded Colt .45 in a holster slung lazily around his waist. He was unshaven, and, really, were it not for the fact that he should not have even been there at all, Sortt would not have taken the time for such a rudely disheveled visitor. But this figure appearing out of nowhere in the office and disappearing again whenever Sortt made too fast a move, then reappearing again, gave Andrew pause. Then as Handy began to tell the story of what Farson Uiost had done and what had happened to the Earth, Sortt knew there was something bigger required here than his old ways of reacting. He knew that he was the prisoner, as was everyone, of a struggle so far beyond his control that it was more like ants to Gods than man to man. It was sobering and debilitating to a man like Sortt who struggled all of his life to be in charge and to be in a position to make good decisions for others. Now he was perhaps nothing at all. *Because, if Farson fails, and it looks like he could, we will disappear for real. The ScreenMasters will never allow Earth to resume its previous destiny. Never. They can easily destroy what's left of us. If or when he fails.*

Sortt knew that Farson was attempting to fix a ScreenRent that appeared around Earth by changing history, one way or the other. Either it could be repaired, or Earth could never have existed. *Fixed, one way or the other.* Farson had bought some time with stasis, but it couldn't go on forever. Stasis time seemed like normal time as always. But from what Handy was saying time was actually passing faster than the wind over the Potomac River during hurricane season.

"It's a real tough situation for me, Handy. I want to do something. Everything in me screams to do something, anything. I don't know of anything that I can do that will have any effect whatsoever."

"Well," Handy said, "there is one thing."

103. Handy Pushing

Farson was considering the makings of a ScreenMaster and the way the other ScreenMasters discussed how truly rare they were. He was sitting on the butte overlooking the city. He had watched as Handy passed through the gateway into the city and had eavesdropped during his meeting with Sortt. It was a clear evening, the air was fresh, and Farson's thoughts were deep. He knew that his Ascension was really quite easy for him compared to the stories the other ScreenMasters had told him of theirs. His was legend. He knew that levels and layers were just there for him to move over, under, and around on, while to others they were barriers that stopped them cold. What had been impossible for them had been natural and seamless for him. He was a breed apart as far as ScreenMasters go. *I am just a human being.*

Before Ascension he had been an assistant professor of political science. He had been a teacher and a published researcher of some note, known primarily for his spacial concepts and timeline theories which built on others' genius work. He had always dreamed of being in space and being an explorer, but life had not worked out the way he had dreamed.

Like many people in those days, Farson had settled in to something that worked. His life had been happy. Karina was always the key to things for him since she joined the Chamberlains' little family so long ago.

He watched Handy move around inside the city. Farson wondered if the course they had chosen was correct. Karina had now joined him as a ScreenMaster. He had walked her through the appropriate levels, much to the dismay of the others. The others clearly could not see what he could see. She was an excellent ScreenMaster, an unquestioned ally, and someone he could really trust. That he had chosen her, that he had taught her, that he had made her a ScreenMaster was historic and upsetting to the others. To Farson, it was just another step along the way.

<<*Handy, what exactly are you doing?*>>

<<*Just what you've been doing.*>>

<<*And what would that be?*>> There was a long silence. Handy had turned in the distance of Emerald Earth, beyond normal sight. He was looking back at Farson as though they were standing next to each other. Farson could clearly sense Handy's reach into his mind's eye. There was a knowing quiet between them. Finally, Handy answered Farson's question.

<<*Pushing the envelope, Farson. Trying to find a way.*>>

<<*You're looking in the wrong place, Handy.*>> Handy laughed enthusiastically at this remark. He walked off into the fields shaking his head and laughing some more.

<<*You are such a card, Farson.*>>

104. Big Changes

Farson's Ascension had had some tough times. The loneliness, the sense of loss, the responsibilities were sinking in. After all, up to that moment he had been just another assistant professor struggling to teach and stay up with his chosen field. Up to the moment the ScreenMasters arrived, his life seemed to be fairly well mapped out. *A plan that went far astray.* Sitting there on the butte – to be known eventually as the Butte of Decision – Farson knew that the secrets of the ScreenMasters were nothing to what he now knew. The possibilities for good and evil were enormous and much more than enormous. Earth's stasis was the starting gate out of which would rush changes that would change everything. It seemed a matrix of quiescence, but in reality was a confluence of consequence.

Emerald Earth, although deep in stasis, was still providing food for other worlds, and Farson knew that the many other capacities of his species could do far, far more. He also knew what had caused the ScreenRent and that it could happen again. *People are people, and a planet of ten billion can get into a lot of trouble.* It wasn't, as the ScreenMasters posited, that human beings were inherently bad for The Screen. Rather, it was, as Farson now knew, that unlike other races, human beings could really damage it. Uvo had said that in all his travels and in all his mental searches he'd never heard of or seen anything even close to the amazing process of a human being achieving ScreenMaster status. *<<I'm not surprised that you turned the normal definitions upside down and totally redefined what a ScreenMaster is. Looking back now it seems inevitable.>>*

Farson knew that Earth had to be spared. It was a treasure beyond all treasures. He knew only one way to do it. Freeing Earth's people without the proper precautions would trigger a devastating ScreenMaster response, and Farson was not sure he could currently counter their combined efforts. *<<Don't think you can count on my acceptance or assent, Farson,>>* Uvo had said. *<<I will not retire.>>*

Farson knew their friendship had limits. The other ScreenMasters' enmity was a source of mere chagrin for Farson. *For they know not.* But Uvo was special. Uvo was a friend. *Uvo knows.*

Farson was listening when Handy said to President Sortt, "There is one thing."

<<*Don't screw this up, too, Handy. You've made enough mistakes.*>>

<<*Farson, are you talking to me?*>> Handy's reply came instantly.

<<*Yes, Handy. Don't tell Sortt too much, too soon.*>> Then, suddenly, Sortt was in Farson's mind. Farson felt Sortt's confusion and frantic attempts to figure out what was going on.

Farson! It's you! I can hear you. I can see you! Farson was upset with Handy.

<<*Handy, you're going way too far. Don't push this. You'll just make it harder for them.*>> Handy was quiet now.

Why 'harder,' Farson? It was Sortt again, a little bit less confused, a little bit sharper. *He's learning fast.* Farson could hear Sortt's thoughts trying to latch onto him as he began to leave, the purple hue intensifying around, encasing him. Sortt continued to attempt to reconnect like a little boy running after his father's car.

Now, Farson was traveling faster than light times light, faster than imagination. *Alone on The Screen. Peaceful.*

<<*Where are you running to, Farson? You can't hide, you know.*>>

<<*Uvo, I know. I know.*>>

<<*Not going according to your plan, Farson? Why do you suppose Handy is doing that?*>>

<<*Uvo, why does Handy do anything?*>> Farson's speed continued to increase. Even Uvo's thoughts were fading out in the blinding rush.

<<*Farson, where ARE you going?*>>

Faster and faster. Farson was traveling through dimensions of times. Layers of worlds. Things were everywhere at once, and yet he was so alone.

<<*Not alone, Farson.*>> Came a thought sharp and clear. Handy was beside him, then gone, like a flashbulb going off suddenly in a dark room.

Farson was still seeing spots as he went on.

"Happy Birthday, Farsy," said Hattie. "Now blow out the candles." Sam was sitting at the table, too. So was Karina. Farson puffed up to blow, but Sam interrupted him. "No, Farson, make a wish first!" Farson closed his eyes and thought deeply. He was thinking about this wonderful moment and how he wanted it to go on forever. Sam, Hattie, Karina, and him together, happy. He looked at the cake Hattie had made for him. "Happy Birthday, Farsy!" it said. Even the exclamation mark was three flavors of frosting. Farson kept thinking and wishing. Suddenly, Sam bellowed out, "Farson! Blow!!" Just before he blew out the candles, Farson was still thinking, *I wish I could have this beautiful cake and eat it too.*

<<*Fat chance, Farson!*>> came Handy's thoughts clear as a bell. Farson stopped. In his secret thoughts he knew that Handy couldn't be doing what he was doing. He absolutely knew it. <<*I've sort of gotten a new lease on life, you might say, Farson. You should try it. Honesty works wonders.*>> Then, he was gone. Completely gone.

Farson was just standing still on The Screen. He was considering Handy and all of his machinations. His incredible drunkenness. His debauchery. His silly attempts to start things and then never finish them. His insistence on having fun and being surprising and unpredictable. Handy was a LevelTen ScreenMaster, and Farson was now far beyond the 15th Ring, each ring having one hundred levels. Handy was a caretaker on LevelTen and the most unreliable ScreenMaster The Screen had ever known. Handy was also the most vexing and inventive of the ScreenMasters, and he was Farson's friend. Suddenly, he was back again. With Farson in the far reaches of The Screen, Handy couldn't be there, but he was. <<*Farson, let's get a drink or something. All of this running around has gotten me powerful thirsty.*>>

<<*Handy, you can't do to Sortt or the others what you're doing. It will hurt my plans.*>>

<<*What are you planning, Farson?*>>

<<*To set them free and to finally repair The Screen.*>>

<<*That's my plan, too.*>> Farson grew more concerned.

<<*But, Handy, it must be done as I have envisioned.*>> Farson watched Handy wince.

<<*Christ, Farson! Can't a guy have ANY fun anymore?*>>

105. The Penumbra

As the shock wave approached, the selected crew of MoonBasers worked with the remaining Skers to redeploy the genoa, all in compliance with Midshipman Bensn's minute specifications. This additional sail, along with the mainsail and spinnaker, it was theorized, would increase the space station's velocity just enough to let them duck in front of the Moon, very closely, just before the shock wave hit. Once the sails were hauled in (no easy task) and the station's retros were slowing it down in the highest reachings of the Moon's scant atmosphere, it was the considered opinion of all involved that

SkyKing would be sheltered from most of the wave's effects. The odds of survival were good once SkyKing was tucked in place. The two crucial tacks were an enormous and complicated undertaking. The crews were theoretically knowledgeable but inexperienced. No one had ever actually done it before.

John Hanson Silver was screaming profanities and thinking worse. He was a big man, so people were jumping to meet his commands. "Goddamn it, Smith, get that line secured and get the hell out on the fucking boom! If we don't clear the hypo-block in the next three minutes, we're fucked! You hear me?" The Skers standing nearby were at their consoles watching and listening, but it didn't take much of an insight to see that the personal adjustments they had made to working with the profane, physical, boisterous, and emotional MoonBasers had been difficult for them. To the Skers all was planning, preparation, and then careful, methodical execution in silent coordination. For the MoonBasers, action was everything, right or wrong. The MoonBase theory of "Do something, stupid!" was in full implementation as the crew crawled over the rigging and throughout the command center. "Stop jerking off, you asshole, and get moving! NOW!" Silver was red-faced, sweating, and the veins up and down his arms and neck were bulging. He wasn't really mad. It was just his style of action, of leadership, of motivation. Silver felt that the louder he yelled, the faster people carried out his orders. Watching Smith don his spacesuit in a panic and get into the hatchway, depressurizing and then launching himself into space without hesitation, tetherless, toward the distant hypo-block, Silver's theories were hard to argue with.

The Skers moved quietly and independently around Silver in the command center. They continued to manipulate their consoles and holo-processors, moving levers and switches in front of them. Midshipman Bensn was there, too, of course, at the navigator's station. He was the Sker who had conceived of the genoa in theory and developed its mathematical possibilities in conjunction with the other sails. He had performed years of elegant and hypothetical equations that resulted in the computer complex that now managed over 600 square miles of micro-thin solar sails and the accompanying lines, sheets, halyards, and shrouds, which were really whisper-thin filaments, to control the shape and trim of the sails. He was the one person, more than any other, who was responsible for the maneuverability and the increasing speed of SkyKing. As the prophets had foretold, "One shall arise among you, and he shall know the way."

Bensn was struggling in the Sker way with intense discomfort at being around Silver. Silver could feel it, and it made him laugh. Bensn turned to glare at the sound of Silver's scornful laugh. Bensn's look made him laugh harder. "What's the matter with you, Skerboy? Never seen real men work?"

"No, Sergeant. I've seen real men work. I've just never seen a vile man screaming such obscenities while real men work."

"'Vile?'" Silver turned toward Bensn and grabbed his chair, spinning him face-to-face. "'Vile?' you say? You listen here, shithead. I was in space when your best features dribbled down your mommy's leg." Bensn was trying to figure out what that meant when Silver shoved him back against the instruments in disgust. "Just stay the hell out of my way, asshole." Smoothing his ruffled uniform, Bensn calmly went back to his work, to his monitors, without any thoughts of animosity. He saw something on the monitor.

"Sergeant Silver, it would seem that Smith has missed the block."

"What!?" They both looked at the monitor, and it was obvious that Bensn was correct. Smith had misjudged the trajectory and now was drifting past the repair site out into space. "Holy shit!" Silver grabbed a communicator. "Smith! Come in! This is John Silver!"

"Sergeant, I'm sorry. I thought I had it right. We were in such a hurry that I ... !"

"Hang on, boy. I'll be right there." Hanson's communicator dropped to the floor. As every head in the control room turned to see what was going on, John Silver was already gone. The hatchway hissed-closed in his wake. He was running full steam for the suit locker and air lock. He rammed his legs into the suit, arms stuffed in, reached into the gloves. The helmet wasn't even on all the way as he hit the decompression button. Just as the last collar latch clicked in place, he was already flying out of the hatch into space, seemingly without any thought of trajectory or for his own personal safety. Midshipman Bensn watched in disbelief as the only crew member who was actually capable of commanding the MoonBasers, and hence in making the station's movements successful, put himself at extreme risk without a thought.

"Sergeant Silver, this is Bensn."

"Yes, what ... the ... fuck ... do ... you ... WANT ... Bensn?" The words were stretched out to emphasize Silver's exasperation with the Sker navigator. "I'm kinda busy, *Bensn*." The Sker was watching the trajectory, and his fingers were flying on the console in front of him.

"I believe you also will miss the block by about twelve feet."

"Fuck the block." This surprised Bensn. He had never considered any other scenario than that of Silver attempting to reach the block and save the station.

"Sergeant, if we don't clear the block, we will miss the tack. If we miss the tack, all is lost."

"Fuck the fucking block, asshole! I've got a man out there. That's what matters now." On the monitor it all seemed so calm and orderly. One space-suited figure drifting softly away as another slowly headed toward him. The station was seemingly motionless in the moment, hanging there as a backdrop. The blackness surrounded everything. Lieutenant Bensn had taken the moment to recalculate.

"Sergeant, my calculations indicate that," and now Bensn was holding the mike key open so Silver could not interrupt him, "if the block is not cleared in just under four minutes, the tack will come too late to shield us from the shock wave." He continued to hold the mike open. "That will be devastating to the systems of the station and will imperil all of us." The mike remained open, the squelching irritatingly loud in everyone's ears. "Sergeant Silver?" Bensn released the mike to allow Silver's response. The connection was dead. "Sergeant Silver, come in." Nothing. "Sergeant Silver? Come in." Nothing. It was dead. Severed from the other end. It was clear that Silver had turned his radio off. All eyes turned to the monitors.

The two figures were converging. Bensn's eyes narrowed, and for once his hands were off the keyboards. *There is nothing I can do.* Silver reached Smith. Bensn looked at the digital chronometer, less than two minutes and forty-five seconds (2:45) left. There was some tumbling of the two figures, and then Smith and Silver were heading back to the station. *What is happening? He can't be doing that.* Then it became obvious what was intended. Silver was building up some momentum and then propelled Smith toward the station and was now hanging back. *He's staying out there.* Now Silver was slowly moving off in the direction of the block. "How is he doing that, Lieutenant?" Bensn swiveled toward the female officer who assisted him. She was a Sker. Clean, clear-headed, all in white. Her eyes blinked. Bensn could see the quizzical, but unworried look.

"I believe he has punctured his suit and is using the outgas as a propellant."

"What!?" Repoul Bensn was shocked. This maneuver was nowhere in the manual.

John Hanson Silver was freezing cold. His suit's pressure was depleted, and some functions were now shutting down. He was in a slow drift toward the hypo-block assembly. He still had about a hundred yards to go. He looked at the chronometer projection on his inner face shield. 1:43 left. His teeth were chattering. *Jesus God Almighty! This is too fucking slow!* Back at the station Bensn was watching the countdown. He knew there were more than three hundred thousand people, perhaps the last of the race, who were depending on what Silver was up to. On the Moon they were all huddled in the temporary shelter of the tunnels, overtaxing the life support, no long-term capacity capable of sustaining them. Without SkyKing they were all dead.

"We have a line on Smith. We'll get him in ahead of the wave."

"SkyKing to Sergeant Silver." Silver had turned his radio back on, volume on the lowest setting. Bensn could see the suit's readings. "Smith is safe." Silver was now closer to the block, but he had miscalculated. He was staring at the block, just out of reach. Bensn looked up from his now frantic calculations. Forty-five seconds left. Silver would miss by about seven feet. His suit telemetry indicated system shutdown in about twenty-five seconds.

Silver saw it. It made him laugh. For all of the Skers' great technology and science, there it was. He looked at the small, fragile trimming device. To set it free would only take the smallest yank on the line. It had twisted over an entry ratchet in the oldest malfunction known to sailing. A fouled lead. A small tug on the line and it was free. The hydraulics could not free it because they were designed for the other, working end of the winch system. All its strength went in the other direction. This would have seemed impossible to the Skers with their micro-system expertise. But anyone who had ever held a tiller on the high seas knew that the command, "Ready about!" always caused the crew to clear the blocks and lines before the tack. Silver laughed again as he unlatched his helmet.

"Sergeant! No!" Bensn's call was at the highest volume, but Silver never heard it. His helmet drifted effortlessly toward the block. Long John Hanson Silver was beyond all help. His body exposed to space, his suit was slowly turning. The helmet struck the lead just below the block. Bensn forced himself to focus on the console, telemetry was active, the line was free, the block activated. The station began to alter course slowly into the solar wind. Bensn looked at the chronometer: 3.5 seconds. *Time to spare, John.*

"Lieutenant, Smith is in the station. All secure."

"Engaging now. Stand by." Through the window Bensn could see the far edge of the Moon coming into view as the sails moved out of the way. In the dead silence of space – the Sker equipment and technology was perfectly efficient – fifty winches and forty miles of micro-thin lines and the vast sails synchronized as the mainsail and the genoa trimmed, and the spinnaker crew prepared to tack. While no one could really feel it, there was a sensation of the station surging ahead. Like a ship of old on the high, spirited seas, they were heading for a safe harbor before the storm.

<<*Did you see that, Farson?*>>

<<*Yes, I did, Handy.*>>

<<*Are you going to save him?*>>

<<You are slipping, Handy. I'm a little disappointed in you.>>

The intercom beeped.

"Report, Lieutenant." It was Voul, from his quarters where he had been closely following events.

"All is well. Steady as she goes, Captain." Voul toggled a switch, and the monitor changed views. Viera was smiling at him across the gulf between SkyKing and the Moon.

"Are you going to make it, Voul?" She was so beautiful to Voul. Even in the midst of the emergency, he loved to look at her. He loved her. He wanted to hold her. Events between them were confusing him. Now was not a time for divided attention.

"I think so. Bensn is our best. It's going to be close. We'll be in the penumbra in time, but our simulations predict a warping gravitational effect of the shock wave around the irregular curve of the Moon and its craters. We're still going to feel it. Plus, because of our speed, we may have to tack again to synchronize directionally with the Moon at the last minute. Otherwise, we might weather the shock wave – with damage – and then be drifting perpendicularly away from the Moon, unable to rejoin. These are all difficult things to do, Viera. We'll have to begin the second tack successfully in about two hours, and that will determine much. Before today we've never done this tack even once. Simulations indicate that to accomplish a full about requires time. If we miss the slot by anything more than ten minutes, it will be bad. I don't know how we've done what we've done so far."

"That's why you've got my boys up there with you," said Viera. "They're strong, they're smart, and they've done their homework. You built the plan, and they'll execute it." Viera's face showed absolute conviction.

"They are also very brave, Viera." Voul had just been briefed on Silver's heroic action and his death in space. He looked at Viera, and knew she was unaware of the tragedy. He did not want to say what he knew he would say next.

"There has been a casualty, Viera." He saw her wry smile, and the slight shake of her head. Viera was full of appreciation for the honesty Voul was showing. For his courage, too.

"If you mean, John Silver, Voul, he is here on the Moon with us. He appeared out of nowhere. We thought he was dead, too. He thought he was dead. But he's here." Voul was shocked and then relieved beyond what he would have thought. John Silver's demeanor was always abrasive and annoying, but the way he threw his life away without fear or hesitation to save everyone else was truly heroic. How could he be alive? "We think it was Farson. What do you think?"

"What else could it be? He took his helmet off."

"Yes, he did, Voul, and I have already written him up for that breach of protocol." She smiled and waved gamely at Voul as the monitor faded out. Voul was still relishing the news of Silver's being alive, and then as Viera faded out, his heart began to ache for her all over again.

<<It's a good thing you threw the helmet quickly, John. There's only so much I can do in a nanosecond or two.>>

<<Farson, thanks for doing that. It never occurred to me that you were there.>>

<<I am always there, John. You were magnificent. Who knew that such a beast of decadence and vulgarity could be so wonderfully unselfish?>>

<<Now you're pissin' me off, Farson. What the fuck did you expect? Of course, I would do that. I am human after all!>>

<<Yes, you are, John. Yes, you are.>>

Bensn was watching the Moon slowly drift toward them from leeward, now looming over them, as the successful weathering up took effect. They were a little behind schedule, but the plan had been aggressively conservative. Bensn and the Skers had calculated and recalculated the tack once they were within the penumbra, and the result was always the same. It couldn't be done in the time allowed. They had made adjustments to get SkyKing into position sooner, giving the crew longer to do the tack. He had unfurled the royal topgallants and calculated winging the new genoa as the station crossed the point of wind. Still it was going to take three hours and twelve minutes if there were no problems. What would ten minutes of the shock wave's warping turbulence surging over them from the Moon's edge do to SkyKing's fragile solar sailing capabilities, its rigs, and spars? Even with full retraction, there would still be damage. Bensn was still recalculating that scenario and the final course settings. The Moon was at 036 degrees. SkyKing would round to 033 and then stiffen up to come to 040 in about ten hours. The Moon would still be a little faster. Could SkyKing speed it up enough? Could the crew of Skers and MoonBasers do it in time? How and where could the damage be minimized? How much could be saved by more precision in the calculations? Or lost by a wrong one?

Bensn was worried. He knew the situation was more dangerous than others thought it was. No one could be sure what would happen. What if the sails were smashed, but the station made it through the penumbra only to drift away into space with everyone else marooned on the Moon? Starvation. Loss of life support. Slow death in lonely defeat. Bensn himself was drifting away, lost in his thoughts. It was uncharacteristic for him, but, in the end, Skers were still human. If Silver were in the control room, he would be screaming at Bensn. "Hey, asshole! What in God's name are you doing? Get your ass in gear! You give me that stuff." Silver would have grabbed the sheets of calculations. "I wanna know what the hell's goin' on! And right now!" Bensn would have jumped to his feet, squaring off, looking into Silver's dark, impenetrable eyes. Their faces would almost be touching. Bensn always thought that Silver would smell bad up close. Silver's fiery breath would be in his face. His gigantic hand would probably grab a clutch of Bensn's white shirt at the neck, and he would shake the Sker lieutenant into compliance.

The other six Skers in the control room were watching Bensn slumped at his console. Bensn became aware of their attention. Their concern. He straightened up in his chair and returned to his work with a shrug. The other Skers continued to watch Bensn for a moment. They had all known each other for years. They had all seen the indefatigable, and famous Bensn never waver, never show emotion. Skers all knew that beneath their discipline and rigor they did feel things, perhaps even more than most. The Sker culture was controlled and predictable. Bensn's lapse at his console and the shrug of his shoulders were unheard of. A sea change. If they had been able to share Bensn's inner feeling, they would have known that the change was profound indeed. Silver's brash, crude nature, and his unselfish death that saved them all had reached into Bensn's soul. The tears that filled Bensn's eyes, and that blurred his view of the Moon as it began to shield the station from the coming unknown, would not stop. Bensn didn't seem able to stop it.

"What the fuck is wrong with you, Skyboy? Shouldn't you be calculatin' or something, instead of sitting there playing with yourself and getting all misty-eyed and shit?" Bensn whipped around in his chair upon hearing Silver's booming voice. He was standing in the door. "Jesus H. Christ, boy. You'd think you missed me or something." Silver walked to Bensn's chair and put his hand on the Sker's shoulder. Repoul glanced at the hand, the rare actual contact with a non-Sker, and noticed a faint hue of purple. Long John Silver smiled at him. "You'd THINK. But we know different, right, shithead?"

The Moon's penumbra, the cone of protection it cast in front of its path, represented theoretical safety from the coming shock wave set off by the ScreenMasters' "Patch" of the Rent around the Earth, now placed in stasis. Good Old Earth, now changed irrevocably, had set off a cataclysm of events resulting in devastating changes. The Moon was orphaned. The space station was cast adrift now desperately trying to avoid being rammed by the Moon or crushed by the shock wave, or, worse, just drifting away into wounded and helpless oblivion. The people of Earth, once alive and thriving, were now in stasis and reduced to a coma of timelessness where the smallest activity was measured in hundreds of years. The inhabitants of SkyKing and the Moon were the only remaining, fully alive human beings: sparse remnants to be sure. Perhaps the sole survivors of the race.

These hardy few had inherited the whirlwinds of history, and the storm was bearing down with a fearful vengeance.

"Do you understand my calculations and projections?" Bensn was speaking to Corporal Benjamin Franklin Smith. Bensn knew that Smith was the MoonBasers' third-in-command after Silver. Smith had come directly to the command after removing his suit. When he had first appeared, everyone had just witnessed his amazing rescue and the death of John Silver. He was to be Silver's replacement, but, with John Silver's miraculous return, that was all changed now. Smith was young, knowledgeable, and always followed orders without hesitation. He was no John Silver. Bensn looked up at Silver. Silver laughed out loud.

"Now I don't look half bad to you, is that it? Well, you're going to like Benjy, too." Silver began to leave the control room, with his signature guffaw. "Benjy, watch out for Bensn." Silver was laughing at his own exaggerated pronunciation of the alliteration. "He's a real mother fucking cocksucker." This made him laugh even louder. "But he knows his shit almost as well as you do." This barrage of vintage Silver profanity and laughter echoed in the hall as he made his way out of the compartment. Bensn could still hear him long after the door closed behind him. Somehow, it didn't bother him in the least.

Smith responded to Bensn's question without missing a beat. "Well, I see what you are doing, but you're going to have to help me with this final vectoring. It seems we are cutting it awfully close." Bensn looked at Corporal Smith. They were in silent mutual contemplation for a tick or two of the ship's clock. Thinking. Bensn was surprised at the young man's concentration, perspicacity, and grasp of the situation.

"Any ideas, Corporal?"

"Hmmm. I think I know how we can do it, Lieutenant." Bensn crinkled his forehead. The other Skers took note of this display of emotion by Bensn. Things were changing. "First, we dip jibe as we come round the Moon, right?"

"Correct. We are in the process of doing it now," answered Bensn.

"Then, as we round up, we shift the sails to close haul, right?"

"Correct."

"Then we have to try to hold our relative position and slow down at the same time, if we can, right?" Again, Bensn assented. Smith was on a roll, his confidence expanding. "Then, there are two problems: getting the sails shifted quickly enough, and getting to the right place at just the right time, at the right speed. Correct?" Again the nod, but slower now, more thoughtful as though new ideas were emerging. "Then, when we jibe, why not just shift the station instead of the sails? Then we can just drop the sails, and slow our momentum with the retros. With the sails down, but unstowed, the situation should be manageable and the station much more maneuverable. The shock wave will pass around us. We'll be safer and in position sooner, with more time to prepare. We will basically have changed direction with one-tenth of the effort." Bensn was thinking. Smith didn't know that he had just fulfilled another Sker prophecy, "A stranger to our ways will know." Smith's way would save at least one full tack and hours of effort but with uncertain results.

"The sails unstowed?" Bensn already knew the answer and why no Sker had thought of it.

"It's what we call in the mines a 'bail and rail.' You sacrifice the equipment to save the crew. So, the sails will be damaged, but the station will be far, far better off."

The conversation became more heated after that. Things like arranging for crews to detach and handle the sails, synchronizing the movement of the station, and the stowing of the spinnaker became a priority. Smith felt there would be no time or personnel to do it, but the Skers were adamant. They talked about practice drills and started looking for volunteers for the exterior assignments. Smith said, "If you insist on attempting to stow the spinnaker, it could cost lives." Bensn looked at him sternly.

"To us, mobility and independence are life. We will need the sails after the shock wave." Smith looked back at Bensn. The wheels of his mind were churning.

"What if we ram-stowed the sail in a forward compartment with auxiliary winches? What's the most forward compartment?"

"Near Commander Peterson's family quarters there is a companionway that runs the distance between the whorls. It is the longest on the station."

"Then let's try that. The sails will at least be inside, and it'll be better than leaving them outside, right?" Obviously,

Smith was not aware of the Sker tradition of meticulously and ceremonially stowing the sails. Bensn was thinking it over.

"Maybe." Bensn's response was not all that enthusiastic. The sacred flaking of the sails was a ceremony so cherished that this compromise would cause problems among the Skers, but Bensn knew Voul would support it and that would make it all right.

"God Almighty, Bensn, this is an emergency. Maybe? What other choice do we fucking have?" The typical MoonBaser dialect was emerging.

"Contain yourself, Corporal. These are matters of some theological weight as well as emergency issues."

After this exchange, Bensn and his Sker team turned to the mathematics of the new plan. *Any port in a storm* was a thought that Bensn held on to. That, plus hope and a prayer.

106. Farson Wants to Have Dinner

Voul and Viera were thinking about each other. He was in his study, his father's books neatly stacked in front of him. He had been searching through the pages for permission to feel the way he felt. Viera was directing mining operations deep under the huge Copernicus crater. More accurately, they were mining the smaller Pytheas impact crater, inside Copernicus, which was a rich lode indeed. Her presence had come as a surprise to the miners. She had a broad smile from all the banter they were throwing at her. "Why didn't you say you were going down on us? We'd have been ready!"

"It's dark down here, Commander, But, don't be afraid. We'll hold you." To Viera, the men and women who operated the shafts were the best: happy, good-natured, hardworking, and hard playing. The anti-fraternization rules were cast aside long ago. The crew loved Viera as a woman and as the best commander they could have, and the fairest manager any of them had ever known. Her style had won them over. She was one of them.

In her own way Viera, too, was seeking permission to feel the way she felt about Voul. How would her crew feel? Would they feel betrayed because she had fallen in love with not just a Sker, but the king of the Skers?

It was a tough time for both Viera and Voul, except for the fact that it was also indescribably wonderful and exciting to be in love with each other. When they were together, their minds together, what they shared was not to be denied, not to be forsaken for any reason: ever in life. *And beyond.* She was startled at the thought's clarity and wondered, for a moment, if she had actually spoken it aloud.

This particular moment, for Farson, was almost a personal stasis period in which all was readying. He could feel her every move, her breath on his neck. With them, there was always this moment in their lovemaking when, not pausing, but pacing with each other, catching up, slowing down, synchronizing, they neared a perfect result, not an end. It was a time of sheer delight. All was well. All was as it should be. Everything was going to be perfect. Together they could drift along in this dreamy moment of ecstasy for quite a while, as they were now. *But not forever.* <<*It's so perfect, Farson. You are so close.*>> He could feel her eyelashes. The mental and physical messages came unmistakably to Farson.

<<*Yes, it is, Kari. Or should I say, 'Sitwory'?*>>

<<*Oh, Routier, now would be a good time to stop talking.*>>

Afterwards, they stayed in bed for a time. It was a soft bed, a feather bed, in North Conway. It was snowing outside. The reports said it could be the biggest storm of the winter on top of a heavy snowfall year. <<*Farson?*>> Karina's mental voice was clear and distinct in the quiet of Farson's mind,

<<*What are you thinking about?*>> Farson, for once was not far off, but rather he was right beside her.

<<*I was thinking that I feel like cooking. Something really nice. A paella, perhaps.*>> It was a Spanish dish that in the past had been a disaster for Farson, but one that he could cook, sometimes brilliantly, sometimes just okay. Then there was that one other time. Karina switched to speech, as she rose up on her elbow to look at Farson.

"Are you sure? Paella?" Karina remembered his embarrassment that day.

"Okay, that last one was awful, I admit. But I can do it. Being a ScreenMaster has some advantages, you know." They both thought that was funny. As though being a ScreenMaster finally meant that Farson could cook as well as he always thought he could. "But who to invite?" Now this really made Karina laugh, because while this discussion was always interesting, she knew the decisions had already been made. Paella means at least eight people, and Farson knew exactly who they would be. Farson's ScreenMaster advantages over her were not so daunting now. Karina had most of the ScreenMasters' skills, too, thanks to Farson, and they were growing stronger in her every day.

Karina offered a "suggested" guest list, just to continue the conversation. "How about Voul and Viera, you and me, of course, Commander Peterson and Brittany, Handy and Uvo?" Farson was happy about everyone, except for the last two.

"Leave Uvo out of it. I thought about Sortt, but that's premature. Invite ZZ<<Arkol25609. He can be a lot of fun sometimes, you know." ZZ<< was, as always, strobing silently, nearby Farson. "ZZ<<, you like paella, right?" The robot seemed to wake up at the sound of his name, his strobing increased slightly. and the vague purple and gold hue that always surrounded his metallic presence intensified.

<<I do like to analyze the flavors and consistencies of this traditional Spanish field dish, but I must say I haven’t eaten in years. What would be the point, Farson? Those systems would need rebooting at this point; others would have to go off-line. There are trade-offs in my capability structures. So, I’ll pass. May I ask a question, Farson?>>

<<Go ahead.>>

<<Are you expecting trouble?>>

<<Yes, of course.>>

<<Then I will follow normal protocols.>> Karina had followed the mental exchange closely. She looked at Farson.

“Trouble?” Farson smiled. He was thinking of the rice cooking over the stove’s fire and then transferring it to the preheated oven at just the right moment. Too soon, and the rice would be hard and crunchy. Too late, and it could burn badly, like a used ashtray at the bottom of the paella pan during the long oven phase of the dish.

“Well, trouble comes in many forms, Karina. I’m worried about burning the rice. Let’s let ZZ<<Arkol25609 worry about the other stuff.” The robot’s strobing was somewhat irregular. Farson knew this meant he was traveling on The Screen.

<<Farson, why am I not invited?>> Uvo’s question came swift and sure.

<<Because your appearance would be unsettling to them all, except, of course, to ZZ<<Arkol25609 and Karina.>>

<<Not to you, Farson?>>

<<Uvo, you’re so insecure.>>

“ZZ<<Arkol25609, would you please invite everyone for about eight o’clock tonight? Apologize for the short notice. I know they’ll understand.” ZZ<< bowed his head slightly as if to his king and in a brightening gold and purple glow, he dematerialized.

<<*Invite, Farson? You are trying to be witty, aren't you?*>>
<<*I know you enjoy a good laugh, Handy.*>>

They all asked the same question. "How do we get there?" They all got the same answer. "Be ready at 8:00 p.m. precisely. You will not need to clear your schedule. It will be a leisurely dinner, informal attire. The ScreenMaster doesn't want to take you from your duties, but he does want you to enjoy yourselves. Dress for warmth. The local temperature is eight degrees Fahrenheit, and a heavy snow is falling. You will be going to North Conway, New Hampshire. You will be briefly out of touch, perhaps for no more than a few seconds in real time. If anything important happens, Farson Uiost will know, and he will tell you. Be prepared."

<<*Farson?*>>
<<*Yes, Twill?*>>
<<*Why have you done this to me?*>>
<<*I will give you a hint, Twill.*>>
<<*Is it a good one?*>>
<<*It's a good one.*>>
<<*Go ahead, Farson.*>>
<<*Think of it as a level. Try to surmount it.*>>
<<*It's a test, Farson? Is that what it is?*>>
<<*Twill, I gave you a hint. Get to work.*>>

Farson had the menu planned in detail, and Karina was suspicious. Chorizos, lobsters, shrimp, mussels, clams, chicken, partially cooked rice, saffron, all together in a single pan. It was the fastidious way Farson tended to do everything, making sure everything was just right. "It's like the last supper, Farson. Why so cautious?" Farson looked up from his studying of the recipe.

"Karina, there could be a few surprises tonight." Karina was scrunching her eyebrows.

"What? Something I don't know about?"

"Maybe even something I don't know about."

He then returned to the recipe's description of how to time the rice with the raw ingredients.

107. The Dinner Party

Everyone was in the cabin by 8:00 p.m. sharp. ZZ<<Arkol25609 had arranged it. Jim Peterson and Brittany were looking out the window at the falling snow. Karina and Farson were making drinks for everyone, and Voul and Viera were sitting by the fire in a warm silence. ZZ<<Arkol was actually in the room as any other guest would be, instead of assuming his usual silent, stoic strobing mode in a secure corner. The room was full of wonderful bubbling paella smells, and it was a warmly lit room with soft yellow light. The room was large enough for twice as many people with extra-soft chairs and sofas. It was definitely very cozy.

Karina seemed a little worried. "I wonder why Handy is not here yet?" Farson laughed softly.

"Karina, Handy marches to his own drummer – really, to his own band. Don't worry about him." She nodded slightly in acknowledgment as she was remixing the sangria to make it a little fruitier. The sound of her wooden spoon pushing the ice against the glass pitcher filled the silence.

<<*He actually is here, isn't he, Farson?*>>

<<*Yes and no, Karina.*>>

<<*Where is he?*>>

<<Can't you guess?>>

As dinner neared, everyone was settling in around the fire, on couches and chairs. ZZ<<Arkol25609 continued to stand, but his carriage was less tense, and he seemed, in his own way, to be relaxing. Voul had been talking to Brittany, and ordinarily Voul, whose strict esthetic nature would have him naturally hanging back somewhat in social situations, now found that he was sitting very close to Viera pressing in warmly beside her. He was actually resting his hand on hers. Viera was happily talking to her friend, Jim Peterson, and conversation was soft and intimate. Karina and Farson were talking in the kitchen as Farson pulled the bubbling and aromatic paella from the oven. It was as though everyone had decided that this suspension of reality was perfectly okay. For these passengers and crew of SkyKing and the Moon, the life-and-death struggle was far, far away. For Voul and Viera the danger to their respective worlds was in abeyance for now. For Farson and Karina, all was as it must be. She whispered in his ear.

"When are you going to tell them, Farson?"

"Tell them what, Kari?" he said softly.

"That Earth is not what they think it is."

<<Careful how you answer, Farson. I am listening.>>

<<That's good, Twill. And you ARE getting better.>> Then he spoke out loud. "They already know."

<<Farson! You can't be serious.>> Twill's thought invaded Farson's mind like a harsh wind.

<<Twill, what are you thinking? These are human beings. Of course they know. What else could possibly be true?>>

Karina's gentle thoughts pervaded everyone else's. *<<Farson's right, Twill. I already knew.>>*

<<*He told you.*>>

<<*No, he didn't.*>>

<<*Then why did you ask when he's going to tell them?*>>

<<*Hey, I'm human. It's the way we start conversations sometimes. Asking questions that we already know the answer to. That is perfectly normal for us.*>>

<<*You are not exactly normal anymore, Karina. Farson took care of that.*>> Farson and Karina looked at each other and smiled happily.

They continued to prepare the meal. Farson noticed that she was a little tense from the exchange, and he took her hand momentarily, warmly. She relaxed and turned back to the wine, knowing things were as they must be.

Voul was thinking about what was happening in the little cabin in North Conway. Everyone had been brought here by ZZ<<Arkol25609 instantly and would be sent back within a few seconds of leaving. So, everything: The cocktail hour, the dinner, the inevitable discussion would all take place in less than a few seconds of real time. Voul recognized that this meant that Farson not only could move around in time, he could also control it, or perhaps, more accurately, he could change it. Farson seemed to be able to do anything he wanted to do with time. Voul had noticed that Farson and Karina had been engaged mentally for a few moments, so he assumed that there were other ScreenMasters watching but not present. He wondered why and what was going on. <<*Voul, they cannot join us in this place. It's beyond them. All they can do is monitor from out on The Screen. They are trying to interfere and would if they could.*>> No response was needed to Farson's communication. Voul was never going to get used to the feeling of it so deep in his mind, even though Skers were naturally telepathic in some ways. He appreciated Farson's willingness to communicate, his wonderful openness, but he wondered if it would really all work out. His world, SkyKing, was nearing disaster or, perhaps, liberation. MoonBase was safe physically from destruction but logistically in deep trouble without SkyKing. Then there was Viera and him. Love so deep on his part that the thought of living without her was impossible to even consider, and yet she was so different. They paralleled the differences of MoonBase and SkyKing, and those differences brought the entire situation into focus for Voul. Viera was sitting beside him. "What are you thinking about, Voul?" she asked gently.

"Probably the same things you are, Viera. It is nice to be here, isn't it? We know nothing significant is going to happen while we are gone, that we're not missing anything or ignoring our duty. For a moment, we are free to relax and enjoy a snowy evening on Earth. It's amazing, really."

"Yes," she said, "it is," and hooked her arm through his as their thoughts also joined together.

Farson continued the conversation even as he was bustling around preparing the main dish of the evening for serving. "You know, Kari, if I had been a ScreenMaster last time, the 'Paella Disaster' would never have happened."

"Why do you say that, Farson? Your skills as a chef are renowned." She was smiling as she said it.

"Well, when it came out burned in the bottom of the pan, I could have made a quick time adjustment and then pulled it out at the right time, before that happened."

"Wouldn't that have changed other things too, Farson? Like the way I tried to make you feel better, after the party was over?" Farson was remembering that moment enthusiastically.

"No, because, as you know, I can adjust nanoseconds and then sort of flare the small changes back into the final outcome."

"You are a true virtuoso," she said sarcastically. "It wouldn't be exactly the same, would it? Because, while all of the guests had a wonderful meal, paella at its best, you had to eat the small burned portion, and act like it was still the greatest thing in the world. You even had seconds. It was smart of you to get everything out of the pan so quickly." She smiled, content with her interpretation.

"Don't you see," he said, "if everything had been perfect at dinner, things would have been *even better* afterwards." Farson was considering Karina's theory that any change would change everything, working back through those moments looking for proof for his point of view. He could sense where the mistake was made and was toying with another slight adjustment, when Karina frowned at him disapprovingly. Then another intruded.

<<*Farson, how do you do that?*>>

<<*For me to know, Twill, and for you to find out.*>>

<<*Well, I know that you have created some kind of a barrier around you and it's like a mind-baffle to the rest of us. You seem to have localized a similar effect to what we've done to Earth. There is a little hole in time and space around you. We are circling around it. None of us can penetrate it.*>>

<<*Keep trying, Twill. You seem to have learned to communicate through it. To answer your questions I will give you one more hint. This one will hurt.*>> Twill recoiled with that thought. Farson was so powerful. A warning like that was to be taken seriously.

<<*How can I prepare?*>>

<<*Sorry, Twill, if you want your answer it's just going to hurt. Relax and get ready. No pain no gain, as they say. Try to*

isolate one or two of the effects.>> Suddenly, Twill's mind and soul and being were assaulted by thoughts so huge and enormous, so loud and cacophonous, so deep and wide, so sharp and pounding that he lost all sense of normal consciousness. Like a gunner who no longer hears the blasting of his guns, Twill began to float on the overwhelming agony and confusion. He was numbing inside the excruciating pain and barely able to focus. He heard a baby cry, and someone asking to change the channels. He heard a man saying, "Fire, fire!" And many other anomalous phrases. He heard someone laughing, and he heard someone die. Then, just as quickly, the sound was gone, and he was floating in his room again, his elegantly gimbaled chair attempting to straighten him up. He was unconscious and staying that way. He felt like he was nearing death.

Farson came walking out of the kitchen carrying a large platter of perfectly done paella and said, "Let's eat!" Everyone was gathered around the table ready to begin.

<<*What was that, Farson?*>> Uvo's thoughts came along with the main dish.

<<*What do you think it was, Uvo?*>>

<<*Your games tire me, Farson. I think it was Earth.*>>

<<*You THINK, Uvo? Or do you know?*>>

<<*I know. It wasn't necessary to kill Twill.*>>

<<*If he dies, Uvo, it's his own fault. He will live, this time. You're correct. It wasn't necessary. But it was still the right thing to do.*>>

"Delicious," said Karina. "Farson, this has that special taste to it. You know, when it's just perfect?"

"Thank you, Kari," he said with some pride, "when I take my time – all the time I need – things generally turn out better." That made them both laugh.

The Petersons were enjoying their dinner, and Voul and Viera were well into their salads. All was well. Farson turned to the robot. ZZ<< was looking at him.

<<*The truth will set Earth free.*>>

<<*As you say, ScreenMaster Uiost.*>>

<<*You are not in communication with the others?*>>

<<*Correct.*>>

<<*I have nothing to worry about regarding you?*>>

<<*I have been assigned to you from the beginning. Nothing has changed.*>>

<<*Will I know if it does?*>>

<<*You will be the first to know.*>>

<<*Is that going to happen?*>>

<<*There are some possibilities, but I doubt it. You and I will see this through, most likely.*>>

<<*Good.*>> Farson liked the robot, and had from that first moment. In fact, wherever ZZ<<Arkol25609 had been away, he missed him. The robot's presence was reassuring. <<*It's hard to imagine that there are 25,608 others like you.*>>

<<*I am a middle construct. The manufacturing did not stop with me, ScreenMaster Uiost. There are many, many more than that.*>>

<<*But you are special, right?*>>

<<*I am assigned to you. That makes my 'mission' special, as you put it.*>>

<<*What are all of the others doing?*>>

<<*Are you sure you want to know?*>>

<<*Tell me.*>>

<<*They are standing guard in preparation. Waiting for what you know is coming.*>>

<<*What were they doing before my Ascension?*>>

<<*You use the word 'before' as though you are unaware of time's complexity. How can I answer a question based on a word that has so many meanings?*>>

<<*Can you answer the question directionally?*>>

<<*Do you mean 'in general' or do you mean that I should combine all of their activities and try to find an 'average' to offer as an explanation?*>> Farson was stumbling trying to keep up with the robot's train of thought. He knew it was going nowhere.

<<*Just forget it.*>>

<<*That is impossible for me to do, ScreenMaster Uiost. My programs are inclusive.*>>

<<*Well, then let's just leave it right there.*>>

<<*Agreed.*>> Farson looked at the robot standing like a statue in the corner. Strobing smoothly, unruffled.

He could stand there forever. Farson was shaking his head in wonder.

Voul looked over at Farson, as though he heard the conversation. Farson knew of Voul's abilities, but to hear a conversation between a ScreenMaster and a ScreenKeeper robot of ZZ<<Arkol25609's caliber was unheard of. Still it seemed to Farson that Voul had "heard" something. "Voul, where were your parents born?" Farson knew Voul had been born on SkyKing.

"Our tradition does not encourage that sort of history. We were all born to be free in space." Farson was thinking, *that's two conversations I've started that ended up going nowhere.*

<<*Nowhere, Farson? I thought you could do anything, whatever you want. That's what I hear.*>> Farson noticed Twill's caution. *He is recovering.*

<<*I wish it were true, Twill.*>>

<<Wish, Farson? I've never heard you use such a word before.>>

"Pass the sangria," said Viera. She was hoping to warm the moment. Farson was enjoying his paella *(perfect)* and took a sip of Kari's well-prepared and delicious sangria. He gave her a warm smile, and quietly, distantly, felt his way through Twill's mind for a spot of recognition. Twill would live. In fact, he had done quite well. What Farson was looking for, what he had been testing for, a sense of remorse, just wasn't there.

Disappointing.

From far away Uvo came the clear following thought, *<<What did you expect?>>*

Farson sent back, *<<Where are you?>>*

<<Farson, I'm preparing. What you are doing is going to have profound effects. Preparations must be made.>>

<<Uvo, yesterday is only as different from today, as is today from tomorrow. Change is the natural order. Don't worry. We are dealing with enormous perpetuity. It just feels like oblivion coming, when really it's only tomorrow, as usual.>>

<<But, Farson, you are ScreenMaster of Earth and now supreme. You are doing things no one else can understand.>>

<<There is still Twill and his aspirations. Then, there is you, Uvo. Wouldn't you say you've grown a lot in our relationship?>>

<<Yes, but ... >>

<<And, then, Uvo, there is Handy. Remember him.>>

<<What exactly is he, Farson?>>

<<He is who he is, who he has always been. Look carefully. It is plain as day.>>

After dinner, Farson stood and offered a toast. "As each of you: Voul, Viera, Jim, and Brittany, as well as you, ZZ<<Arkol25609, and, of course, my sister Karina, return to your duties and your lives, take me with you in your thoughts

and hopes. What happens next will determine much. Whatever happens, remember my dream of a free humanity living to its potential in peace with all, finally at peace with itself. You will learn much in the days to come, but there is one thing you should always remember: Humanity is good, yesterday, today, and tomorrow. The bad came from false beliefs about limits that are now outmoded and will seem foolish to all of you, as they now do to me. Mankind is good, thoroughly and completely good. We have been living in a dream of good and bad, but as Shakespeare said, 'There is nothing either good or bad, but thinking makes it so.' So," standing up, he raised his glass to all, "here's to humanity! Long live mankind!" Everyone stood and joined in the toast, downing their sangria, enjoying the warmth and camaraderie of a moment stolen from time.

<<*I was not the first. I will not be the last. Mankind is forever.*>> Farson's second toast was in their minds as ZZ<<Arkol25609 began a more intense strobing, preparing to transport all parties back to their respective homes and duties and times. Brittany moved over next to Farson and took his hand in hers. Farson looked at her.

"Farson, when you say, 'mankind is forever,' does that mean that SkyKing will survive the shock wave?" Farson tensed his lip, and his brows furrowed slightly.

"Brittany, in these matters there are no guarantees. The free swings of human will and history will go on and on. Voul has planned and trained carefully. Viera's command is in position. All is ready for success. That is all we can ask. Life is to be lived ... not planned to be lived, Brittany. These are amazing times, so go live."

"And die, Farson?" She was still very concerned. Farson remembered the death of her mother, and the years of loneliness and heartache she went through. He knew she was wondering if it could all happen again.

"People die, Brittany. You know that. You have gone on with your life. How was your meal tonight?"

"Great."

"Are you happy here?"

"Yes, very happy. I want to stay here forever."

"If you stay here, life is over, your life. Your life is out there waiting. It's not here. Do you understand?" Brittany was watching Farson's eyes. She felt his thoughts washing through her. She did understand. She felt braver and more certain. She closed her eyes for a moment.

"Yes, I do. I do understand."

Now addressing everyone, he said, "Then, all of you, take this night, this dinner, these feelings and do what you must do."

"Where will you be?" asked Viera, for them all.

<<*I will be with you.*>> These thoughts appeared in all of their minds at once as Farson suddenly disappeared so completely, that they all wondered if he had ever really been there at all. The room was still filled with delicious smells and the memories of their laughter together and the fun they had just had, but now ZZ<<Arkol25609 had already begun transporting them.

The history in the room, of that evening, seemed to go with each of them. No one doubted that Farson would be with them as they faced the challenges ahead. Then they were all instantly back at their previous locations. The people around them seemed not to have noticed. It was as if they had never left.

As Karina was cleaning up around the cabin when ZZ<< Arkol25609 returned. <<*Did you enjoy yourself, ZZ<<?*>>

<<*Well, yes, I did. With Farson's permission I indulged some circuits long dormant, and I did enjoy it, if that word suits your*

meaning.>> ZZ<<Arkol25609 was in a rare mood. He strobed for a moment or two. <<*But, now I must, as we all must, return to duty.*>> Karina could tell that circuits were being switched on and off.

<<*Will you miss it?*>>

<<*Yes and no. I will miss discoursing with Farson.*>>

<<*You are a friend. You know that, ZZ<<?*>>

<<*I appreciate the sentiment, Karina, but no, I am not a friend. I cannot be.*>> With that the robot glowed the golden purple of his transit and left with a soft rustling sound. Karina's inquiry followed the robot. She knew it would catch him. The robot's thought returned. <<*Because The Screen will not permit it, as you well know.*>>

<<*We will see, ZZ<<. You might be surprised.*>> No further exchange occurred and in the silence of the New Hampshire snowstorm, Karina continued with the domestic chores until Farson returned.

<<*The robot was quite talkative tonight. Don't you think?*>>

<<*It must be the recircuiting. He was still his old noble self, though, after you left.*>>

<<*Of course. I noticed that Brittany has reached a point of clarity that surprised me. Somewhat ahead of time.*>> Karina continued with the dishes and cleaning up.

<<*You noticed that, too. She is really something. The future is coming our way.*>>

<<*Well, if you're done doing the dishes, there is one more thing coming our way, Sitwory.*>>

<<*Only one, Farson? You're not going to start boring me now that my wings are spreading, are you?*>>

<<*Routier. My name is Routier. And I will never be boring.*>>

One by one the lights in the little cabin went out until there was only the warm glow of the fireplace, dimly visible from outside through the snow. Not that anyone was watching.

108. It'll Be Something

The shock wave caused by the Earth's disappearance in space was approaching fast. SkyKing was jockeying for the perfect position in the penumbra of the Moon. The crews were in place. The evacuation was complete. Drifting along in space, the station, the Moon, and all the people were ready; there was a quiet spreading everywhere, even as preparations continued. Com links were open between the windward face of the Moon and the afterdeck of SkyKing.

The Moon had extended its sensor tendrils about sixty miles out as an early warning system. It didn't really give them a lot of time or a lot of warning. "It may be some help," Viera said to Voul. "Better than nothing."

When the sensor technicians on the Moon first monitored the increasing pressure that they had been expecting, its power still surprised them. They noticed an anomaly at first, but then they became aware that the pattern of the shock wave was quite different from what they had planned for and had discussed at such length. All the experts felt it would be a radiating pulse traveling at a predicted speed, but what the scopes were showing now was a swirling effect which whipped the sensor tendrils in all directions. It was much stronger than they had predicted.

"We have a force 15 storm now, and it's gathering the closer it comes, as though it is compressing around us." Voul heard this report and for a moment he felt a sense of hopelessness, despair. That was way too strong a force. Things would be destroyed.

"Confirm that again." His order was short and quick with urgency.

"Confirmed. SkyKing may not withstand the impacts and force. It's coming on too quickly." *Impacts.* "We were expecting a rising gale, perhaps even at hurricane force. This is a killer."

"Batten down." This was the anticipated first command once shock wave proximity detection was established; it was a call to general quarters and for all hands to prepare.

"Command to Moon Alpha Station, come in." No answer from the windward face. Then an intermittent and scratchy transmission came through.

"Commander," the fading transmission was barely audible, "the readings here are off the scope."

The technician beside Viera looked at her. Viera looked at Voul's face on the monitor. Then it hit them. Everything went out, things were flying, and the last thing she remembered was an ominous and increasing pressure. It all happened so fast they were just swallowed up.

No Sker – or human being – could have predicted the nature of the shock wave from the ScreenMasters' deletion processors. The physics were incredibly complex. What the processors did and how they did it was a great mystery of The Screen. It was clear, in attempting to repair The Screen, they had to completely erase all cause and effect. It had to be as if it had never happened, and more, as if it could never *have* happened. The wave that hit the Moon was so pervasive that there was no escape. Like trillions of e-lasers and subsequent implosions, the shock wave was clearly destroying the Moon's surface habitat.

As Farson said, "Life is to be lived ... not planned to be lived. These are amazing times." The plan to protect SkyKing had worked better than all planning anticipated. As the wave passed, damage was done, more from Moon debris than the shock wave. The station hiding in the Moon's shadow was saved, but damaged badly. It was several hours before partial power was restored in a few places.

"How many?"

"Hard to tell right now, but I would say there are multiple casualties. It was too quick. We were not prepared for that." Voul was downcast. The room was dark and in ruins. The crew member who had asked the question was covered in dust. What of the people on the Moon, how many there? Of the Skers, how many? *These are awful thoughts.* Voul was in turmoil.

It was much worse than expected. Each death was final, no replacements ever coming. It was not ultimately catastrophic to the station or to the Moon. Both were now limping through space, recovering. MoonBase had over two hundred dead. The Station had fared better with just under fifty dead, mostly on the after whorls and decks. The ram stowing of the sails had worked, but repairs would still take months, if not years. Both the Moon and SkyKing were in shambles, physically and emotionally. The people from SkyKing sheltering in the mines were safe.

<<*Our plans have all come true.*>> Twill was gloating, looking into the emptiness where Earth had been. <<*In the end, you did nothing to stop it. Your plan was a miserable failure. I would have expected something more from All-Mighty Farson Uiost than just standing there and watching it all be destroyed.*>> Twill had seen what Farson wanted him to see.

<<*Twill, you will never learn.*>>

<<*I agree with him, Farson. This does not look good,*>> Uvo's private thoughts were halting and uncertain. <<*What has just happened?*>>

<<*Uvo, we have lost much, it's true. We have also gained much, much more. Be not afraid, my friend.*>>

<<*'Thinking makes it so,' 'ey, Farson?*>>
<<*Exactly, Handy. I couldn't have said it better.*>>

Voul ran to the transporter chambers. It was chaos. People, machines; everything was being pushed out of the way to make room. There was crying and injuries, mayhem. He was going to leave SkyKing to search for Viera in the debris and confusion. His uniform was covered with the dust of the Moon that had come blasting through almost every SkyKing compartment. There was blood on his hot and messy tunic. Skers were everywhere, trying to help straighten things out, bandage the wounded, repair the vast damage. He was crying out in mental torture, reaching out for her with his mind. One of the crew members had opened a communication channel with MoonBase. In the dark and destruction he still scanned for her, yearned for her. Then, there she was on the monitor. Bending over a crew member, silhouetted in the dim light, her hands were covered in red. She saw him on her monitor looking at her. Their eyes met. She shook her head and went back to the task before her. Voul's heart was pounding as he left for the stern of SkyKing and the devastation waiting there. In the midst of ruin and disaster, the pain and anguish, the death all around, he was relieved that she had survived and he was guilty for feeling such elation, for taking the time for such mere personal matters, for knowing that he would have abandoned SkyKing in the midst of its greatest trial to find her.

She was safe. That was enough.

Brittany was just regaining consciousness. Her father was standing up as she opened her eyes. "Dad, are we all right?"

"Yes, yes. We have survived."

"How could we? That was awful." She looked around. The normally perfect order of SkyKing, its pristine cleanliness and shining promise were shattered and scattered in ruin. In disarray. "How could we have survived this?"

Commander Peterson looked at his daughter's face, scratched and bruised, twisted in fear. "I don't know, honey, but we did. That's all that matters. Everything else is just stuff. We can fix it." Brittany looked at her father. His uniform was torn. There was some blood.

"Dad, are you okay?"

Karina had returned to her quarters on SkyKing after Farson had left the cabin. She had been in there when the shock wave struck. She was pinned by a bulwark and strangely not in pain. She could hear people trying to reach her, but it didn't matter. Take your time, she thought. *We've got plenty.* That thought perplexed her. Where did that come from? She waited and waited. A light appeared. Then air streamed in. It was so fresh. She heard voices.

"We are too late," they said. "Look at her. She's dead." Karina tried to move, but nothing happened. Everything was strangely muted and muffled. She tried to look around, toward the light. She smelled a log fire and a felt a winter chill. Her hand was on her chest, and she tried to move it to her face. It was lightly glowing. She tried to look again. In her fingernails there was a faint purple hue. As she watched, it extinguished. "Did you see that?" one of the workers asked. "See what?" another shouted. "Just keep working. Get her out of there." They moved a leverage device into place and pushed down. The wreckage moved. They pulled her free. "Is she dead?"

"Who knows? Let's get her to sick bay."

Voul had reached the command center, and things were just as bad there. "We are spinning," said a crew member, "but we are getting it to slow down." Voul knew that was the first good news. "Keep at it."

109. The Afterwards

The destruction of Earth really did make sense. At least that was the argument put forward. Earth had caused the Rent, and Earth should pay. <<*We did what we had to do. We did it when we had to do it. It worked.*>> The Rent was repaired. The Patch was gone. All was well with The Screen again. Twill had foreseen it all. He was nearing preeminence, even now presiding. Farson was eliminated with the success of their ScreenPatch. There was reason to celebrate. The station, the Moon, and Earth itself were gone. The Screen was whole again. That's what mattered. Earth's dangerous history and nature had been entirely erased. All the ScreenMasters regretted the disturbance, but they were all relieved to be done with it now. All of them except one.

<<*You guys think it's over. Don't you?*>>

<<*No, Handy, we know it's over. It's what we created him for. He did it for us. It's all over. The Earth and Farson are gone and now fading into insignificance.*>>

With this Twill laughed heartily and patted Uvo on the back of his folded wings; the sound of his appendage on the feathers was hollow. Uvo was not laughing. Twill had enjoyed the sensation of the feathers in his tendrils. Uvo shrugged him off.

<<*I had hoped, Twill, that this darkness in which we still reside would be lifted with the end of all of this, as you had said. I had hoped that you would have learned from Farson, as some of us have.*>> Uvo was rustling his feathers back into place.

<<*What's to learn, Uvo? Are we to learn that we are less than all? That with every passing event, our existence and our powers would be lessened or become more and more subservient to the passing salience that we ourselves created ... subservient to Farson Uiost? Are we to learn that with every assault, we are altered and must retreat?*>>

The ScreenMasters on The Screen were listening and watching and silently agreed. Their thoughts were palpable. There was a celebration of sorts reverberating through them all. There was a restored happiness, a wholeness, on The Screen. <<*Uvo, you know. What was, is. What is, always has been. It is what it was, and ever will be. We again are whole. There are no 'layers' anymore. Farson was great, but to a fault. He overstepped. We all knew about what he was going to attempt long before he tried it, and each of us chose to maintain The Screen as it has always been. That's what we have done. There can be no exceptions. You knew it all along. We all did.*>> Uvo was pensive and confused. Farson would have spoken to him at this point, but now there was nothing in his thoughts. Silence. He missed the touch, the reassurance. Uvo looked over at Handy.

<<*Your thoughts, ScreenMaster Townsend?*>> Handy, too, felt the pause in things, the emptiness where Farson should have been.

<<*It seems to be back to normal. I cannot detect anything. And I am looking. The Screen seems secure and very stable.*>>

<<*Seems?*>> Twill's powerful thought drilled through Handy, causing an abrupt sensation. It was like a command more than a question. <<*'Seems,' Handy?*>> Twill was insisting, authoritative. Almost punishing in tone. <<*You played with him, Townsend. You enjoyed it. How foolish do you feel now? And you, Uvo; you were the worst.*>> Handy knew what Twill meant. Uvo had facilitated Farson and helped him. He had encouraged him in his own way, and there would be a

price to pay, perhaps. He looked over at Uvo. Uvo was twisting in his seat, and his screen glow was brightening, Twill's action inexorable. Handy's response was almost a scream.

<<*Twill, this is unnecessary!*>> Twill's attack on Uvo was sanctioned and sudden. Uvo was dissipating. He was in agony. He was being executed in front of them all. Handy thought about Uvo's beautiful mind and his far-reaching abilities. He thought about Uvo's years of leadership and his nurturing nature. Tears streamed down Handy's tortured features as he watched Uvo's excruciation. It was all happening too quickly, so differently than anticipated. Twill was winning, after all. Then Uvo was gone, but his last thought lingered in the air.

<<*Farson, I'm coming.*>>

Twill laughed again. <<*You're not coming, Uvo. You're going. You're dying. All that you were, all that you stood for is dying with you, now. Your plans and your dreams of a different Screen were delusions, and that has taught the rest of us who remain much indeed, Uvo. That is your legacy. Total failure.*>> Uvo was gone.

Twill turned to Handy, again. <<*And, you, Townsend, will fare no better. You are banished to a forgotten time, and place. To us, you are dead as well. Never to be heard from again. Unlike Uvo, whose service earned him a quick result here, yours will languish and have no honor or purpose. Yours is useless, as you deserve. You have never belonged and, unlike Uvo, you will not be missed.*>> As Handy Townsend, the oldest, most senior of all ScreenMasters, began to disappear, Twill was laughing. It was malevolent and final. He moved into Uvo's seat: the new situation, the new order. Twill was settled in. His thoughts were expansive. *Handy, Uvo, Farson, Karina, Earth, Moon, that stupid space station ... it's been a good day.*

The barge, formerly Uvo's, now hanging in black, empty space where Earth used to be, swept in a swift turn, at Twill's command, and departed in a flash of finality. Nothingness was left in its silent, relentless wake. The ScreenMasters were finally gone.

The technology of the ScreenMasters had repaired things. Exactly what they had come to do, they had done. Farson had tried his best, and failed. As Twill had said, it was a good day for the ScreenMasters. Or so it seemed on The Screen.

They all remained within the expanses of the familiarity of The Screen they had always known and resumed normal operations. Twill felt a great contentment. He had been tested and tried, and he had overcome it all. He had watched the destruction of two adversaries with relish and had eliminated a disturbing nuisance. He had achieved his wildest dreams of supremacy. *Sweet vindication.* He had not actually witnessed Farson's end, but his ScreenSense confirmed the result. It made him laugh. <<*For all that, Farson, you were the easiest. So much trouble, all for nothing. I got what I wanted. You got nothing. You thought you were so smart, but in the end, everything you did, everything you sought, it was all for nothing. You make me laugh, Farson. You are nothing in the end.*>>

Twill's thought went out across The Screen. All ScreenMasters heard it. It echoed throughout the omniverse, now Twill's. He waited, somewhat cynically for the reply that always came from Farson in the blink of time. He waited. He waited. It never came. He laughed a deep, cleansing laugh. A last laugh.

Handy was singing:

Things have changed in this old world …
    This old world.

Things have changed in this old world ...
    This old world.
Once things were deadly and things were
    Dyin' ...
Now the world's a peaceful place, and only the
    Babies're cryin'...
Oh, yes, things have changed in this old
    World ...
Things have changed, things have changed.

110. The Flow of The Screen (1) Farson's Teachings. (Excerpted from his log)

Farson and Karina were in a classroom. He was lecturing and she was listening. The four hundred students were fascinated with Farson's topic and, perhaps even more so, with having the two most famous ScreenMasters in the room with them.

"You can look at The Screen for eons and never know the Truth. So many feel it is a given, never shaken, always constant and dependable. I knew right away that that was untrue. It is so dynamic and changing that when you finally see the patterns of The Screen, it changes right in front of you. All we know is prologue, not reality. The Screen is way ahead of us, and that is its incredible power. Earth's fissure – the Rent as they called it – was not damage. It was just natural erosion. In truth Earth's crime was to be part of a visible change they could not control. Earth was the scene of major Screen activity, that's true. Of course. Earth was the site of amazing things constantly, and as I searched for a reason, I found some hints, but they were only walk-ons in a well-plotted scene of colossal and galactic events. Screen geology, if you will. Like glaciers tracking along, Earth's events were preeminently natural. They also revealed much, if you knew what you were looking at. So far we have only seen what happened in the past. The trick is to correctly interpret the future. I was the only one who did that. It drove the ScreenMasters crazy. In the end, their enemy – Earth and its 'horrible' people – were the saviors of them all. I saved Earth, and, most importantly, its people. Humanity was the ultimate cure, not the disease."

This truth always made Karina laugh. She couldn't control herself. The rest of the class joined in and laughed, too, infected by her. Farson was watching it all.

"You see? Her frivolity, her humanity was the one thing that has always made sense to me. Her irreverent joy in the face of so much gloom spoke volumes of what we, yes we, are all about. From the very beginning, she wanted life to resume, to flourish. She wanted change and lots of it. The other ScreenMasters just could not keep up with her. I knew she was only the first. Thinking about that inspired me. Being with her is life for me."

Now they were both laughing. The students were smiling, knowing they were part of something special. The freshman seminar that they had signed up for held that promise. It had just delivered.

"Technology doesn't really do it in the end. It is nature, exemplified by The Screen, that is truly amazing. Nature generously hints at us, almost to the point of total laughability when suddenly you realize how obvious it all is. Karina always knew this from the beginnings of our relationship and in her intuitive comprehension of The Screen. Our voyages on The Ship proved it.

"The bad news is that from the point of view of maintaining status quo, humanity is almost too malleable. Because every time we touch, or kiss, or whatever, we introduce infinite possibilities, changes never ending; as we interact, we change everything with every thought. Boy meets girl, and everything changes. Human procreation is beyond the pale of prediction. It is so random, so invasive and circumventing, and almost devious, that it remains to be seen what really happens when something like that happens. People are so naturally complex, so intricately intersticed that there is seemingly no way to predict anything, really. Aside from humanity's adaptability – its incredibly flexible versatility, its unfailing determination to survive and be free – it is this element, this faceting reproductive approach, that gives us immunity to the vicissitudes of events and to the notion of fate. Humanity is truly alone in this. We are so complex in our combining that we move through change swiftly and seamlessly. Normality – status quo – for us *is* change. We accumulate vast experience and intricate knowledge so naturally and easily that there is no question that in an essential and cellular way, we advance farther, faster, and more thoroughly than any other race ever even imagined. That is our secret. Now the secret has to find new places to hide. This hiding is not a good thing, except for one reason: Winning is impossible. While others figure that out, it will give us precious time."

The class was taking notes, but the test had already begun.

111. MoonBase and SkyKing

Time is the greatest healer, mostly because it keeps moving along, and people must focus on things at hand. Sometimes people linger in the past, but with the way things are, with the way things always have been, looking backwards doesn't work for long. It's hard to drive one's way through life in reverse. So, in the end, with the Rent patched, SkyKing and MoonBase went off on their way, and the ScreenMasters went theirs. It was as though there was an intransigent schema that was playing out on The Screen, and no one could stop it.

The repairs on MoonBase and SkyKing were completely engrossing and all-consuming for all hands on that side of things. Twill's giddy assumption of preeminence was far and away enough for him after playing second fiddle for so long. In his dealings with the other ScreenMasters, he felt he was magnanimous and forgiving, but those around him saw the flaws of aloofness, arrogance, and self-righteousness. The memories of Farson's way remained strong. Going their separate ways, humanity and the ScreenMasters were both moving on to other things, other places. The battles were over.

Babies were born, families formed, and, in just three years, the now-combined world of SkyKing and MoonBase had seen a sizable increase in population, perhaps in celebration. The issues of education and farming were paramount now, and research into the new capabilities of the new union with the Moon occupied the Skers in their planning for the future. Their obsession with "walking among the stars" had dimmed somewhat after the "Flight into the Penumbra," as they called the escape from the storm's full fury. The damage and death, the injuries, and the uncertainty of facing space together as sole survivors had caused some serious rethinking of the popular interpretation of some of the Sker scriptures in vogue up to that point.

The debate was interesting because it involved a basic tenet of Sker faith: that the spiritual interpretations of Ban Jonsn were infallible. Voul himself was the first one to put forward the position that this was not, and could not, be true. As the son of Ban Jonsn, and the leader of the Skers, this was risky in a magnitude that made the Skers receive it with astonishment and doubting reflection. If Voul could say such a thing, then it might just be true. Because in the way of the Skers, they assumed his infallibility, even as he, himself, called it into question. When he questioned this precept of infallibility, it only increased his stature in the hearts of the loyal, hardworking, and unassuming Skers. If you question infallibility, then your own infallibility is doubly assumed.

The Skers were now even more focused than ever on the operational perfectibility of the MoonBase and SkyKing combination. The gurney and the transporters were now a fully operational transportation system. One could travel anywhere and everywhere on and between to the two sites with almost instant ease. The space between had blurred.

Voul and Viera personified the emerging reality. Because they were helplessly in love, they began to appear, more and more, in public together. It wasn't too long before people both on the Moon and the station came to see them as the co-leaders of this last desperate assemblage of humanity.

Jim Peterson and Brittany were very content in their lives. The routine of completing the education and upbringing of a newly minted young woman was more than enough for Jim. After years of command, he found the rich details of life that he had often missed in the midst of his career responsibilities, now interesting and satisfying. In the three-year aftermath of the storm, Brittany had completed the transformation from the little girl who lost her mother to a strong individual coming into her own right and ways. She now fully realized the reality of their situation, and that safety was a fleeting thing, not an unshakeable fact as she had thought as a child. Now, she knew that her world required her presence as a fully participating partner, not just a passenger. This realization brought important changes in her relationship with her dad. Ever since her mother's death, Brittany had always been close with her father, but now she started to take some of the responsibility from his shoulders. She knew SkyKing from stem to stern, but she also knew its people. To the Skers, she was one of them. To the other crew members, she was one of them, too. Even among Viera and the MoonBasers, she had learned to move effortlessly. She was universally popular because she was a beautiful female – always a hit on the Moon – but also because she was so energetic and happy and so obviously intelligent. Some noticed the change after the storm, and those who knew her best saw her coming into her young womanhood over the past few years with grace and with her mother's good looks. To Jim, it was unbelievable and unsettling how much she mirrored his memory of his precious Joan. At fifteen, going on twenty-five, she was almost fully grown, and she had a voracious appetite for knowledge, for new experiences, and for helping him.

After taking care of his child-rearing and other domestic chores, Jim spent most of his time in the navigation station on SkyKing. Figuring out where they were going, how long it would take, and the myriad options available to MoonKing (as the two communities had started sometimes calling themselves) captivated him. They were now traveling faster and faster. The Moon was keeping up by carefully using their nukes on the surface, learning better systems all the time. Everyone knew that the explosions could not continue indefinitely, so alternative measures were being studied by the Skers, of how best to actually take the Moon in tow. SkyKing's sails had been repaired and were in the process of being fully redeployed. Currently only the jib and the spanker were flying and trimmed, but before long the main and genoa would be back up again. After that, the full suit. That would be a problem for the Moon. The sails were so large in comparison to the station, that from space the station itself was almost invisible, dwarfed by comparison. On the recutting and repairs of the sails after the storm, their size was increased again. The raw materials were now readily available. There was no need for secrecy. The Skers went all out. Voul had openly asked the sailmakers to increase the size and capacity of the entire suit, with the thought of greater speed and greater towing capacity. In the vacuum of space, the weight of the Moon meant nothing, but its mass was another issue. Turning, stopping; these were matters of physics that the Sker scientists were persistently working on. The subtle changes in attitudes and the amalgamation of two former mutual anathemas had created an atmosphere of action and accomplishment. For the always-motivated Skers the changes were not overwhelming, but certainly for the crew members of the Moon and the non-Skers of SkyKing they were amazing to watch. Mind-boggling. Suddenly, MoonKing was full of can-do people who got along, who loved and joked about their obvious differences. The open love between Voul and Viera went a long way toward encouraging the normalcy of all these new elements.

At first, people wondered about the two of them. Obviously, the commander of MoonBase and the captain of SkyKing must have dialogue and contact. Lots of it. But the obvious enjoyment in each other's company and then the late nights together caused some discussion. During those first days after the storm Viera and Voul couldn't have cared less what people thought. They were alive.

As things had settled down after the shock wave and the repairs had begun, Voul wanted to transport over to MoonBase to see her. She said, "Fine," but he knew he would have to find her, and that he probably would not have her undivided attention when he did. He found her on the windward side in the bunker they had used to manage the sensor tendrils. She was shouting at one of the workers. "Jesus H. Christ, Frank! When John Silver gets here, he'll kick the shit out of you for that." She was speaking to Benjamin Franklin Smith, third-in-command. Now newly promoted Sergeant Smith looked at his commander fearfully. It wasn't his first experience with her hot temper, but it was the first time it was focused directly on him. "You're telling me that with John almost dying to clear that winch, you couldn't even lock down the main sheet so we could see what the fuck was coming at us?"

"No, Commander. The lines were tangled from the beginning. We worked hard to straighten them out. Our analysis only started to answer in the last few seconds of the emergency. We took huge risks with our hydraulics. Sergeant Silver's actions freed the system so we could operate. We did get the sails working. But another effect of his courageous action was to allow us to record some of the storm data details. Alternating our requests in with the sail trim instructions, we got it. That data has proven to be enormously useful. The energy we absorbed and the damage we sustained are far more understandable with that data."

"What good is it?"

"Commander, without the data we gathered, the sails would have been trimmed inaccurately. Perhaps lost. Even with the data coming in at the very last second our research shows that we certainly saved the mainsail, and we saved SkyKing from direct exposure to the shock wave on the starboard side." Viera thought about that for a moment. The starboard side was where the Skers' quarters and most of the scientific and operational stations were located. Where Voul was located. She looked at "Frank," as he liked to be called. He was not the usual MoonBaser. He dressed in neat uniforms, favoring light colors, while most MoonBasers liked the darker colors because they hid the stains and dirt of their hardworking lives. He was handsome, but not sensual handsome like her favorite ensign. He sometimes seemed to be weak, but always stood his ground with intelligence and persistence. He got his point across without argument or recrimination. When he thought he was right, he was more than up to dealing with Viera's heat, or with anyone who tried to intimidate his methodical evaluations and actions. *He is more like a Sker than a MoonBaser. That's probably why I like him so much.*

"Well, thank God Almighty that you guys were there. You single-handedly saved us all, right, Fraaaank?" In her sarcasm she drew out his name mockingly.

"No, Commander, but we should not be belittled as ineffective either. The opposite is far closer to the truth. It was a team effort, and we were part of the team." With that comment, Viera noticed Voul had found her and was now watching the exchange.

"Hi, Viera," he said with a smile that was just a little too expansive.

"Well, look who's here, The freaking messiah himself." Viera knew her Sker books too well, and she made the most of the religious trappings that surrounded Voul and his family. She noticed that his uniform was not perfect, but mildly wrinkled with some oil spots and other stains. His face, while happy to see her, showed the signs of worry and stress. She immediately wanted to comfort him, but not here. "Let's go to my quarters, Voul. I have the schematics there as well as the damage reports for you to see." She turned to Sergeant Smith. "Frank, keep me informed. Give your crew a 'Well done' from me." The sergeant smiled with appreciation, not because he won, but because she had listened to him. He watched them walk away together and noticed that Voul's hand brushed hers at their side. Knowing the Skers' assiduous avoidance of any contact, he realized that there was more to Voul and Viera "going to her quarters" than just the schematics and reports. To Benjamin Franklin Smith, third-in-command, that was very reassuring, even if he couldn't fully understand why he felt that way. As time went by, that became a general feeling throughout the Moon and the station. Voul and Viera symbolized the joining of the two cultures. People liked it.

Voul and Viera were not alone in the attraction of seeming opposites, as it turned out.

112. Look at These Two

"This is a brother and sister act, I take it?" the skydiving instructor asked. "Well," Farson said, "it could be or we can go separately." The instructor looked at the two of them. They were both attractive, but Karina's style outshined Farson's in his rumpled clothes and tousled hair. They were both fairly tall and fit, so it wouldn't be a problem in the air. "Well, go watch the waiver video and sign all the documents. I'll meet you at the staging area in about forty-five minutes." Farson and Karina went into the video lounge and began to watch the video.

"They are trying to scare us, Farson." She thought that was hysterically funny and was almost unable to control herself.

"No, I don't think so. They are just worried. Liability and all of that. Then there's the issue of deployment." She nestled into him a little bit more. He could feel her warmth. The video played along. She looked at him forming a question. "Not everyone is going to understand us, you know, Karina." She laughed, and they watched the video.

<<*Do you think I understand, Farson?*>>
<<*Yes and no.*>>

When the instructor looked in on them, they were happily signing all the documents, almost ready to go skydiving.

<<*What can I do, Farson?*>> He thought for a moment before answering.

<<*Remember, all of the times we have done this before? Watch for any changes. No matter how slight.*>> Her nervous laugh came along quickly on the heels of that suggestion. She knew he was trying to tell her something. The instructors were entering the room, full of their authority.

"They act like this is our first jump," Karina said out loud, softly. Farson was watching her closely.

<<*Are you sure?*>> The instructors began gathering up the papers. One of them looked at Karina.

"Ms. Chamberlain, you forgot to initial this box." She looked at the document. It was the section on medical history. The box unchecked was "Claustrophobia?" She turned to Farson.

<<*That's odd.*>>

Farson laughed. <<*Answer the question. Let's go.*>>

<<*How many times have we done this, Farson?*>>

<<*Who knows? Do you still enjoy it?*>> Karina smiled at him.

<<*What do you think?*>> She looked out the window at the drop zone. <<*It has such an otherwhere and otherwhen feeling. It's amazing.*>>

<<*It's always fun to take a break, Karina. Somewhere where nothing else matters. In free fall, for example.*>> This made her laugh, and she started to playfully lip-sync with the instructor's explanation of the coming skydive that they had heard so many times. She was doing it just to make Farson laugh. It worked.

<<*If they knew what we are up to, they might not let us jump.*>> Farson laughed out loud.

<<*Now that's really funny, Kari. That is really, really funny.*>>

He was still laughing when the instructors came in and asked, "Are you ready to skydive?"

After gearing up, they walked to the plane, hand-in-hand. One of the instructors said to the other, "I never even liked my sister. Look as these two." Karina and Farson were lost in just being together, happy and ready to jump out at 14,000 feet. They were checking each other's gear over and clowning around. "You'd think they'd done it a hundred times," said one of the two instructors. The other one said, "Let's just do our jobs." The four of them climbed into the small plane, and it taxied to the end of the runway for takeoff. Once they were at altitude, the plane's jump door was opened, and everyone positioned themselves for exit. Just before she left, Farson heard Karina's thought. <<*Once we're out, anything can happen, right?*>> He had to admire her brave perspicacity, her never-ending ability to equal any occasion. He knew his message was getting through.

<<*Correct. Nothing is foreordained. Blue skies.*>>

<<*Blue skies to you too, Routier.*>>

Karina left the plane in high spirits.

The circumstances were overtaking Farson as he watched her jump from the plane. Karina and her instructor tumbled in instability at exit. It took some seconds for them to stable up. By that time they were almost out of sight for Farson, but he continued to stare helplessly at them until they were stabled up. Then he jumped.

113. Handy and the Bottle (2)

Handy was outside watching the "Bottle." The glare of the vast stasis barrier was obvious to him. He wondered if they even knew he was there.

"Well, here I am," he said out loud to Farson, "just as you said I would be." <<*Now what?*>> No thought came instantly back. Farson's thoughts were missing lately, and it bothered Handy. He stood up, dusted off his pants from the dirty rock he had been sitting on, and started off down the hill away from his special "Area 51," as he called it. "These people have no idea," again speaking out loud. <<*Why shouldn't I talk to myself? No one else is talking to me.*>> He sent his thoughts out to The Screen, the way someone might shout into a canyon; an imaginary echo the only response.

The people in the bottle were in stasis, but not the way Handy had thought. He had originally thought that Earth had been slowed down, but now he understood that that wouldn't have worked at all. Slowing them down would have killed Earth from the ScreenMasters' point of view, permanently ending the threat, in a long, slow death in a distant meaningless past. So instead, to get them totally out of the way, Farson had speeded them up into a far distant and more meaningful future, which still would look, to the people of Earth, like nothing had changed. Looking out, he knew, they would eventually detect a universe in slow, slow motion, but it would be years and years before they figured out that it was actually their world that had been speeded up. That way, Emerald Earth could be contributive to Farson's plan: extra harvests many times a year; super-short life spans – so to speak – with a lot of important changes crammed into a relatively short period of real time.

To the ScreenMasters, their plan would seem to be right on schedule. It would seem to Twill and the other

ScreenMasters that their planned elimination of the Earth and the repair of The Screen was complete and thorough.

If they only knew.

As Handy walked down the hill, it was clear to him that something unusual was going on. *Something unusual indeed.* He could tell that the people "in the bottle" were advancing at a speed that was evolutionarily shocking. He could see changes inside: the lights, the colors, the organization of things. He wanted to enter their time, but he knew there could be no return from that decision. The time he was in now, though, was way too slow for him. Without Farson, things made no sense. He had lost direction with his friend gone. He remembered Farson's description of the advanced levels of The Screen. "You can relive things, Handy, and enjoy them. Sometimes I go back to a moment in my life, and just let it happen over. For me, it's like sitting down in a comfy chair by the fire and closing my eyes. Those happy moments which we all have had, they are all there for me to live over and over again, still knowing all that I know now. Sometimes I change things a little just for fun. Sometimes Karina comes with me. Can you imagine that? We can relive our first kiss; it's one of our favorite 'trips,' as we call them."

Handy could hear Farson's voice in his mind, but now, in this slowness, it was only a memory, not a vital reality as it had once been. Handy worried and wondered about that. Farson was so powerful, so important: a ScreenMaster above all others. What happened? *Did Twill really win?*

Handy sat down. He had a small campsite, and it was getting late. He reached down into his knapsack and took out the silver flask, flipped back the lid, pressed it to his lips, and tipped back his head taking a deep draught of the booze. It soothed him. He thought he heard a sidewinder moving around in the sand. Then he saw a trace of purple hue where the sound had been. A purple ripple in the sand. The color of lore. ScreenMaster purple. "Now, who's that coming from?" He took another drink. He stared out into the world of the bottle – not the flask, although he was also thinking about looking into that as well, hoping there was still a little more in there.

In the world around him there were new colors everywhere. *They are very busy in here.*

The flask seemed to lift itself to his lips again, and the night became quieter. Handy was getting tired. His old song was playing again in his head.

Things have changed in this old world ...
        This old world.
Once things were deadly and things were
        Dyin'...
Now all's a peaceful place, and only the
        Babies're cryin'...
Oh, yes, things have changed in this old
        World ...
Things have changed, things have changed,
        Things have changed ...

He was nearly asleep as he pulled his bedroll up to his chin, tucking himself in. It was a chilly night, but his little campfire would do the job of keeping him warm. *There are sounds in the night, tonight.* Soon Handy's snoring was the loudest sound. As time went by, it became a slow, rhythmic breathing with just a little snore to it. All was quiet. The stars were bright; the night was clear. The fire reflected on Handy's face softly. If Handy had been awake, he would certainly have seen the blurry face looking at him sleeping there. He slept soundly until sunrise, and by then so much time had passed in the bottle that that first face, the first instance of Emer-engineered stasis-eddy, was just a triumphant footnote in their ever-advancing history. Just before Handy's dawn came, that same person's face, much, much older now, had returned and was waiting impatiently for him to wake up, as were the others standing behind him.

114. The Flow of The Screen (2) Farson's Teachings. (Excerpts from his log)

The history of the old ScreenMasters recorded their efforts to keep The Screen from changing. They thought they were preserving it, strengthening it, and keeping it safe when, in truth, they were destroying it, weakening it, and putting it at high risk of such total disaster that, in the end, they will have to be forgiven. Far from saviors, they were obstacles to be overcome. The strength of their numbers was in their favor in those days, but, in The Screen's time, those early chapters proved to be only a beginning.

As though a vast forest, harboring a potential infinity of seeds and seedlings all growing at different rates in different soils, The Screen is a vast nutrient, a wide source of constant change. It rolls on and on through time, wanting more and more and more. Then the ScreenMasters discovered Earth.

Earth itself was the answer to the question they had never asked. It was the answer for which they were not prepared.

The first ScreenMasters were not masters at all, but servants. They were good servants. They saw the direction of change and raced after it. The great philosophy of The Screen was so clear to them: Goodness and giving were all; evil and taking were the opposite. How could you take from something that was illimitable? In such inclusiveness, where was evil's place? What evil had The Screen ever championed or given genesis to? The great growing forest knew no death or dread. The nourishment of universes, a great building of things beyond all imagination, it was all very clear to them in the beginning. The faith to leap out of one's own comfort was the key. It was revelation, and it was hard work for them. The revelatory phase was first and primary.

But no one explained it to that first ScreenMaster. He just became an accidental time traveler, and he had to figure it all out. He stumbled onto the answers. It was inadvertent, almost a mistake. It happened in the blink of an eye. He was the first, fallible and flawed. He knew what he had, but he also knew right away it was not him who The Screen was seeking. He was just the first. Within the great forest, it was as if he had been swept up, sifted out from the others and reborn into a vastly different life. Metamorphosis. It felt like he had been spit out at first. He wandered The Screen for many years. Time was out of sync for him. He wandered in time and space. The vast forest grew and grew around him, so many changes and new places. He felt lost. Alone.

In the flow of The Screen, Earth's eruption was inevitable. The Rent that developed was a cause of alarm for the ever-growing number of the old ScreenMasters. They had all been swept up, sifted, and reborn. Perhaps spit out, too. Each one of them knew of all the others, but their links were weaker then and their purpose was not as clear as it became. Twill, like Handy, was a true intellectual prodigy, so his thoughts gained a high prevalence. His prescriptions of decorum and stability, his preference for questioning change, and seeing change as something needing to be fixed or slowed became the currency of their realm. For Twill, his Grand Ascendancy was an epistemological epiphany. His narcissistic world of Essor was all about self from birth to death. Life there was always defined in self-referential ways. Always. It was a quid pro quo kind of place. The Screen's gift of great unbounded freedom was a threat to be contained. Twill took it to heart. His innate, visceral resistance to change was beyond his control. He did what he could, but he was who he was. He saw the foundations of this new world in terms of his old one and understood all too well its implications. It was a classic mistake of the devil we know. Old Earth had a saying, "If all you have is a hammer, everything looks like a nail." That was Twill to a T. His elegant intellect was susceptible to self-deception, and his industrious and audacious disquisitions on all topics of The Screen became the matrix of misdirected discussion. In every way that mattered, Twill's shallow interpretations became what was known about The Screen. It was all so new in the beginning, the discovery so overawing. Twill emerged as a leader, not by universal acclaim, but more by industry and his persistent certainty. Quantity not quality. That was Twill's secret. He thought for the others, and they allowed it.

When those ScreenMasters ultimately came to Earth, they had already agreed the planet needed to be "fixed." That is, destroyed.

Handy was first and pure. Twill came along later and was not.

Then there was me.

As a forest grows in the flat lands and then up into the mountains, so The Screen flowed over all obstacles, all terrain, a menstruum of change, on and on. The small being looks at the mountain and sees no detail from the distance, but once in the midst of the climb, all those details become realities, some beautiful and encouraging, some harsh and halting. The rarest of all mentalities is awareness. Especially when things are changing. To remember early childhood in old age is almost impossible, and certainly rare. To see something up close and remember it as something you saw from far, far away is a trick that few can master. For most, it's an almost insurmountable challenge to hold values constant in wildly changing times. Adaptability is the key to evolutionary success. Unchangeability takes stubborn intransigence, a deceiving form of ignorance. To truly understand The Screen – its flow and its reality – one must emotionally, intellectually, and physically be in many places at once. One must be able to move seamlessly between time and place, never missing a beat. Some call it omniscience, but in reality, if we really think about it, it can be quite normal and natural. We humans are all transiting through time, albeit in small segments versus The Screen's enormous expanses. What is a moment anyway? Is it a place as much as a time? A moment in time, as they say. We all wander in and out of moments and memories all the time. It's routine. We never think about it that way, though. It's just living, to us. To the ScreenMasters, that truth was incomprehensible.

When they "repaired" the Rent, I saw the window closing, and jumped to be on the other side, taking everything with me. The ScreenMasters thought I was gone, or dead, or, even better, just not.

Like a willow that grows best in its native soil, I chose to stay close to home. "A ScreenMaster from Earth," they said. My defenestration was an act of high principle that looked like cowardice to them. My choice was a beautiful thing that they just couldn't or wouldn't comprehend. Handy always understood. His selfless act, of isolation and loneliness, transformed our world; his sacrifice and imprisonment, as he put it, freed everyone.

It will take a long, long time for the old ScreenMasters to catch up with us, if they ever do.

In the end, our path was not the path of least resistance, of course. But it was a path. I just held the door open for the human race to move from the old to a new place where they could all be safe. It worked like a charm. Everyone waltzed right in.

115. Voul and Viera Discuss the Future

Before Voul and Viera finally reached her quarters, there had indeed been schematics to go over, and Voul's nature precluded avoiding work for any reason. He didn't give it a second thought as they walked together through the Moon's compartments, reviewed the damaged sections, and spoke to department heads. They worked through tentative schedules and rewritten logistical plans. They visited multiple sites to verify conditions and encourage overstressed personnel. In the end, tired and worn out, the two of them returned and faced each other, finally alone again, back in her apartment.

Though they were tired, they were attentive to the rich feelings that had grown so strong between them. The bond was warm and steady. Voul, who had spent his life in abstemiousness and asceticism, watched Viera as she moved around the rooms. He knew she was wanton, hedonistic, and yet truly loving in a way he had never known, no, in a way he had never even dreamed of knowing. She seemed happy to give up her ways for him, and yet the uncertain morality, the subliminal threat of her libido breaking loose, was always there. He had seen it happen. When their hearts beat hard and fast together. When he was like a person verging on disaster, and it was causing his body to shake and his mind to recoil and embrace all at once. Emotions he had worked so hard to control coursing through his veins in the victory of abandon and release. Viera was looking at him. Their eyes were more than just meeting; they were boring into each other. She had felt his mind before and wanted it again: that sharing of desire so deep that no physical contact was needed. The Sker way of love. Skers could just sit beside each other and with practice have pleasure unattainable to others. She could feel it stirring inside her now. It always started with Voul, but she was learning to join in. She could feel her mind warming up, her eyes watering, rolling back into her head. She could feel that feeling rising. *He does this without outwardly showing anything.* While she was in ecstatic turmoil, he seemed so quiet and centered. She was unraveling, and he was calming and almost meditative. She could now hear his thought. *You are exploring the world of mental embrace. I long for the forbidden world of physical embrace. I ache to touch you and to sense and feel your physicality. This is the Sker way, Viera, but I want your way.* Her breathing accelerated.

You took the words right out of my mouth.

His mental voice was soft and soothing, and she loved it. Her eyes were open now. The disaster just survived was fading, and the aches and pains of her bruisings were abating. It had been a long, long day. She loved his soothing mental loving so deeply it was hard for her to move, to risk fading the pleasure, but she did it anyway.

Unsealing her jumpsuit, she turned gracefully away from him, the garment falling to the floor. She said out loud, "Okay, Voul, let's start with a shower." He couldn't help but laugh. *No Sker woman would ever do that.* Voul knew he couldn't do that. Breaking off a Sker embrace before it was over was unheard of. Showering together was an unbelievable transgression. In the midst of riotous thoughts approaching sacrilege, Voul felt a joy of recklessness as he followed her toward the shower. He would have followed her anywhere.

As she walked into the shower, she looked over her shoulder at him and laughed. "You men are all alike." With this, her laughter teasingly increased as the warm sprays of the large shower came on and she leaned into them as naturally as an animal in a rainforest downpour. Voul, of course, was right behind her.

"What's ahead of us, Voul? Can you see anything?" Viera was reclining in bed. They had bathed. They had eaten. They had loved. They had rested. This was her time to relax and talk. Throughout her life she had always been an action person. Resting was only a necessity, never a pleasure. Things were changing.

"Well, much depends on Farson, of course. The sails are full and bye. The crews are working together. Food is plentiful, and atmospheric control and long-term life support shows promise. Our speed is increasing. We are getting somewhere. The future looks good." Voul found these moments with Viera after lovemaking particularly interesting. First, that he was here with her, and, second, because he enjoyed the respite from his duties. There seemed to be no reason for lounging around with her but for that very reason, he loved every minute of it.

"Farson." Viera had spoken the name very slowly and softly. It had taken her a long time to buy into the idea of Farson as all-important. MoonBase had always been distant and isolated from the others; the MoonBasers liked it that way. All of that had changed. With Earth's disappearance, the Moon and its crew were far more interested in SkyKing and much more involved. "Where is he? Dead?"

"No, not dead, but like that, really. We have been waiting, but there's been nothing. Karina seems happy, so that means a lot. She remains in her compartment and seems to be doing something, but no one can determine what. She walks around talking; she sleeps as though someone is with her; but she stays alone most of the time. Brittany sometimes gets in, but she's the only one. Karina's injuries healed suddenly about two days after the storm. Since then her spirits are consistent with Farson being alive and in contact with her." Voul was feeling the stirrings of duty during this conversation and started to move off the bed. Viera held him from getting up.

"You are not going anywhere, Voul. You promised to teach me more." Voul stiffened and gently shook her off, standing up. Viera was not pleased.

"Let me check in." He tapped his wrist, and the holographic screen appeared with Repoul Bensn's face in it. "Report." Repoul responded as though Voul had been in constant contact, even though hours had passed. Hours passing without contact with Voul in days gone by would have been reason to raise a high alert, but now things were slowing down, even for the Skers.

"All is well. Nominal operations all within expected parameters. The crew is quiet. All whorls are functioning normally. MoonBase is exactly 160 nautical miles behind us and maintaining its position. We are traveling at just under half speed. Acceleration is increasing at a diminishing rate, as predicted. Commander Peterson would like to talk to you when you get a moment. All sails are engaged and trimmed. John Silver is working on MoonBase's forward shielding and will not report, but that is also as expected. Transporters are functioning normally, and all surviving shuttles are fully operational. Most of the injured are recovering; there were four additional deaths, all crew and MoonBase, no Skers."

"That distinction is unnecessary, Repoul. These are new days."

"Very well, sir." As Voul ended the communication, the communicator peeped again.

"Yes, Repoul."

"Sir, I forgot to mention that ZZ<<Arkol25609 came aboard around 2300 hours. He was in the Peterson quarters, and now he is on the Moon."

"Did he check in with Karina?"

"Not that we could tell, but it is likely that he did."

"What is he doing on the Moon?"

"He seems to be searching for something."

Viera heard the transmission about the robot and was up dressing. Voul knew their private time was coming to an end. "I'll be on the bridge in under ten minutes, Repoul. Jonsn out."

Viera was standing very close as he signed off. Then she was in his arms.

"You have a lot to teach me, Voul. Come back soon."

"You have a lot to teach me, Viera. But, I'm learning."

"Yes, you are, Voul. Yes, you are." Then they were off to their respective duties.

ZZ<<Arkol25609 was actually in quite a hurry. Where what he was looking for was located he had no idea, but Handy had said it must be there somewhere. When the ScreenMasters had put Earth in stasis, the Moon had been cut loose, but up until that moment the lunar station had been considered by Earth to be a military listening and watching post. To put aside the Moon's active population of thousands and to consider the Moon merely a military listening post was a mistake and mirrored the reasons why the planet was considered out of touch concerning its two colonies. It was true, however, that in keeping records and telemetry, the Moon had no equal. Handy wanted the data and visual recordings of those many hours when the ScreenMasters were deploying their devices, and especially the precise moment when the Earth disappeared. He had been told there would be something interesting on them. ZZ<<Arkol25609 knew that

it was Farson who had told Handy. When ZZ<<Arkol25609 asked Handy where exactly Farson was when they had spoken, he answered, "Through the looking glass." ZZ<<Arkol25609 knew that Handy was living near the transport station on Earth; and that he was the only "clear" individual on the planet. Handy's "campsite" was located on the edge of the vast fields, clearly off the farmer traffic routes, so he had plenty of room in which to move around. As always, he stayed close to one particular area he called "Area 51," which he clearly considered home.

With Handy's penchant for indecipherable responses and allusions to situations only he could define, ZZ<<Arkol25609 found it was far easier to just carry out Handy's instructions without too many questions. ZZ's intellect was prodigious, but his patience was sometimes wanting.

When Viera arrived, ZZ<<Arkol25609 was scanning through one of the most damaged areas of the Moon. Workers were everywhere conducting repairs.

"Do you need any help, ZZ?" The robot had assumed his full height for this assignment, about nine feet tall, and the golden purple glowing of his metallic covering gave him a definite appearance of invulnerability. The disarming strobe across his face varied inexplicably in colors and intensity. Now it was purple, but not the Screen purple, something slightly off from that.

<<*No.*>> Viera winced at the strong telepathic touch of the robot's response. She decided to just watch and see what happened. ZZ<<Arkol25609 continued scanning the area for whatever it was he was looking for.

Viera's communicator indicated an incoming message. "Viera? Voul. What's he doing?"

"I know it's you, Voul. You don't have to announce yourself." There was a slight pause. Then she continued.

"ZZ<<Arkol25609 is scanning around like crazy. I asked him if he wanted any help. He declined. Have you talked to Jim yet?"

"On my way to the Petersons' compartment now. See you later. Keep me informed."

"Is that an order?" She was looking into his eyes on the little floating screen over her wrist.

"Yes." He was laughing. She laughed, too.

"You are learning, Voul. It's really quite amazing."

She turned back to look at ZZ<<Arkol25609. He was walking toward her at a hurried pace. He was holding an object about the size of a bread box. She could feel his thought forming in her mind. *<<Coming with me?>>* It was not really a question, but before she knew it, she was running to keep up with the robot as he passed her headed for MoonBase's control central. "God Almighty, ZZ, that's about three miles from here." Slowly, a bright yellowish golden light engulfed her, and the next thing she knew they were in the control room with several startled crew members. ZZ<<Arkol25609 was already working on opening the object. "Be careful, ZZ. We've got the key. Don't damage it." She recognized the recording lasercell unit. ZZ<<Arkol25609 made a wide sweep with his hand and arm, ending with his arm extended toward the object. It was the old human gesture of "after you." She shook her head with a mock smirk. "Oh sure, you come out of nowhere and start bossing me around. Now you're a chivalrous Knight of the Round Table. What's the matter? Can't figure the box out?" ZZ<<Arkol25609's arm had remained outstretched as though continuing to reemphasize the gesture. With this confusing remark and question by Viera, he dropped it to his side, searching his memory for references for round tables, finding nothing germane. His strobing had changed to a reddish hue, and it

was a little faster. Viera noticed his hesitation and walked to a console, opened a connector link, and a beam reached out to the object. A screen appeared, and it was obvious that data was downloading. "This'll take a few minutes, Z. Just relax." The robot stood as still as dead, strobing smoothly now in the standard soft yellow. *He could, of course, stay like that for years.*

<<*It shouldn't take that long, Viera. We're kind of in a hurry here.*>> The robot's thought was softer but still insistent. Viera found herself possessed of an irresistible urge to hurry. She realized the robot was mentally urging her to go faster. She forced herself to slow down. "Just hold your horses, Z. Haste makes waste. Let me do it my way." His strobing oscillations varied momentarily from slow to fast and back to slow, then very slow. "Good boy, ZZ. Stay," Viera said, showing the robot the palm of her hand.

On the monitor screen before them was the clear black of space broken by the bright lights of the ScreenMasters' devices being deployed and appearing one after the other. The scene was speeding up at laser-fast rates and soon invisible to the human eye, but the robot saw it all. He was recording it and transmitting as fast as it downloaded.

<<*Good boy, ZZ. Stay.*>> Handy repeated Viera's joke secretly to the robot, just to annoy him. He thought it was very funny that she had said that. *If she only knew.* The humor was wasted on ZZ<<Arkol25609 who was far busier than he appeared to be.

116. Inside the Bottle

"How long will it take?"

Andrew Sortt, the first and last president of the United States of Earth, was sitting in a room that initially seemed to have nothing in it, but on closer inspection was jammed with subtle controls and multiuse furniture. The sleek, clean design was the artful concealer. As he moved around in the room, soft lights shifted and view screens appeared and vanished in a phasing motion that revealed high-value engineering. As the scene developed, it was clear that this was not a room at all but part of a much larger space, and there were innumerable people in attendance, all in personal matrices of their own. People were moving from matrix to matrix, and they were also able to instantaneously move anywhere throughout the entire space. Farson had taken awhile to fully grasp the situation when he first arrived. It had taken him several minutes to emotionally catch up with the speed of development inside Emerald Earth. ScreenMasters are very good with time, but typically all time was developing at the same speed. This situation was like stepping onto a fast-moving treadmill from a static sidewalk. *A really fast-moving treadmill.* So, Mr. Sortt's question was not an easy one to answer.

"Well, it depends. In their time, probably less than a few hours. In our time, it will be about two months or so."

<<*We've got to slow this pace down, Farson. We know how to do it, but the timing is so critical we really need that information more quickly. Can Karina help?*>>

Karina. Farson's thought lingered on the mental harmonics the word created in his mind every time he heard it. The ScreenMaster of Earth, now on Emerald Earth, still had access to Karina's thought, although it was never easy through the stasis field. It was her physical presence that he missed so badly.

<<*Not really. We don't communicate on that level of complexity yet. It is getting better. The transmission of action requests is very, very oblique. To have her actually do anything – and she wants to, you can believe that – might be disruptive to her process. Everything is hanging by a thread. That's good news.*

For the ScreenMasters, what Karina and I are doing is inconceivable, even though they are the ones who made it possible.>> Farson was thinking about Emerald Earth, and he knew it was becoming a powder keg; its magnitude of success was also its greatest danger. They had become something so empowered and advanced that the stasis was no longer controlling them, but, their freedom was not yet attained. The stasis field was strong and vital; it worked in the essential way of containment, but no longer in any overall way of control. The Emers had changed all of that. His thought swept across the planet. He saw the encompassing vast city and the all-surrounding "farms," as they called them. The old oceans and land masses that had been combined in remarkably ingenious ways. The distinction between liquid and solids on Emerald Earth's surface had been blurred. That was as it had to be since the lunar and solar tidal influences had vanished and the traditional climates had eroded. The Emers had not only achieved universal peace and prosperity among themselves, they had tamed the planet itself into a harmonious whole that worked perfectly in their hands.

Now Earth had only two environments: urban and rural. Really, ultra-urban, and techno-rural. The city was one vast, interwoven and interlinked "room," with inhabitants free in ways never dreamed of in human history. Virtually living as one, all Emers could move freely anywhere on their new planet almost instantaneously. They were free of want, free to simply be anything and everything their culture could offer. What they were achieving was amazing, even to a ScreenMaster. As Sortt had simply said, "We are." The fields of Emerald Earth were a true example of abundance and freedom. Huge agricultural devices, cities on wheels really, roamed the virtually unlimited land, planting, harvesting, delivering, and improving. The city itself was a huge single, seamless institution with education and research as its only goals. Life was very good on Emerald Earth: a far, far different existence from what the old ScreenMasters had planned. The level of automation was evenly spread throughout the society, leaving some work for the inhabitants but only the work that required human intellect, not menial or manual labor, unless it was desired. The tutorial education system had resulted in quantum leaps of progress and invention. For generation after generation the peaceful pursuit of knowledge and its practical applications had achieved a utopia in human terms.

Now they wanted out. From what Farson could see they had it all figured out. "We just need the timing," Sortt had said. "And *that* little piece of information is still beyond our reach. Though hopefully, not yours, Farson."

Farson was thinking of Handy, how peacefully he slept outside. That there were no stars in the Emerald Earth sky didn't bother Handy. What a good soldier he had always been. There had been no questions when Handy had seen Farson looking at him from inside the bottle. The communication had been difficult, but it had been achieved. Whether Handy thought he was saving Farson, or something else, didn't seem to matter. The details were complicated, but Handy got it. It was almost as though he had been watching the stasis barrier alter itself, a little more each year, year after year. Farson knew, without being told, that Handy had noticed. He had indicated that there had been a little more change over the past few years, but Farson doubted that even Handy could have guessed why. Farson looked out the window onto the view outside. It was so beautiful, so perfect; what a gift the ScreenMasters had unintentionally given to mankind in their rush to judgment and punishment. Happiness, peace, prosperity, evolution, and purpose. United, humanity was an awesome force. Andrew Sortt was watching Farson and asked, "What are you thinking about, Farson?"

"About what is going to happen." Sortt nodded his head.

"It's pretty wild, isn't it?" Farson turned and looked at President Sortt. Andrew had been born in South Carolina, in the little town of Beaufort. He had been a local high school swimmer who set records. He went into business, and then into local politics and in a career of less than twenty years, he had been elected president of the United States and then of the planet. He had been the first and only person to achieve such a status. When the ScreenMasters came, it ruined his life, but now nearing an age beyond belief, he was ready for anything. "If anyone had told me this story back then, I would have laughed them out of the room. This is totally new territory. For the Moon and SkyKing it's been just under five years, for us, over six millennia, so far. We think we are ready."

Farson looked at him a little more closely. He was still a handsome guy. Despite the years, he still looked vigorous and engaged. Farson liked him. He liked him a lot. The years Sortt had spent on Emerald Earth had been good years. Now, all seemed ready. "Well, Mr. President, ready or not, here we go."

<<Call me Andrew, Farson. We're leaving all that behind now.>>

117. Karina Becomes Involved. Handy Delivers the Data.

She was falling. Her instructor was with her in free fall. He was overly attentive to a young woman he thought had little skydiving experience. Her log showed thirty-five jumps and an A-license, the first level. She played along. How could he possibly know? Farson was there in the sky somewhere, but she couldn't see him yet. He had left the plane after her. After about a minute of free fall she pulled the rip cord, and her canopy opened softly, smoothly. Under the canopy, her instructor well below her, she could enjoy the view from

4,000 feet, and she knew Farson would be right along. The instructors had waited for each of them to pull and went lower as their job required, so they were essentially out of Farson's and Karina's sky, just as planned. Alone in the sky, all that was needed was for Farson to catch up to her. No problem. In a minute he was flying even with her. They both were laughing.

"Hi, Kari." She looked over just as Farson's canopy gently touched hers.

<<*You keep changing things. Won't it cause problems?*>>

<<*I'm trying to tell you something.*>>

<<*What?*>> She couldn't hear his next sentence, but his lips were readable. Then, his canopy bumped hers again, slightly more firmly this time. Suddenly, he pulled sharply on his left toggle and spiraled hard down and down and down. From her perspective it looked like he was going to go all the way to the ground. But at the last minute, his canopy leveled off and she relaxed as he safely planed across the grass to the center of the drop zone's target circle.

She was upset at his "hook-turn" maneuver, but she understood that reality and what they were doing were two separate things. She was also wondering what it was he wanted to tell her. The afternoon sky, dark blue and cloudless, claimed her attention again, and she continued her slow, peaceful descent. As the target grew larger, she knew she was spot on, as usual. Her tiptoe landing was on the "X," but Farson was nowhere in sight. *That never happened before.*

<<*Karina Chamberlain, you are needed.*>> There was no mistaking the sensation of ZZ<<Arkol25609's dry thoughts. It wasn't that the robots had no emotion. They did. It's just that their emotions were texture-less and flat in communication. Not human. *Farson's thoughts are much, much different.* For a moment her mind warmed to that thought,

thinking of him in her arms, her lips on his, his dependable response. In that mental state his last nearly inaudible words that she lip-read, flying under the canopy, still rang in her mind. She had learned to prepare for the unexpected. She remembered what they were now. She remembered his encouragement. <<*You can do it. Don't be afraid.*>> Thinking about him and his skydiving antics, she was shaking her head and smiling to herself. *He'll never grow up.*

Then she was back in her cabin on SkyKing. ZZ<<Arkol25609 was there, strobing away. If a robot could be impatient, he definitely was.

<< *This must get to Handy immediately.*>>

<< *Why don't you take it there?*>>

<< *I am a ScreenKeeper, Karina. Earth is off The Screen now. It would kill me. I will go if I have to, but I thought it would be more efficient if you did it. You are the only ScreenMaster available who can do it.*>>

<< *You know there is one part of the planet ...* >>

<< *For you Karina, not for me. That space is still within the field. For me, my mission, the very existence of that field is painful and disturbing even from here. That close and I would cease all functionality.*>>

<< *Twill? Uvo?*>>

<<*Very funny, Karina. You know they are, shall we say, unavailable for this mission.*>>

<< *Are you feeling inadequate, ZZ<<Arkol25609?*>>

<< *A little. You should decide now. There is not a moment to lose.*>>

Handy was waking up. His little campsite was the picture of rustic tranquility. He had decided to stay in this part of Emerald Earth, without really knowing why. He could have lived anywhere, but here he was for all these years. He stood up, pushing his bedroll aside, naked to the waist, and walked to a small bush nearby. His morning urination was accompanied with a robust and relieving session of uninhibited flatulence. It made him happy. He was laughing to himself, shaking himself dry as he turned around to find Karina standing there. She was dressed in Sker whites, tight-fitting, her blonde hair fresh and clean. Her eyes indicated that she was pleased to have surprised him and to have caught him in the act of being ... well, being Handy. "Oh, shit!" he said, zipping up a little too quickly to be sure all was in its proper place. "Ouch! Goddamn it, woman. Why are you sneaking up on me like that?" As she shifted to telepathy, Handy knew this meeting was important.

<<*ZZ<<Arkol25609 said to give this to you and say, 'It is time.'*>>

Handy looked at her. <<*You know what's in there, right?*>> Karina looked at him. He looked like a bum. His bedroll was filthy, the coffee pot looked like it had never been cleaned, his beard was getting way too long, his pants were stained, and she imagined she could smell him from where she was standing. He was looking around for something, found it, and put a small stub of a cigar in his mouth and lit it, almost burning his nose with the igniting flame. He exhaled with a big sighing blow, licked his lips, and took another deep inhale. He reached for the coffee pot and looked in. He then drank directly out of it, spilling a little black, viscous coffee down his bare front. He smeared it around in a feeble attempt to wipe it away.

<<*Don't you think you're taking this act a little too far, Handy?*>>

<<*What act?*>> He laughed as he put on his shirt, unbuttoned. Karina eyed him in disbelief. He walked up to her and took the small purple object from her hands. <<*I hope you've got a backup.*>> This made him laugh. She just looked at him. He was still pretty close. He took her

shoulders in his hands and pulled her to him. He kissed her on the cheek and then hugged her. <<*You are a beauty, Karina.*>> Then he walked away, as though toward something, becoming a blur. There were other blurs around him now. She was looking at the scene intensely. Was Farson nearby? Her heart was beating. The blurry Handy turned to looked back at her. <<*I can feel your love for him, Karina. He's a lucky, lucky guy.*>> He was disappearing now. He looked at her one last time. She noticed serious intent on his face. An odd thing happened. The brightest purple she had ever seen exploded toward him, engulfing him and quickly dragging him as he disappeared. With a flash he was gone. Karina was alone as the air reverberated with ripples running off in all directions, left, right, up and down. Then it smoothed out again, as before.

She stood there for a moment, the smoke from Handy's cigar still lingering in the morning air. She was thinking. *When he kissed me, it was sweet and warm, no odors or grossness.* When he hugged her, black coffee stains should be on her pristine white clothes, but they weren't. Close up, Handy was hygienically perfect. She remembered the smell, like fresh linen. *To look at him, you'd never guess.* It all confused her a little, but she remembered what Farson had said, "Handy is more than he appears. Much more." She was wishing she had had a little longer with Handy. It had been a long time since they had had a really good talk.

She looked around. Was there blurring again? *Is something slowing down?* Just the thought of that made her very happy. Things were starting to happen again. That thought made her even happier.

Far away, but not so far, one of the many functionaries surrounding the new leader knocked on Twill's ornate office door. He turned in his gimbaled chair. "Yes."

"Something is happening back in the previous ScreenGrid." Twill knew it was about Earth.

"What is it?"

"Well, it's hard to know. Nothing has changed, but there was a small perturbation."

"Just that? Or something more?"

"Just that. We thought you should know." Twill thought for a moment. Reviewing events and schedules. Then he spoke.

"Well, occasionally things do adjust, and satellites will shift constantly in orbit especially after their mission is complete. Continue to monitor the situation and keep me informed." *There really isn't much that could happen now. It's all done.*

Twill went back to the planning of his great event. It was taking all of his time and attention. *It won't be long now*, he thought. All on The Screen would soon fall into line behind his leadership. The day was coming when there would be no doubt who was supreme. Farson? Earth? He swept his tendrils through the air as though shooing insects away. *They just don't matter anymore, if they ever did.*

118. Handy, Farson, and Andrew

"Well, we've analyzed the data, and it turns out you were right, Farson. There is a brief window, according to our scientists, of about eighteen nanoseconds. It is a moving target dimensionally because of the time facets, and we have unintentionally exacerbated that problem with our stasis controls, but we've got it under control now. It's really quite amazing; first, that it took us so long to notice the opening, and, second, that the ScreenMasters were so sloppy." Andrew was reading some details of the report as he spoke. He looked up at Farson and Handy. They were both looking at him.

"They weren't really sloppy, Andrew." Farson said. "It occurred at initiation. It's part of their system. It was because of your scientific advances inside stasis that you could detect it. That, plus one other external factor." President Sortt had more to say, but Farson was moving away.

"We calculate that it's going to happen again when they terminate, Farson. Are you leaving?" Andrew asked the question, but now the seemingly inattentive Handy was obviously watching Farson for the answer. Farson looked back at them both and smiled.

"I think I'll take a walk."

Sortt moved slightly as though to stand in Farson's way, more to illustrate the importance of the moment than with any hope of changing Farson's direction. "We need a decision, Farson. Time's awasting." Farson smiled at Andrew Sortt. He noted that, with all of his years, and all that had happened, Andrew could still be pushy. *And ambitious.* Farson saw that Andrew's shoes were the ones now popular on Emerald Earth. They floated slightly off the floor when the wearer was still. It reminded Farson of the robots. The shoes had a slight under-strobing when they lifted up. He noticed that Sortt was still standing there. Waiting. Pushing lightly, but with purpose, on the moment.

"Andrew, time is the one thing we have almost too much of," as he gently moved past Sortt and headed off alone for one of his favorite spots on the planet.

The effortless transportation system made it easy for people to move around on the planet, but Farson's mastery of it was different, more elegant. To Handy and Andrew it looked like he had just walked through the wall. Farson felt

Sortt's mental voice as he traveled. It was growing in strength, and that made Farson happy. Andrew's leadership meant everything.

<<*Farson?*>>

Sortt looked at Handy questioningly. "Will he be back?"

"Well, as you know, Farson is what he is. So, he either will be back or he won't. We still have our work to do, and it ain't going to be easy what we're up to."

"What is the 'one other external factor' he mentioned, Handy?"

"Something to do with the robots, most likely."

Farson was now nearing what he referred to as his "fishing hole" on Emerald Earth. It was a quiet place on the edge of one of the great fields. The smell of the wheat and soy and other crops filled his senses. It appeared to be a small "pond" where the plant material was shorter and the soil was richer, almost liquid. The "fish" he knew were descendants of the ancient and highly intelligent mammal dolphin. Farson liked the continuity of their evolution. His fishing pole was a holo-laser with a projection on the end that looked to the creatures like their favorite food. When they took the "hook," the sub-fields around the "bait" grabbed the animal painlessly, and that always precipitated the most exciting and fairest fights in the long history of sport fishing. The reel-end force fields protected Farson from being dragged, but gave the animal an unlimited length of line to run and fight. The mechanism measured the skill of the fisherman and the instincts of the "grass dolphin," as they were called, and simultaneously weighted things in favor of the better of the two. Too hard a tug by the fisherman and the line broke, freeing the dolphin. If the animal fought too hard and panicked, then the line stiffened in favor of the hunter. It was a true balancing of the hunter and the hunted, giving each an even hand in the fight.

Farson had never landed one yet, in many tries. *They are very smart.* It was a beautiful day, and he was thoroughly enjoying the casting of the line and the knowledge that there were hundreds of animals beneath the field watching and waiting. He could see the vegetation undulating with each cast, as the creatures followed it, inspected it, assessed its value, its veracity in terms of their world. Farson knew enough to wiggle the rod and to reel in the line just so, to taunt them. Sam had taught him well. In truth, Farson was happy just playing at fishing. A strike was not necessary for his satisfaction. He remembered what Sam had told him: "Fishing is what it's called, boy. Not catching."

As Farson continued casting, he was also remembering Sam. He had really loved Sam. Still did. Sam had been a sort of father to him. He had been a hard man to get to know, but as time went by, the two of them became very close. Farson was just an orphan boy from nothing, really. His mother and father died in the backwoods of Ohio, just as he was born. The beginning of his life remained part legend, part conjecture. Some say Farson changed his own beginnings after his Ascension to ScreenMaster of Earth, but he had never spoken of it. Sam had been a worker in the house of the Chamberlains, but far more than that to Farson. The Chamberlains were away so often that Sam and his wife Hattie had raised Farson, and in due course, Karina, too. Sam died a few years after Farson and Karina left. Perhaps tobacco did it; perhaps his broken heart did it. Hattie was still alive in the Indianapolis area, although nearing ninety now. Her strength was the catalyst for so many things in the lives of Farson and Karina. Hattie had been the first to see the love between them when they were still young. She had seen it long before anyone else.

"What in the name of God Almighty are you two doing?" Hattie had come into The Ship unannounced. The situation was clear. Farson was in the process of kissing Karina. It was going to be a very light kiss, but it was a kiss nonetheless. On hearing Hattie, the two of them leaped apart, embarrassed and off guard.

"Hattie! You are supposed to knock! You scared us." Hattie noticed the "us," and remembered how in the beginning Farson wouldn't even acknowledge Karina's presence in the Chamberlains' home. Now, they were both making frantic moves to get out of the attic and away from Hattie's astonished stare.

"Hold it right there!" They froze in place. "What is going ON?" Farson and Karina were recovering from a moment when, with eyes closed, they had slowly, exquisitely moved their lips to almost touching, where the innermost limits of close-but-no-contact had created a magnetic-like attraction, to the point where they both knew it was going to happen, no doubt remaining. They could feel each other's soft but excited breath. The emotions were surprising to them both. Karina had asked Farson if he had ever kissed a girl because some of her friends were doing it. He had sort of hawked up something in his throat and made a gagging sound, proclaiming that that would never happen. Girls were icky. Karina had asked him if he thought she was "icky." He said no, she was his friend and someone who helped crew The Ship. She had asked him if he had ever thought of kissing her. He said no, they were brother and sister. She said not really. Then she said that she was very curious what it felt like and would he do it with her so she could find out? He said no, of course not. She pleaded with him, said he was afraid. He denied that. She said what if they went to a planet someday where kissing was like handshaking there, wouldn't it be valuable to know what to do? He began to waver.

Just as their lips touched, Hattie had barged in. They were both in a high state of enthrallment. Hattie was feigning anger, but she *was* surprised.

"Come on, you two. Tell me what's going on." Neither of them spoke, heads down. "You were kissing, right?" Farson spoke first.

"Not really." Karina's head turned quickly in his direction for some help.

"I was just showing her how to do it."

"How would YOU know, Farsy? Ever kissed a girl before?"

"Well ... not really." Karina looked at him and mouthed the words back at him. Not *really*? He had told her flatly "no" when she had asked him. He smiled at her. Hattie just stood there, arms akimbo. She was an imposing figure, and one that meant so much to both of them. Her loving ways had made new lives possible for them both. With the Chamberlains away, Hattie and Sam were really the adults in the house. But all four of them were orphans in their own way.

"It's time for dinner, you two. We can talk about this later." The subject was closed for now. She had often wondered what would happen when these two "young'uns" became more aware of their changing bodies and increasing maturity. *Well,* she thought, *I guess we're there now.*

Sitting there at his "fishing hole" on Emerald Earth in a time far distant from the one he had just been thinking about – "reliving" would be a more accurate description – Farson knew, with the certainty only ScreenMasters can have, that Sam was still with him. He remembered when Sam had died and those years when Hattie and Sam had been part of every meal, almost everything he had done, or learned. He remembered the sense of family and stability they have given him. He remembered Sam's tough kindnesses, and Hattie's warm embraces, extravagant and infinite, wells that never ran dry. His gratitude was unbounded. He knew now that they had given their lives over to the care of two children of other parents, and yet had loved Karina, and him, without doubt or equivocation, as if they were their own. To Hattie, Farson was her son, and Karina was her daughter. To Sam, it was pure instinct to love them both. He was different from Hattie in his way of loving, but Sam's still waters ran just as deep. *It is important to remember these things.* In Farson's world there were issues that swept across all time and space. There were decisions that were his to make and his alone. He had already made some, and some more were on the docket right now waiting to be made. This base of his emotions, Hattie, Sam, and Karina, and worlds he had come through, were the matrix of his determination. Alone, he was filled with uncertainty. He constantly went back over his thoughts and actions in the past. Fortunately, as a ScreenMaster, he could relive them; he could change and adjust them somewhat. In the end, he knew he was just human. He was thinking about how Sortt had asked for a decision. Why had he spent so much time contemplating Sortt's shoes? *What makes me do that? Why am I so preoccupied with minutia? I can't seem to stay on a topic for long enough to reach orderly conclusions? Am I doing the right things here? It all feels so disjointed.* Farson's mind, relaxed and released from discipline, filled itself with disorder and doubt. Depression, always lurking around the edges, was always pushing in. Karina's absence made it all much worse. The time alone on Emerald Earth had been hard for Farson.

He was starting to fade into his own special brand of self-oblivion when he was abruptly startled back into reality. Someone was whistling, screechingly, in his ears.

"Will you pay attention, Farson!! You got a bite." Sam was mad and excited at the same time. Farson's rod was bending, precariously on the point where the fish could tear loose. He knew he had to ease the line or all would be lost. "That's better, boy. Ya'd think ya never got taught nothin' about fishin', for God's sake. Ya almost lost it." Farson knew immediately which fish it was. The biggest one of the day. The one that would make Sam jealous when they returned home. The one that Hattie would grab first for dinner. He had been here a hundred times before. He looked at Sam. Sam's eyes were intent on the fight, watching Farson, watching the fish, as though seeing it all for the first time. Farson looked in Sam's eyes. There it was. The unselfish love of a true father. Sam didn't care who caught the big fish of the day. He was living the moment with Farson. His eyes jumping back and forth, his hands wringing in anticipation of a successful catch. It was the most important thing in the world to Sam: Farson's fish. Farson's doubts and worries were gone. He was working the rod with all of his abilities. It was a big fish. It took all of his fishing skills. It was a moment to live fully, and he was doing that. Exactly that.

When Handy had entered into Emerald Earth's time frame for the first time, he carried with him the keys to a future that would change everything. As he transitioned to the inside of "the bottle," many things happened. Access had always been blocked. But on this day and in this place, Handy had known it would be otherwise. As he walked in (it had taken almost six full steps), he felt things, and he sensed much more. Crossing the threshold, he was immediately swept with a soft, warm breeze. He quickly noticed that everything he wore, and every inch of his body had been cleaned as thoroughly as anything in his life had ever been cleaned. He felt refreshed as though from ten hours of deep sleep.

The world he had just entered had embraced him technologically. It was temperatureless. The air was unnoticeable and clean. It was supremely comfortable. There was quite a crowd there to greet him, a ceremony really. Thunderous applause welcomed him. He sensed the whole world had been waiting and now was watching. He was right. Andrew Sortt greeted him, but the first thought he encountered was Farson's.

<<*It took you long enough, Handy.*>>

<<*Yeah, I'm a little slow, aren't I?*>> An attempt at humor.

<<*I have been trying to tell you.*>>

<<*Well, I'm here now. Am I too late?*>>

<<*Not at all. You have done magnificently. We have been planning for this moment for a long, long time.*>> Handy looked around at the strange, tall, golden people all around Farson. *There must be a thousand of them.*

"Welcome, ScreenMaster Handy Townsend. On behalf of the people of Emerald Earth, we are honored to greet you on this historic day."

Andrew Sortt was performing the leadership duties he had agreed to. Even in a world as highly egalitarian as Emerald Earth, there were still times when the one spoke for the many. As Sortt's life had been extended – as the lives of all Emers had been extended – he had accepted the role reluctantly, arguing there were others more worthy; it was time for younger leaders; he was ready to move aside, but it all fell on deaf ears. Emers believed a reluctant leader was the only one worth having.

The ceremonies were concluded efficiently and in a meeting of key scientists and President Sortt, Handy had turned over the purple object and the revolution had begun. In the subsequent days, the Emer scientists acquired total orbital field control and were ready as the moment approached. By agreement, only Farson could activate the new system. Handy described the process by comparing it to the old-Earth art burglary scenario, where the robber lifts the valuable object and replaces it immediately with another valueless object without setting off the weight-sensitive alarm system. Farson liked Handy's analogy, but he said the difference was that the getaway would take a long, long time and that they were now replacing a doomed and unwanted object with two new things: a priceless planet and its people and a massive dissimulation that must not be discovered. "It's the old bait and switch," he said.

Everyone, on that day of days, knew it was a lot more than that.

Handy had, of course, been looking around for Farson after his departure "for a walk." He found him sitting on the edge of a meander in one of the small canals that still honeycombed the fields in this area. He was way, way out in the middle of the northern expanse. There was a creature beside him, wiggling and anxious to get away. Handy recognized the grass dolphin of course. <<*What are you doing, Farson?*>>

<<*Do you know these creatures are highly intelligent? It thinks it was fishing for me. It's very pleased with itself for catching me.*>> The creature was golden in color and had a soft furry layered coat that appeared at first to be wet scales, but the sheen was really part of its beautiful coloring. Its blowhole and gills were large and working hard, breathing the air and meta-liquid mix composition of the slushy subsurface too. <<*Amazing what the Emers have done.*>> Farson seemed preoccupied with the creature's anatomy and obvious awareness. Handy was, ironically, impatient with Farson's distraction. The grass dolphin's orienting response at Handy's speech pleased Farson immensely. <<*This is one smart creature here, Handy.*>>

<<*Are you ready yet, Farson? We've got a world of things to do.*>> Farson knew Handy's nature well. The impatience Handy was reflecting was a product of the Emers' enthusiastic industry and assiduousness in so many years of isolation and preparation. It was more than forgivable. They had been waiting for 6,500 years. Now the time had come.

<<*Not quite. One more year, Handy. That's when it will happen.*>> Handy laughed. He knew that meant he and Farson would be together for a while longer and that made him happy. But he also knew that it meant – on the outside – that it would only be a short time, about a half a day, before everything changed. He had time to enjoy himself, but the revolution was already upon them. It was the best of both worlds. Plenty of time, but none to waste. He also knew the Emers would not be happy waiting another long year.

<<*What do you think Twill will do?*>> Handy asked. Farson gently pushed the creature back into the swishy field, giving it a friendly pat on its back. It swam away in the green and amber slurry, finning its way through the vegetation, moving down into the thick, rich subsurface below.

<<*You ought to know. You're the one who created him.*>> Handy put his hand on his forehead and shook his head back and forth, slumping slightly in self-recrimination. In his early ScreenMaster days, exploring, he had known Twill and shown him the way of The Screen. Not his proudest moment, in retrospect.

<<*What in the name of Jesus, Mary, and Joseph was I thinking?*>> Farson smiled at him.

<<*You did the best you could. You were all alone in those days.*>>

<<*Except for you. You were always around.*>>

<<*Well, Handy, I was hardly 'around,' as you put it. My mother was pregnant and dying. My father was lost and abandoned. It was pretty bleak for me until you came along. So,*

it was always you, Handy, not me. And your doing 'the best you could' was, without a doubt, the most important sequence of events in all of human history. You are the one, Handy, and you know it. You've always been the one.>>

<<*I've been trying to forget it. I'm not up to it, never have been, never will be. I just do what I'm told.*>>

<<*As do I.*>> That made them both laugh. Farson stood up and walked over to Handy. Standing right in front of him, he took him in an embrace and hugged him. <<*I've been wanting to do that for a long time, Handy. You have been so important, and your struggles have been so unappreciated.*>> Handy knew this time on Emerald Earth was the first time he and Farson had been in the same real time and real place over so many years. *How long had it been?* It was impossible to know because of the times involved and the places. It had been a long, long time. The warmth of their friendship had always been there, but Handy always wondered whether it was real or just his imagination grasping at the straws he needed to continue to persevere. Now, here, he knew it was real. No delusion. Farson Uiost was his friend. Forever. <<*That has a new ring, doesn't it, Handy? 'Forever.'*>>

<<*I need a drink, Farson. Let's go.*>>

<<*Bring your guitar.*>> This made them both laugh again as the two of them simply, but slowly, disappeared, the telltale purple ScreenMasters' hue remaining briefly almost like a shadow fading at dusk. The grass around swayed in the breeze with their passage. Their footprints in the spongy surface filled in again, and soon it was as if they had never been there. In all directions, as far as the eye could see, the amber waves moved gently, life teeming above and beneath the surface of Emerald Earth with the clear, amber sky over all.

Handy had one more thought for Farson. <<*You know he is preparing his own Grand Ascension.*>> Farson knew.

<<*Yes, but for whom and to where? That is the question.*>> Handy laughed at the irony of Farson's question. He felt a new thought forming with Farson's last comment.

<<*I've got an idea for a new song, Farson.*>>

<<*I can't wait to hear it.*>>

119. Karina, Viera, and Voul; Brittany and Her Father

It was dark in her compartment. She liked it that way. But for once she had decided to turn on the lights. Since the penumbra shock wave hit SkyKing, Karina had been avoiding things. When ZZ<<Arkol25609 asked for her help, she knew it was important. The robots were a conflicted species. On the one hand, their devotion to Farson was obvious. On the other hand, they were driven by deep programming and cherished traditions that were not always in perfect sync with him. Farson knew full well that there were scenarios where the robots could be a problem, but that had not happened yet. It was one of the reasons he had elevated Karina so early. ZZ<<Arkol loved her. *If the robots love.* The robots also knew that when all else failed, Karina's connection with Farson was a constant they could count on. In her compartment, Karina was thinking about her current level of connection. Even though she and Farson were communicating, it certainly wasn't the type of contact that she wanted. *When you grow up with someone, you'd think you'd get tired of them eventually.* Clearly, that was not the case.

Their beginnings had been tough. She could vividly remember that ride to the Chamberlains' house from the space port. She could remember the smell of the upholstery in the vehicle's luxurious backseat. She could remember Sam, and how formal and standoffish he had seemed driving the car. *Doing his job.* She remembered the street lamps of the town going by through the windows. When the big white house with red shutters came into view, she wanted to get out and run away, but, instead, she allowed herself to be guided inside; she felt trapped. That day she was on automatic pilot. When she got to her room, she turned off all the lights and sat on the small bed, alone in the dark. Just as she had after the shock wave hit so many years later.

Her sixth year had been the saddest time of her life. It had been the most fantastic time, too. Her parents had been assigned to the space station the year before, and moving into space from a college town in Maine was fearful and exciting and captivating, all at the same time. The Jacobson family had to make the transition quickly because the opportunities and demands for her mother's specialty were growing by leaps and bounds. Her skills were desperately needed on the station right away. Space botany was now a profession that had many practitioners, and its conceptual framework was held to be intellectually challenging and fascinating in its far-reaching potential. But the realities of initiating self-sustaining vegetation in an entirely artificial environment were complex and daunting. Easy to begin but perhaps impossible to perpetuate.

Karina's mother was the foremost scientist on Earth in this highly specialized field. She had built and argued the case, successfully, that once the natural environment was discarded, it would take all of humanity's collective knowledge and experience to build a complete biosphere with an autonomous, self-sustaining, growing climatic environment. Further – and this was the theory that had gained her international fame – she had stated that the artificial environment would become far, far simpler than its natural progenitor and, because of that, there was no reason to even attempt to replicate nature. The key to success, she postulated, would be ingenious chemistry and not merely environmental replications.

To the botanists, this bordered on philosophical heresy, because instead of a natural environment determining reality, her theory was that botanical engineering, independent of "nature," could generate a brand-new, perhaps better, environment. Better for plants, and, most controversially, for people too. Her laboratory proofs were elegant and persuasive. Her depth of research into fermentation, yeasts, and, interestingly, seaweed and crabs, had brought tremendous accolades and honors.

But then, in the opinion of many, she went too far. To her critics, her laboratory experiments were interesting and innovative, but how could they ever be proven in practice?

Then the "Jacobson Chain" *was* proven. Catherine's experiments resulted in a brand-new group of vegetation, rich in nutrients, delicious in taste and texture, and in the end, infinitely manipulatable, creating new foods and a whole new approach to cultivation.

Her system of fertilization within a "closed" environment won her the Nobel Prize two years in a row. The second prize's citation noted that she had defined the "closed" environment with a series of experiments that proved her hypothesis of life's self-sustaining quality: Nothing, in a purely molecular sense, is either destroyed or created. In her microscopic filtrations, nothing was wasted. Some of the implications of this system were disturbing to moralists, but Catherine Jacobson overcame them with her famous "re-assemblers" that utilized the most basic component of matter as its building block. She made the case that all matter was equal in her equations and that it was human intelligence, and spirit – she granted – that made some combinations so distinct. Vegetation was the potter's clay, she said, not flesh and bones. The arguments persisted that she was playing God, but her assiduous attention to detail, and her persuasive, non-combative nature, made friends of potential enemies. The new highly nutritious foods were overwhelmingly popular, and in a surprise side effect, even though they were filling, they, miraculously, guided consumers to their natural body weight and clearly extended life spans considerably. What medicine's "miracle drugs" had done for pain, Catherine Jacobson's "ChainFoods" did for dietary obesity and other food and eating disorders. The full impact of humanity moving away from animal tissue and other products in the traditional food chain was just as startling as the miracle drugs of previous generations. Somehow, the world knew that with her discoveries and achievements, something fundamental had changed for humanity.

When the call came with the invitation to SkyKing and the Moon, Catherine could not have been more excited. There were many offers, but space was the vacuum her nature longed to fill. It was the perfect assignment.

"Oh, my God! Oh, my God! Oh, my God!" Karina heard her mother's happy screaming all the way down to her little playroom in the basement. She looked up from her holoscreen, tapped her wrist to shut it down, and ran toward the stairs, scattering toys and tripping over blocks, vicariously excited. She ran to her mother, leaving the playroom, as usual, in the apparent chaos and disorder that only she could understand. Karina knew something wonderful had happened. When Catherine Jacobson saw her daughter coming, she ran and picked her up, and the two of them were spinning around and then jumping up and down with glee. "Wait until your daddy hears this one!"

The timing could not have been better. Tom Jacobson was about to be fired. He worked at a division of General Motors that specialized in air integrity systems. His primary responsibility was to manage a section that produced airlocks for the growing space station. He knew there was something wrong in the alloy systems they were using, and after months of research and investigations, he was about to blow the whistle on the company's self-serving apathy to the risks involved. He didn't really have a problem with his employer's preoccupying dedication to profitability, but there were limits. His senior vice president immediately saw Tom's scathing report as a problem. "Oh, come on, Tom. Those doors and hatches have been working perfectly for over twenty years. Upgrades have been seamless. The new schedule is accelerated. What's the problem? It's not like the doors will fail. They could just leak a little, right?" Karina's father was a thoughtful man. He was a man who liked to have tools in his hands. He liked to actually do the work. Theory was one thing, but practical working with the objects manufactured from those theories was where reality met the papers pushed around in the office. Practice was always different from theory. Over the years, Tom had seen it many times. The quiet sequencing of controlled experiments versus the chaotic roar of reality's unintended consequences; he knew that the best laid plans always alter once the battle begins. He had learned that lesson. History's argument is irrefutable. Tom knew that turning back when you're on the wrong path is the only choice. He tried again.

"You are talking about the theory, Bob. I am talking about the reality of the metals in space. Twenty years of people coming and going, carrying things, doing things without thinking while doing something else. You are right. They may 'just leak' first, but if you look at that report more closely, you'll see that 'leaking' doesn't always mean the same thing in one situation as it may mean in another. On SkyKing there are always a series of airlocks in the most critical places. If one leaks, it increases the likelihood that the next one will leak.

The carefully controlled pressure differentials are what give the elegance to our products. When you walk through our airlocks, they open and close around you in a series of pressure changes that make it seem like you are just walking along, but those transitions are highly complex, both mathematically and from an engineering point of view. Those years you hold up as proof of invincibility are also the variable we cannot control. As one of the predicted pressures changes, even microscopically, it causes slight recalculations in all of the others. This has been going on for years. There is a situation, where all of these minor changes, cascading along other chains of integral and responsive changes, could cause a serious problem to develop unseen. Look at the scenario section in the appendix." Bob Baker wasn't really listening. He had heard it all before. Tom Jacobson went on anyway. "The probability of loss of life and loss of whorl integrity could be very high. Unacceptably high. The records will exist to paper trail it right back to us, Bob. We've got to do something. We've *got to*, Bob."

"What? Close the station? There are 285,000 people up there now and more every day."

"I would stop new assignments, clear the oldest whorl, and fix it on a whorl-by-whorl basis."

"And, how long would that take, Tom? How much would that cost?"

"Years. Billions." At this point, the conversation always broke down. They had been there before. His boss just looked at him.

"Years, Tom? Billions? Are you crazy? There's no stopping SkyKing now. Your idea would be an operational catastrophe. A monumental setback. A public relations nightmare. Why not just continue the refit?"

Tom knew what his boss was talking about. The famous "refit" theory. It held that a new whorl, the sixth, would be built and followed by a partial "isolation" of the famous "WhorlOne" original compartments. This would clear that section of the early station for a dynamic systematic refit of its doors and other facilities. It was part of the original maintenance design. It would not interrupt anything. Like a caterpillar creeping along a branch from leaf to leaf, the refit would eventually update everything: from the oldest to the newest. It would be a bonanza for General Motors, essentially building a whole new, much larger, more intricate space station right over the old one. There was a possibility that it would actually work. The aging early systems on the station were the most susceptible to a cascade. Even Tom Jacobson acknowledged that, but, for him, the risks were just too high. "Can't we agree on this, Tom? My higher-ups are not happy with your intransigence on this. Your documentations have not been well received." Tom shook his head, but said nothing. It was becoming useless. His boss wanted to conclude the conversation. "Well, let's not go too far here today, Tom. It's late. Let's call it a day. Think it over. We'll talk again tomorrow."

The meeting broke up, and Tom was headed home with a heavy heart. Married to one of humanity's most popular and famous people, he was about to be fired. *What's wrong with me? Why can't I just shut up? Why do I have to be the guy that always sees the gloom and doom? Why can't I just go along?*

Riding in the levi-lola train, speeding along at 300 miles per hour without a vibration or any sense of speed, it was as though he was just standing in a room. He was relieved when he felt the slight vibration on his wrist. It was Catherine. She was excited.

"Hi, honey," she said. "We're going into space."

Karina was young, but she still noticed the struggle her mom and dad had with leaving Earth. Their house was everything to them. Catherine's laboratories were there, Karina's playroom. Her dad's den and workshop. She heard her dad say that the move was actually going to be a great thing. "A hard thing," he said, "but it's going to be great for us." Karina thought she sensed some worry in her dad's voice.

The company had immediately assigned him to manage the "refit," and that got him away from any pending employment issues. They said he was the perfect person to oversee the repairs. When Tom had started to depict the refit as wrongheaded and dangerous, his boss held up both hands and said, "The timing is perfect."

"Let's have a going-away party," Catherine said. Karina liked the idea. No, she loved the idea. It was a chance to say goodbye to all her friends and to start her new life all at the same time. Catherine was excited, too. Tom feigned exuberance. He was under no illusions: The transfer would solve some problems and create others.

"It's going to be a big, big party, Tom. You know that, right?" He laughed at Catherine's comment. Of course, he knew it. He took her in his arms in a big hug. His wife's gregariousness was well known from long experience together.

"Not for me," he said. "There'll only be two people there for me." When Karina heard that, she rushed into a three-way embrace with her parents. Arms all around, they hugged each other, Mom and Dad bending down to put all of their faces together, kissing her, and laughing. It was a happy moment for them all. Especially for Karina. New worlds coming.

<<*Karina, what are you doing?*>> It was Farson, of course. His thought startled her in her deep remembering.

<<*You know exactly what I'm doing, Farson.*>>

<<*You're indulging yourself a little with that hug sequence, aren't you?*>>

<<*You're just jealous.*>>

<<*Well, I do have you, dear sister.*>>

<<*Really, Farson? I hear it's another year before we're back together. When WILL we be hugging again?*>>

<<*Close your eyes.*>> Karina resisted his mental embrace, wanting more.

<<*THAT is not what I mean. I want to actually hug you.*>> She could feel the coming changes on The Screen. Some of the changes she saw worried her.

<<*What difference does proximity make really, Karina?*>>

<<*It makes a big difference, Farson. A big difference.*>> There was a long pause in their conversation. She could sense him in her mind, waiting. She had to admit that this level of contact was not all bad. She could feel him holding her. She could even sense his heartbeat and his soft breath on her neck. *It tickles.* It was nice. It was reassuring. But still … Farson kissed her and looked into her eyes. He could sense her resignation to things as they are. He didn't like the sense of incompleteness either. He knew this was the best they could hope for. *For now.* He also knew there were still things they could do to make things better. He smiled at her. She knew what would come next.

<<*Let's go have some fun.*>>

It was their first skydive as licensed jumpers. The first time they could jump together alone, without instructors. They were on the plane, heading to altitude. There were nineteen other jumpers with them. They would be the next to last out because they were scheduled to pull high, as inexperienced jumpers do. Farson was looking at her. Her jumpsuit was tight; it had to be. She was fairly light and fairly tall, so her fall rate would be slower. He was even taller than her, and heavier. They were both fit, so Farson wore a looser jumpsuit to slow him down. He guessed that their fall rates would be close enough. In free fall, proximity makes the jump fun, and fall rate is crucial to maintaining proximity. They had planned a skydive that they really had no business attempting, but for them things were not always what they seemed to be. This jump was one of their favorite "places" to be together. It was like a carnival ride to them. How many times had they done it? Only they would know, but as Farson said once when Karina asked him, "Who's counting?" They laughed at that question again, as they always did. Counting would be meaningless because the "number of times" one does something implies that time is a limiting factor. For Farson and Karina, now, time was an element of their ways and means. They could manipulate it the way others walked from room to room, but there was more to it than that. It would be like being in one room studying for an exam, and also being in two or three other places, say, sleeping (and getting the physical benefits), playing cards with three friends, and exercising in another. Being in many places at the same time, independently living each time, and, overall, knowing exactly what was happening; this was now natural for them. And, it was even more. They could use the dreams from the sleep room, to help them win the card games, and while exercising, use the improved oxygenation to improve their exam score. As Uvo had said, "It's a whole new sort of existence."

The load organizer shouted out, "Two minutes!" holding up two fingers for those jumpers in hard helmets who couldn't hear over the roar of the twin-engined plane and the insulation of their helmets. Farson and Karina were giving each other final gear checks; it was part of the fun. Farson would check her chest strap by tugging on it and running his fingers along the fastener. He could feel the swelling of her breasts and the warmth of her body through her snug suit. He would carefully check her leg straps and attachment points and then go to the back of the rig to check her reserve and main pins. Finally, he could check her "hacky," a soft pullout device at the bottom of her rig that activated the parachute system at pull time. Once all of that was done, Farson would give her an affectionate pat on her butt and always think <<*That's my favorite part.*>> Karina enjoyed the pre-jump gear check ritual as much as he did.

<<*Now, it's my turn.*>> She went through the same routine on Farson, but when she got to the leg straps, her fingers seemed to find something that required extra smoothing and checking. <<*Don't want that out of position during deployment.*>> She moved in closer and reached behind him with both hands to check his pins with her fingers and to check his "hacky." She patted the back of his rig, and they moved closer into a long hug. Then it was time for them to helmet-up and prepare to leave the plane. As Karina was smoothing her hair and putting on her open-faced helmet and goggles, she looked toward the front of the plane where a student and an instructor were waiting for their turn to leave. Her instructor was there with the student. He was looking at her. He had seen their embrace and "gear checks." She smiled at him and sent a thought rocketing into his brain, <<*You should be preparing your student and not watching me.*>> He bolted upright, eyes wide. Uncertain of what had just happened, he turned to his student with a little extra alacrity and attended to business.

<<*Karina. You are bad.*>> She looked at Farson with a mischievous grin on her face.

<<*He deserved it, gawking like that.*>>

<<*His sister is probably not quite so friendly.*>>

<<*Too bad for him.*>>

When their turn came, they exited the plane together, diving toward the tail, at around 14,000 feet. In no time they were linked, hands to hands, facing each other. Falling at around 115 miles per hour, they moved closer until their lips were touching. Then they kissed deeply. *A kiss pass.* Farson pulled her into him, and they held tightly. Kissing and now tumbling, they stayed together for almost sixty seconds. In such an intense environment, they were exhilarated and stimulated. It never ceased to excite them. They split apart and tracked to separation, safely deploying their parachutes simultaneously but at a safe distance apart. Farson could hear Karina laughing as their chutes settled in at about 2,500 feet above the drop zone. As arranged, they flew side by side to the drop zone and landed right beside each other, both easily standing up their landings, instead of the awkward, off-balance, tumbling landings most beginning jumpers are so well known for.

With the parachutes still lying on the ground, they rushed together and embraced again, falling down into the wind-billowed, high-performance nylon and lines of their canopies. It was warm, and the material smelled like fresh air as they snuggled together and kissed each other with brief, exhilarated abandon. Eventually, they stood up and gathered their canopies for the walk back to the packing area. As they walked together, neatly coiled lines in hand and canopies thrown over their shoulders, they noticed that people were watching them. One person watching was the instructor. Again. He was escorting his student to the hangar after the jump. Karina looked at him and their eyes met. <<*Don't.*>> Farson was half-playing with her.

<<*Farson, you're getting bossy.*>> He knew she was right. Her strength as a ScreenMaster had grown exponentially. He could tell that beneath her quip, the truth was obvious.

<<*Sorry, I'll be better next time.*>> Holding hands and laughing as if they didn't have a care in the world, they continued on to the packing area of the hangar. The instructor had turned away.

She stood up in her room on SkyKing and went to the door of the compartment. The chime had sounded, indicating that her invited guests were arriving on time for the meeting. Karina had kept them waiting for a moment or two, but it wouldn't matter. Just before she opened the door, she paused for a moment. She was still reliving that last moment on the ground, "under canopy," as Farson called it. She could feel his hands on her, his lips exploring hers. The immense intimacy of that moment was lingering in her thoughts: She could still smell him; she could still feel the sensory overload; her hands were still full of him. <<*It's just the skydive, Karina. You've always found that exciting. Perhaps you're confusing amorousness with adrenaline?*>> So far from the truth, she knew he was trying to be funny. "Goofy," as she often put it. She knew how much he loved her, how he longed for the very same things she did, how he loved the way she loved him. Her eyes were welling up a little as her hand turned the handle on the door to let the guests in. Just his joking thought that her feelings were less than genuine was upsetting. All she wanted was a normal life again. When would that happen? When would things settle down? *When?* <<*What difference does it make, Karina? Weren't we just there? Just now? It was real.*>> She knew he was lingering around her, just as she was lingering, her hand hovering over the door handle, extending the moment. His ability to master his emotions left her unsettled. He always seemed like he had such control. She knew it was an act, but even that seemed out of her reach.

<<*'What difference?' Farson? You've got to be kidding.*>> She couldn't hide the effect his comment had had on her. He

knew exactly what button to push to get the desired confirmation he was looking for. He knew when he seemed to doubt her, even in the smallest degree, it just made her crazy. She could never accept anything short of absolute in that regard. It was the one thing they both had. The one thing that saved them both.

Now she was opening the door handle. <<*I'm too easy. Too much in love with you. You take advantage.*>>

<<*I do? We can straighten it out when we get together, Kari.*>> He was enjoying his own joke. She started to turn the handle.

<<*You are so funny, Farson. I forgot to laugh.*>>

She opened the door and everyone filed in. Farson was gone.

Brittany was first to enter. She looked at Karina and instantly grasped that something was going on. "Karina, have you been crying?" Karina looked at the thirteen-year-old. She was an amazing with her luxuriant auburn hair, she was not tall, but very pretty. Striking. Her soft hair was just touching her shoulders. She was wearing the bright Sker whites she always preferred. She looked great. Sadly, Karina knew that Brittany was growing up. Her father was coming into the room right behind her. Karina couldn't help making a comment to him, somewhat kidding, but she knew there was truth in it, too.

"Jim, you're letting her go out looking like that?" Brittany's whites were a perfect fit. "She might upset the Skers." Jim Peterson laughed. He was a strong-appearing man, obviously used to command, comfortable with himself. She could tell that he had mellowed over the years on matters concerning his daughter.

"She's a big girl. I can trust her." Karina had noticed the slightest suggestion of color beneath the pressed white of Brittany's uniform.

"She's made a few 'improvements,' I see." Jim's eyes swept over his daughter and back to Karina. His eyebrows shot up without comment. Brittany was watching all of this, of course, now hoping to change the topic.

"Is everything okay, Kari?" she asked. Karina's nickname rolled off her tongue. She was the only other person besides Farson who ever called her that. An intimacy that Karina strictly avoided and discouraged with most people. Somehow Brittany's easy affability carried an exemption. Karina let it go as usual. The truth was, she liked it when Brittany called her that.

"These are crazy times, changing times. A lot is going on." Brittany nodded as Karina answered her question. "Actually, I was laughing before you all came in."

"Has Farson been around?" Brittany knew he had been. How she knew, Karina could only guess. Farson had been away for a long time as far as the people of SkyKing were concerned. But somehow Brittany knew that just wasn't true for Karina. As the years had gone by, Karina had noticed that Brittany was precocious in a number of interesting ways. Karina's hesitation to answer the teenager's impulsive question was interrupted by the late arrival of Voul into the room. Brittany's attention shifted and her excitement was obvious.

"Voul," she said happily and moved to hug him. The two of them had always been close ever since Brittany had been born on SkyKing. Voul was a big brother to her. She loved him and always let him know. Hugging him, she asked, "Does this mean we're finally getting married, Voul?" He laughed and, after a few moments of hugging, gently pushed her away and smoothed his pristine uniform. As she stepped back, she had scuffed his shoe. He bent down to quietly smooth the mark away, as any Sker would. Brittany went right down with him and moved his hand away and said, "Let me do that." They were having a minor struggle over who was going to buff up the shoe. Their hands were fighting over it, and the scuffing was not getting fixed. This was just the sort of situation that Brittany loved the most. She had his undivided attention, and she was having a ball. Finally, Voul stood up in frustration.

"I can fix it later," he said. Brittany was still down there, buffing away.

"Brittany, behave yourself. Leave Voul alone." Jim Peterson had seen it all before, many, many times. Brittany slowly stood up, looking at the door. Viera had entered.

"Well, Brittany, have you gotten him to propose to you yet? I sure haven't." Brittany was conflicted momentarily but not for long. She hugged Viera with almost the same intensity of feeling that she so often exhibited for Voul. Viera loved her too. Brittany had something special that was secretly precious to Viera, something she herself had never had: the stability of a warm relationship with a loving father. She looked at the young girl's face and stroked Brittany's brown hair. She could smell the sweetness of the young teenager. Viera knew that even though Brittany was still young, she was probably the most popular person on the station. Everyone loved her. Her skills in navigation and in organization had grown immensely from being at her father's side. Her education was proceeding way ahead of schedule. She had accepted the fact that she was a role model for the coming generation. *She is still just a kid.* Viera was still holding her, and looking her over. "What have you got on under there, Brittany?" This question caused Brittany to quickly move back, her face reddening.

"Probably the same things you do," she said a little too quickly. Viera knew that Brittany was just defending her undergarment choices, but Viera also knew that under her own orange MoonBase jumpsuit there was absolutely nothing. She laughed and said, "I don't think so, kiddo." Voul looked at Viera. They exchanged a moment together. Karina was about to start the meeting. Everyone turned in her direction. Brittany was relieved that everyone was now focusing on other things.

Karina began to speak about things to come.

Farson was back at his desk in North Conway. The snow was piling up outside. It was cold so the snow was fluffy. Earlier he had cleared the walk and taken out the trash. *Fat chance there'll be a pickup today.* The air was so fresh that he had lingered outdoors. The weather was fascinating. *On Emerald Earth all of this has changed now.* The planet now had one climate, one global weather, one people. *At least I can still come here.* That thought made Farson pause with a new reality. *I'm not alone anymore.* Being in many places at once, roaming in and out of time and space; his world had become so much bigger, so much more interestingly complex. He was constantly amazed at his ability to handle it all, to know where and what and when he was. His abilities had grown with a central awareness and consciousness. But he had always been alone on The Screen. In the olden days of old Earth, explorers had used the sun to navigate their world. Now his navigations were almost spiritual, at least metaphysical. The only way to *know* was to *be*, and to be aware of being. He could sense all the other times and the other places. He knew that Voul and Viera, Brittany and Jim were with Karina. He knew what Handy and the people "in the bottle" were doing. He knew that Twill was still plotting. He flexed his mind for a moment and was flying down a MoonBase tunnel on the gurney. It stopped, and the doors opened. He could see John Silver working at the consoles. He could tell things were getting ready. He could also sense Twill doing his thing, relentlessly.

Farson moved his chair away from his desk, stood up, and went to the window. It was a strong New Hampshire storm. Even the trash he had just taken out was already covered.

<<*Karina?*>> Farson's voice was soft, almost a whisper.

<<*I'm just about to start, Farson. Is it time yet or not?*>>

<<*Not quite. Time in the bottle is passing quickly, so you can sense their urgency, but we need to be careful now. Twill is still a ScreenMaster, if a little old-fashioned. If we are not careful, he can and will cause trouble. He's preoccupied with his plans for his Ascension, but he remains a factor.*>> Farson looked down at the document on his desk that he had been reading. Karina could see it through his eyes.

<<*That isn't your famous 'Letter to the Skers,' is it?*>>

<<*Yes. You remember Uvo implied that I went too far with this.*>> Farson knew she did. <<*So, I'm rereading it.*>> There was a silence for a few minutes, which seemed natural between them. Silence was not an indication of inaction in their relationship. Karina was the first to speak.

<<*Voul is making the transition well enough. Leaving all of that behind is not easy for him.*>> Farson shuffled the papers. He tapped them on the desk to jog all the edges back to even again. He looked up, feeling an intenseness pushing its way in. He knew that Voul's struggles were scriptural. The times were demanding big and rapid changes. Without clear guidelines, in a world he had never imagined, things were hard for the King of the Skers. The document in Farson's hands had been an important addition to their history.

<<*But, creeds are just 'systems' for belief structures, and too often they have to be written down. Static doctrines will no longer suffice. We all have to be engaged in reality and involved together. All together. There can be no exceptions. As the*

Americans used to say, 'E pluribus unum.' Out of many, one.>> Karina smiled at him, softly shaking her head. *Now I know why Uvo was concerned.*

<<*The next thing you know, Farson, you'll be singing 'The Star-Spangled Banner.'*>>

<<*Let's leave that to Handy.*>>They both laughed. It was one of those well-timed comments that created laughter that wouldn't stop. Handy singing the national anthem. Every time they paused and tried to move on, it started up again.

<<*Karina, you know there's really no reason to be concerned. The Skers understood completely. Uvo was just being overly protective.*>>

<<*I know, Farsy, but many times Uvo was right.*>>

<<*True enough.*>> Still looking out the window, Farson noticed that even his own boot tracks, in the deepening snow, were almost gone.

Twill was snarling. *How can they be so unconcerned? So preoccupied with such minutiae? Everything they wanted is being destroyed, and they can't stop it. That has always been what's wrong with Farson and his horrible sister. They are irrelevant. I wish I had Uvo to ask about this. He knew them better than I. He liked them. But he's dead now. As they will soon be.*

Twill's mind swept over The Screen, adjusting it, moving things, encompassing it. It felt good. Strong. Secure. *It's better than ever. Except for Earth. That one little spot. Why does it take so long? We've fixed The Screen elsewhere far more easily. It's because of the nature of humanity. What they have done was far worse than any other. It'll take time to fix. But it'll be done.* His mind fastened on the Patch and the Tear. They were both holding strong, and the defect was getting smaller. *Yes, it's all going according to plan.*

Farson and Karina were not laughing now.

<<*See, Kari. He's there; he's right there.*>>

<<*Yes, Farson, I see. Did you feel it?*>>

<<*The extra pressure on the ScreenPatch? Yes, I did. It was surprising.*>> Farson thought for a moment to himself. If Karina noticed it, others probably did too. <<*Time is running out.*>> There was just a hint of worry in his thought, Karina noticed.

Karina turned to the four other people in the room. "It's going to be a little hairy from here on in. Let's go over the plan one more time." Everyone started working out the details together, including Brittany who was sitting at the table between Voul and Viera, occasionally looking back and forth.

120. The Welcomed Truth

The plan was simple but not easy. The Emers' assumption of co-control of the orbital stasis barrier would be seamless in its operation, and there would be no way for the ScreenMasters to know anything had happened. Everything would be exactly the same for them, except for the slightly increased, deeply embedded alternate authority protocols, which were undetectable. According to the engineers overseeing the project, the plan was foolproof.

The Emers had a fully integrated program to secretly manipulate the switchover and to continue the stealth ghosting of Emerald Earth while Farson did the rest.

The plan was now in full implementation mode, and everyone was hard at work.

Nearly eight-year-old Farson softly knocked on Karina's door. He waited, staring at the crack where the door and the frame met. He waited. He was deeply hoping against all hope that there would be some sort of movement: The crack might widen or maybe there could even be just a shaking. He fantasized that it might shake a little as she approached, her light step causing a vibration on the old wooden floors within. Something. Then there would be a slight change in the light around the crack as she touched the doorknob. It would be slight, but in his heightened state of concentration he would discern it. Then there would be the telltale increase in distance between the door and the jamb. Small at first, perhaps infinitesimal, but nonetheless discernible. Then ... and then ... he saw that it just wasn't moving at all.

<<*Farson, why do you insist on playing with history?*>>

<<*It was our only disagreement, Karina. Wouldn't you like to have a perfect record?*>>

<<*You can't change history, Farson, at least not for us. I will remember no matter what you do.*>>

<<*How would you know?*>>

<<*I'd know. You know I'd know.*>>

<<*Well, why didn't you answer the door?*>>

<<*This is stupid. You know exactly why I didn't answer the door.*>>

<<*Tell me again.*>> She was not happy at this recalling of a bad memory. It had been the one time in their life together when Farson had been completely unreasonable with her. His case had been based on the high calling of his efforts and "distractions." That was what he had called it. "Distractions." So, she had closed the door in his face. He had left in a huff. He came back.

<<*No. I won't tell you again.*>>

<<*I said 'distractions.' I didn't say 'unimportant distractions.' I don't think that the situation called for such a drastic response.*>>

<<*You've never said it again, even though things have heightened and grown even more complicated and crazy.*>>

<<*I was wrong. You made me see it.*>>

<<*Made you, Farson? Oh, come on! You were begging, and you know it.*>>

He was back, staring at the crack again. Still nothing. <<*I do think you were right there at the door. I think you had decided it wasn't worth it to lock me out like that.*>>

<<*Ha! I didn't move a muscle, and I had decided that it was worth it. All of your machinations and visions of grandeur were hard to endure, but when you belittled something that you knew was indispensable to me, that broke the camel's back. Why must we relive this over again and again?*>>

<<*I think I gave up too early.*>>

<<*You gave up when you saw that you were wrong, wrong, wrong. You always try to have things 'perfect,' Farson, and some things are never going to be 'perfect,' in your sense. Relationships are complicated. You were wrong, and you admitted it; that's why I opened the door, eventually.*>>

<<*What if you were wrong, Karina? What if you had waited too long?*>>

<<*I wasn't. I didn't.*>>

<<*What if you had? What if you did?*>>

<<*Sometime in our far distant future. Is that what you mean? That's the only meaning 'had and did' could possibly have in this conversation. True?*>>

<<*Yes.*>> Farson was acquiescing but not surrendering.

<<*Then, we'll cross that bridge when we come to it.*>>

Farson did feel something begin to move. It wasn't what he thought it would be. But something definitely moved. Sam had said it once: "The leaves swirl in the direction of the current." Farson could remember Sam always cast his bait down current so the fish would come upon it rather than the other way around. Sam said that the fish would think they were great hunters and seize the bait that way. If it came floating up to them, they would wonder why. "Fish are predators. If it's too easy, they won't be fooled."

He was still watching to see if the crack of the door would change, when, in the end, the change he wanted and was so desperately hoping for had already happened within him.

<<*Karina, I didn't give up too early. I didn't start early enough.*>>

Sortt called down from Emerald Earth to the Sker team on SkyKing. "How's it going?" he asked.

"It's going," they responded.

From anyone else this might have been considered a smart aleck answer. But he knew, from the Skers, it was the welcomed truth.

Farson's rod bent into the current, bowing down with the weight of his prey.

121. How Is He Doing That?

Repoul Bensn had his hands full. It was more work than even he had thought it would be. Managing the thousands of tiny satellites was one thing, but fighting off the security protocols that the ScreenMasters had built into the system was daunting. The sophistication of their systems was so complex that Repoul had come to realize that it wasn't really "sophistication." It was really just the way they were. To them, working on multiple levels of time – *simultaneous, shifting dimensional anomalies* – was as natural to them as praying constantly for understanding and guidance was to him. The more he thought about it, he knew that without Farson's intricate and elegantly timed and tuned assistance, what he was doing now would have been absolutely impossible. With Farson's help it was "going," as Repoul had said to Andrew Sortt. *Meaning injected.* The people in the bottle were all watching and hoping. Handy's presence on Emerald Earth had really helped, too. The Skers were now part of the new team in co-control of the ScreenMasters' system.

All they had left was to break Emerald Earth free, replace it with a "virtual Screen saturation," as Farson described it, and then wait for what he referred to as the "movement," which apparently was some level of minute activity from the ScreenMasters' monitoring structures that would signal a transition underway and that would trigger the all-important shift. Then the Emers would take over. In meetings prior to co-control, Farson had said that while it all seemed so complicated, it was really so very simple. "All we are doing is reaching into the fabric of the future where the ScreenMasters think Earth is and redacting some of those moments, compressing them and resaturating them here and now. The timeline we are working on is brief in ScreenTime – about 6,500 years in human time – but it will be long enough for an irreversible shift to occur, for the co-terminal injection, and an irreplaceable micro-patch to the damaged portion of the local Grid to be permanently put in place. In some ways, it is what the ScreenMasters were trying to do anyway with their complex little orbital devices, but our way is far more inclusive, allowing Earth and its people to reemerge in real time and to really live again; plus as the timeline rejoins in about 200 years there will be no disturbance because the saturation will decline over time, like a hand slowly coming out of a glove. It is, in truth, the 'healing process' for The Screen that the ScreenMasters are expecting. Earth will be gone from this place, but 'this place' on The Screen will slowly make the adjustments, and in the end it will be as if nothing ever happened. Exactly as they are anticipating. Another benefit will be the blossoming of the greatest secret of humanity." He then added the one word, from the ancient creeds, that truthfully describes what was really going on. "Salvation."

Andrew Sortt was a contemplative man, especially in these later years. From the days of his presidency to now, he had softened considerably. He used to always dress to the nines, but now a softer attire package had emerged. He liked to feel relaxed. His hair had receded with distinction, not too much or too far. His physique was still strong and slender although, a softness had crept in. His face was still the same fascinating tableau that the media had loved to speculate over. Those furrows in his brow still shadowed up there, but now it all blended into a man in whom people saw maturity and a level of contentedness.

His eyes were still hawk eyes.

They were the last telltales of his fierce youth when he rode to power on sheer ambition, will, and indomitable determination. Those eyes were the lights that shined through the tunnel of a troubled youth, erratic school times, terrible decisions in love, and two failed, but passionate, marriages.

Women still found him interesting and sometimes nearly irresistible, but Andrew Sortt knew too much now. He knew too much about himself, about his matrix of happiness, and too much about his enormous responsibility. When he had stepped aside for those first years in stasis, when he had timelessly walked the farms and fields like a nomad, he had relearned the joy of solitude and peace. His return to politics, now of Emerald Earth, was thrust upon him and at him; he did not want it. Life in the bottle had been perfection for Andrew Sortt. He knew that Earth's people were "safe" –

whatever that meant – meaning that their situation was what it was, no changing it. A tautology of irony. A politician's nightmare. Nothing either good or bad could be done to improve it or make it worse. Human beings had lost control. So, their leader wandered in the world, not unknown, but unfettered by responsibility. In those years he discovered love again. He discovered life again. In a moment of opportunity and discovery, through his friendship with Farson and the time they spent together in Farson's cabin in New Hampshire, he inevitably became the third truly enlightened human being since the arrival of the ScreenMasters.

Let's hope.

"Farson, you've got to be kidding."

"That's what Twill said once, Andrew. Look where he is now."

"Right, Farson." Sortt said that with heavy sarcasm. "Twill is standing there with a gun to our heads, finger on the trigger, twitching with fate, anxious to shoot."

"No, that's not correct, Andrew. He has a gun he thinks is pointing at us. It's really a brush making the final stroke on a canvas that will paint a vastly different world than what his limited vision is now showing him. We want him to 'shoot.' I'm just wondering why he's waiting."

Farson knew the movement he was waiting for was coming. The advancing event seemed glacier-like to him, even slowing down as it approached, as if it would never really happen.

For the others it was on them like a flash of lightning, then gone.

Twill was thinking about his planned Ascension and how glorious it would be. Not only would he be the über lord of all the ScreenMasters, he would destroy the ever-troublesome

Earth and bury Farson Uiost, once and for all. He spun his gimbaled chair around and looked at the monitor and control panel floating there. *All I have to do is complete that little connection, and all is done.* He saw the holographic switch like a little finger pointing at him, beckoning him perhaps. *It's strange how all of eternity rests on that little switch and all the plans that created it.* He turned away from the monitor and returned to his ruminations on the grand event. He was thinking of what he would wear and who would sit where. The cast was all set. Word had gone out. Everything was ready. *Everything, except for me.* He loved that thought. He was just sitting there, relishing it, rolling it over and over in his mind like a tasty morsel in his mouth. Suddenly, his mind was filled with Farson's smiling face, and he bolted upright in the chair, almost toppling over. "God Almighty!" Twill shouted, but the vision was gone in a second, leaving a mental image burning into his brain. *What made me think of that?* He decided it was nerves or just a slip of his control, or something minor like that. He returned to his plans. Now he was impatient, restless. *I'm moving up the date. I'm tired of waiting.* Just before he stood up to leave the room and inform his staff of the change, he saw Farson's image again, ever so briefly, like a strobe in his mind. This time Farson was beckoning him as though he wanted Twill to come closer. *What's wrong with me?* Twill was angry as he pushed himself out of the chair. He marched across the room and slammed the door, leaving the room empty behind him. His chair was slowly spinning in ever slowing, gimbaling circles, as if searching for the perfect position.

Repoul had completed his study of the ScreenLock system and wanted to bring something to the attention of Karina, Viera, Voul, and Commander Peterson. He asked for a conference. It was not arranged easily given the "locations" of all the parties. They were to meet on SkyKing in AlphaCommand's observatory overlooking the new sixth whorl. This room was smaller than it appeared from outside. The large window created the illusion of great depth, which the room did not command. It was generously furnished in a typical Sker motif: very soft colors, a muted ambience with excellent acoustic security. The ubiquitous background noises of everyday life on the station – now there were over 310,000 people living there – were thoroughly filtered out. As they entered, it was clear to everyone that the privacy of the room was assured.

Viera came in last and closed the door. The complex quietness deepened in the room, and she had the feeling that she could hear heartbeats and sense thoughts. *This is nice.* She was aboard the station for all the official reasons: supply line schedule refinements, arranging R and R for her miners, some adjudication issues, visitor exchanges (Skers seemed to enjoy their time on the Moon as the MoonBasers did theirs on SkyKing.), the technical issues of proximity maintenance, and, of course, planning for the reappearance of Earth into their little space-faring formation. She was very busy on all those things, but there was one more thing. Voul. In the three days she had been on SkyKing she had woken up every morning with him. Their relationship was not exactly open for all to see, but they clearly were not hiding it. *Things are changing.* She was accepting the fact that without him she was just not as happy. Waking up with him was better than anything else. Their lovemaking was endlessly interesting to her. Not nearly as wild as she had come to expect in other relationships. Voul, like all Skers, was conservative by nature in that department. Yet, there was something vastly different with him. *He is on my mind.* She remembered their first mental embrace; it seemed like ages ago. *It just keeps getting better and better.* With this thought she had looked over at

Voul, who was also in the room. He was watching her. He smiled slightly, in his inimitable, low-key way, conveying ferocious desire almost imperceptibly. *He never used to even smile.*

Karina spoke first. She clearly wanted to get on with this meeting. "Repoul, what's up? Is everything still ready as previously reported?"

"Yes, it's true that we *are* ready. It is also true that we thought we knew the timetable. It now seems that we were inaccurate in that. My study shows that every element that could have caused delays, for security or for command and control circumspection, has now been overcome. Suddenly, there is full readiness on their end. We are in a hair-trigger situation now. They can now execute their plan on a moment's notice. I have isolated the exact initiation point. We all know that a perfectly timed response on our part is essential. In all of our previous modeling there were sequences of interconnects that would key our foreshadowing co-replication sequences for a good 'dovetailing' effect. No such protocols now exist. They are gone. 'Ready' and 'aim' phases are over as far as I can see. 'Fire!' may occur without warning."

Commander Peterson found Repoul's use of the traditional preparation for "open fire" sequence phraseology pleasing and disturbing at the same time. In his concern, Jim also found pleasure in how the team was now working together. Voul's and Viera's alliance went a long way both symbolically and in actually removing the previous tension between their two communities. That unease and mistrust were now gone. The Skers were the glue that held everything together. Born in space, knowing only the station as home, these wonderful people cherished their place and its promise. *They are teaching us all.* It had been some time now since the Skers' role as leaders had ceased to be a question. They had earned it. Karina was, well, Karina, almost a disembodied presence now, like Farson, but not like him at all in other ways. She retained a strong humanity and a presence much like she was before all of this began, back in the simple days when the ScreenMasters had first come. It seemed like a century ago, but it was just over a year to them.

Peterson asked the question that was on everyone's mind: "Does this affect the probability estimates we've been relying on all along or not?" Everyone looked to Repoul for the answer, but it was Voul who spoke.

"No. It doesn't affect them, Jim. It destroys them." Voul's mind was calm in the midst of the maelstrom of details and changes flooding in. This was more new territory for Sker operations, but it was good. Working in irreconcilable uncertainty had brought them all even closer together. In the Sker way, solutions were being explored, of course, but this situation was different.

"Now," Voul said, "we need Farson. Since there is no other way, we assume he knows it."

Voul Jonsn said this as though it was common knowledge.

Commander Peterson was again in full command of the space station orbiting the Moon. SkyKing was now the central hub of everything. He said something so common in naval history that it rolled off his tongue smoothly like water coursing under a ship's keel. His words expressed the innate faith and courage that had powered so many vessels on the treacherous high seas throughout history. "Stand to your stations. Steady as she goes." They hugged and shook hands and left the observatory, already working on what was to come next.

Repoul returned to his calculations.

The large window framed vast and endless space stretching far, far away, a mighty blackness, stamped with hauntingly beautiful lights that twinkled as if in encrypted signaling that no one could ever truly decipher. The station and the Moon, strange companions in a strange setting, sailed on, seeming not even to move at all in the vast, black Brobdingnagian immenseness around them.

So small were they now, so exposed, so alone, so vulnerable; there could be no turning back in the directionless wonder surrounding the space station and its companion. There was no forward, no sideways, just "Steady as she goes."

Commander James Peterson, who was now with his daughter Brittany in their comfortable quarters, had said it. The derivative option paths were thinning out even as the cold grip of their destiny tightened. *The stakes are really high.* He looked over at his daughter. She was not happy.

Brittany, like all teenagers, was angry with her dad about going to bed. "Dad, it's early. I've got homework and ... " She saw the look in her father's eye and knew there was little hope that she would win this one. But she smiled anyway, knowing from their history that an extra effort could occasionally pay off and then said, "Come on, Dad. Let's just watch the late news. Then I'll go to bed."

Over the years he had noticed that Brittany needed less sleep than most people. He slowly and reluctantly nodded and joined her on the sofa. "Just a few more minutes then." He acquiesced, perhaps for his own reasons, perhaps to make her happy. He loved his time with Brittany. They were alone in a world not of their making that had swept them up as it raced along. So much sadness had given them a way to finding a closeness now so important to them both. *The Late News Tonight* was about the solar sails and the new Sker innovations, how the Moon's crops were growing, and how the miners were planning their annual "Mardi Gras," a drunken brawl that they loved to distraction. The Moon and New Chicago were becoming tourist attractions, and the Mardi Gras was a highlight. By the time the announcer was halfway through her reporting of Chicago's plans for crowd control on the parade route, Jim was nodding off. Brittany laughed and said, "It's you who needs to go to bed, Dad. Let's go." She took his hand and encouraged him up. He was exhausted. As he turned out the light, he saw a faint purple glow beginning to fill the room. He said to her, "You go ahead. I won't be far behind." As his daughter drifted away to her room, Commander Peterson was awake with awareness as Farson's thoughts and instructions came into his mind. He tapped his wrist communicator and initiated a transmission. "John," he said to the face that appeared in the air before him. "Here we go."

Sergeant Long John Hanson Silver said, "It's about fucking time."

122. Essor

It was truly a momentous occasion on The Screen, and the ScreenMasters were gathering. Not necessarily out of respect for their new, self-appointed leader, but they were coming nonetheless.

Farson's leadership had always been sort of a bare-bones variety, without pomp. For Twill there was no other way than all out. It seemed as though all of his long, long existence had been building toward this occasion. Escaping death, fighting off change, and, finally, in his opinion, triumphing magnificently – all that had happened – deserved more than an interoffice memorandum, to say the least. So all the stops were being pulled out, and the extravagant trappings of Twill's Ascension to Grand ScreenMaster were soon to be revealed in their effulgent glory. Never before had all the known ScreenMasters assembled in one place. The logistics were not complicated for them – being in two places at once was easy – but the mere fact of the assemblage and the Ascension of one of their number to supremacy raised the event to millennial proportions. On Twill's host world, however, it was not so easy to stage such an event. Buried beneath 1,900 kilometers of dense ice, Lake DurR was the driest place on the planet. That's why they all lived down there. The drier the better. The colder the better. The lake was really a dead sea in the abysmal dark. The Essors, as the population of the planet was known, eschewed the light and the surface, which was bright and oxygenated: deadly to them. Perhaps this antonymic relationship to what all of humanity loves imparted the initial revulsion that Twill felt when he first came to Earth on Uvo's barge. He knew there was nowhere on that blue planet, not even in the depths of their fading polar ice where he could feel even remotely comfortable. On his home world, Essor, he was in the very definition of Heaven. There was only one other species, which had a ScreenMaster, that could actually attend the glorious celebration in person, and she was not coming. The ScreenMaster population was almost entirely averse to traveling in person to other locations. Some had conjectured that this reluctance to travel was the genesis for forming the ScreenMasters in the first place. There had to be a way to coordinate things. *No one can be everywhere.*

Most races had one or two ScreenMasters, and because of the rarity, these individuals and their importance were coveted and protected as nothing else. When a planet lost a solo ScreenMaster, the chair was left empty, there were no standby replacements, and the planet and its race typically declined in importance. Twill had made the case that with the Ascension of a Grand ScreenMaster, lesser ScreenMasters, or even non-ScreenMaster placeholders (an individual appointed to administratively fill the position until a naturally evolved ScreenMaster appeared indigenously to assume the mantle) would now be acceptable. Every race, Twill predicted, because of his exultation, would now be represented. Many worried.

Some races had two or three or even four ScreenMasters but that was rare; usually one or, sadly, none. Twill was the only Essor to ever achieve ScreenMaster status. Uvo's world had two, partially because of their vast numbers.

Twill wanted to make a complete statement of his power and his consummation of The Screen on Essor in a way that none could ever question. In attracting the other ScreenMasters to "passage" there, he was preparing a dark deception for them. They would all participate hoping for the best, but, in the end, Twill's plan would change everything they knew.

The robot CT<<Dinsil2371 was the key to Twill's designs. With that robot beside him, doing what Twill knew it would do, whether the ScreenMasters agreed or not would make no difference whatsoever. He was very self-assured and pleased with himself. *A perfect plan.*

123. CT<<Dinsil2371 and Farson's Secret

CT<<Dinsil2371 was a mild-mannered, very ancient, ScreenKeeper who was very seldom called upon. ZZ<<Arkol25609 had the higher calling on The Screen. He was Farson Uiost's ScreenKeeper. He had all the technical advantages over CT<<Dinsil2371, who was part of The Screen's antiquity. The rules were that ScreenKeepers ruled ScreenKeepers. Period. They marched to a tune that only they could hear. Attempts to interfere had led to disasters, so over time they had come to be almost a sort of background theme on The Screen. Always there. Always watching. There had been occasions when they raised their level of participation to preeminence. ScreenKeepers at times were clearly more powerful, in their aggregate, than even the ScreenMasters themselves. Since the coming of Farson Uiost that role had

reared its head once more, but with less effect than expected. Farson's protection, and the assistance he needed, seemed to be the "pet project" of the ScreenKeepers. But Farson was not like other ScreenMasters.

When CT<<Dinsil2371 first recruited Hattie, it signaled a big change. Bringing Hattie and Sam together first with Farson, and then with Karina and Farson, had had far-reaching ramifications, from the ScreenKeepers' point of view. The reasons were all good, even if some were surprising. Farson and Karina first actually saw the robots with the arrival of the ScreenMasters' barge, and at that time they naturally assumed the robots had come with them. As things developed, Farson came to see that that was not true. As he began to move around in time, especially after LevelTen, it became abundantly clear that the robots served a function above and beyond that of the ScreenMasters. In time, he saw the independence of the robots for what it was: essential. The ScreenKeepers, of course, appreciated this insight immensely.

All ScreenMasters could summon certain robots. The robots would accommodate almost any request made by a ScreenMaster. Sometimes secretly, sometimes openly, ScreenKeepers always accompanied ScreenMasters wherever they went. With one exception: Farson Uiost. He could and did choose to travel alone sometimes. ZZ<<Arkol25609 found that there was nothing he could do to stop Farson when Farson wanted to go alone. It worried the robot, but as Karina had said to console his frustration, "He always comes back."

Farson learned, early on, that the robots served many important functions and one was as "relays" on The Screen, facilitating ordinary traffic and communications for the ScreenMasters. He had formulated a theory that they were "boosters" for The Screen. The ScreenMasters weren't always as strong as they seemed to be in myth and lore. This variation from ScreenMaster to ScreenMaster was one of the first things Farson noted. Twill was one of the strongest. Handy was the one he understood the least. Karina was the only one Farson considered to be in his own league. Uvo was the kindest ScreenMaster he had ever known. But once Farson had actually achieved LevelTen, he realized that the robots were everywhere. He learned later that Twill also had this information.

CT<<Dinsil2371 had an interesting history. Perhaps the most interesting of all the ScreenKeepers, although, ZZ<<Arkol25609 was not far behind. Between the two of them, and their far-reaching activities, a relationship had formed and stood the test of time, and more. Much of what they had labored to achieve was now hanging in the balance on the far, far away planet of Essor, and in the tenuous link between SkyKing and the planet Twill was about to destroy. CT<<Dinsil2371 was on Essor to strengthen it, and ZZ<<Arkol25609 was trying to get into position near Earth, as a relay, but the robots had limits in how far they could go and how fast they could move. It had never been a problem when there was time enough. Since Farson came on the scene, time was just not what it used to be. Everything was speeding up.

"ZZ<<Arkol25609, where are you now?" It was Repoul Bensn following the planned protocols exactly, of course. ZZ<<Arkol25609 admired the Skers for their irrepressible dependability. They were far different from other human beings in that regard. However, their cumbersome form of communication left a lot to be desired.

<<*I am where I am, Midshipman.*>> The ScreenKeeper's thoughts always came as mental fulguration to the Sker. Expected but still startling. They penetrated space's distances and times with such ease.

"Commander Peterson said he saw a ScreenKeeper's purple aura in his compartment a few moments ago. That observation is the source of my inquiry."

<<*Physical presence is not required for action, Midshipman. My location is of no concern.*>> ZZ<<Arkol25609 knew more about the needs and phobias of human beings than he would ever let on, especially in a conversation with a Sker. <<*CT<<Dinsil2371, however, is in position at Essor. This you do need to know.*>> One of the problems with such an old robot as CT<<Dinsil2371 was that the mobility issues were exacerbated. The alacrity of his movement to Essor, while slow in ZZ<<Arkol25609's terms, was still well above the capabilities of an average ScreenMaster. ZZ<<Arkol25609 reflected for a moment on the state of ScreenMaster evolution, which, before Farson, had been disappointingly slow to him, but predicable. With Farson, his estimation of what the future held was now uncertain and incalculable, a step in the right direction and a fast step indeed.

"We are in a situation of anticipation right now. All is ready." Repoul was preparing to break his connection. Suddenly, the robot's voice was audible in his ears through the communication device on his console.

"Do not think, 'all is ready,' Midshipman. There are variables in play that do not lend themselves to your self-delusory feelings of adequacy. *En garde*, Mr. Bensn. There is much of great importance in your hands." Bensn found this last exchange troubling. Skers did not like to question themselves, especially in emergencies. He was going over the plans and calculations intensely rechecking everything just as ZZ<<Arkol25609's last thought came to him. He knew that clear thinking and corrective action in the coming emergency would create the moment he had been waiting for all of his life.

Unlike the many other circumstances in which he had faced uncertainty, this one seemed to be beyond his control.

<<*Do not worry, Midshipman. Your work has always been excellent, and this time will be no different. Just stay alert. It will all be over soon. When the time comes, do not hesitate, no matter what. You are the center.*>>

CT<<Dinsil2371 was standing within an arm's reach of Twill. He was covered in the ScreenKeepers' ceremonial uniform, which was surprisingly ornate, reminiscent of the Swiss Guards of the ancient Earth Papacy in Rome. CT<<Dinsil2371 had been in Rome twice: once in the late twentieth century to handle the death of one pope and then to assist in the selection and installation of another. He assisted at the end of one of the shortest reigns and the beginning of one of the longest. *Even those days of joy and sadness pale before this day's importance.*

Twill was magnificent in his confidence and supremacy. If what he wanted came to pass, CT<<Dinsil2371 would be in a bad position. If what Twill wanted was thwarted, CT<<Dinsil2371 would be killed. *It's been a long life.* CT<<Dinsil2371 contemplated his fate impassively. His outer skin checked and manipulated his clothing to perfection. He remained still. The only sign of life was the telltale strobing of his visual perceptors and his unique aura. Twill turned to him. <<*Why is your glow gold, CT<<Dinsil2371? Why is it not purple?*>>

<<*I am an older model than most, and perhaps defective.*>> Twill continued to focus his attention on the robot.

<<*How old?*>> CT<<Dinsil2371 remained still, unanswering, though his strobing slowed. Twill could see that no answer was forthcoming and turned his attention elsewhere with a shake of his head in disdain. *Stupid robot.* Twill's thought was not unnoticed, and he suddenly started

with a bright image in his head, undefined. It was so bright it frightened him and reminded him of Farson's image appearing earlier. He stopped and turned back at the robot. The strobing had stopped to a steady stare. CT<<Dinsil2371 could have been dead. Then imperceptibly at first, then slightly more, the strobing resumed. Someone called Twill's name, and he started to walk off. CT<<Dinsil2371 remained still and stoic, if looking a little eccentric in his colorful coverings. Twill looked back and saw that the tasseled hat had changed positions slightly. He faced the robot for a moment. *<<Well, anyway, I'm glad you came here for the ceremony, CT<<Dinsil2371. It is an honor of sorts. Your presence lends a special feeling. When was the last time you traveled this far?>>*

<<I don't get out much, Twill. This occasion demanded my passage here.>> The voice in his mind was sharp and focused. Twill had the thought that the words and the meanings might not be exactly the same. Soon his name was called again and he was off to the preparations.

Farson's voice was a soft stillness in CT<<Dinsil2371's ever agile mind. *<<Remember our friend Uvo, CT<<Dinsil2371. Caution is always appropriate in these circumstances.>>* CT<<Dinsil2371 didn't move at all. Farson was lingering for a response.

<<I remember well, Farson. Uvo's stories will fill you again soon. Your path leads to truth, and I will be exactly where I must be and do exactly what I must do when the time comes.>> Farson's thoughts came ricocheting back instantly but, again, very gently and softly, respectfully.

<<Someone once told me, 'Every path leads to the truth if you follow it to the end.'>> CT<<Dinsil2371 remembered.

<<I was much younger when I said that, Farson. Now that I'm here at 'the end,' I hope it's true.>>

<<Oh, ye of little faith.>> Farson was thinking of Uvo and having his counsel and stories again. It was a pleasant

thought, but for the first time, he knew that CT<<Dinsil2371's view of things could be wrong. *But then, who is infallible?*

CT<<Dinsil2371 was alone. Solitude did not bother him after all these years. In fact, solitude was the one thing he was at peace with. Farson was so sure of everything, but CT<<Dinsil2371 had seen too much. True, he had never seen anything like Farson, but still there was a certain hesitation in his knowledge and acceptance of Farson's uniqueness. When CT<<Dinsil2371 had first encountered Farson, it was during his Ascension at LevelTen. He had known Farson was approaching, but the new ScreenMaster's speed surprised him and even with all of his experience and knowledge CT<<Dinsil2371 could only delay Farson for a short time. What might have been a death blow to others was just a mild sting to Farson. From that moment on CT<<Dinsil2371 knew there was much to do. His meeting with Farson was only the beginning. Standing there on Essor, waiting for the moment of moments, he thought to himself, *Things have moved so far, so quickly.*

He could see Twill moving in the crowds, and he noticed that the crowds were growing. The gathering was underway. CT<<Dinsil2371's strobing stayed steady. Inside, where the truth of his existence resided, he felt emotions that had been unstirred for so many years. Years alone and not alone. *For the longest time now, alone.* A sadness. It was good to be part of Farson's plan, but still, it was a challenge he never thought he would have to endure.

<<CT<<Dinsil2371, I did it on the 'planet of troubles.' This will be no different.>>

<<Farson, that is a myth of your legend. You can't fool me.>>

<<You are wrong, CT<<Dinsil2371. It really happened. You'll see.>>

CT<<Dinsil2371 was still alone, despite the presence of Farson's thoughts. It was comforting to know that true virtuosity allowed Farson to achieve such omniscience, but the robot knew a moment of truth was coming.

<<Every moment is a 'moment of truth,' CT<<Dinsil2371, and well you know it.>>

<<Some 'moments of truth' are more true than others, Farson.>> Farson laughed warmly at the robot's response.

<<I haven't seen your sense of humor in a long time, CT<<Dinsil2371. It's good.>> Farson's laughing was anomalous to the moment facing CT<<Dinsil2371. Farson might be enjoying the moment, but CT<<Dinsil2371 was as still as a statue.

Handy was playing his guitar, and he noticed that the air inside the bottle, as he had always called Earth in the ScreenMasters' stasis, was clean and easy to breathe. Despite his years of abusing his body, it was none the worse for wear inside. The song he was singing was really a poem he had written:

The time is comin'
Though people are plannin'
One thing and another's
Going to happen.

They are all goin' to be
So surprised when they see
The truth sure ain't something
That's just that fancy-free.

On Essor, it's building
On the station it's ready
Here on Emerald Earth
We are waiting to be free.

"Hi, Andy." Sortt had joined him on the small hill overlooking what had once been Topeka, Kansas. As Emerald Earth had evolved over the years in the bottle, the population had thinned out to a fraction of what it was in the late twenty-first century. More importantly, the remaining people had spread out, initially away from the former cities and the congestion of the coasts, to almost an even spread around the new world. Improving on the now ancient gurney technology of MoonBase and the crude transporter system of SkyKing, transportation on Emerald Earth had become easy and efficient. The vast farmlands had spread and grown. Crops were varied in a division of agricultural labor that had never been possible before. Of course, pollution had faded into mythology. Wildlife had changed and evolved as had the people of Emerald Earth. It was, as Andrew Sortt had said on many occasions, the Garden of Eden now. Handy loved it here. The social and religious barriers that had alienated populations had been dismantled and dissolved. The planet was ready for what was coming, or nearly so.

"Farson says we are operational."

"He said that?" Handy was doubtful.

"Well, what he said was, 'Prepare to go forth.'" Handy knew all too well. "He also said, 'Tell Handy, that I said, Salvation is at hand. Repent.'" Handy smiled.

"That's exactly what he said he would say." Handy – at least the Handy that Farson knew – understood well what those words meant. The human race was about to be saved. All the implications of overcoming the ScreenMasters' stasis, camouflaged by Twill's Grand Ascendancy, and, once and for all, would result in the establishment of the true future of The Screen. It was here. It was now. Handy was thinking of Mrs. Handy and his sheep, not about the universe or the "omniverse," as Farson called it. He was thinking of a troubled world and then of his life as a troubled, unreliable

ScreenMaster who pretty much screwed up everything he ever tried to do. He knew about his primacy, that he was the first ScreenMaster. That was before anyone knew what it was really all about. *Farson taught that lesson well.* Handy was flawed as an individual and flawed as a ScreenMaster. His only claim to fame was that Farson considered him his best friend. After Karina, of course. *What did I ever do to deserve a friend like that? Gandhi, Jesus, Buddha all rolled into one, raised to the umpteenth power.* Farson made all the other ScreenMasters look like wannabes. Then there was Farson's Secret. *How many know now? Karina, obviously. Me. Who else?* Handy looked over at Andrew Sortt. Farson had taken a liking to the ex-President. Handy liked him too, probably. *That's it. Just the four of us. The total sum of my friends.* Handy wondered about Uvo. Uvo's fate was problematic. *Would it matter?* Handy seemed unsettled with that. Then he had another thought. *Soon enough, we will all know.*

BOOK III

The ScreenMasters

"This time, like all times, is a very good one,
if we but know what to do with it."

– *Ralph Waldo Emerson*

"Anyone who can handle a needle convincingly
can make us see a thread which is not there."

– *E. H. Gombrich*

Chapter Eight

Realization

124. Karina's Dream

"Sitwory, watch out!" Farson was full of doubt and worry. It was her first time at the helm for a landing. She had long maintained that she could do it, but with Farson hanging over her, it was proving more difficult than she had imagined.

"Routier, give me some room. I can do it." Landing on Beach was not easy. The planet was covered with sand everywhere, except for the water. The warm winds could be stiff, stirring up the fine, soft sand, affecting visibility. A landing on Beach had to be made evenly; otherwise, The Ship could tip over if one landing pod went in too deeply. Landing on Beach was touchy because it had to be done perfectly or there would be problems, as Farson knew only too well. As he backed off a little, Karina seemed to relax, and she brought The Ship in perfectly for a three-point landing. "There, you see, Routier. All I needed was a little room to maneuver."

<<You changed it, Karina.>>

<<No, that is how it happened.>>

<<How can we remember things so differently? I clearly recall that I had to take over or The Ship could have been flipped over.>>

<<'The Ship,' Farson? Is that what we're talking about?>>

It started out as if it would be just another day. Karina had been aboard the space station for just about fourteen months now. Her mom and dad, Catherine and Tom Jacobson, had settled into their new positions. Catherine was building ChainFoods replication sites on both SkyKing and on MoonBase. She had found that the pristine environments lent themselves perfectly to her systems, and all prototypes were functioning with the same dependability and were developing the same popularity that had so quickly spread around Earth, and her many assistants were all learning the initiation process quickly. People really liked the food. Predictably, the MoonBasers had discovered a way to distill a highly intoxicating version of gin from one of Catherine's derivatives. She knew there was nothing she could do about it. Inevitability and ingenuity always flow together toward human predilection. The new "ChainBrew," as it was known, was surprisingly potent and yet, a pleasant new feature: no disagreeable aftereffects. In her calculations and analysis of the MoonBasers' imaginative perversion of her formulae, she actually found a new direction she had not thought of. She had long known and written about the clear health benefits of her diet, but the MoonBase brew's unique euphoria showed her that the chemistry of ChainFoods might not be just preventative in health issues, but also possibly might have a health engineering capability as well. She made some directional notes, and planned to conduct further research to consider this new feature when she had some spare time.

It was safe to say, in these months in space, though, she was busy, successful, and very happy at her new job.

Tom Jacobson was working on air quality issues on the station and noted that his wife's introduction of her synthetic food processes was having a positive effect. "It's as if the process has the same effect on the environment around it as it does on the bodies of the people who use it for food."

Catherine had only said, "Of course, what blesses one, blesses all," quoting Sker scripture, which she was also studying. She wanted to understand the Skers as deeply as she could.

"Well, aren't you adapting well," her husband had said with his customary humor. He had noted the affinity that quickly developed between his wife and the Sker Nation, as they liked to be called. It was predictable. The Skers were trained from the earliest days of their lives to live pure, uncomplicated lives, avoiding all the "contrivances" and myriad assignations that people created to complicate their lives. Sker food preferences had always been simple and natural. In Catherine's ChainFoods they immediately saw the purity of a process derived from elemental ingredients. The Skers had developed many interesting additions to her line and were fairly independent in their production. The Skers were now producing as much of the ChainFoods on the station as she was. And they were exporting their new recipes to the Moon as well.

The Skers, as they did in so many areas of their interests, became partners in Catherine's science.

Tom's problems with General Motors, however, did not end with the family's emigration from Earth. True, he was much happier now on the station. His family had been assigned to the oldest portion of the station, WhorlOne, so that meant that Tom's operations were also centered there. His well-known concerns about the integrity of the station's complex airlock systems had made him the perfect selection for this assignment, and every day he was getting closer to a solution. There had already been a failure of an airlock prior to his arrival. It was the system that connected WhorlOne with WhorlTwo, passing through the command center of the station. That particular series of lock and passage complexes was not the oldest one, but it was the one that had been installed to bridge system versions, after a major upgrade from the original program. That upgrade was the pathway to the next system generations. So, in this area, the controls and the alloy-match matrices were necessary hybrids of the old and new systems. It was also the most heavily used series of locks and passageways of all four active whorls at the time. The new fifth and sixth whorls were still under construction.

As each of the new whorls had come online, WhorlOne had become, more and more, the bedroom of the station because its spaces were larger and less intensely designed for multiple taskings. WhorlOne rooms were sometimes just rooms, not multifunctional spaces. People liked WhorlOne. Its location offered fantastic views of Earth all the time. In real estate nothing had changed. Location still mattered.

In his investigation of the airlock failure, he had reviewed the data records over and over. He knew that the only thing that saved WhorlOne from complete and catastrophic decompression was the original redundancy built into the final chambering of the transition elements. That is, those first designers had actually installed a complete second pass (all five stages) after the first one, just to be safe. People walking along the corridor didn't know it, of course, but they were actually going through the process twice in that area. Throughout the station, the aerosol seals between whorls and passageways opened and closed around the people transiting so efficiently that it was unnoticeable except at the first and last stages, where they had to actually step on floor plates to open the double seals. Once inside the chambers it was a walk-through in pleasantly light breezes as the transitions were made. Except, that is, for a particular transitional corridor on WhorlOne where there was one extra floor plate in the middle of a longer transition area with large picture windows all around. Over the years, this particular location had become a favorite wedding ceremony site and had a certain reputation as a sort of a "lover's leap" spot on the station. As far as his investigation went, Tom Jacobson knew that this popular location had done more than start and formalize relationships and serve as a quiet reprieve from the busy life on the station. He knew that the hybrid technology and foresight of the builders had saved the lives of perhaps everyone on board SkyKing. This was not widely known because General Motors, in the repairing of the breach, had kept a tight lid on the situation. Tom's initial discontent with that secrecy, back on Earth, had created a chain reaction that, if Catherine had not been selected for service in space, would certainly have led to Tom's unemployment.

Now he was in charge of the station-wide refit operation. Using the knowledge and foresight of those early engineers, he was managing a program to install a similar redundancy throughout all of the other whorls. Already, he had fixed the problem at WhorlOne, which had really occurred on the newer WhorlTwo side where his parent company had made "considerations" in determining the data and material systems for the new upgrades. In his air quality research, he had discovered a minute degradation from the oldest whorl to the newest. The degradation of the air quality, from whorl to whorl and passageway to passageway, though slight, was getting worse with each new addition. This problem needed to be fixed, and he was fixing it. It would take time. Tom and his crew had already fixed WhorlTwo and were beginning work on WhorlThree. The newest section, WhorlFive, still under construction, seemed a long way off. Three additional new sections, far bigger and far more complicated, were planned, and they were scheduled to hold as many people and operational functions as all the others combined. Tom knew there was no time to waste.

Karina was in her family's home on WhorlOne, trying to talk her mother into the idea of it being her sixth-and-a-half birthday.

Catherine knew she was facing another goofy celebration of their daughter's birth, not because she really wanted to, but because she knew there was no avoiding it. It was only three months ago they had celebrated Karina's sixth-and-a-quarter birthday. When Karina got an idea into her head, there was no turning her away from it. "Mom, we can make a cake! We still have the party hats from last time, and we could invite the other kids. It'll be fun!" Karina's mom was trying to ignore her. "Come on, Mom. Please, please, please, please, please!" Catherine could feel the inevitable surrender gaining strength within her. She looked around the apartment. Everything had just been cleaned.

"Could we do it somewhere else, Kari?"

"Four, four, four, four, four!!" Karina loved the fourth whorl. Especially the community room and its warm swimming pool. She was already running out the door to tell her friends.

"ScreenMaster Twill?"

"Yes." Twill was surprised at the interruption. It seemed that no one interrupted him anymore. *Especially now.*

"I just wanted to bring something to your attention." The speaker was one of Twill's technicians. This particular technician was part of a team coordinating the satellites around Earth with Essor's system of subterranean comlasers. Like little virtual communication tunnels throughout the planet, Essor's scientists had constructed, over the years, a system of steady and powerful lasers that functioned as an intricate network for many purposes including planetary system controls. As in so many things Essor, this system was complicated far beyond its original concept. Essor's scientists were in perpetual motion intellectually and constantly upgraded and modified everything. They referred to "invention" the same way other races thought of "evolution." One of the most interesting spin-offs of this scientific method was an infinite amount of specialization. So, the technician interrupting Twill was actually assigned to monitoring the waveforms of the stasis field around one, and only one, "prong," which was defined as a 1/100th segment of one satellite's sensor-tendril's contact with the stasis field. Essor had assumed control of the entire stasis field from the beginning, because, after all, it was Farson's idea, and Twill never had and never would trust Farson. Twill knew that the technician, by the very nature of Essor, could not in any way be a significant part of what was going on. He looked at him. It was actually a her, he noticed. *Even more so.* Twill indicated with one of his appendages that whatever information this insignificant female had should be coming forth with dispatch. "There was a bump, sir."

"A bump?"

"Yes, sir."

"What kind of a bump?"

"Well, sir, it was like a vibration in the air after something closes. It was almost undetectable. Very, very small."

"Has this sort of thing ever happened before?" Twill was not really interested. He was just articulating the next logical question in an event inquiry.

"Yes, sir."

"Well, then, what's the big deal?"

"Well, sir, it's not that it's a big deal, sir. It's actually that this time it was such a small deal. It was so small that no harmonic isolation or even non-harmonic analysis can explain it, and, of course, you know I've been trying." Everyone knew that technicians operate in an almost "stream of consciousness" mode, and follow everything that comes up regardless of where it goes or how long it takes. That's why there are so many of them.

"If it's so small, why are you bothering me? I have some pretty big things on my mind right now." Twill was already starting to move away, physically and mentally.

"Well, sir. It's so small, infinitesimally small, that there is no explanation … " the technician hesitated. The next comment was obviously difficult to say. "... unless it is an enshrouded mis-addressing adumbration within our system structure of control." Twill turned and looked down at the technician.

"Of *control*?" The technician indicated an affirmative response to Twill's harshly posed question. Her eyes were wide open and obviously in some state of advanced concern at Twill's intensified interest. She answered quickly, slurring her words together in her anxious haste.

"Yessir, butasIsaiditwasverysmallsir."

Now, Karina was thinking about the cake. What kind of cake and how big a cake were her agenda items. "Mom, it doesn't have to be really big. Chocolate, though, it HAS to be chocolate." Catherine was thinking about her own work schedule and how overdue some aspects of her plans were. Still, one of the biggest reasons she accepted the job on SkyKing was that it would force her little family to be together more. As she looked at her daughter, Catherine Jacobson knew that there was nothing she wanted to do more than make a sixth-and-a-half birthday cake for her daughter. It was amazing to her to watch how excited Kari got over even the most insignificant things. It seemed that everything was magnified in Karina's mind. Once Catherine got used to translating Karina's ideas into the terms her daughter was believing, then it became perfectly clear what she was doing. Karina knew her parents loved her, but she also knew that they had important things to do. So, to compete with those schedules she simply used their love for her to make them overestimate the importance of her desires: to the point where they were afraid to dismiss them. Karina never used the downside of her personality – her ability to cry with all her heart and soul – to manipulate her parents, even though her capacities in that regard were exceptional. She felt that that would be unfair. The use of the upside of her personality – the ability to make everything seem like the most exciting and fun event in the history of the human race – was fair game indeed. Karina had game. If she could get her mom laughing and smiling about something, well then, Karina knew, she was going to win. Meaning, she would win more time with her mom and dad. At six-and-a-half, Karina already well knew how special her parents were.

When Tom heard that the party was going to be on "Four," it was a relief to him. It meant that he would be able to return to work on WhorlThree afterwards without packing everything up and moving it again. His crew would be within easy reach, and if he was gone for an hour it wouldn't really matter.

Karina and her mom were now standing before the finished cake. It was a beautiful chocolate cake with chocolate frosting and six small candles.

"Do we need another one, Mom?"

"You're six, not seven, Kari."

"I'm more than just six, Mom."

"There is no such thing as half a candle. A candle is a candle. It has to be six or seven. Not six and a half."

"What if I could get one in half length-wise?" Catherine Jacobson looked at her daughter and shook her head slowly side to side.

"If you can do it, that would be OK." Kari ran out of the room. She knew exactly who could do such a thing for her, candle in hand.

Farson knew she was coming. <<*Kari, this is a little strange.*>>

<<*Why, Farson. It's nothing compared to what you've done.*>>

<<*Give me the candle.*>> He knew it was no use arguing with her. They were in the cabin in North Conway. Farson got up from his chair, put on a coat, and went outside through the snow to the shed. Karina was right behind him. They went inside. It was cold. The little room was small but well organized with many tools. The old structure still blocked the wind. He was looking for the razor knife in the pile of things on his workbench.

<<*Don't you worry about hurting your fingers digging around in all that old junk?*>> Farson felt around in the small tools and bolts and sawdust until he finally found what he was looking for.

<<*No.*>> He was now concentrating on the candle, leaning in close with the knife. A few moments passed, and then he held up two neat halves. She smiled. *Even the wick.*

<<*Nice job, Farson. I knew you could do it.*>> Off she went. Farson looked down at his hand. There was a small cut on his index finger.

Catherine looked at the two half-candles. "How did you do that?" Kari smiled and laughed the laugh of a six-and-a-half-year-old girl living on a space station floating around a beautiful blue planet heading for unimaginable change and challenge. She knew way too much to answer her mom eye-to-eye, so she turned on her heels, seeing that she had won the six-and-a-half-candle argument and waved over her departing shoulder.

"I DO have FRIENDS, you know, MOM."

The "half" party was scheduled for 4:00 p.m. Karina's closest friends were coming: mostly adult crew members because there really weren't that many children her age on the station yet. Most of them were either younger or older than Karina. She invited any children in the area, though, because she knew only too well how few things there were for them to do on the busy, growing space station.

It was getting better. There were 125,000 people and around 800 children now spread through the large and growing station. Most people had been reluctant to bring children or to have them born on SkyKing. But that was changing rapidly with each passing year.

Around thirty-five kids were coming to Kari's party, plus parents and the crew members. *This could be big.*

Tom was explaining to his crew what was up. It was about 3:30 p.m. and time to get moving. "I've got to get going to the party. You guys move the gear and then come on up and have some cake and lemonade." The crew made sarcastic noises like that was their fondest dream in life. "Then I'll meet you at Four's entry ports. Run a quick check. People will be coming and going so don't start anything. Just look it over and give me a report when I get there." He left for home and a quick cleanup and then off to the party. The crew was still laughing over the cake and lemonade prospect. They had all been down to the Moon a few times for *those* birthday parties. They knew that even a good party up here on SkyKing was tame indeed by Moon standards. Still, it was Karina, and they all loved her.

It was bedlam in WhorlFour's recreation area. Kids were running around, swimming in the pool, tossing balls, and Catherine was loving it all. She was trying to get enough towels for the partiers and to keep them from slipping on the slick pool deck. The table where the cake had been placed so neatly at the start of the party now looked like a war zone. Kids are lot of things, but neat is never one of them. As Tom walked into the happy melee, the concerns of the day's labors weighing on his mind suddenly disappeared, and he was quickly drawn into the fun. It was, after all, "a birthday party ... and a half." He watched the pin-the-tail-on-the-donkey contest. Pinning the tail on the picture of the animal was the furthest thing from the youngsters' minds. It was all about running around with a tail and pinning it on anything that got in the way. The pin, of course, was a sticky yellow repair strip that Karina had wheedled out of her dad's crew. Once it stuck to something, it stayed there (without a special nonstaining solvent – which the kids did not have – it just could not be removed). This only added to the hilarity as several children already had the long, colorful "tails" attached to various parts of their clothing and were unable to take the yellow strips off. As Tom was watching, he felt a slight touch and turned around. Karina had pinned the tail on the back of her dad's pants. She was already running away, tearing off the "blindfold" which, of course, had been totally ineffective. He watched her exuberance and thought about his daughter's sense of determination and self-worth. Tom remembered his own youth and a father who was abrupt and sometimes harsh. Tom had promised never to do that to his children. Now, with one child, a daughter, he knew that his own experience had helped to make Karina's life better. Identity, he knew, was a fragile thing. To have her identity of happiness and confidence so strongly set so early was a good thing. *It will come in handy later.*

After the games, came the cake and singing. Adults and children were happy and contented as the party finally broke up. Nearly one hundred people had attended. Catherine had performed the quiet, behind-the-scenes role of scenery crew chief, moving games out of the way, and bringing in the dessert table, and then cleaning up the room as the kids and their parents, and the other crew members drifted away, on to the other things in their lives and jobs. Tom walked over to her, approaching from behind. He knew she was the source of so much good in his life as he touched her shoulders and began to massage the area he knew always got the same reaction. Catherine relaxed and leaned into his hands and as her head gracefully burrowed into his shoulder, she whispered softly to him, "Hmmmm, that feels so good."

"I've got to get back to the repair crew, Cat."

"Help me with this trash and I'll walk with you." Too good to pass up, the offer of her company spurred him to help with the party debris, and soon they were on their way. Suddenly, Karina was with them. "Where did you come from, Kari?"

"Wouldn't YOU like to know, Daddy." She liked to seem to possess the magical and mysterious ability to appear out of nowhere. She wedged in between them and took their hands and they walked toward WhorlFour.

When they arrived at the repair site, all the partygoers had already gone through the transition point, and the crew was beginning the repairs.

"We're going to have an issue with the spacing of the redundancy units, Tom. They kept making things cheaper and cheaper from whorl to whorl." The crew chief knew that Tom didn't have to be told this. He already knew it. But it was his nature to restate the obvious. He was standing over the original plate. One of the other crew members was bending down, looking into the mechanism.

"Hey, Tom, this is awfully hot." He was pointing to the machinery that opened and closed the airlocks. "It's way too hot." Tom came over and looked at it. What he saw made him stop cold.

All eight crew members and Catherine and Karina were inside the transition tunnel. They had walked through the first two airlocks to reach the center where the repairs were being made. Tom knew right away. For years he had studied the deterioration of metals in space. His theories about overexposure of the five old airlock systems versus the ten new airlocks of his design had predicted sudden and catastrophic failure without immediate replacement. No one had taken him seriously.

He was looking the reality of his theory in the face. He turned to his wife and began to wave a hand in the "get away" signal, but the floor caved in under him, buckling like a hot piecrust. The men tried to grip onto something, but there was no time. The emptiness of space was sucking the corridor out through the breach. Catherine pushed Karina back through the fourth airlock and told her to run. Karina fell down and struggled up, the rubber soles of her sneakers getting a grip as she instinctively streaked back the way she had just come. Just as she went through the airlock, a safety shield slammed down, sealing her from her parents. She looked through the little window and saw her father sucked out into space and her mother face down, desperately trying to hold on. Then the vacuum dragged her across the floor and out through the hull breach. Karina stood there, staring into the area beyond the barrier that protected her. It was empty. Open to space. She stared, wide-eyed and speechless.

Alone, Karina was looking at the gaping hole in the corridor between the two whorls. Cut off from the disaster, in the stillness of her shock, sealed off in the safety her mother had pushed her into, locked outside looking in, her heart cried to be with them even if it meant her own death. Her hands still felt their hands. Her sense of happiness was being sucked away by the emptiness and finality on the other side of the window. She slammed her hands against the plate glass and screamed for her parents. No answer came back. The silence seemed unnatural and surreal. She slumped down to her knees, her head against the bulkhead. Tears were streaming down her face. The party she had wanted so badly, the donkey tails, the cake, the singing seemed a nightmare now, all leading to this.

In the vacuum that followed, she knew nothing would ever be the same. She was alone. She slumped to the floor. "No, no, no," was all she could say. Then, all she could do was cry.

Twill was spending time assessing the technician's so-called adumbration, and even at his high level of mathematics and insight it was beyond his comprehension. "What are you talking about? I don't see any problem." The obsequious technician restated that the level of salience was extremely low.

"I may be the only one to notice it, Master Twill. I was assigned to deep background modulation analysis on that single frequency. So, I would notice anything anomalous in the spectrum to which I was assigned."

"Who assigned you to that function?" Twill was still annoyed. The technician gave a detailed report of the assignment structure, which included innumerable others, each assigned to the tiniest function analysis, all working independently, tracking nominal operations of the system.

Twill thought of Farson's parable of the anthill, and was further annoyed. He asked one more question.

"What could possibly be causing whatever it is you think you see?"

"Oh, no, Master Twill. I didn't 'see' it. The machinery 'felt' it. The reporting structure took note of it in the binary math segment. In reading the output, naturally, I came across it." Twill knew those reports and how they were just one long formula recording the process in such detail that the reports were always lengthy. Some technicians spent their lives reading just one.

"When did this occur, technician?" The technician seemed to think the question over and after a long pause, she responded.

"Impossible to say, sir. One part of the report seems to suggest it occurred over 6,000 Earth years ago, and another seems to say it was only since we began our final preparations, within the hour. In both reports the phenomenon is exactly the same: infinitesimally small, but highly ordered in its occurrence. That paradox is not resolving in ongoing analysis, so the only conclusion now available is that what is being reported is what happened."

"Is there any effect that is discernible?"

"No, sir. None that we can detect or predict." Twill was beginning to move away. But he asked one more question.

"So, if there's no effect, did it or did it not occur?" The technician had reached the end of her information stream.

"Impossible to say, Master Twill."

"Then why did you bring it to my attention at all?" This the technician could answer and did.

"Because it was impossible to confirm that something happened or that it did not happen but it is very clear that, either way, it never happened before. We thought you would want to know." Twill's annoyance was turning into anger.

"Know what?" He raised his voice. "That you don't know if anything happened or not?"

"Exactly, sir." She seemed happy with this conclusion. Twill stormed off, waving his tendrils at her over his shoulders. At first she thought he was going to hit her.

"That's ridiculous. Let me know when and if you ever have anything to actually report on this matter. Otherwise, don't interrupt me again." The technician watched him storm off and then returned to the data stream to which she was assigned. She quickly realized that she was now way behind schedule, and catching up would not be easy; she checked the volume of the data once more. She realized, with the interruption to discuss the matter with Master Twill, that catching up would now most likely be impossible.

<<*Why did you want to go through all of that again, Karina? It's so painful.*>>

<<*Farson, do you know what my very last thought of my dad was?*>>

<<*What?*>>

<<*That donkey tail I pinned on him. I saw it as he went out into space.*>> Farson didn't respond. He could think of nothing to say. <<*When I think about it,*>> she went on, <<*I find myself dreaming hard that it was different. That Dad repaired the flaw and we all lived happily ever after. Why can't I have that dream, Farson? We can do almost anything. Why can't we do that?*>> Farson moved beside her. He took her hand. His other arm went around her shoulders, and he hugged her close to him.

<<*The truth is the truth, Karina. You know The Screen well enough to know that.*>> She moved even closer to him. He was thinking of the frightened little girl he remembered so well.

<<*I still dream it and redream it, Farson. Maybe I shouldn't do that. Maybe that's just something I shouldn't do.*>> Farson

kissed her cheek and stayed close with his lips still touching her. He could taste her tears.

<<*We can always dream, Karina. It's only human.*>>

125. Brittany's Log (Miscellaneous Entries: 2102 to 2104 C.E.)

(1) Karina had been gone from SkyKing for a little more than five years when I was born. When my mother was killed, I was about the same age as Karina was when both of her parents died. So, of course, I learned about her at that time. They told me that she was living on Earth with an adopted family. I figured that I was better off than she was. I had my dad, and I was still on SkyKing.

The birth rate in those early years was low. SkyKing was still a risky place for kids, so there weren't many of us. I was not the first to be born on the station, but I was among the first. Most of the other kids became Skers – as we all know now – and in some ways I did, too. Not the same way they did, though. Because of my dad and his position we remained more traditional than the others. He had been ordered to SkyKing as its third-in-command, and he always served under orders which, of course, could change. So, we never really knew if we would be staying on the station or if we would be ordered back to Earth and on to another assignment.

The station has definitely been my home and my world, that's for sure. When I was really young, I went to Earth with my dad twice on official business. Didn't see much. I hardly remember it. In reality I have spent my life on SkyKing. I've have been to the Moon a couple of times, but just over and back. Again, on official business. Dad's no sightseer.

The Skers say I'm Sker, but my dad says I'm an Earther because of him and Mom. To me it doesn't matter so much where I'm from, as who I'm with and what I have to do.

The seven years between my mother's death and the appearance of the ScreenMasters' barge were really something. The ensuing years have not been boring either.

(2) The first person I really remember is my dad. Mom would argue with me about how that could not possibly be, but it's true. He was changing me, as the story goes, and while he was at it, he was teaching me, or trying to teach me to say "Daddy." All I could say was "Dutty." For the first years of my life I always called my dad "Dutty." That was the best I could do that day when he first heard me attempt to answer his ever-repetitious "Come on, Brittany, you can say, 'Dad Dee,' 'Dad Dee,' 'Dad Dee.'" I got the first sound and the Dee part. So it came out "Duh Dee." He ran around the house saying it, singing it, and being sure that my mom got the message. "She said, 'Daddy' first. Not 'Mommy.' She said 'Daddy' first." He was ecstatic. I've always reminded him that the way I said it rhymed with nutty.

(3) The space station always had places where some people could go and others could not, but I went wherever I wanted to. My dad was eventually promoted to Commander of the station so people hesitated to tell me to get out, and if you ask me, they just liked having me around. I had been taught to be careful. I have dressed in the Sker whites from the first time I could choose my own clothes, which was early on. My dad always said that he had no control over me at all. This was not true, of course. It gave him an excuse to allow me to roam free in the station's environment. There were two major separations: Skers from everyone else, and the mechanical side of the station from the living quarters. The living quarters

included the "lake" and all the recreational areas, plus the living apartments and communal rooms or "public areas." The mechanical areas, on all whorls, were like an unspoken danger, and I should have stayed out of them, probably, but a boy by the name of Voul Bensn was always working in them. He was a lot older than me, but it was really fun to bother him. I was five, and he was seventeen. Now I'm twenty-three, and he is thirty-five, and I still feel like he was my first love. His wife, the MoonBase commander, has never minded this situation, as far as I can tell. Even though given the chance, I might give her reason to worry, I really don't think Viera Nichols has a jealous bone in her body. Her love for Voul, and his for her, is a story in itself. MoonBase was always hedonistic from the beginning. The Skers are ascetics, and chaste. When those two finally married, it joined us all into one family. MoonBase, SkyKing, Farson, and whatever is left of the human race. When I stood as a bridesmaid at their wedding, my tears and my joy were the same mix of emotions felt by everyone that day, with a little extra because of my long relationship with Voul. So much has happened since the ScreenMasters came. Even now we still don't know everything.

Farson did say, somewhat prophetically, at the wedding reception during his brief toast to the newlyweds, "For Voul and Viera, this is a beginning. For us all, it is a confirmation: Just as humanity's survival is inevitable, the love of these two people was also inevitable."

Inevitable or not, things have really changed, that's for sure. When I first came to SkyKing, the Earth was still supplying everything, and the shuttles were constantly coming and going. People from Earth vacationed here, and there were always new people coming aboard. Entertainment, education, and almost everything was still Earth-bound. We had broadcasts constantly from Earth. Our com network was from Earth. Except for the Skers, most people both on MoonBase and on SkyKing considered themselves on a tour of duty, but now we know that that was never true. The 350,000 people on SkyKing are, as of now, the largest known gathering of free human beings anywhere. The 10,300 on MoonBase are the second largest. Farson says that Earth will be back, but how can we know for sure? What will they be like now? Farson has spoken about the stasis field and the way he had to speed up Earth's time to hide them from the ScreenMasters. He said that in the years we have been separated and traveling on our own with MoonBase, the Earth has advanced by over 6,500 years. He has told us of what he calls "Emerald Earth." It's a place of peace and an evenly spread population that lives in harmony and in abundance. The trashed environment that we all remember has been cleansed completely. Farson tells us of a new species of amphibian that roams the planet's vast farms and fields.

No one on SkyKing or MoonBase has seen anyone new, other than the babies born here, for thirteen years now. Imagine, the babies born now are coming into a world where Earth does not exist. In one more year it will be our year of 2104, but what will it mean if Emerald Earth reappears in their year of 6517?

What can a twenty-four-year-old woman do about any of that? I was just becoming a young woman when all of this happened, so I remember everything. Today, my life is part Sker and part daughter to my father who really is still an Earther. He wears the same clothes he always wore, even though styles have changed. I wear the Sker whites. I am a Sker, really. My father is not. So I'm still between two worlds, maybe more. I still love Voul, but in a different way, I suppose. Viera was always too wild and too rough for him. She was the leader of MoonBase for Heaven's sake. That place. It symbolizes all that was wrong on Earth. Drinking, smoking, debauchery, wild parties, irresponsible use of resources, and a certain raw animalism that evolved into a free-sex society among other things. She is its queen. Not because she was so good, believe me. It was because she was so bad. She told me that the first time she ever saw Voul he walked into a room where she was ... shall we say ... in the act with another man. I've asked her about this many times, and she always says it was as if he didn't notice the nudity or the situation's awkwardness in any way. He was calm and businesslike. "Polite," she always says. When I've asked Voul about it, he always says that he does not judge other people. He was there for a reason, and he did what he came to do:* save the station. Something happened between those two that day, that's for sure. The combined crews of MoonBase and SkyKing were shocked beyond all other shocks at the announcement of their intention to marry. Skers don't marry. MoonBasers don't take it seriously. Voul Jonsn, king of the Skers and the son of the founder of the Sker Nation, and Viera Nichols, the commander of the wild and crazy MoonBase: They did marry. They did it in regal and gala style. It was an extravaganza like no other. The ceremony was held in MoonBase's New Chicago (the first domed community on the surface of the Moon). The "reception" was held in the Great Hall of SkyKing. The transporters and gurneys ran all night. The only comparison I can make is to the old presidential inaugurations of Earth. There were several parties, and the newlyweds went to all of them. Again, this was an aberration for Voul, who had never attended a party in his life. By all accounts, he was having a ball. Now they've been honeymooning on MoonBase for two weeks, if you can believe that. Sergeant Long John Silver is in command of MoonBase while Viera honeymoons, and Repoul Bensn has assumed Voul's Sker duties while Voul is away. If anyone had told me that any of this was possible, I would have told them they were nuts. My dad is taking it all in stride. "I knew all along, honey. Those two were in love from the minute they laid eyes on each other. There was nothing that could stop it."

Too true.

(4) I still love him. I looked at him at the altar and wished it was me with him up there. I remember running into his arms as a little girl and loving every second of it. He had to peel me off. I used to wait hours and hours for just a brief look at him. He is the most handsome man I have ever seen, and he is the nicest man I have ever met. He is a Sker and not just any Sker. He's the founder's only son. Since the wedding, Viera and Voul seem happier than ever.

He loves Viera. I think she may be pregnant now. Maybe I'm suffering from transferral, but I have seen the signs in her.

My mother died when I was six. Voul was always around: tall, immaculate, and handsome. He filled a void for me. For seven years before the ScreenMasters, he was my friend, my "uncle," my little girl's fantasy. So, who can blame me? Now, perhaps, I'm like those "people in the bottle," as Farson calls the people on Emerald Earth. I'm waking up in a new world. My father relies on me to assist in managing the space station. I travel back and forth to MoonBase, and my days are full. Other than work, my life is sort of empty. Farson has spoken with me about it, secretly as he always does, and he says that <<*All will be well.*>> I know that my work on SkyKing is crucial. My father is getting older. So, I'm busy and fairly happy. Being born here and living all of my life here, then watching Voul fall in love and marry someone else, sometimes I feel like I'm losing control of my life. That things are carrying me along on forces that I cannot control. Alone in bed at night, I feel out of control, on the verge of losing something that is so important. I can't put my finger on it, but I know if Mom were here, she would know what to do.

That's gone, too. I remember her, but not thoroughly. I look at the pictures and movies of her and me, and it seems like two people I don't know. Sometimes, lately, I find myself crying at night. In the morning when I put on those crisp white pants and tunic and ponytail my hair, I feel like I become someone else and go out of my room as a masquerader, in disguise. Behind the quietude of Sker patience and peace, there is a little Earth girl screaming for help. Help for what? To do what? With whom?

126. Viera's Plan

There was nothing complicated about it, really. Her plan had always been straightforward and ambitious in its simplicity: First, develop every component and potential of the Moon into an industrial powerhouse to benefit the MoonBasers and support SkyKing; second, find happiness and keep it.

This wasn't the first time in her life that Viera thought of marrying, but she knew it would be the last time. Her dalliances were legion, but those devotions had been purely physical. She went through lovers like a Sker changes clothes. Something new every day, but everyday sex had worn thin in more ways than one for Viera. Her senses of command had sharpened, her emotions had toughened. But now she found that things within her, personal things, were also changing even as the Moon around her was changing. The stark craters of the lunar surface had lent themselves to the stories of stoic characters stomping around in that infernal dust, from the earliest days. But with the life and death challenges of the shock wave, the true sophistication of the miners, their incredible proficiency, skill, and adaptability were now well known. Viera also now knew that the true nature of her relationship with Voul was also becoming no secret now.

The power of the Moon had risen in the emergency. The people on SkyKing knew that the Moon had saved them. One thing had not changed: Viera Nichols was the unquestioned Moon commander. The stories of how she could fight and fuck with the best of them were still out there, but now when her name came up it was spoken in a softer, more respectful tone.

She was really pretty, for what that was worth. She always thought it was a mixed blessing. Men didn't really listen until she kicked them hard where their brains were. Then they always listened, but not to what she was saying but to her throaty intonations and the way she said things. Any sign of weakness and it was game over. For Viera the game was never over. She liked men, loved many of them, and they knew it. She was really smart. She could outwit anyone anytime and always did. She was MoonBase commander by Earth appointment, but when Earth disappeared, and through all that had occurred, there was no question of changing leadership on the Moon. Viera was there to stay.

The gurney and the technology of the laser drills made the ever-enlarging scope of MoonBase possible. In the process of drilling so many miles in the compacted silt, a byproduct appeared. A silicon-like substance that was compared to those big bubbles that kids on Earth used to stream out of soapy loops on summer days. These Moon bubbles had tensile strength and could be blown larger and larger. Plus, in the cold of space they hardened like stone, but held their transparency and multi-axis tensile strength. MoonBasers learned to manipulate the material and started to make small surface shelters out of the material. It was easy, and there was an endless supply in the wakes of the drilling machines. Soon, the shelters were combined to make them bigger and bigger, and then the honeycombing began. Thousands of bubbles were stacked higher and higher in a giant arching dome. Using the ancient tools and rules of geometry and construction, the possibility of a surface city began to materialize. It wasn't planned, but once it was started, New Chicago became an inevitability. In addition to the tunnels and the mines, a city in the sun was now becoming a growing suburb of MoonBase where almost everyone wanted to live. Viera's plan included making New Chicago a true surface city, and she was moving quickly in that direction as populations increased. The power of the Moon was in mines, but the miners longed for the starry, starry nights.

The mines were bountiful. As it turned out, the Moon was really a little Earth, in its chemistry, with the capabilities of water, wind, and fire, and of supporting a rapidly growing population.

Some of the MoonBasers were troubled by the domestic side of New Chicago: babies and families, schools and shops, but still, in their free time it was New Chicago with its nightlife, open spaces, and nascent culture that always drew them back.

Surprisingly, Viera frequently stayed with Voul on SkyKing. "Long weekends" she called them. It was clear that the Sker ways were affecting her. When she was on SkyKing, she took to dressing like a Sker. "I am a Sker, you know, Voul. I was reborn in your arms." Voul looked at her. She appeared to be made of white porcelain in her perfectly fitting uniform over her perfectly fit body. He was still looking at her as she stood up. "No comment, V? You usually say something when I say that."

"What is there to say? I was reborn in your arms, too." She walked over next to him and looked into his eyes. She felt the tendrils of his mind touching hers. It was a familiar arousal now. She knew he was exploring her most secret places in the most sensitive erogenous zone there could ever be for her. Her heart rate increased, her breasts swelled, and as sometimes occurred, she could see his thoughts and feel his body as he was feeling her mind. She kissed him, although it took an effort to move at all. "You are getting stronger, Viera. I used to paralyze you doing this."

"Well, I'm getting used to it. Soon enough, Voul we'll be doing it my way while we're doing it your way. Won't that be something?"

"I like your way," he said.

"And, I like your way," she said. "Soon it will be our way." She laughed knowing "our way" was inevitable now. Marriage to a Sker had always seemed a little boring to Viera, but now that she was in it, she knew much more. Boring it was not. With Skers, appearances are deceiving.

"Deceiving, Viera? That is certainly not the Sker way."

"Oh, you have your secrets too, Voul."

"Really? Like what?"

"Like you can't hide your thoughts from me when we make love. You've taught me how to listen, and listen I do."

"You always seem, shall we say, preoccupied in those moments. I've never noticed your attention wandering." He was smiling. "So, what secrets, Commander, are you talking about that I have?" Viera moved away a little. Proximity and Sker mental contact went together. As she moved away, the contact diminished a little.

"Like, what is that gigantic planet that Repoul is watching so closely on the long-range scanners?" Voul moved close. Viera was whispering now. "Secrets, Voul. They are hard to hide from your wife."

Voul was searching and finding. She did know. Of course, she did. One thing he knew about Viera was that whatever she was planning, it was not going to happen in the dark. She always spilled the beans. She always got to the truth.

He felt her mind gently probing his, like soft fingers through his hair.

"So now you're a MoonBaser and a Sker?"

It would seem so, she said to him, but no words were spoken. Voul closed his eyes and felt her lips on his. His thoughts were awash in softness. He was floating in sweet surrender.

127. Voul's Excuses

As the inevitable conversation with Repoul Bensn drew closer, Voul knew that he would need excuses and lots of them. Like the secret of the solar sails had been, the secret of Sargasso had been deemed sacred since Bensn's discovery of it. Almost like new scriptures being written, the Skers' evolving knowledge of the planet from the extremely long-range sensors telemetry had been guarded closely. Now Voul had let the secret out through close contact with Viera. In the Sker ways, this was a breach of security of the first magnitude. If anyone other than Voul had done it, serious repercussions would have swiftly ensued. The son of the revered founder, Ban Jonsn, occupied a special place in Sker history. Even though he was all but unassailable, the coming conversation with Repoul still loomed darkly. Repoul had earned respect among the Skers and was second only to Voul in regard and rank. Repoul was a scriptural purist and frowned on Voul's infatuation and impetuous marriage to the MoonBase commander. He saw the synergy of the match, but still, even though his friendship with Voul was deep and cherished, this new relationship was perplexing.

As Voul approached, Repoul was working at his station, as always. Voul was working at his excuses. Obviously, being in close contact with Viera so often opened doors that otherwise would have been closed. He was thinking about that excuse – how valuable she was – but realized that there was so much raw pleasure in those moments that it would not be an impressive diversion to Repoul's disapproval. Pleasure was not sanctioned. Then he calculated that Viera's nature could easily account for the breach of security. She just wouldn't and couldn't take no for an answer. Voul realized that that would make him look weak in Repoul's eyes. Finally, he thought that perhaps Viera could have learned it from Repoul himself when she was on the station. Perhaps he could make that work. No, Repoul would never accept it. In the end he decided to just tell his friend the truth. As he approached, he was wondering what had possessed him to even try to think of excuses, and then he realized that Viera had been in his mind, and, of course, he was in hers. Shaking his head as though to clear it, or perhaps to enjoy the lapse a little longer, he walked into the control room.

"I have news for you, Repoul."

"As I do for you, Voul."

"Viera knows about the planet." Repoul looked over his shoulder. He was surprised, but only in timing, not in substance. They looked at each other for a minute. The exchange was poignant. Voul broke the silence. "What's your news?"

Repoul hesitated for a moment. He looked down at the equations and at the obvious conclusion. "It's not a planet."

Voul tilted his head and stared at Repoul. "Then what is it?"

128. Sargasso

It was like nothing ever seen in space. "Sargasso," as Repoul had named it, appeared to be a vast, dense mist with giant islands of icy green all over it. It was still so far away that actual descriptions were not possible, but Repoul knew that while it was potentially Earth-like in atmospheric chemistry with some elements of topography, it was like nothing humans had ever seen before. "We will have to learn everything anew." Repoul was looking at Voul. Voul slightly bowed his head in silence for a moment. The scripture Repoul had paraphrased was over a hundred years old. The two Skers looked at each other. It was as predicted. "There shall be a new world in heaven and earth and all things shall begin anew." Voul was thinking of his father. He was wondering if Ban were here what he would say. He wished that he had the depth of faith and awareness his father had had. In his heart Voul knew that would never be.

Among the Skers only Repoul and Voul had the knowledge of Sargasso. SkyKing with MoonBase was now moving through space. More than 350,000 souls now and growing. The two groups, one on a space station built for orbit now preceded by enormous golden sails, and the other a vast gray moon, marooned from its companion planet, propelled by explosions once deadly but now its life force. *An odd couple,* Voul thought, *but so important.*

"Well, Voul, what do we do now?" Repoul sitting at his console, in immaculate whites, seemed young and intense.

"Now, Repoul, we do what we were meant to do. We prepare and explore."

The transit to Sargasso would still take years, and there was much to do. All the excuses and reasons had altered with the discovery, but in another sense nothing had changed. MoonBase would continue to build its cities, and SkyKing would continue to grow technologically and socially. The populations would continue to blend together. Even now the food production was stabilizing, and life support systems were again rebuilding reserves lost in the shock wave. The combination of Sker insight and human nature was working. The human race had changed into something new. The changes were continuing. Time was passing.

129. Commander Peterson's Memories

When Jim was in college, he had a friend. The exact time and place of their initial meeting was difficult to recall, but John Vander came along at a time when Jim had just married. The year was 2066. Jim and his young wife, Joanie, were living in an apartment in College Park, Maryland. He was studying history, and his wife was working to support them. He had served in the U.S. Navy during one of the middle eastern wars. He had been on a small ship off the coast of Jeddah, Saudi Arabia, in the Red Sea. The war had been fought over oil and religion. The Western powers were attempting to constrain what they considered religious fanaticism and to protect the flow of diminishing oil supplies. In those days there was little discussion left in the world councils, and the fighting had turned brutal and consuming. Jim had volunteered. He regretted it. Afterwards he went back to college and was trying to restart his life.

John was single and wild. Jim was struggling to find meaning. They both loved motorcycles. Jim remembered the long rides with John. They rode fast and furious. Once caught in a rainstorm they huddled under a highway overpass as the rain poured down. He remembered John's face dripping with water as they had parked their bikes on the side of the road and sat together on the stone embankment. John's beard was soaked, and water spewed out as he spoke through the whiskers. "This is great, Jim. We were rooster-tailing there!" They both laughed and sat together, waiting out the storm.

They fell asleep and were awakened by a state trooper who told them to get moving. It was still raining, but off they went, rooster-tailing away into the night, electric engines screaming at the acceleration. That night was a night they both remembered. Jim, thinking about it now, far away in space, was reminded of what John had said as they got back on their motorcycles. "When you gotta go, you gotta go." It still made him smile. Despite the fact that there were no motorcycles on SkyKing, Jim was still going and going. *But where?*

Voul was calling. "Yes, Voul?"

"We now have a destination, Jim. It's a long way off, it's directly on our course, and it's really something." Jim walked over and looked into Brittany's room. She was asleep. The room was quiet and peaceful. She always slept with a soft light on in the room. He could see the rising and falling of her rhythmic breathing under the covers. He returned to Voul, who was waiting patiently.

"I never doubted you," he said.

A year later John had been killed in a motorcycle accident with his girlfriend. Jim attended the funeral and stayed with John's family for a time. John's mother, in the hospital that night, tried to comfort him. "What will you do now, Jim?" she asked. He didn't answer her. He couldn't find the words. After a while they walked out together. They were both crying. Jim's anguish was deep. He had encouraged John's motorcycle riding. He had told him it was freeing, exciting. For Jim the adrenaline rush was an antidote to the war's mixed-up and debilitating memories. John's death seemed somehow to be his fault. John's mother must have known his thoughts when she whispered in his ear at their parting, "He loved riding with you." Her kind words felt like the bullets

Jim was trying to forget, tracing past him in those bloodied nights of confusion and despair in the war. He tried to smile but his regrets smothered him. "I loved riding with him, too."

In his anguish and memories, he knew that sometimes there was just no escape.

130. The End of the Beginning

Farson was sitting alone in the fading yellow light of the sunset. *The things that we have done. So many things.* In all the years he had traveled, he had seen too much. The human race had thought one thing and done another. Its "great destiny" was like a false reputation that mankind had carried for all these years. Now it was gone – at least that destiny. Farson thought, *That which had seemed so real, for so long, for so many. Now gone for all time.*

The burden of Earth's "progress" had taken a deep toll for its meager results, like a mother laboring in a difficult birth, full of hope and dreams, full of glorious agony, and now, holding the child, wet, bloody, real.

Now our true destiny is forced upon us, no more wondering, no more justifications for unjustifiable actions. Now the burden is gone. The rose of that world has withered away. Much greater lies now ahead.

The truth had first arrived with the ScreenMasters, but little did they know. *Mankind has changed. I was just the first.* It was hard for Farson to look back, because he knew that to fully know the past was to see mankind for what it really had been. This meant that looking forward was the only way to go. Still, he had been there to see it all. The ScreenRent had demanded that he solve the problem, and he had done that. The knowledge of all the killing, all of the wars, the prejudice, the cruelty *ad infinitum*, the avarice, greed, hatred ... all of it now had to be fixed, once and for all. *What was it all? Was it just us growing up, or something deeper? A flaw beyond repair?*

Emerald Earth was the only answer he knew. Farson wondered, was he the savior of mankind, or something else? Something darker? The prospects for Emerald Earth were amazing and daunting. Farson knew that all he had done was stop history and start over. *A new beginning.*

When he was in President Truman's White House on that fateful day when the second bomb so smoothly dropped through those B-29 "Superfortress" bomb bay doors over Nagasaki, he had seen the eyes of the old man who had commanded the slaughter. Truman had attempted to stay ahead of events, but events had overwhelmed him. Like so many before him, President Truman had seen what mankind had always seen. Kill or be killed. Truman had done it while speaking of the power of the Sermon on the Mount. He thought that the Sermon was a call to action, but Farson knew it was not. It was a knowing prediction that had finally come true. *The Kingdom of Heaven.* Farson laughed, but not disrespectfully. He laughed at the irony. The meek, the poor in spirit, they that mourn, they who hunger and thirst after righteousness, the merciful, the pure in heart, they who are prosecuted for righteousness's sake. Farson knew that the prophets, and all who had suffered and died in Earth's history had always been a growing, living entity, gathering power for a day to come. *And that day did come. I was in my cabin in New Hampshire when it began.* The ScreenMasters did not come to Earth to save it. They came in fear, dragging the baggage of their own dark histories and profoundly false beliefs with them. *They came for me. And my sister. To use us and kill us.* Farson stood up. He was in a desert. The sand was blowing. *I have changed that.*

He was dressed in his usual loose pants and a loose white shirt. *No cardigan in this weather.* He wore sandals on his feet, and his hair was long now, his beard full. *I dress like a pauper. I own nothing. I want nothing for myself. Yet I wander through time looking. Always looking.*

Karina appeared beside him. She had changed as well. Her clothing was almost identical to Farson's now, soft slacks, a loose white blouse, sandals, but she routinely wore a flowing ScreenMaster's robe. Her long hair blew free and in the fresh, warm air. She took his hand. <<*We still have so much to do, Farson. Let's keep going.*>>

<<*I know.*>> Her hand was soft and warm in his. He knew what was coming. <<*It's not just us anymore, Karina. Will that be hard?*>> She was looking at him.

<<*No, Farson. It'll be easier. Think of all those who came before and still are. Think of what we can do now. All together.*>> Farson knew. SkyKing and MoonBase, alone in space for now, had set the course for Sargasso, but unknown to them, Emerald Earth was on the verge of its recrudescence. It would soon join the other two in their journey. <<*We have taken what the ScreenMasters did and turned it against them without harming them. There is nothing to fear.*>> Farson had seen too much. He knew it wouldn't be that easy. Karina almost laughed out loud. <<*Farson, what can they do? Time is on our side. The TrueScreen will protect us. We will be gone. They will think they have won. Twill will be satisfied with his primacy. We are so strong now. They will never know the truth.*>> Farson was nodding but with a deeper reason.

<<*Ultimately, Karina my love, that will be the problem precisely.*>>

There were a few more moments for the two of them. They kissed and whispered things to each other. They stood up and disappeared. The desert winds began to cover the prints of their soft sandals in the sand.

Repoul was at his station as they appeared beside him. He was startled slightly, but he had been waiting for them. The simple command that changed everything and restarted everything surprised Repoul. Not the action it commanded but the mundane wording. Farson had said it simply, with his hand on Repoul's shoulder. "Push the button, Repoul." The midshipman's hand moved to the console, and without a second's hesitation his finger depressed the gray activation switch.

Far away, CT<<Dinsil2371 moved next to Twill, as the newly risen Grand ScreenMaster toggled another holographic switch. Twill sensed something and turned to look at the robot, but it was too late. The robot had moved away again. Twill at first thought it was an attack, but then in an overwhelming moment of lucidity his countenance changed. Twill saw his moment of triumph occurring and took it all in. In his own Essor way he laughed out loud. "Now that was just too easy," he said. With a wave of his hand, the robot collapsed in a heap beside him. Twill's aides came rushing over. He waved them away. The commencement of his Grand Ascension celebration and the destruction of Earth were both underway at the same time. With his aides in tow, he moved quickly into the palace. The crowds were waiting and welcomed him with the acclaim appropriate to the new ruler of all the ScreenMasters and now of The Screen itself. The thought of Earth destroyed and the end of the human race did not occupy his mind for more than a second or two. Then only to gloat on his vast victory over Farson Uiost. In his mind he knew that the silence he could feel meant that Uiost was dead, and he, Twill, was finally free of that curse. He

adjusted his cloaks carefully as if straightening them was the only thing on his mind as he walked to the podium. His first words, the first words of the new Epoch, were, "My fellow citizens of The Screen, I bring you tidings of great joy. The ScreenRent is repaired. We are all safe again. Long live The Screen and the ScreenMasters." His words were met with tumultuous approval, and the celebration had begun. For Twill it was the ultimate moment of giddy success, and he meant to enjoy it fully.

In the exultation of the moment, few noticed that the robot's collapsed frame had disappeared.

Just inside the outer range of their telemetry, a large disturbance echoed. Repoul was looking at the monitor in disbelief. A beautiful amber and green planet had appeared and, with astonishing speed, was moving into close proximity. SkyKing's instruments were already registering the gravitational pull and a vast increase in the station's velocity. *The sails must come in.*

On MoonBase, Voul and Viera were also watching as telemetry registered the same events. The all-systems lights were flashing overloads, but one call came through clear as a bell. "SkyKing and MoonBase, this is President John Andrew McKinley Sortt. We have matched your course and taken you in tow. Acceleration is underway. Furl the sails. Shut down your propulsion systems. The next few days will be very interesting." There was a brief pause and then he continued, "But you already knew that." He was smiling brightly when the transmission faded out.

Voul, Viera, Repoul, and Jim Peterson were all looking at the instruments. The rate of acceleration was astounding. The sails on SkyKing were being quickly stowed, and MoonBasers, in typical form, were preparing to party.

Celebration was the universal thought among the odd space-faring formation as the joyous rebirth of Earth became apparent to them. The rebirth of them all.

As the new reality sank in, the residents of MoonBase, and yes, SkyKing too, were all thinking the same thing: "It's our new birthday. Let's have some fun."

First, though, they turned off the engines and shut down the nukes, made sure the sails were stowed, and then they let the celebrations begin.

The human race began to truly relax for the first time in its long torturous history. A call came in from New Chicago, "Commander Nichols, you are not going to believe who just walked into City Hall." She smiled because she could guess. Farson and Karina had joined the party, with two golden robots in their company.

ZZ<<Arkol25609 first and then CT<<Dinsil2371, moving somewhat slower, took up their stations off to the side, standing silently, strobing, watching.

131. The New Mission

Farson and Karina's first child was born in North Conway on February 5, 2098 (c. 6506 E.E.) at 12:01 a.m. Their second was born at 12:09 a.m., just minutes later. They named their twin red-headed daughters Felicity and Valgary and vowed to never say who came first.

SkyKing and MoonBase eventually achieved orbit near the giant Sargasso. All their resources were focused on investigating Sargasso and its mysteries. The silent and inscrutable Emerald Earth had moved off to a location of its own, but well within sight.

The first explorational operations of Sargasso were being planned, but even these momentous events were overshadowed by what people were calling Farson's New Emancipation Proclamation. This brief speech of 119 words revealed a truth like none other in human history, and changed everything.

"Every human being is and always has been a ScreenMaster. We are a race of ScreenMasters. This is what the ScreenMasters wanted to stop. This is what they wanted to kill. In the days ahead, you will learn and experience things and do things unimaginable before today. Also in these days ahead now, you will each begin to comprehend the truth of mankind and the truth of our nature and our new, everlasting mission. You will see that all that I have done is just the preamble. You will do more. Much, much more. The Farson Uiost you have known is no more. Now, we are all equals, in power, in peace, and yes, most of all, in love."

132. Farson's Log (1)

I, a stranger and afraid
In a world I never made.
– A. E. Housman

"TIME IS A HOUSE OF MANY ROOMS. THAT YOU CAN'T REMEMBER YOUR OWN BIRTH OR IMAGINE YOUR OWN DEATH IS ALL TOO TRUE. HOWEVER, AS A SCREENMASTER YOU MUST DO EXACTLY THOSE TWO THINGS – IN VIVID DETAIL – OR YOU CAN NEVER CLAIM THE TITLE. ONCE YOU ARE ABLE TO FULLY EXPERIENCE THEM OVER AND OVER – AND EVERYTHING IN BETWEEN – THE DOOR OUT OF THE FIRST ROOM OPENS. YOU HAVE ACHIEVED A BEGINNING."
– *FARSON UIOST*

Oh, I know they now quote me with reverence (sometimes inaccurately), but it wasn't always like that.

The notion of time, as complicated as space itself, was not a quickly accepted concept at all, to say the least. People had always felt that time was time, one long strand running from the beginning to the end. I knew that time was like a screen so vast and intricate that it had gone virtually unnoticed. Far from the one-strand theory, time always was, and always will be a complex, interwoven structure. The strand theory was linear and too easy. Change one thing in the past and change everything. The ScreenMasters knew that wasn't true. I saw even more than they did. A lot more. "The ScreenMaster of Earth" they called me. What a misnomer that was. As human beings we instinctively work in multilinear time concepts constantly. In its simplest form, it has been called multitasking. We also manage relationships in different time lines, and we know that changing one thing often has virtually no effect at all, in the past and in the present or in the future. We humans enjoy time travel and do it all the time. Some of us live in the past. Some of us live in the future. Very few human beings, if any at all, ever live in the present. This was a fact overlooked by the ScreenMasters when they came here, and it has to be said that that oversight has cost them dearly.

To us it was obvious to the point that stating it could seem to be a terrible exaggeration. The well-known fact that humans communicate nonverbally 90 percent of everything they do communicate is exactly like that, too. To say that we are mind readers automatically generates dismissive incredulity, as though that could not possibly be true. It's the elephant in the room. It's so true that no one will acknowledge it. If you say you can read minds, people will laugh, so you don't say it. If someone else says it, you laugh at them so they regret saying it. Some things, as the saying goes, are better left unsaid. Which is the hilariously convoluted way that human beings render fact into myth so that everyone can agree that something is, of course, true without acknowledging that it actually is true. Human beings are time travelers and mind readers, but it can never be recorded thus or proven because we won't allow that. It's as if the species itself is programmed to keep our secrets secret. Even though, as the saying goes, "Everyone knows," especially the people on Emerald Earth.

When I was chosen as ScreenMaster, it seemed that I had been singled out, but events have proven it was far, far more than that. In the ensuing years, my attempt to explain what happened to all humanity was met with that very fact-into-myth syndrome just mentioned. Since I was the first, I have a special, perhaps, position in history, if that is the correct word anymore, for what has happened and will happen. Just being the "first" implies that there will be others, and, of course, there were. As the numbers grew, being first, ironically, grew in importance to a grateful planet. However, it was always a two-way street, even when no one would listen. Things change slowly. There is strength in numbers.

Time is a house of many rooms. They say, "You can't remember your own birth, and you can't imagine your own death." It's true, I suppose. But, as a ScreenMaster, until you do exactly that you cannot even begin. Once you are able to fully experience your birth and death over and over – and everything in between – you will find that the first door to the first room of The Screen swings wide open.

You will have achieved a beginning.

133. Farson and the Robots

<<*Well, what now, you guys?*>> The two robots were there with him in North Conway. It was cold outside, but warming. In New Hampshire people can tell. The other parts of the country think it's always cold in New Hampshire. Colder than other places. But New Hampshirites can tell when it starts to change. "We've made it through another one," they will say. It makes them laugh. The snow was still piling up outside, and the temperatures were in the teens. "We've made it through another one," was now being heard around town. Farson had already heard it. He had gone into town looking for a juicer. He was fascinated with making juice. His blender's ability had been stretched to its limit. The spinach juice did not work out. He needed a juicer. The grocery store had a really good one, in the appliance section, for about $200. It came with a bunch of utensils to use for different kinds of juices. There was a crank squeeze attachment for wheat grass juice. *And spinach, too.* There were blades to pulverize turnips and beets. There were various sizes of containers including a milkshake-size glass that attached directly. Farson's recipe called for adding spinach juice to beet juice, celery juice, and the juice of an apple or two. *It will look like blood and taste like sweet Mother Earth.*

<<*An interesting concoction, Farson. Especially from you.*>>
<<*That thought occurred to me too, CT<<Dinsil2371.*>>

As he watched the cashier ring up the juicer and vegetables, he noticed the people in the next bay were looking at him. The woman said, "It'll be a while before *our* beets're up." He realized she was talking to him. She was with her husband, Farson supposed. They were picking up a few things in town. They had several packages of ice salt on the counter.

"You're right about that," Farson said. He knew that there wouldn't be fresh local beets in the supermarket for months. *These will do for now.* Then he thought. *A world where you can get beets from Slovakia in the dead of New Hampshire's winters isn't all bad.* He looked down at his beets. *They'll do for now.*

<<*So many things are interconnected, Farson.*>> CT<<Dinsil2371's voice was clear and strong. <<*Sometimes I feel like it's almost too much for me.*>>

<<*You are such a joker, CT. Do you really expect me to believe that?*>>

<<*I did quit once, you know.*>>

<<*I know. And look where that got you.*>> CT<<Dinsil2371 looked down at his robot hand, his robot body. His head swiveled toward the window and he noticed that the snow was slowing. He could see the blue skies starting to show through the clouds in his reflection.

<<*Indeed.*>>

Farson noticed that ZZ<<Arkol25609 continued staring out the window, without another word.

Felicity was usually the happy one. Valgary was the explorer and wonder worker. Karina was trying to get Felicity to the dinner table. "Your dad will be back soon, you know. He is not going to be happy."

"He's always happy, Mommy," Felicity was correcting her mother, as she often did. "He's one of the happiest people I know."

"He won't be happy hearing that you won't do what I tell you. So, let's get to the table." Valgary was already there at her plate. Felicity was hesitating.

"I think I saw lima beans, Mom." Felicity would eat almost anything. She was famous for it. She even drank her father's juice mixes. (Karina thought her daughter feigned that affection.) But she knew Felicity definitely hated lima beams.

"They are very nutritious, Felicity. They are just another kind of bean. You like baked beans, black beans, green beans, and chickpeas, especially as hummus. True?" The little girl was listening intently. She did like other kinds of beans.

"True."

"So what's up with lima beans? They are considered one of the most nutritious foods."

"That's the second time you've mentioned that. Everything is nutritious, Mom. Even ice cream and popcorn. Everything has nutrient value. I hate lima beans."

"What makes you think they are on the table?" Karina had worked hard to conceal them. She had added onions, fresh corn, mushrooms, red peppers, three kinds of lettuce, and a delicious poppyseed vinaigrette.

"You can't fool me."

The woman in the grocery line said to Farson, "Well, we've made it through another one. That's something." Farson smiled. *There it is.* He nodded in agreement. The couple was leaving now. She turned and added one more comment. "It wasn't easy this time, was it?" Farson continued nodding.

"Truer words were never spoken."

Felicity was at the table. Not completely in her seat. Her posture indicated less than total commitment to staying for dinner. She noticed so many of her favorite vegetables in the salad. She saw the lima beans. "Yuck." Mom was unhappy. This struggle between Felicity and lima beans was never easy. It was a matter of principle. Karina felt that Felicity should see the logic of it. She liked every kind of bean except limas. Felicity felt that with so many beans acceptable, her distaste of lima beans should be allowed. Karina knew her daughter had a point but continued to try to win the battle. "They are just like the other beans you like, 'City. Just the same."

"Oh, no, they are not. Limas have that extra yucky dryness and an awful aftertaste that ruins the whole meal. I gag every time. Every time. As you know." Karina did know. Watching Felicity gag and choke on lima beans at the table was not her favorite family dinner event. Valgary ate limas with enthusiasm and diligence, sometimes covering for her sister by eating both helpings. Farson was oblivious to the distinction that waylaid Felicity at every serving of the dreaded bean.

"Here, watch me, 'City. See?" He was demonstrating by exaggeratedly chewing the beans and overacting his enjoyment. He finished with a clean mouth inspection, tongue out. He was teasing her. Their tongues were now pointing at each other across the table.

"Just watching you do that makes me want to throw up." She turned her plate so the beans were as far away from her as they could be and began to eat her rice. "Mom, the juice has spread over my whole plate!" It was true. Karina had tried blending in a little butter prior to serving the limas, hoping this could help. Instead, in Felicity's view, the melted butter had facilitated the lima bean contamination sliding easily into the other occupants on her plate. "It's all ruined." She pushed it away and sat back with crossed arms. Looking at the other three people at the table, she said, "It must be great for everyone to have a nice dinner."

Sitwory was on Beach. Routier was there, of course. "Well, that should do it," she said.

"What?"

"That should do it for our official entry to Beach." She smiled at him.

"Yes, I suppose you are right about that."

<<*Farson, you didn't say that.*>>

<<*I know, Karina. I know.*>>

<<*That just proves it.*>>

<<*What? That you can always have what you want?*>>

"Routier, you are such a rascal."

134. Farson's Log (2)

We did play with time. *Sometimes.* If we changed anything it was for the good. *Long John Hanson Silver.* It's not like we wanted to. Things were really pretty good for Kari and me. We lived. We grew. We loved. We've stayed together through it all. Now we have our children. Felicity and Valgary. Happiness and sacrifice. Peace and trial. Joy and faith. They are identical twins who look nothing alike. *Except for their hair.*

People wonder about the girls. That goes without saying. They are wonderful. They center me. They keep us both in the moment. *Focused.* They are so important. They remind me of so many who have gone before. Mostly, I see Karina in them. But I also see the others in them. I try not to. It seems unfair to the girls. But watching them, I see it all: the past, the present, the future. In their eyes I see The Screen growing strong in all directions. I see the hope of thousands of years. I see my own weakness and strength. I see Karina's love. In their eyes, and their lives, I see everything.

135. "Stop!"

"Farson, you are never going to learn if you don't slow down. Coal burns slow. You have to ease it around. A little push here. A little tap there. Be patient." Farson had the door open and was coughing in a cloud of smoke and coal dust. His gloved hand was still in the chamber. "Stop!" Farson looked at Sam, and slowly removed his hand. He closed the door. The coal was burning smoothly. He eased the grate to just a slit, almost closed. "It'll still be burning in the morning, Sam."

Sam looked at Farson, arms covered in soot. "You're learning, insect. *Finally.*"

136. Now Here, Now Gone

TIME TRAVEL
by Farson Uiost

Our memory
Is a preservative
Of things that easily
Could go bad
If just left out
In the open.

The little ziplock seal
Slides along even as
We listen, knowing
That that must go
Quickly into
Storage.

Then one day, strolling
Along the motherboard
There it is again: fresh
And crisp and sour
Or sweet, reserved
As planned.

Time travel is not
Unusual for us, we
Walk in and out of
The past like
Blinking. Now
Here, now gone.

<<The end.>>

Front and Back Matter

with appendices

Complete Works
Table of Contents
Diagrams
Chronology
Dramatis Personae
Glossary
Poems
Sequel Preview
"About the Author"

Complete Works

W. Mahlon Purdin

Published and unpublished

Poetry

I. First Poems (1967-1974)
II. No Place to Wash Our Hands (1975)
III. The Ballad of Hayden Brown (1975)
IV. And Is Mine One? (1976)
V. Go Forth Companionless (1976)
VI. July Poems (1976)
VII. Self Poems (1977)
VIII. Touch & Eddy (1977)
IX. Forty Days, Forty Nights (1982-1990)
X. Untitled Poems (1987)
XI. Pencil Poems, Fading Poems (1987)
XII. Untitled Poems II (1993)
XIII. Songs (compiled 1994)
XIV. Spoondrifting (2001)
XV. Working Poems (2001-2002)
XVI. Welkin Blush (2002-2004)
XVII. Selected Poems: A Chrestomathy (2003)
XVIII. Poems/2005
XIX. Poems/2006
XX. Poems/2007
XXI. Poems/2008-2009
XXII. Poems/2010
XXIII. Poems/2011-2012
XXIV. Poems/2013
XXV. Pathetic Poems (2014)
XXVI. Time Running Out (2015)
XXVII. Pathetic Poems 2 (2017)

Short Stories

The Last Remains (1972)
Abyss (1973)
Waiting for the Truth (1975)
Wish You Were Here (1978)
Iznaya (1979)
Kill Zone (1979, updated 2002)
Zachary Doane and the Cat Who Came in from the Cold (1987)
Ratworld (2003)

Novels

I'll Ask Her in the Morning (1978/2017)
The ScreenMasters:
(Volume I) The Rise of Farson Uiost (2014)
(Volume 2) Sargasso (2015)
(Volume 3) The Dreams of Ida Rothschild (2016)
(Volume 4) The World of Nor (2018)

Nonfiction

(Available on www.legendinc.com)
Essays, blogs, and comments
Magazine articles
Dear Rebecca: Letters from Vietnam

TABLE OF CONTENTS

Illustrations

SkyKing

2017

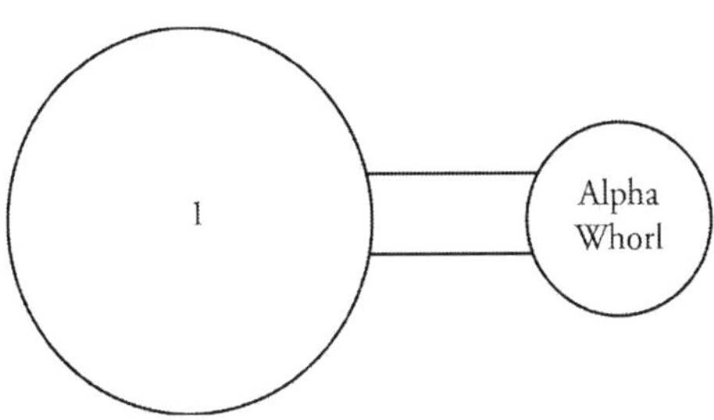

2020

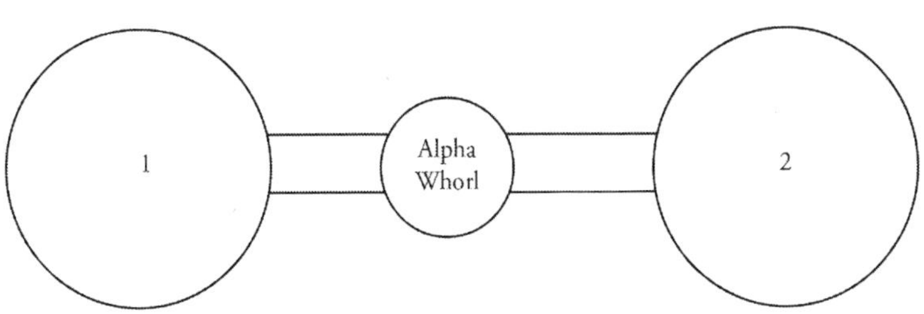

2044

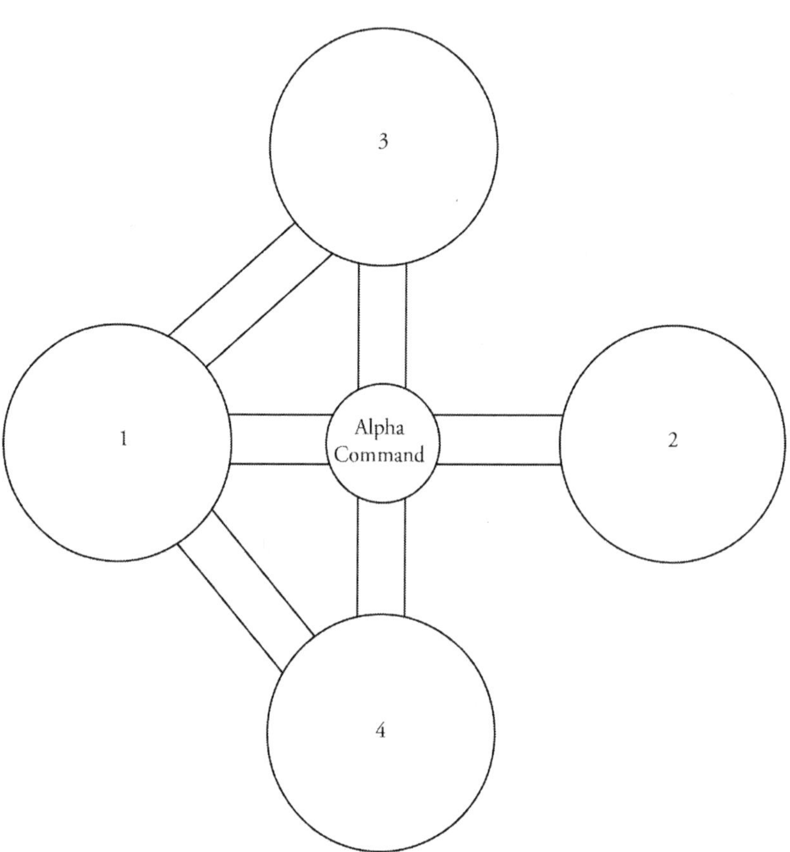

2094

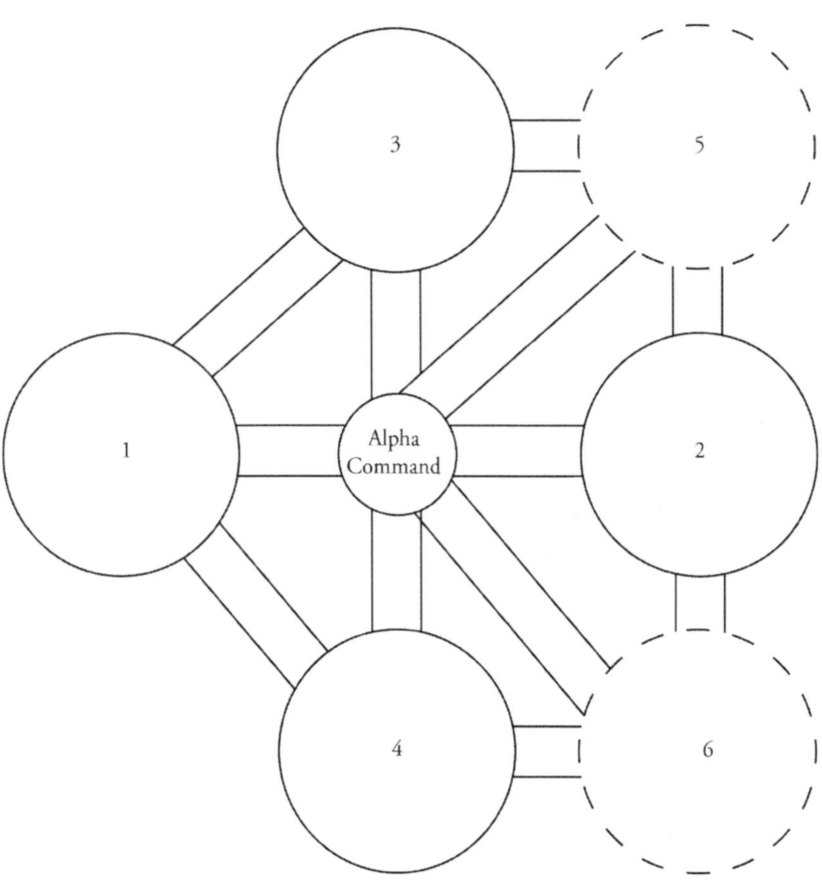

Chronology

A.D. / C.E

1945	Nagasaki is bombed, August 9, 11:02 a.m.
1957	Ban Jonsn born, December 25
1991	First faint hints of The Screen are discerned by scientists as reported in *The New York Times*, February 25
2010	SkyKing first goes crudely operational
2014	MoonBase settlement is planned
2020	First permanent Moon settlement established
2039	James Peterson born, August 19
2044	Joan Peterson born, July 27
2057	Gerald Antonoff born, January 1
2063	Farson born, February 5
	Mary and David Uiost die, February 5 and 9
2064	Voul Jonsn born on SkyKing, July 30
2065	Karina born, July 31
2069	Viera Nichols born, March 23
2071	Karina's parents killed on SkyKing
2071	Farson (almost eight) and Karina (almost six) meet for the first time
2075	James Peterson moves to SkyKing as third-in-command
	Ban Jonsn dies, March 12
2076	Brittany Peterson born on SkyKing, February 14
2080	Laso-Nuclear Exchanges end
2082	Joan Peterson dies, May 17
2084	Jim Peterson becomes commander of SkyKing
2088	Andrew Sortt elected president of the USE

2091	ScreenMasters arrive, January 15 Earth is placed in stasis, March 30
2094	Voul and Viera marry

——————— E.E. ———————

6000	Farson and Karina quietly marry, in a private ceremony, on November 27
6002	Handy notices a fluctuation in the ScreenLock
6505	The Mending
6506	Felicity and Valgary born to Farson and Karina, February 4

DRAMATIS PERSONAE

The ScreenMasters
Farson Uiost [yüst], ScreenMaster of Earth
Karina Chamberlain, his sister
Twill, Uvo, and others
Handy Townsend

MoonBase
Viera Nichols, Base Commander
Sergeant Long John Hanson Silver, second-in-command
Corporal Benjamin Franklin Smith, third-in-command
Ensign Reginald Chambois

SkyKing
James Peterson, Station Commander
Brittany Peterson, his daughter
Lieutenant Gerald Antonoff, third-in-command

The Skers [skī-erz]
Voul Jonsn, Sker leader, and second-in-command of SkyKing
Midshipman Repoul Bensn, a Sker theorist and Voul's assistant
Ban Jonsn, Voul's father, founder of the Sker nation
Lieutenant Barny Patrsn, Voul's trusted co-pilot and friend

The Robots
ZZ<<Arkol25609, a ScreenKeeper
CT<<Dinsil2371, an ancient ScreenKeeper

Emerald Earth

John Andrew McKinley Sortt, the first president of the United States of Earth

Strapper Jordan, an Emer farmhand

Earth's population

Others

Tom and Catherine Jacobson, Karina's parents

David and Mary Uiost, Farson's parents

William and Mary Chamberlain, Farson's and Karina's adoptive parents

Hattie and Sam, worked for the Chamberlains

Joan Peterson, SkyKing Commander's deceased wife

Glossary

EarthStasis. The ScreenMasters' plan to solve the problem.

E.E. This is a time designation, like A.D. and B.C. in other eras. It means Emerald Earth and denotes the actual date for the inhabitants of Earth including the years in stasis.

E-Lasers. Erasure pulses created to clean and protect satellites in space. They later evolved into highly destructive weapons, and later gave birth to the transporter technology.

Emerald Earth. First mentioned in section number The renamed planet Earth, now totally devoted to agriculture, arts, education, and some forms of entertainment. Known everywhere for its good food, clean atmosphere, and water, it is now peaceful, a very natural setting, and easily hosts the extremely generous export system it developed for sharing its bounty. The only social organization on Emerald Earth is that of families. People come to Emerald Earth in tribute and on pilgrimages. John Andrew McKinley Sortt is its leader.

Emers. Residents of Emerald Earth. Also known as "lubbers" to the people of MoonBase and SkyKing.

Farson Uiost. Born, 2063 A.D., elevated to ScreenMaster, 2091 A.D., age 28.

FirstLevel ScreenMaster. Perhaps the easiest to attain, this ScreenMaster level involves solving a current, somewhat minor problem affecting The Screen.

GateWay. A transfer opening to higher and higher Screen levels achieved by traversing layers of The Screen.

Gridframes. The basic measure of The Screen, calculated in lightyears, for distance and time.

Laso-Nuclear Exchanges. From 2077 to 2080, they disrupted all societies, especially the United States.

The Mending. Farson's original plan to reunite Earth, SkyKing, and MoonBase as independent entities, but it also would become the name Twill used for his planned Grand Ascension to supremacy among the ScreenMasters.

Phanta. A Screen phenomena that only the highest-level ScreenMasters have ever seen, and one that only Farson understood.

Right of Privacy. The cherished Sker postulate of organization, which allowed each individual to live as he or she sees fit within the one rule of "Do no harm." The Skers consider it the absolute guarantee of the rights of religious freedom and freedom from prejudice.

ScreenBurn. The period of time after a repair is made and before the repair completes itself. Like a healing period. It is a period of strength because great things are happening. It is also a period of exposure because things are changing, but not yet complete.

ScreenChange. The change of an aboriginal being into a ScreenMaster. This change is not always successful or completed.

<<ScreenCommunication>>. For those who inhabit and travel The Screen, this is a natural form of deep connection, telepathy; an attribute; a distance-insensitive system of communication … among other things.

ScreenDeclension. A system where the overall control of The Screen is redivided among a new number of ScreenMasters. Previous to Farson this always meant there had been a reduction in the number of ScreenMasters. After Farson Uiost, and what came later, it sometimes was the opposite.

ScreenFabric. The Screen in its vast composition is held together by many factors, large and small, all having varying measures of intent, from which its overall strength or local weakness is derived. The substance of The Screen.

ScreenGlow. Another reference to a ScreenMaster's ScreenLite, which usually lingers after departure.

ScreenGrid. The fundamental element of The Screen.

ScreenKeepers. The robots who generally accompany some ScreenMasters in their travels. The origin of the ScreenKeepers, until Farson, was unknown and unquestioned. They just were. After Farson, it was a different matter altogether. They are highly intelligent, can alter their appearance and height, were and are telepathic, and in possession of many attributes of ScreenMasters themselves.

ScreenLayers. Groups of 100 levels.

ScreenLite. A purple hue that surrounds a ScreenMaster when he is activating his or her Screen powers.

ScreenLock. In conjunction with the Earth stasis field, The Screen concentrated around the planet and created a time lock in which the planet's time altered while space around remained unchanged. The removal of a lock was thought possible. The Earth's ScreenLock cycle was occasionally visible from the planet it surrounded.

ScreenMaster. Master of The Screen, able to harness and direct its power through time, existence, dimension, and space, without limit, although ScreenMasters vary in the depth and reach of these abilities.

ScreenMend. The procedure that results in upgrading a ScreenPatch to a full, seamless repair of The Screen. Highly technical, and very unusual, in ScreenMaster terms, and accomplished only by the most advanced ScreenMasters, and even then success was never guaranteed.

ScreenMoiré. A pattern discovered at Level9.96 that implied a way to slew a ScreenMaster's passage.

ScreenPassage. A ScreenMaster's movement on The Screen.

ScreenPatch. A temporary solution to a ScreenRent.

ScreenRent. A cascading syndrome of disintegration that begins with a small "rip" and, if allowed to continue, eventually will cause fragmentation (tearing) in The Screen and – in the theories of the ScreenMasters – can lead to complete destruction.

ScreenSense. The awareness that all ScreenMasters have of the Screen's completeness and ever-presence.

ScreenTear. The catastrophic effect of an unrepaired ScreenRent.

ScreenTime. Roughly 10,000 years to one Earth year.

ScreenTruth. Fabled among ScreenMasters to the "Word" of The Screen itself.

ScreenWeb. A ScreenMaster's individual aspect that moves with him through the fabric of The Screen. Highly individual in size and characteristics. In many ways a ScreenMaster's Web is his defining signature.

Sker. People born on SkyKing, who accepted the teachings of Ban Jonsn. Pronounced to rhyme with "higher."

Star>Day. Approximately 24 light-years+.

Stasis-Eddy. An Emer intervention from within the stasis field, allowing them to observe and communicate through its effects.

TrueScreen. Farson's discovery.

Poems

THOSE IMAGES

by W.B. Yeats

What if I bade you leave
The cavern of the mind?
There's better exercise
In the sunlight and wind.

I never bade you go
To Moscow or Rome.
Renounce that drudgery,
Call the Muses home.

Seek those images
That constitute the wild,
The lion and the virgin,
The harlot and the child.

Find in middle air
An eagle on the wing,
Recognize the five
That make the Muses sing.

(1937, 1938 C.E.)

MAG

by Carl Sandburg

I wish to God I never saw you, Mag,
I wish you never quit your job and came along with me.
I wish we never bought a license and a white dress
For you to get married in the day we ran off to a minister
And told him we would love each other and take care of each other
Always and always long as the sun and rain lasts anywhere.
Yes, I'm wishing now you lived somewhere away from here
And I was a bum on the bumpers a thousand miles away dead broke.
I wish the kids had never come
And rent and coal and clothes to pay for
And a grocery man calling for cash,
Every day cash for beans and prunes.
I wish to God I never saw you, Mag.
I wish to God the kids had never come.

Feeding the Sheep
by Handy Townsend

Farson and Karina
Moving through all time
Touching place to place
Touching face to face
Farson and Karina
Love's best purity
Farson and Karina
Oh, sincerity ...

AMERICA
by Handy Townsend

Let America be America again.
Let it be the dream it used to be.
Let it be the pioneer on the plain:
A home where we roam free.

(America never was America to me.)

Let America be the dream the dreamers dream.
Let it be that great strong land of love,
Where no kings connive nor tyrants scheme:
Where no one is crushed from above.

(America never was America to me.)

"I've never been that perfect."

by Handy Townsend

I've never been that perfect.
I've never been as wonderful.
But I've seen a lot of times
And I still sing in rhymes.

Those people in the bottle
Need to meet me over a drink.
They'll never expect it,
Won't know what to think.

A man who moves in real time,
While the world crawls home.
A man who can see them and
Tell them they're not alone.

THINGS HAVE CHANGED

by Handy Townsend

Things have changed in this old world…
This old world.
Things have changed in this old world...
This old world.
Once things were deadly and things were
Dyin'....
Now the world's a peaceful place, and only the
Babies're cryin'...
Oh, yes, things have changed in this old
World....
Things have changed, things have changed.

"Time is comin'"
by Handy Townsend

The time is comin'
Though people are plannin'

One thing and another's
Goin' to happen.

They are all goin' to be
So surprised when they see

The truth sure ain't something
That's just that fancy-free.

On Essor, it's building
On the station it's ready

Here on Emerald Earth
We're waiting to be free.

TIME TRAVEL

by Farson Uiost

Our memory
Is a preservative
Of things that easily
Could go bad
If just left out
In the open.

The little ziplock seal
Slides along even as
We listen, knowing
That that must go
Quickly into
Storage.

Then one day, strolling
Along the motherboard
There it is again: fresh
And crisp and sour
Or sweet, reserved
As planned.

Time travel is not
Unusual for us, we
Walk in and out of
The past like
Blinking. Now
Here, now gone.

Sequel Preview

THE SCREENMASTERS VOLUME TWO

Sargasso

W. Mahlon Purdin

Chapter One[4]

The Ice Canyons of Sargasso

1. It's Really Big

Gerald Antonoff was at his station. He was looking at the planet they were now calling "Sargasso." At least a very small part of it. *Very small.*

The planet was so large as to be almost indescribable. The largest ever known. *Solar system size.* The small piece he was looking at was an object of great interest. Throughout the portion of the vastness of Sargasso that SkyKing could see, there were multiple millions of little areas of brightness. Antonoff had no idea what they were. No one did. Nor did Farson apparently. *At least, he's been no help despite our requests.*

The lights were uneven in a somehow predictable way. Antonoff had been scanning this part of the planet for months. Through the viewer, he could always tell where he was, by using the lights. Even as the planet slowly turned, Antonoff always knew. He wasn't the only one. The entire bridge crew was aware of the intuitiveness of the lights.

Then he noticed that one was blinking.

---

[4] For readers of the first volume, The Rise of Farson Uiost: It is now approximately 2104 C.E. and 6517 E.E. For the past several years, the Moon and SkyKing, and the silent, impenetrable Emerald Earth, have all been orbiting at Sargasso recovering from all that happened, assessing things, researching, investigating each other, and generally resting, recuperating, and enjoying life. The events of volume one have taken their toll.

At the conclusion of this book is a section entitled, "Front and Back Matter with Appendices," which contains a dramatis personae, a glossary, a chronology, and other information for you.

Andrew Sortt and Farson Uiost were having a brandy. Actually, it was an Armagnac. Sortt spoke first, looking at his glass. "You know, Farson, we used to have these all over the White House."

Farson took a slow, savoring sip. "It's very nice. Many things of old Earth were very nice." Farson was looking into the glass, thinking of the aging oak casks and the flavors and colors of the brandy. This easily led him to thoughts of oak trees and camping with Karina.

It was their first night. The little converted van had all the trimmings. A queen-size bed, a bathroom, a kitchen, a shower, hot water, a refrigerator with a freezer, a generator, and even an outdoor shower. They had brought a pop-up tent to cover the picnic table, two folding chairs, and an L.L. Bean outdoor kitchen that folded up to briefcase size for stowage. Farson had spread out the doormat and hung a few strings of lights. In the twilight there were several of the little bulbs that didn't come on.

"Getting careless, Farson?" Karina was making a joke. Farson was fastidious in details.

"Not at all, Karina. I picked this one because it wouldn't be too bright." Karina looked at the lights. Then at Farson. Her eyebrows went up.

"We wouldn't want that, would we?"

2. The Blink of an Eye

Lieutenant Antonoff couldn't believe it. *Did it really just blink?* He closed his eyes and then looked again. *It is blinking.* He grabbed a pencil and started marking in time with the blinking to record them. The pencil was making little lines with spaces at varied distances in timing with the blinks. Antonoff was hoping it would mean something. With his other hand, he tapped the device on his wrist. A holographic image of Voul's office appeared. Antonoff was still making lines and watching the light. "Commander, we've got something." Voul came into range of his screen. He was perfectly dressed in the Sker way. Crisp whites. Groomed to perfection.

"Report."

"One of the planet's lights is blinking. It was right in the middle of my screen."

"What area?"

"Just below us." Voul was thinking. He knew that area was of interest. There had been inconsistent readings, or rather consistent readings that shouldn't have been there. The Skers were concentrating on it. Their probes had been unsuccessful. There seemed to be little or no atmosphere.

A thousand miles on Sargasso was like traveling an inch or two on Earth. Or less. Maybe much less. It was impossible to know. The size assessments of Sargasso were far from complete.

"Is it continuing?" Voul could hear a scribbling sound as Antonoff's pencil grew duller.

"Yes, I am mirroring it now on paper."

"Are you getting impressions as well?" There was a slight pause, and then a heavier tapping.

"I am now," he said, pressing harder.

President Sortt was still speaking. "It's true, Farson. We both know it is. There were good things on Earth, good people on Earth, good times on Earth.

"I always wonder, though, if in all of the good, there on old Earth, was there not always something of the terrible as well."

Farson knew what he meant. The will to survive, the ambiguous philosophies, the manipulations, the wild moralities, the greed. "It's been a long time, Andrew."

"True again."

They sipped their drinks. Farson thought of Handy's incessant smoking and drinking and how it seemed to help. The situation on Emerald Earth was weighing heavily on him. So much had happened. *So many gone.* He thought that Handy would be lighting one up at this point. *And pouring himself a generous refill.*

<<*Feeling a little weak, Farson?*>> Handy's interruption was not unwelcome.

Farson's dad had been a smoker, and Farson sometimes smoked his pipe. It was an old, gnarled, hand-carved piece of white briar. It always felt good in Farson's hand, but he was no smoker. Karina always laughed at his amateurish attempts.

"You've gone too far with the professorial, Farson," she would say. *How many times has she said it?*

Farson knew Handy wasn't talking about smoking. He was talking about The Screen.

<<*All is well, Handy. As you well know.*>>

<<*Just checking.*>>

The Moon, SkyKing, and Emerald Earth: The three of them, so different and yet so bound together, had moved far, far away. They were now their own little solar system, orbiting a giant wall that went on forever.

It went up, down, and in all directions. It appeared to be perfectly straight. Its curvature was beyond comprehension.

The Moon had grown in population as they traveled through space over the years to get here. They had finally completed New Chicago, and built two more surface cities. Memphis had nearly a thousand people living in it. Bangor was the newest; designed for a colder climate, with snow and wind. MoonBasers were moving into Bangor with stoves and blankets. They seemed to love the rugged terrain and climate.

SkyKing had eight whorls now, and the ninth – by far the largest – was under construction.

Emerald Earth remained home to 6.8 million people. Their culture and technology were a constant source of discussion and study by SkyKing and the Moon. It was difficult to do with no contact allowed. Clearly, in the way that the planet had reappeared and had taken the Moon and SkyKing in tow, everyone knew that something significant had happened there.

When the stasis field came down, everything had changed. Emerald Earth was now a force to be reckoned with. Farson had told everyone only one thing about the people living there, "The ancients are no worry. They are us."

The three separate worlds: worlds so different. The raucous MoonBasers and their commander, Viera Nichols, living lives of complete freedom. The MoonBasers had proven to be a remarkable team. SkyKing – with its ascetic Skers and their leader, Voul Jonsn, and with commander Jim Peterson and his always-ready crew – had grown by leaps and bounds in the ensuing years of peace and predictability. Emerald Earth, with Andrew Sortt and the mysterious Emers, kept its distance, silently, completing the formation.

It had been an interesting ten years.

On Emerald Earth, it had been the longest ten years in the last 6,520.

Time had changed its flow on Emerald Earth. "Time is time," Farson had said. To the Emers, ancient history had involved something called SkyKing, something called the Moon. Their lives had been imprisoned and, in almost every way, freed at the same time. They had lived "in the bottle," as Handy had called it. To them the universe was finite and controlled.

Over the centuries, Emers had developed a philosophy of sustenance and balance. They learned to live peacefully together even as the population steadily declined. The Combing. It involved a planned, slow attrition, unnoticed at first, and then feared, and then cherished. Life became everything as the thinning population spread out. There were the people in the city, ultimately almost half of the population. There were the farmers who made up the other half. Farmers came to the city, and sometimes the city people went out to the farms. It was not an artificial segregation of the two groups. It was real. They inter-communicated and interacted and intermarried and inter-everythinged. Their lives were very, very different, but all Emers are in harmony. In the end, Emers were either ultra-urban or ultra-rural. The farmers moved over the ambered waves like nomads in their rolling cities called harvesters, and provided the raw materials for everyone. The urbanites lived in their amazing vertical world and achieved scientific wonders that set them all free.

By the time Emerald Earth took control of the ScreenMasters' stasis field, they were certainly the most advanced civilization ever known, if severely misunderstood. Over the 6,500-year-long stasis period, with unlimited resources and the amazing adaptability and potential of human beings, as a group, they created a confluence of circumstance and opportunity – with Farson's help – that could only be called salvation. The reborn humanity that now was in orbit near the giant, mysterious Sargasso was really something. Physically, the Emers were as profoundly different from the people on the Moon and SkyKing as the people of the twenty-first century were from the people of 4400 B.C.

Emers were taller and thinner on average. They were all one color, one race. There were wild variations in hair and eye color. There had also been careful genetic alterations. On the whole, these new people were similar to the old, antecedent human race, and yet strikingly different: the unpredictable, anaphoric conclusion to a long historic statement, with one exception.

This new humanity now knew the secret of their own natures that Farson had so thoroughly hidden from the old ScreenMasters. It had been a secret so powerful that its discovery would have resulted in the immediate destruction of humanity, as Twill had always so savagely recommended. It was a secret so powerful that the secret itself dictated the solution. Long before the ScreenMasters began to have an inkling of what was really happening, it was already too late. It was a secret that changed all of reality, hiding itself within. Even now, the old ScreenMasters still think they won.

That Earth still existed and was reunited with the station and the Moon; that Farson and Karina were living with their daughters on SkyKing; that Viera and Voul had had a daughter; that Andrew Sortt had emerged from stasis with immense age and wisdom and power ... all of these facts were still unknown to the old ScreenMasters, as was the truth of humanity's power. To them, Twill's plan had worked. Earth was gone forever. The space station and the Moon were destroyed. The Rent was repaired. The Screen was safe. To those old ScreenMasters, all was well; all was as it should and must be. Everything was exactly as planned.

How wrong they were.

<<*Farson, are you following what is going on?*>>

<<*Of course.*>>

<<*Sargasso is blinking?*>>

<<*Something like that was to be expected. It's a big place.*>>

<<*Ten years. Nothing. Now, something?*>>

<<*Well, that something was always there. We just hadn't seen it yet. Or maybe it hadn't seen us.*>>

<<*The magnitudes are a little scary, don't you think?"*>>

<<*Compared to what, Uva? Even Sargasso is small in the scope of things.*>> The avian ScreenMaster adjusted her wings

and brushed her hand through her soft shoulder feathers. She settled everything back into a smooth profile of dignity and power, looking at Farson.

<<*Yes, Farson. Everything is huge, and yet everything is small. When I think of Uvo, it's not the expanse of space and the great, vast Screen I think of. I think of the outer vanes of his inner feathers. I think of the soft aroma when he settled in beside me. I think of his quiet laugh and tender love. When I think of how much I miss him, I feel small, tiny, infinitesimal. Your grand scheme seems misplaced somehow – wrong to me – in his absence.*>>

<<*I feel it too, Uva. I loved him.*>>

<<*I know you think you did, Farson. My love and your love are very different, though.*>> Farson was looking at her with his mind. There was no denying the truth deep in her thoughts. <<*Imagine Karina is gone. Then you'll know.*>> Uva's mental voice had an odd twinge to it. Not threatening, but something like that. She was wishing he knew the pain she was feeling. She was wishing Farson would someday know her loneliness.

He had learned from Hattie that love has many faces: some kind and nurturing, some harsh and tough and teaching. Uva's were the latter in this moment. He knew she was screaming, with her agony, inside.

That thought remained. *Imagine Karina is gone.* Farson concentrated. Karina was currently on the Moon with Viera. Felicity and Valgary had a playdate with Prms Bensn. He had just turned three today. Farson knew everything was fine in their world. Karina was happy in Viera's company. Their friendship had grown and grown. They were more like sisters now. Farson scanned The Screen. All was well. He looked at Uva again. She was looking at him.

Farson found her unblinking stare disconcerting.

Those four words still hung in the air.

3. The Idea

Young Farson was restless. He hardly ate his breakfast, but Hattie had stood over him until he did. At school he kept looking out the window, looking at the clock. At lunch he just pushed his food around, although the ham salad sandwich did look good. He noticed Hattie had put in a Tootsie Roll. *Oh, what the heck.*

The afternoon dragged on and on like a church service. He was the first student out of the building after school. His bike seemed heavy and slow.

When he got home, he went straight up to his room. Hattie noticed. *What's he doin' up there?*

Farson was writing a note to Karina.

STAY RIGHT HERE

I wonder sometimes if I'm so isolated
That I lose out experientially.
I mean those camels, those pyramids,
That Eiffel Tower, that Lenin's Tomb.
But then I watch you falling asleep
On the couch and think of the days just past
Driving, measuring, moving furniture,
Hanging curtains, painting touch-ups,
Going out for pizza (not for me),
Talking with our daughters all day
Thinking of what my day was like,
I doubt it.
It might be nice, but in an odd Thoreauvian way
I think it might be distractive. So many new
Things to factor there than here, in fact,
Here I can concentrate on things.
Plus I do get out and about, six states,
Ten towns, shopping at the supermarket,
I average around 11,000 miles a year
Just around here. I know a lot of people,
Which makes life fun, and I still have long, long

Periods of working alone, singing alone, and
Writing alone to satisfy the soul.
So going to Fallujah or even Tikrit,
Maybe taking one of those river cruises
Down the Murat, or back to Australia sometime;
Are thoughts I have and have again.
But when one is happy where one is
It means something.
And I'm going to stay right here
Until I figure that out.

When Karina came home and saw the "note," it made her laugh. She read it again, and then she tore it up into little pieces, still laughing.

<<*You are so predictable, Farson. And yet, you think you are so clever.*>>

<<*Can you figure it out?*>>

<<*Wait a minute. Let me think. Hmm. You miss me?*>>

Farson leaned back in his chair and listened to the peepers just now starting to set the mood for long-awaited spring evenings to come.

<<*Well, of course. That's a given. You know that.*>>

<<*Really. It seemed in your 'note' that you were trying to talk yourself into something. Either that, or you were just feeling sorry for yourself. Or dreading your mundane routines. It was perfectly clear, however, that all the effort it took to get it to me, including going to school all day and risking an encounter with Hattie, showed a sincerity – really, a devotion, that is hard to overlook. So when you say so casually, "You know that," remember when you taught me "Everything hangs by a thread?" Without clarity of message, you must agree, anything can happen.*>> No answer.

<<*Farson? Knock, knock.*>>

Farson was in North Conway. He had decided to go skiing at a mountain called Attitash. It was early April, maybe the last day the mountain would open for the season. He had arrived late morning, geared up, and was sitting in the middle of a high-speed quad chairlift alone, swiftly ascending to the summit for his first run. The cool air, the bright blue sky, the beauty of the mountains filled him. It was a day off. The chairlift moved swiftly over trees and trails.

On the way up the mountain, he noticed that there were bras and beads hanging from some of the trees along the lift trail: an aftereffect, he assumed, of the last big event on the mountain's yearly schedule, Mardi Gras Weekend. He watched as a particularly close tree with at least seven bras, and even more strands of brightly colored beads hanging on it, passed underneath him. He smiled. The caprice and impulses of humanity always warmed him with their whimsy. He loved the unpredictable nature of people everywhere. He knew it was one of humanity's greatest strengths: having fun. He had gone back to write the poem for Karina for that very reason. That he had chosen that day would not be lost on her. Her laughter confirmed he had made his point. It was their Door Day[5] anniversary. The day he had hesitated. The day she took control. They both knew it. It was an endless argument. She said he had waited too long and could have ruined everything. He said he had done it perfectly, timing it to the second. The poem was his way of saying that he had everything under control. Her laughter and, in his view, wrongful insight, made him ask for the confirmation: "Can you figure it out?" Time being no barrier to them, her request that he "wait a minute" was funny. Farson knew that he could never win the argument. He knew in his heart he had waited too long that day and that Karina had saved everything. He could rewrite history and move worlds, but the truth with Karina was always the immutable truth. They could play.

---

[5] For readers who have not read volume one, The Rise of Farson Uiost – "Door Day" is further explained there in the first one hundred pages and throughout the book. For purposes here, it was the day that Farson and Karina became equals. They were ten and eight years old, respectively.

They could joke. They could be in many places, in many times at once. They were true ScreenMasters of The Screen. But even with all of that power and ability, Farson knew. Karina loved him enough to risk everything. And she would do it every time without hesitation. Farson knew that that degree of certainty, of resolution, was beyond him without her. Her thought interrupted him.

<<*It sounds like surrender to me, Farson.*>>

<<*We've been here before, Kari. Nothing new.*>>

<<*Where? The place where you can't do it without me?*>>

<<*You wish.*>> They both laughed.

The ski lift arrived at the summit. Farson stood up from the chairlift and skied down the ramp. As he put his hands through the ski pole straps, he noticed Mount Washington through the bare trees. It was pure white, brilliant at the peaks, and Farson could see the tree line was just starting to green up. *It won't be long now.* The winter in New England was coming to its ever slowing conclusion. It was coming for sure, but people always wondered, "Is spring ever going to get here?" He pushed off, his skis gathering speed through the mashed potato snow. He took the easier, intermediate trail, the Upper Saco, but was thinking of the two or three expert options along the way. *It could be my last run of the year. Why not?*

On Emerald Earth he turned and looked toward the far horizon. The sky was a perfect soft orange. Those fiery red sunsets of lore were long gone now. No sun. Day and night were mechanically generated to suit human nature. This made Farson smile. *Human nature, the one truly unstoppable force.* This, to Farson, was the one truth that no one could fully dispute. The vast, past changes – great and disastrous – that it had caused, and those unknown changes still yet to come, had all been, or would be, recorded. But understood? *Never completely.* Farson faced a deep truth secretly to himself: He preferred the past, or pasts, to be more accurate. His childhood with Karina, North Conway in the winter, standing in the grocery lines, these he loved. Driving his old truck around the mountain roads and along the lakes' shores, he relished. Even the war and his experiences there, before being a ScreenMaster, were memories he revisited with frequency and emotion.

Farson looked out across the horizon of the world as it now was, so many years later, and wondered. *Does anyone remember?*

4. Farson's Log (1): The Problem with Emerald Earth

They were ahead of us: way ahead. Contact would have been destructive. The Emers had all been ScreenMasters, aware and confident, for thousands of years. They had seen so much and learned so much more. They lived on a ScreenMaster world. They had taken what was given to them and made the most of it. It wasn't easy. It never is. Over the centuries they had gained control. Not in the traditional way, but in the True ScreenMaster way: order, peace, freedom, humanity, all together.

In the beginning, the planet itself was dying. What choice did they have? I was there and that helped. There were arguments about which way to go. In the end, like fighters worn down in struggle, the two sides gave it up. There were no signed documents, no written agreements, no records. It all happened for everyone at the same moment. Unanimity. Ascension. Salvation. The TrueScreen was born. They learned to control it together, and life became heaven on Earth. The population was thinned out by design and always with care. The planet's ecology evolved perfectly in their hands. It was a world of grains and science. "The exports," I told them, "are important." One planet feeding many others. A people blessed with wealth untold who have no money.

Emerald Earth became humanity's brightest light, long shrouded in stasis, but soon shining again.

They kept asking me questions. They'd show me their amazing inventions. Some went with me when I traveled. Some went other places.

There is only one old ScreenMaster on Emerald Earth now. Handy, of course. He still lives out in the open air and shoots eagles. He was always there whenever I stopped by and still is.

I keep thinking about the little stream where Sam and I fished. Long gone now.

<<*Really, Farson? Gone?*>>
<<*Handy, don't you have anything better to do?*>>
<<*They're readying a mission. Want to go?*>>

Sam used to tell me that if you sit in a place long enough, the fish will come to you.

"Is that why you're sleeping half the time?" Sam sat up a little less slumpy. He straightened his shirt front a little. He reached into his pocket for his beat-up old pocket watch. "That thing never knows what time it is, Sam." He looked at the watch and was somehow reassured. He leaned back against the tree, checked his line, and closed his eyes again.

Voul looked at Farson, who was dressed in the usual cardigan sweater and corduroys. *There's something new about his shoes.* Farson noticed Voul's interest. "They're gyro'd. Much easier, Voul. You never feel tired at all. Nothing can penetrate the sole, and they never actually touch the ground. Traction in all situations. I can even walk on water." Voul knew Sker scripture as well as Farson did.

Voul had come a long way during all the changes. Even with the sacred scriptures being assaulted right in front of him, from events out of his control, and now by the mechanical shoes of the man standing right in front of him, he just shrugged it off now.

"Do you have an extra pair?"

"No, just this one, Voul. Want to try them on?" Farson laughed at his own joke, knowing the Skers' very strict clothing traditions. He knew only too well the things that Voul was dealing with now. Being a Sker and being in love. Dealing with MoonBasers everywhere. Joking that Voul might actually switch shoes with him was a clear sign. They were friends. Voul reacted only slightly when Farson put his arm around him and said, thinking of the coming trip to Sargasso, "Cheer up, buddy. How often does a mission like this one come around?"

People always wonder if I am really there or not. The idea of being in two places, or more, at once takes awhile to get used to. There are things you have to do first. None of them easy. It takes time to understand. That's why there are levels. It's indescribable. It is a matter of awareness. Walking and chewing gum is a good directional example. Think about it. You have to watch where you're going, chew the gum without choking, and maximize your alertness, all the time intensely enjoying the flavors. How many places at once were you, just doing that simple human act?

Anyway, my answer to their question is, "Yes, I am here." That's enough usually. "He's one of us," they would say. Acceptance of things unknown can be a sign of great intelligence.

So when I went on the mission to the ice canyons of Sargasso, I was really there.

You wouldn't want to lose even one hair if it didn't need to happen, would you? What if you knew another one would never grow back in its place?

So, yes, I was there with them on Sargasso. It was as real for me as it was for them.

5. The Ice Canyons of Sargasso

The exploration crew had been on the shuttle for a long eight days. The preparations for departure on SkyKing had been exciting. There had been a lot of activity and even a small departure ceremony. The crew waved from the launch pad, and everything went perfectly as the shuttle, filled with hope and dreams of adventure, left for Sargasso.

Farson and Voul were together on the shuttle. There were twenty Skers and twenty MoonBasers. Viera and John Silver were on the Moon. Karina was on SkyKing with Felicity and Valgary. Captain Peterson and Brittany were on the bridge of SkyKing. Repoul Bensn was with Lieutenant Gerald Antonoff in their respective stations, as usual. The time had passed slowly. The shuttle was a large, generous vehicle with room to spare. It wasn't a luxury liner, but the food was great, everyone had their own room, and there were plenty of things to do to prepare. Everyone kept busy.

When the call came in, the idle time of waiting and preparing quickly changed into action.

"You are within range, Commander. We estimate two hours to touchdown."

Voul and Farson were talking as they got ready. Farson was telling Voul about some of the things he had learned about Emerald Earth. "They have implemented the fourth role of government activity. The basic first three were always known: fairness, operations, and planning. But then they added the fourth: humanity. It all happened at once. It was like waking up. 'The world born anew,' as the Skers like to say. President John Andrew McKinley Sortt was their leader at that time, and he still is, if we can still call it that.

"The planet is now a powerhouse beyond our wildest dreams. The population is much sparser now, but that had been a planned evolution over a long, long time.

"Now all across the vast plains and throughout the beautiful, sprawling city, there exists, universally, in all of its people, the rarest of all human qualities. The one trait that gives us hope, that allows us to build, that drives us to love. The one thing that shows that we really understand. Patience. In the quiet rustle of the vast fields, in all the work at desks and plows, there is now a beautiful sense of timelessness and patience. People work hard at their hearts' desires. Education flourishes and has created a world of highly intelligent, completely aware people who are building a wonderful new existence. Technology has evolved into a fabric that they weave into a connected community where everyone knows everything.

"In the changing planet there were decisions to be made. Habitats disappeared, and new ones were developed. Water and soil mixed. The best water anywhere. The best soil anywhere. Slowly but surely they have made the planet theirs. Fairness. Operations. Planning. Humanity. In their hands, the garden they were given has flourished in its new reality." Voul was wishing he could have recorded the conversation. Its impact was revelational, approaching a sacrament. His attention was avid, and he found himself anticipating and relishing each word, hoping he could remember every one.

"Other than loving my sister and all that that entails," Farson said, "watching Emerald Earth being born has been my greatest pleasure. I spend as much time there as I can.

"Karina. I love her name. I say it sometimes just to hear it. Uvo was my friend. But Karina is my wife. She always has been my sister, my best friend, really. It was definitely love at first sight."

Voul was thinking of Viera in much the same way. These two men, so different in many ways, shared something deep and unspoken. They both loved forbidden women. Their growing friendship was a precious oasis where they both enjoyed relaxing together. Voul felt honored. Farson felt his aloneness soften in Voul's company. He looked at Voul and felt relief and trust. *A friend?*

Farson continued. "I wonder sometimes about Karina. Seeing her parents die. Coming to a strange home. Fitting in." *She makes me want to be in only one place all the time.* Voul was looking at Farson. Voul knew that he might never feel exactly what Farson was feeling, but he knew how powerful his own experience had been. *Viera.*

<<*Farson. Why do you say such things when you know the truth very well? You know exactly what I feel. Poor Voul struggles so with his feelings. You are almost taunting him.*>>

<<*Just making conversation, Karina.*>>

There was a silence for a few moments. Karina realized that Farson was longing for her out there. It tore at her heart. Even though she could be in many places at once now, sometimes she could not be where she wanted to be. Her own loneliness welled up. Farson noticed the silence as she departed. <<*Where are you going?*>> Faintly, he could hear the two girls laughing as their mother reentered their room on SkyKing. He smiled and turned back to the job at hand. Voul was ready to go. A voice was blaring out of the communication speakers.

"All right, drop the cocks and grab your socks, boys and girls. It's time to saddle up." Long John Silver's guttural voice over the communicator from MoonBase caused them all to start moving to the air locks. Farson was hurrying to get his suit on.

The ice canyons of Sargasso were in the deep, cold, unforgiving vacuum of space. The planet seemed to have very little gravity at all. Barely enough to stay down. The one-fiftieth G of Sargasso's outer surface was hard to explain, given its inestimable mass. The Skers "conjectured" that the nature of its mysterious interior must have something to do with its apparent defiance of physics. Repoul's theory was that the source of Sargasso's gravity was deep, deep inside. Being on the surface was like being in a plane diving through old Earth's atmosphere or a roller coaster down the steep first plunge. They would feel the stillness of the surface, Repoul had predicted, like an astronaut on a space walk from a vessel traveling thousands of miles an hour, and the near weightlessness of a steep dive all at the same time. The exploration crew on board were all mentally preparing for the long-anticipated experience of standing on Sargasso's surface as the shuttle made its final approach. They were getting into their positions and reviewing their plans to reach the blinking light at its source. "To see it with our own eyes," as Farson put it.

The ice canyons were like the valleys between huge, sharply peaked mountains. As far as the eye could see, the patterns repeated themselves, like a mirror in a mirror. The view was disorienting in its scope. The Skers had been unable to estimate the land mass of Sargasso's surface, but it was assumed that the entire surface was exactly the same. At the time when Emerald Earth had taken SkyKing and Moon in tow, they had arrived at Sargasso so quickly that the long-range monitors had only seen it briefly from afar, and even then it was still a very partial view.

The shuttle landed, the air locks were opened. The debarkation to the surface was made without delay.

Now they were standing on Sargasso. The suit technology supplied by Emerald Earth was perfect for the job. Their shoes all had little tractors and force fields that held the wearer at a constant distance from the surface. The suits were as comfortable as street clothes. Virtually unlimited in power and life support functions. Little worlds of their own. Communication was also excellent and effortless, with both "all call" and privacy features.

A general transmission came to them all.

"We have estimated that it's about a mile to the base of the mountain where the light structure is." With that information the troop of forty began to walk off in the direction indicated. Farson and Voul walked together in the rearguard. It was quiet as the group snaked around the ground features, over the ups and downs, always moving toward the objective. Voul had a question.

"Farson, when did you know?" Farson knew exactly what Voul was asking about. He knew that Skers didn't really fall in love. They procreated. They worked together. They felt attachment, but 'in love?' That was rare indeed. In their history, it had happened, but that was long ago. The Skers now were dedicated, determined, dependable, and, most of all, metaphysical about the world around them and its allurings. Voul had given up all of that denial in the instant he had met Viera. Their worlds were so different, opposites. But even in that odd and awkward moment of their first meeting, he knew. Farson was answering his question.

"*Some* might dispute my version." Farson knew Karina insisted on believing that he had at first rejected her. But he knew that the moment when he had first seen her was the "when" that Voul was asking about. For Farson and Karina it was much more complicated than that. "The truth is, Voul, there was no 'when,' really. It was more of a 'what.' It's what you know when you realize that any life without her is a life you don't want." Voul walked silently beside him. It was easy going now on flat ground. There was no dust, and no particular hurry. Silently walking along, they were both lost in their thoughts. The troops ahead of them were stopping; Voul and Farson quickly caught up.

"There it is." They were all looking at what could only be called the mountain's peak. At the distant apogee was a structure, which they could now dimly see, even with the aid of their suit's impressive optical visors.

The structure supported the distant light thousands of feet into the black of space.

SkyKing, the Moon, which seemed really close, and Emerald Earth were all floating there above them in stark and crystal-clear view, watching. The explorers turned and looked at Farson.

"Now what?"

(to be continued...)

ABOUT THE AUTHOR

W. Mahlon Purdin lives in Massachusetts with his wife, Joy Hooper Purdin. They have a daughter, Blythe.

He has written poetry, prose, and essays for many years. His eclectic career in advertising and writing has been nurtured by a wide variety of interests in extreme sports, music, and exploration.

The Rise of Farson Uiost is the first novel of The ScreenMaster series, and the fourth he has written.